SAILING TO MONOCEROS
THE SECRET JOURNAL

SAILING TO MONOCEROS
THE SECRET JOURNAL

Marilyn J. Ninomiya

Order this book online at www.trafford.com
or email orders@trafford.com

Most Trafford titles are also available at major online book retailers.

This narrative is a work of fiction.
Inferences to any actual individuals or localities, with the exception of historical references, represent nothing more than coincidence.

Printed in the United States of America.

ISBN: 978-1-4120-1036-8 (sc)
ISBN: 978-1-4269-6379-7 (hc)
ISBN: 978-1-4669-1027-0 (e)

Library of Congress Control Number: 2011905267

Trafford rev. 10/17/2013

www.trafford.com

North America & international
toll-free: 1 888 232 4444 (USA & Canada)
fax: 812 355 4082

This narrative is a work of fiction.
Inferences to any actual individuals or localities,
with the exception of historical references,
represent nothing more than coincidence.

Your work is to discover your world
and then with all your heart give yourself to it.
—Siddhartha Gautama

PRELUDE TO THE SECRETS

Wild specks of tarnish mushroom across the sterling silver. No matter how much polish my mother massages into her picture frame they won't budge. Her strokes are rough and deep, but these blemishes are unmoved by her temper. Whether she uses expensive brands, to restore the prized antique, or takes a chance on bargain stuff, nothing much changes. Sometimes they do fade a bit, just to torture her, because the instant she buys more of the *potion* that "performed the wonder" they resurface even darker than before. They also bring a new crop of ugly pals along with them, to relax at the freebie-spa.

With the frustration of Mother Goose, and that old woman who lived in a shoe, Mom says this *blight* on the ugly frame symbolizes "liver spots" from the stress of aging. She glances at me, giving me the usual dig, letting me know how similar to children they are *very* difficult to control.

Once I told her to have a jeweler dip the unattractive frame in some new silver. She stiffened right up, admonishing me that a *facelift* insults "hard-earned character." When I advise her to toss it in the garbage, or give the church thrift shop a thrill, she cringes saying, "*They* would never appreciate my sacrifice."

In perfect time to my mumbling, "You sure got that right," she marches over to the vase full of assorted fresh flowers, kept on the dining room table. She looks at them with the same compassion she lavishes on the "girls" in her Wednesday bridge group when they moan about their latest operations.

Checking each flower from the stem up, she trims off any browning leaves or petals. "Must I remind you *again* that when the bloom is off the rose, former things of value, including *people,* are discarded?" Then followed by a deep sigh, heaved from the depths of somewhere, comes, "*Out* to pasture they go—heading straight for the glue factory."

The dialogue continues when she runs her fingers through her hair and asks what I think about the condition of her perm. Often it has more kink than body. The tangled mess doesn't look so hot. I always find something nice to say though, such as *everybody* wants four-inches of dark roots now. It's part of a *growing* fad.

Well, you *never* know.

She might *start* one.

Next on the tedious menu, we have the gray hair topic—that "inevitable sad time," when no amount of dye in the world will control the invasion. There's enough peroxide in our bathroom upstairs to stock a hospital, so does she think she's really fooling me when she says, "Some women can't break the harsh habit of bleaching their dull brown hair to vibrant blond using *economical* peroxide. They're in for a counterproductive disaster later on, when salt takes over the pepper. Finding a good substitute, to duplicate the look, won't be easy and a lot more expensive."

She pauses, wringing her hands—trying to lessen those prominent veins—until she says, "The old gray mare ain't what she used to be." I tell her that I agree, since the poor thing now resides in the new tube of *Krazy Glue* on Dad's desk.

She never appreciates my levity. I just get the same dirty look she gave me when, as a generous five-year-old, I donated her mink stole to wrap little Sparky—my best friend's sick dog. Tammy lived in a small apartment, so I did her a favor. We gave him a beautiful pet burial in my backyard. My parents and Tammy's family agreed, until they found out a few weeks later how he went to heaven, all snuggled-up and warm, inside that big, broken toolbox.

I will now yelp my way back to Mom's current problems.

When she is just as exhausted from talking, as I am from listening, she'll ask me, "How many *more* change of life losses must we females expect to swallow, along with the accompanying acid reflux?" I can never answer her. I'm not sure I know, although I *could* venture a guess or two.

Never eating baked beans again, without an air freshener on your lap, would be a good one. And those unavoidable hemorrhoids might turn the *royal* expression she directs at me into a *factual* pain in the ass. Buying a ton of *Preparation-H* won't rear-end her finances. This oily salve erases facial bags and wrinkles too. I hear the stuff's a miracle top-to-bottom solution. Comments like these assure pushing her buttons to a 4-alarm fire, so I keep my mouth shut.

I don't have to wait too long before her lips start quivering *again,* when she cautions me about the overwhelming chore of remaining youthful.

Waving a teaspoon in the air, she says, "Try emptying the *Atlantic Ocean* with this! You'd better learn right now, while you're still a kid, how the clock is set, and *nobody* can turn back the hands."

The best is when she tosses *me* the beat-up feather duster, hoping I'll do something constructive with it. After I catch the thing, and cough and sneeze inside a puff of pollution, I think ending its misery sounds like a great idea. I don't say a word about this either. I just stand there, holding her gift like an Olympic torch, after she collapses on the couch to complain about *Geritol.*

"I am a definite weary wife and mother with that *iron-poor blood.* I cannot understand why the doctor keeps informing me how my checkups are fine, when I have every single symptom they talk about on television—weak and rundown, tired and listless. What *good* is Geritol to a person like me? I can watch those deceptive commercials till the cows come home. No pharmacy could ever stock enough of this glorified pick-me-up to help yank *my* feeble foot out of the greedy grave."

And on and on she goes.

We never owned any *cows,* unless you count those assorted chunks of beef, dangling off icy hooks in the basement's spare freezer, the size a butcher would use. I wonder why she expects a herd of *them* to moo their way over to *our* place. She may be on the verge of losing it, with all of this *pasture* junk.

I think her entire weird obsession—concerning the ancient frame—is because she's afraid to risk setting such a hardhearted example for her own brood. Why give them any more bad ideas than they already have. If you think about her matriarchal duties, she *is* responsible for hosting several hectic social gatherings every year. When they're at full throttle my dad always says, "Holidays and birthdays would be *nowhere* without Mom."

She ignores his compliment. She just looks at him with her eyes rolling and grunts *humph,* before gravitating toward her dumb frame. She'll wave the rattling love of her life around, letting us all know that, "When a *relic* has the courage to survive so many years of familial insanity, the decrepit thing deserves a hierarchal place in the living room to witness a few more—does it not?"

This remark sure silences everybody.

What relic is she *really* talking about?

A smart person knows that the moment has come to take your hand out of the popcorn bowl, get up from wherever you parked your can—both the private and soft drink variety—and make a feeble attempt to clean up the atrocious mess. Only a minimal effort will be necessary. Shifting a few things around, or carrying a plate or two into the kitchen, gets the job done. If you decide to vacuum, she'll just go over the floor again later, so why kill yourself.

Whenever she addresses family members about any of these matters, they better nod in complete agreement. I always do, even if what she's talking about is beyond boring and doesn't mean a thing to me. But nothing could be worse than her spiel about *cleanliness* being next to *godliness,* inferring that God rejects messy people.

I'm doomed.

Out of necessity, I've become an expert at comforting her when she's in *any* of these annoying, reflective moods. All I say is, "How right you are." I can't believe this little insincere comment guarantees me better meals, with heaping portions of dessert.

Referring to food again, leads me right back to yucky liver and those spots. She has two of these *thingies* on her own face and relies on an expensive *wizard* called *Max Factor* to vanish them from sight. "Darling Max is worth every single penny," she tells me. If you ask my father about Max, *he* will tell you, "More like every single *buck* and too bad such *sorcery* can't extend to the corresponding kids."

The picture frame I'm talking about comes complete with an attached spotlight and it rests in peace on the mantelpiece. Ever since I can remember, this ugly thing has always displayed that same picture done in old-time sepia, casting a haunting silhouette over the fireplace.

The amount of soot covering this frame, along with all of those knickknacks, could fill a chimney sweep's bucket. You won't find him in *our* living room though. My mother takes over the job by dancing with her feather duster to Benny Goodman, rocking his clarinet. You'll find every one of his records inside the new *Magnavox* stereo console.

Due to that usual four cups of morning java, she was super speedy on her feet. Swinging with the Big Bands gets pretty wild, when your partner is caffeine-induced jitters. Over the past few years, however, since switching to that instant *Sanka* coffee substitute, she's been doing more of a slow waltz.

I enjoy observing her famous left hook—swishing the feather duster over the stupid frame—in perfect step to *Moonglow.* No prizefighter could send those dark flecks of soot flying into the air, one by one, any better than Mom does. Watching them take off from their runway on the shelf, as they glide to locations of lesser importance, fascinates me. I never miss the ritual, if I'm around.

Putting Benny and airport sanitation aside, the ridiculous photo under discussion shows an infant buttressing between an army of droopy pillows. Despite its theoretical *safety* zone, the poor lopsided baby topples on the seat of a ramshackle recliner. Did the dumb kid cry and act scared? The answer is *no.* Those beady eyes only squinted with puzzlement over such a dubious situation.

To date, things have *not* changed.

The flash of the camera also spotlighted the rest of the little alien, swimming beneath a long and poufy christening gown. From the added framework of a stiff, oversized lace bonnet, a fragile three-month-old peeked out at unfamiliar surroundings. While its forehead rippled like an accordion, it wondered who it is, what it is, and why it arrived on the particular scene.

These questions remain unanswered.

Last year, I developed a wallet-sized print of this nostalgic photo to tuck behind my driver's license. I don't drive too often. Although I have no problem with grasping the steering wheel, where I'm heading is a continual puzzle.

I'm amazed when I hold this picture of my tiny self. I always hear my grandmother's voice coming from somewhere, as if she's standing on top of a distant mountain. Her message soars on the wings of a forceful wind, while her tone remains the gentle breeze, I remember. Yet—the quality is strong enough to reinstate a point in time that evaporated long ago.

She's here once more to tell me, in the simplest terms a youngster could comprehend, how my ancestors emigrated from Plymouth, England when America was still a baby, like me in the picture. I never tired of hearing the story about an angry gray sky that commanded a storm to brew on a brisk September day in the year of **1620.** The water obeyed and shook their ship with a hungry fury, even before leaving port. The passengers gazed out over an endless choppy ocean, which had just swallowed the horizon. Now the wrath waited for *them.*

These family pilgrims were courageous. The heirloom baptismal outfit I wore represented one of the few memories they brought from home. They packed the fragile garment in a small burlap satchel, where dried leaves of spicy rosemary protected it from rot, odor, and mildew.

The relatives took turns clinging to the satchel night and day, fearing a less fortunate passenger might steal it from unlocked quarters—deep inside damp *Mayflower* bilges.

The long, uncomfortable journey frightened them. They suffered extreme nausea and fevers, but this delicate symbol, from the old world they left behind, gave them hope for their uncertain future. New babies meant new chances for a better life in the *New World.* Her voice softened, almost to a whisper, when she told me how descendants continue to cherish the antique. Someday, my own baby will have the honor of wearing the same.

I realized later that this attire goes way beyond *historic* after I saw my father's baby picture. He had on the exact outfit—posing in the same chair—on the day of *his* baptism. *I* looked much cuter. Boys of any age should not wear huge lace bonnets.

Another photo, taken on *my* baptismal day, depicts me *with* my grandfather. He also sits in this chair and holds me, while I sank deeper and deeper into the antique regalia. He made an obvious effort to balance the little marshmallow in the center of his arms, held out as rigid as a yardstick. The look of panic on his face hallmarks an attempt not to have substantial hands crush my billowy legacy.

Or the newborn attached to it!

I don't know why, but prior to seeing *any* of these old photos, I knew this antiquated recliner followed him around eons ago—way before a hyperactive grandchild like me used the tatty thing for a trampoline. I felt sure it hid some exciting stories. Until I knew what they were, I'd have to settle for the workout helping me to tell mine.

The once rich black leather had worn down to a brilliant shine, and became transportation to a castle in the sky. I'd cover myself from tip-to-toe in my grandmother's blue silk robe, with the pattern of white gardenias the size of cabbages. I stared at a beautiful princess, dressed in her gown, on the way to the ball. Shall a handsome prince slide my foot into a small glass slipper?

I also used it to practice crossing my eyes and learning how to make expert funny faces that often got me into big trouble with parental-people.

My favorite recliner fantasy consisted of turning into a rough street kid, while I wore denim overalls with colorful patches of mismatched material. Gobs of raspberry jelly, squishing out of the habitual donut I jammed into my mouth, set the background. Remnants of this jelly on my chin, plus powdered sugar on my cheeks, and a pug nose covered with the hidden dust I trounced out—from somewhere within the chair's shabby cushions—painted my proper urchin-face.

Adding to the chair's biblical age of *Methuselah,* it bore map-like crevices. These meandering lines reminded me of battle scars—etched into the chariot of a storybook warrior. I often wondered what daring struggles took place in such an ancient seat of exploits. I'd alternate placing my right ear on either of the chair's sagging arms, in hopes of hearing a heroic tale—from one or the other. The stubborn body armor remained silent, refusing to share its mystifying history, no matter how long I waited.

The memory of this perplexing chair continues to affect me, most often when I slip into the hazy void between consciousness and dreams. At this quasi-moment, I visualize myself as a rambunctious toddler, in a palpable scene that's the size of a postage stamp, where I bask in the companionship of this rickety contraption. Viewing a miniature me, costarring with the inseparable pal of my childhood, is hypnotic. We're acting in a vivid Technicolor movie from the past, playing out before my eyes. I don't see the show too often, but when the film decides to roll, I equate my attendance with lucid dreaming—with two crucial exceptions.

I am not sleeping.

I am wide-awake.

Aside from owning a fascinating chair that provoked better images for a kid than Walt Disney, my grandfather symbolized a "jack-of-all-trades." Unlike the old saying about being master of *none,* he qualified as master of *all.* I thought he could do just about *anything.* The strongest memory I have, concerning his all-around skill, is when he doused for well water. Somehow, he knew my backyard held an entire lake of the scarce resource. He only had to find out where. Neighbors came and talked about witnessing a "spellbinding event."

He started by sawing a forked branch from a nearby willow tree. After trimming off the greenery, the piece still looked sturdy, but almost disappeared with his big fingers wrapped around it. Holding the bare stick straight out in front of him, he acted like a blind man, testing out his surroundings with a cane—while taking cautious steps around the property.

He hit the jackpot within minutes, when the branch vibrated at a spot near the back porch. Sure enough, as soon as the loud drilling started, a fountain of water surged to the heavens, from deep within that divined sandy soil.

After our rough and ready bath, he mentioned feeling sorry the gusher didn't yield "black gold." I ran inside to retrieve the bracelet I wore as a baby. I used the tiny thing then, as jewelry for my dolls. Although not a true black, with the accumulated grime, the color came close. I handed my token to him. He gave it right back. Patting the top of my head he said, "My family is all the gold in the world I will ever need."

The prolific well is still operational. Our irrigated garden of vegetables, as well as flowers, continues to be the best in town.

My competent grandfather was also a whiz, whenever a domestic crisis arrived on the scene. On rare occasions, when something popped up requiring more than the usual five-minute solution, he'd pace around his entire house. Of course, if I visited there during the dilemma, I'd be right behind. Watching him shake his head around like a floppy puppet worried me. I remember thinking his dear face might fall right off.

Soon enough, his bewilderment led him to his recliner. He'd plop down on the rickety seat with the force of a man, carrying a heavy load. Rotating his shoulders up and down, he'd announce how his "pickle batteries" needed a recharge. Pickles meant a lot to me. How *else* could I fill myself up, whenever I got the smallest bun with the skimpiest hamburger? Hearing him say that homegrown, briny cucumbers could solve any *additional* serious problems was confusing. However, their comprehensive value became clear one strange night when an "official messenger" showed up at my house.

Those ravenous mosquitoes acted like this man's protective sentries, patrolling around the dim porch light. They were weapons, firing moving shadows at the square identification badge—hanging off the collar of his jacket. There, with dense fog setting in, his name flickered like a roadway caution sign. Their frantic buzzing worsened, just before he shoved a stiff manila-envelope at my father. They sensed blood.

In the misty chill of an autumn, dinnertime evening, the stern envoy stood there to inform my shocked parents how their homeowner's insurance would terminate. At the stroke of midnight, the residential area where we lived gerrymandered to a "high-risk tornado district."

While Mom and Dad trembled, *before* any tornado showed up to level the house, I envisioned all of my stuff blowing away. Seeing cool toys propelled toward children in Timbuktu caused a tight knot in my stomach.

I also couldn't believe the energy I wasted the week before, taking laundry bags full of playthings I outgrew, and dragging everything up flights of stairs to the hot attic. Those cavernous rafters made an excellent hiding space for each individual book and toy. This gargantuan heavy collection included twelve metal trucks from my *tomboy* stage.

To pull off my scheme, I wouldn't let scary spiders stop me. I summoned enough courage to ignore the dense netting of cobwebs. I improvised a ladder by stacking a dented collection of suitcases I spotted, way over in a forgotten corner under the eaves. Every step I climbed on this unstable ladder, the more determined I became to prevent my own baby sister from ever getting, and I felt sure destroying, the nostalgic remnants of *my* babyhood.

According to that headless-horseman of a messenger, the sentimental stash is taking off to a bunch of ungrateful babies who, just like her, were always cranky and crying. Only now, they acted up in places I couldn't imagine in my wildest dreams—let alone pronounce. In the dingle of a rusted doorbell, tolling a garbled rendition of *Dixie,* I became *Orphan Annie,* without the red hair. But I sure did have the curls.

Visualizing my house in ruins, I had no other choice than to become an organ grinder, begging on the street, while the adorable monkey I kidnapped from the circus holds a tiny tin cup—one with more dents than those forgotten suitcases. Who could ever resist the special beanie I made for my cutie pie to wear, decorated with multicolored *M&M's.*

The true idea behind "flat broke" meant I didn't have a toy or a piece of my favorite *Tootsie Roll* candy to my name. Since I couldn't afford *any* kind of musical instrument to play, my street-beggar fantasy took off with the twister. Even if by chance I spotted my little harmonica, buried under the rubble, nobody, not even an idiot, would pay to hear *that* racket.

Feeding piles of bananas to a hungry, hardworking monkey, no matter how cute, was impossible. I couldn't even afford to feed myself. When things came right down to it, my ceramic bank—stuffed to its squiggly-tail—just verified, with cataclysmic accuracy, how a chubby pig—covered with huge pink and blue polka dots—*could* fly. But did *my* pig have to be the pioneer? And who knew when or where *Mr. Bacon* might land.

Later the same evening, after gobbling up the dinner I thought for sure a tornado waited to snatch from my mouth, my father rushed everybody over to his parents' house for an emergency confab. Even though they sat me in front of the radio to laugh at *Fibber McGee and Molly,* between the jokes I overheard some of the adult conversation. My mother kept sobbing that changing policies would force us to join the "insurance poor."

How could this be? *Poor* families get their money from charity. I gave these less fortunate people a nickel or two from my healthy pig every Sunday. I didn't want to; I had to. The collection basket, full of dollar bills and coins, landed straight in my lap—while an entire pew of people gaped at me. I thought that for now, I should increase this donation. I'd get all the money back later on—when *I* fell into the homeless category. The church was a much safer bank than that aviator pig.

Before returning with my family to our *precarious* dwelling, I watched Grandpa jump on his chair to deliberate. His agile leap assured me how a higher power would soon solve the dilemma. Early the next afternoon, convincing a different underwriter to put previous insurance-company-qualms aside, he found a more reliable policy for my parents—turning out to be cheaper than the prior one. This improvement contained a clause about "Ample Warning of Cancellation." What this meant, I had no idea. But my father sure grinned from ear-to-ear.

To celebrate this excellent outcome, Mom baked her famous pound cake. I always thought the golden-loaf got its name from the full pound of butter she dumped into the batter. When she carried her creation into the dining room, this culinary masterpiece sat in the center of her green hobnail cake plate. My favorite dessert still looked warm, floating under gobs of melting vanilla icing.

While *oos* and *ahs* made their way around the room, she placed the crowd-pleaser in the center of the festive table, already filled with the delectable buffet she prepared since early that morning. For some reason, I saw something else floating *above* the table. An angel smiled and winked at me, from her perch on one of the overhead beams. Due to her extraordinary presence, the dining room glowed with the brilliance of a beautiful rainbow, painting the *sky* just for me.

I'm positive she flew down from heaven. Her fluffy white wings resembled those generous plumes on Mom's ostrich feather hat. This celestial being, complete with the sound of a harp, came to visit *me* thanks to the extraordinary power of Grandpa's *chariot.* I knew then—while watching those gossamer wings flutter—that a nasty tornado would never even *dare* to take *my* stuff.

And one never did.

I also couldn't overlook the contribution of the magical pickles, being certain the winking angel had eaten them.

As impressive as the status of this miraculous chair continued to be, not only on the occasions I told you about, but also throughout my entire childhood, the incident I'll describe later elevates its supremacy to unsurpassed *forever.*

WARNING

Dearest Secret Journal:

Before the official undertaking of your creation, I have a solemn duty to explain how you're set to undergo a gradual metamorphosis. As your pages creak and groan—along their clandestine path—they will begin unveiling an ominous transformation.

You will find yourself turning into a cloak-and-dagger chronicle, fated to become a buried body of work. In the end, you will rest in peace in a cryptic location—never to witness the current light of day.

But—trust and fear not. I know for sure that any kind of rest, peaceful or otherwise, is difficult to pin down under the best of circumstances.

Forget about eternity!

For this reason, I predict *Providence* will resurrect you. I know she is on my side. I am imploring her to place you into the safe hands of a predestined reader, when the time is right.

I will now address this chosen future reader:

Please, oh please reader—*whoever* you are—*wherever* you are, will *you* be kind to me? I am imploring you not to reveal the sensitive contents of this journal to a living soul. If you betray me, a precious heart will be at stake.

Mine!

Chapter 1

*Old Spice*______________________ **"I only know how it *was*."**

Do you remember when I mentioned the power of my grandfather's extraordinary chair? The following indelible memory, concerning its influence on my life, grips me to this day. Everything began in late fall, on what I expected to be just another predictable Sunday. Other than dreary and gusty weather, nothing special about the beginning of the day alerted me how that afternoon will turn out to be anything but *predictable.*

I recall my mother tacking a huge Thanksgiving poster over the entire front door. The thick paper obscured the usual hallway light, streaming into the entrance foyer, from the triangular window in the center of this wooden door. As I left that morning, I held the railing on the steep porch steps extra tight—fearing the danger of going down them backwards.

I didn't want to waste a single second taking my eyes off the pockets of wind, puffing out the flamboyant turkey in the colorful poster. The proud strutting bird appeared cheerful and very naive about trading its home at the entrance, for Mom's huge cornucopia themed platter in the kitchen, just three short days later.

As usual, for this season of the year, piles of slimy red and gold leaves blew around in swirls—right before landing in heaps to suffocate the ground. I still feel myself slipping on them. My knees throbbed from the scrapes. I remember pulling a bunch of the wet and spiky things out of my boots. This happened to me lots of times before. I never could resist the ultimate challenge of *skating* on them.

Sunday school offered the same old routine, except our teacher kept staring into space. She must have been in a trance when she gave us a generous second portion of oatmeal cookies and apple juice by mistake.

Whatever preoccupied her mind, I hoped her distraction would continue on a regular basis.

As the custom dictated, when this religious education finished, I joined my family inside of the church itself for the regular service. After *that* little catnap, I went with my parents for our usual Sunday afternoon visit to my grandparents' home. I always thought of the happy trip as compensation for a boring morning, as well as freedom's light at the end of a long and baffling sermon tunnel.

As soon as Grandpa finished saying grace, Grandma served his ritualistic Sunday dinner of pot-roast—with all of the trimmings. He never tired of it. Neither did the rest of us, me above all.

When everyone polished off this scrumptious feast, he'd pat his stomach and groan before getting up from the table. The satiated point had come to stroll over to the chair where Grandma sat, encircling his arms around her shoulders. We'd all wait for him to flatter her with his famous bear hug, along with that lingering peck on the cheek. This sweet, anticipated kiss never failed to make her blush and giggle. She became an eighth grader again, participating with friends in an innocent party game of *Spin the Bottle,* and her turn spun that milk jug toward the boy she adored.

Each occasion, when my grandfather's predictable display of devotion took place, it came right before his imminent post-dinner jog. I'm referring to the three-yard-dash from the dining room to entrench in his beloved recliner, situated in the parlor across the hall. Of course, I was his dependable "goldfish tail"—bringing up the rear.

Over the years, everybody in the family—my grandfather included—called his favorite place to sit "the chariot." I guess my childhood perspective influenced them. After dinner, and his tender gesture of gratitude to the cook, he gave this loyal old buddy a firm pat on its baggy-back, grateful to it for taking a ton of bread pudding off his feet.

His Sunday ritual continued, with removal of his tight shoes and those long woolen socks. The next task was to pull the lever that raised the recliner's mechanical footstool, setting the knob to the uppermost level. Within seconds, he stretched his long legs by swinging them high into the air, while sprung toes squiggled. Before long, a fascinating display of slow motion began, as broad feet dawdled downward to relax on this frayed hassock.

While he rubbed his bare feet, until they turned pink, I knew that in only a matter of seconds he'd lean toward a nearby bookshelf to switch on the patient radio, waiting there to entertain him. Whenever I saw this small radio, made with swirls of orange and white Bakelite, my mouth watered. The rectangular shape, and combination of colors, reminded me of a *Creamsicle.* The thought of biting into one, had me imagining the familiar *Good Humor* truck, filled with these frozen treats, making its way down the block. As usual, the friendly man behind its wheel wore a white uniform and jangled those identifiable bells. Hearing loud *dingdonging* convinced me that the truck had already pulled up to the house, until my grandfather said, "The wind plays tricks."

Soon—my favorite "ice pop" resonated with its usual classical music, signaling both of Grandpa's memorable hands to surge toward the floor. Watching him gave the impression of attending a harmonious concert. *He* was a real conductor, guiding the opus streaming from this radio. I knew, though, that his only intention was to fetch the sizeable brown suede moccasins, waiting in their prearranged positions on the floor.

One of the weathered moccasin pair always sat upright, leaning against the left side of the recliner, while the other angled on the floor near the right side. While he put on these comfy slippers, I'd fantasize about cute twin papooses. These little living dolls had black hair the color of coal, and cheeks as round and rosy as shiny apples. They waited for me in the nearby vestibule. After rescuing them, I could put them down for a safe nap in these beaded *bassinets.*

Once established, he unfolded the thick weekend edition of the newspaper. His faithful mission of reading all of the pages, from front-to-last, never bored him. He became so engrossed in current events that every few minutes I'd hear a disapproving *t'sk, t'sk, t'sk* when his tongue tapped against the old wood pipe, dangling from his mouth. My grandmother told me that the nicked thing represented a "pacifier" since tobacco left long ago. He gave up the unhealthy habit on the day they married.

I always counted on his etched brow furrowing deeper and deeper, in perfect unison with his typical *newsworthy* reactions of, "Oh my goodness." And, "Heaven preserve us all." Before long, his customary concern about the chaotic state of the world intermingled with chuckles over comic strips, *Popeye the Sailor* above all.

While music filled the room that afternoon, I remember the weather report daring to interrupt Beethoven's *Ninth Symphony.* Their message had an urgent tone. I wasn't at all surprised when rude hailstones tapped against the parlor's bay window. This jarring sound disturbed my grandmother's abundant collection of assorted African violets, resting on this casement's crescent-shaped ledge that always represented a bright half-moon, in a dark midnight sky.

My favorite grouping of these houseplants continued to be the purple variety. They alone, sat on yellow-velvet doilies she once embroidered. Her portrayal of shiny lilacs, onto this velvet—by use of silk thread the color of lavender—amazed me. This grand arrangement never failed to remind me of a glorious array of Easter baskets, nestling in a secluded garden in the woods; the kind *Little Red Riding Hood* traversed on the way to *her* grandmother's house. I knew she'd be skipping along, reciting her version of my favorite old nursery rhyme, something like, "A-tiskit, A-tasket—a *purple* and yellow basket."

On this day, while Little Red Riding Hood scampered through the fairytale woods, I parked—as usual—on the convenient new *washable* scatter rug, right near Grandpa's elevated feet. Almost as annoying as the rain, I recall several frustrating attempts to mold my new *Play-Dou* into the exact shape I wanted. Using any type of children's modeling clay presented an irresistible challenge. I never could get the knack of forming the sticky substance to match what I envisioned.

This infuriating lack of skill developed into a messy glob, when attempting to create a beautiful Indian mother for those hoped for twin papooses. My earsplitting outburst of temper caused him to drop his paper to the floor and pick me up instead. At this fitful moment, you could call *me* a definite pipe-clicking event. To distract my rage, he whirled me around in a playful way, before sitting me down on his lap.

After settling me, the look in his eyes grew wistful—but not for long. A startled expression, accompanied by a significant moan, took nostalgia's place. Grandpa's obvious discomfort hinted how his diminutive "buttercup flower" might be growing too tall and heavy for his advancing senior-status to lift and spin.

Hearing him gag, from catching his breath, scared me. Regaining self-composure, he appeared bashful about his discomfort. Then, he reached into the deep leather pocket—attached to the side of his recliner. My prior experience with this convenient pouch, subsisted of watching him fish for necessary tissues. On this memorable day, however, he behaved like a proficient magician—there for the sole purpose of my amusement

With a flourish, he pulled a dilapidated woolen beret from somewhere inside the pouch. The old thing appeared more ramshackle than the adjustable seat harboring it. I saw remnants of a once vibrant illustration of a boat, on the front of this now-fading black beret, along with the dynamic embossed logo of a large **A.** The tall letter remained visible in bright red.

This *boat* appeared to be more of a *barge* and had some kind of a little house sitting in the middle of its flat deck; a deck covered with bales of rope. He proceeded to place this strange hat on my head. We both laughed at the sight of me, while the stretchy material flopped down to my nose.

I guess, due to the recent adventures of Popeye, he decided to take this nautical opportunity to educate the first daughter of his only son about *her* future on the high seas. I can still hear the robust *Yo Heave Ho* in his voice, explaining how the moment I floated to Earth—in the safe arms of a celestial "Bosun's Mate"—*I* became a commissioned sailor on the *Ship of Life.*

Gilbert and Sullivan, the musical collaborators of long ago, would have been proud of his interpretation of their operetta, *Pirates of Penzance.* While he sang some of the songs, he adopted the demeanor of a seasoned mariner—being very adept at the role. His acting turned out better than those other "pirates" I saw, just the week before, who performed in a community-theatre version of this classic.

His vigorously bouncing me up and down made renditions of this seafaring trip even more graphic. What a risky move don't you think, with a ton of pot-roast bunking below deck. Lucky for me, and *him,* how my ship retained its cargo for the duration of the trip.

As I recollect this, the endearing aroma of his *Old Spice* surrounds me now, causing me to become as drowsy as I did that day, from nestling my newly *hatted-head* in the infinite nape of his neck.

I always fought sleep. I didn't want to miss a thing. But on this special day long ago, enraptured by my grandfather's cologne, I quit arguing with Morpheus. The instant I gave in and closed my eyes, the familiar zesty-scent triggered an out-of-body experience. The uncanny sensation started with goose bumps on my arms, from a spirited gush of damp twilight air. The chilly breeze carried *me,* right along with it, in a desperate search for a waning autumn sun.

In another split-second, my eyes focused on colorful lights—flashing their cheer on a balsam Christmas tree. It positioned near the large fireplace across the room, while a thirsty fire crackled eager logs. The African violets had abandoned the windowsill. A twinkling replica of a quaint colonial village, balancing on a pile of fake snow, now took the mini-garden's place.

Whizzing once more, I landed back at my own house. My original hatless-head rested on the pliable pillow inside the old familiar hammock. As usual, this secure canvas sling anchored between two of the tall and sturdy weeping willow trees behind my back porch. I touched vivacious spring daffodils, as a determined April breeze swung the hammock to-and-fro.

Before I could even pick one of these delightful flowers, and put it up to my nose for a good sniff, I found myself spiraling toward the summertime waft of sweet, smoky mesquite—sizzling off my father's recognizable backyard grill.

When I jolted awake from this trance, back to base number one on his reassuring lap, my head still swished underneath the, by then, scratchy beret. After this vivid excursion, I expected to see summer fireworks exploding, while I waved my hissing sparkler around the yard at home.

I rubbed white crusty stuff from the corners of my confused eyes. I had to search for my pink Melmac bowl, portraying *Bugs Bunny* waving the American flag, while stars and stripes smothered underneath an irreverent piece of juicy barbecued chicken, along with a scoop of Mom's creamy potato salad.

As any typical sprouting tot, I accepted life around me—except *this* explicit memory never left me. The scene is as clear as yesterday. A message must hide in it *somewhere.* I've tried hard to figure out this puzzling adventure over all of these years, except I can't.

I only know how it *was.*

Chapter 2

*Ship of Life*______________ **"She's free to challenge her journal."**

Up to this point in my journey, although I often get queasy on my prognostic cruise through life, I've been able to steer a safe voyage. Even though maintaining an even keel wasn't easy, I secured the ballast on my own. Minor bumps and bruises from the rolling waves, never altered my itinerary. Now I find the jig is up, along with the untamable flapping jib.

I'm typing this now, sitting alone at the kitchen table, on a Sunday evening. A scary warning hitched a ride with this morning's sunrise and beeped me a jangling **S.O.S.** "Batten down the nauseous hatches *sailor*, a tempest brews in your coffee pot."

How can *I* navigate the crest of a mile-high whitecap? Signals predict an explosion with more foam than a *Colgate* shaving cream factory. My long overdue Ship of Life upchuck can no longer be controlled with *Tums.*

Journal, you are my benevolent port of refuge. Under your warm and endless blank sheets, a girl can weather the worst of squalls. With *you* as her sanctuary, she's captain of her *protected* literary craft. Her pen will always obey orders, because she controls the strokes. There will never be mutiny, while *she* is at the helm.

You crave "incessant thespian whining" in the same way that *she* craves succulent sweet strawberries, dipped in melted milk chocolate. In friendly addition, when she divulges her long list of daily grievances, you won't make that asinine wisecrack. I speak of the grammatically in arrears—as well as disgusting retort—full of typical nincompoopery, "Shove yuh gripes where sun don't shine."

A journal gives its author unlimited space to be obnoxious. Unlike *some* significant others, her sounding board validates a need for histrionics that "raise the house roof." A journal is privy to the *real* reason why its writer hosts those *tightfisted* "rage parties"—the ones without any refreshments.

As a convenient result, she can lift her journal's roof, any old time she wants. She knows that no matter how much of her understanding literary accommodation caves in later on—due to her "temperamental aerobics"—it will stick around for the messy cleanup, without any usual guilt-provoking conditions.

This point is truer than ever, when she suffers from unforgiving mental fatigue. Sitting on the bed, with her open journal on her lap, she's aware of the pen slipping from her cramped fingers. This exhausted writer can only cry herself to sleep.

Throughout the dark night, her tolerant journal waits alongside its worn-out author, who, wrung dry, is now in deep slumber—except sleep is brief. All too soon, her alarm clock decrees another round of difficult daylight, while tousled hair burrows into that still-saturated pillow. She's one of those frantic mice, in the direct sight of *Farmer Gray's* legendary shotgun.

By *this* fidgety point, her tormented tresses are worthy of that mocking commentary, "Washed-out blonde with fried-to-a-crisp ringlets." They always say this, so they think, behind her sore and drafty back—scarred with more holes than a hunk of Swiss cheese.

Loyal as ever, when said writer quits hitting the snooze button, her journal smiles by her scruffy-side to offer unconditional aid and comfort. What's even more sympathetic, a journal will never judge its author, nor speculate why her nose hides under "slimy-green mega-snot."

A journal won't inquire why a pesky skunk's on a rampage to spray its author's expensive new *Adidas* footwear.

A journal can't urge its author to sprint on her "burly legs" right over to the mall, for the one-hour-only sale on *Scope.* Or inform her how to stockpile three supersized bottles of this *urgent* mouthwash—just for the price of one.

An author needs no shilly-shallying in the sock-it-to-me department. She's free to challenge her journal. She's able to fume at will and with fiendish flames blasting out of her "snotty nose," she can smack her journal—right between its pages. As a perpetual good sport, with no connections to law enforcement, a journal relishes—in the midst of this myriad of inadequacies—its writer's "silly juvenile tantrums."

Journal, I have important decisions to make. Taking advantage of your anticipated assistance comes first. Before I officially begin, I should set the scene with narratives from my crazy existence interweaving both past and present. As they evolve, please prepare to support me on this unusual journey—a journey transporting us both, deep into the unknown. Neither of us can predict what's about to come as your pages unfold.

Trust me.

You may as well know now that I use this expression imploring your trust when I'm insecure, so you'll be hearing these two little words often.

Chapter 3

My Crazy Existence

PART 1:

LOITERING IN THE SHADOWS **"Wrong."**

I would be wise to tell you now that I have a slight tendency toward hamming it up. Wait a second! Perhaps I mean more of a huge one. I *do* have an extraordinary talent for exaggeration. Everybody knows this. Now *you* will be in awe of my imagination too.

Since I'm not into self-kudos, I shouldn't take sole credit for my reputation. My father deserves some recognition for my infamous theatrics. Our battles over my "thickheaded persistence," on doing the exact opposite of what he says, *might* play a small part in my fame. We tend to butt heads a lot.

On occasions when we do have what my mother calls, "a spat," but what my dad calls, "abject defiance"—drama does triumph on both sides. There is a strong probability that viewing every one of those great . . . one-thousand, two-hundred, and twenty-five episodes of **Dark Shadows** did push my legendary imagination to his portended point of no return.

He told me, at least four times a day, how naive I am to take any soap opera tripe as realism. This one, concerning the *occult,* produced more "profuse suds" than the eight-ounce bottle of liquid detergent I poured into the dishwasher. He brings up this situation at least once a month, although it occurred over two years ago when I *only* tried to be a good daughter.

Hearing my flu-stricken mother, coughing up her guts day and night, made me fear for my life. *I'd* save the rest of the family, including me, from her feverish and aching fate, as well as the cost of those prescription bottles lined up on the table near her bed. There could be nothing better at killing all those nasty germs than a product for washing dishes, going by the name of **JOY,** so happy to accommodate the chore.

Wrong.

My parents had to replace the dishwasher, hire an expensive carpenter to rip out the entire kitchen floor, rebuild the foundation from scratch, and replace several custom-made cabinets. I never knew it before, but boy, oh boy, do electricians cost an absolute fortune.

Now—since this situation is a different ongoing soap opera, I'll get back to Dad and his dim view of my favorite television show. I guess I must accept the truth. On the surface, he *can* be on his toes, but this excludes teeter-tottering in reindeer clogs imported from Finland. My mother says his future broken leg will be a payback from darling, red-nosed *Rudolph.*

I may like to deny his acuity concerning vampires but can't. According to him, any story on TV concerning a "sympathetic one" should be *somewhat* convincing. In *ghastly* addition, when the *fiend* lies through his *fangs,* while *hell-bent* on converting innocent people to the *sinister* game, why am I the only one wanting to hug him like a *Count Dracula* teddy bear?

But I drew the line at taking *this* sort of stuffed animal to bed with me. My father told me that my astounding advent of "teddy bear commonsense" was a great relief. He didn't want to worry himself sick about such a "sensitive aspect" of my adolescence, concerning *any* kind of male plaything in my bed, "stuffed or otherwise."

He also said many times how *Barnabas Collins,* the central character of this *soap,* is nothing more than a pale and thirsty *unlucky* bloodsucker—with a major *sourpuss.* The despondent loser looks like he's "on the wagon" and substituting his all-time favorite *beverage* with a glass of unsweetened grapefruit juice—using vinegar for a chaser.

In retrospect, I can't argue. What kind of **170+** down-in-the-mouth vampire, with a classic pickle-puss, skulks around his ominous medieval mansion from morning to night, when assorted beautiful women reside in the place on a "revolving door basis?" *Their* voluptuous necks are all his for the taking, while he fends off overpowering *arterial* temptation. If this isn't "self-flagellation" in the vampire world, then what is?

He also thought this ancient *dour* vampire—who will never appear over the age of forty, but go on *sucking* Medicare dry for eternity—suffered from an extreme case of other kinds of *plasmatic* monkey business. All of those sabotaging witches and warlocks, along with an assortment of other entities going bump in the night, caused more traffic at the mansion than a "foggy freeway."

In osteopathic addition, since Mr. Collins could no longer "kill time" by sleeping away the daylight hours in his plush coffin, his stooping posture came from "a poor quality mattress." My dad also thought a vampire character—*compassionate* or otherwise—with the wimpy title of "Barnabas" could never dupe anybody else besides *his* daughter to shed actual tears over this ghoul's depression, concerning a "self-imposed" *undertaking* to kick the "grisly habit."

Likewise, the cast of other "campy gothic characters"—unable to act their way out of a "bloody" paper bag—would warp anybody—above all me—with *my* "perpetual flights of fancy."

Even more ghoul-like, as soon as the show broadcasted in color, the new sponsor turned out to be syrupy red ketchup. As an alarming result, Dad thought about what kind of sticky upheaval he should anticipate on his *own* home front.

Hokey or not, I remained a passionate fan for all of those five-tenuous broadcast seasons, until last year when the batty network ran into a bottleneck and overdosed on garlic. The series flew off the air for good, heading for a more hospitable cave. I sure did love that show. Penning fifty postcards, informing them how infallible *Transylvanian* canon law considers Barnabas their "Patron Saint of Compassionate Incisors" did *not* resurrect him. Oh well.

Some you win.

Some you lose.

Some just give you writer's cramp.

PART 2:

NOBLE ENTITLEMENTS

"Yes—I said *paranormal*."

I must tell you right now, my soon to be overworked Journal, about the huge pile of junk I plan to dump on you. This indicates I should pay you a king's ransom for your service. At the very least, your fee should be the amount a queen goes for. I think the rate of a princess is too cheap, and the low value of ubiquitous lords and earls renders them useless.

Since kidnapping *any* sort of royalty hasn't been on my recent agenda, you have my unending gratitude for being free of charge—unless you count my visit to a certain department store. I love riding on *Macy's* unique wooden escalator. The ancient mechanism rolls on ball bearings, taking customers down with a slow inch by inch to their stationery bargain basement. A plaque dates the squeaky thing back to 1902, when the *Herald Square* location in New York City first opened.

Getting back to bargains found in Macy's modern-day office-world basement, I purchased several long note pads, a hole puncher, a sturdy metal binding clip, a packet of number three pencils, a box of assorted red and blue ballpoint pens, a carton of white typing paper, and a dozen *Remington* typewriter ribbons.

These ribbons *are* cheaper there, but still cost me more than I'd like. I ignore the high price, because quality for you *is* a top priority. I have no other choice but to spend the money, regardless of the reputation I have for being a big tightwad. I'll admit that people find it odd when I tell them about my new strict budget. I guess it's only natural for them to wonder how, by what conceivable means, *I* could be any more of a penny-pincher than I already am.

Explaining my attitude will be easy if they've ever watched the actor Jack Benny doing the famous "masked bandit" skit on his television show.

This classic comedic takeoff depicts him acting as nonchalant as a baby would, gnawing on a zwieback, while he informs the menacing mugger, who is pointing a gun at him, ***"Well . . .*** now let me think this over." He illustrated how a true miser, threatened at gunpoint, wouldn't hand over their overstuffed and booby-trapped wallet to anybody—including an armed robber.

Nowadays, I have an inclination to copy stingy Mr. Benny and the way he acts in his famous spoof. What if a mugger pointed a weapon at me, and asked the same question he asked of him, ***"It is your money or your life?"*** I wouldn't be able to give the perpetrator the obvious quick answer either. "Sure, *here,* take the entire kit and caboodle." I'd find myself thinking over my response too. What's the mugger going to do, other than wedging me between the heavy parental-rock flattening my life, and the hard place known as emancipation?

Yes, I *know* that he could kill me, but without independent monetary security what kind of life could I have, even if I did escape without a scratch. Certainly not the kind I envision for myself. My financial future is *that* vital to me. My main rationale for composing you, however, is due to astounding events manifesting in my life as of this morning, which are nothing short of paranormal.

Yes—I said *paranormal.*

At the minute of my birth, I quit floating in a murky realm of amniotic fluid—filled with meconium. Ever since I contributed this goop to the busy maternity ward laundry, *I've* been bobbling around in the even stranger realm replacing my generosity. As a child, I couldn't rationalize *why* I attract mystical forces. Now I intend to record today's eerie signs with precision, outlining how they've been slapping me in the face since I fell out of bed this morning. Following this, I'll report them in succession, until I solve the present-day unknown.

There's an extrasensory shroud engulfing my life. I'm not exaggerating when I tell you this presence comes across as a major pall-bearing champion, inside of an illusive supernatural arena. With *your* help, cherished Journal, I'll get to the bottom of its eerie masquerade. Or in thinking this over, perhaps I should start at its top. Please be assured, that whatever method I need to dismantle the creepy invader, *I* am up to the task—although I can't do it right now.

No, I'm *not* a chicken.

I just might, shall we say—be a used up hen with a stuck egg.

The real reason for postponing my attack is due, in part, to my father's chastisement concerning the numerous perils of dabbling in "supernatural hijinks." I also cannot ignore the actor Steve McQueen. Both Dad *and* Steve are responsible for my hesitancy about delving into horror.

Until I'm ready to meet my supernatural match, I'll just stick my mitts into a big bowl of *Doritos.* And, while I'm munching away tonight, I'll give you constant reassurance about my perseverance.

But no matter how many circumstances I end up blaming, for my nonstop stalling excuses, my reluctance really originates from the toxic globule that almost ate me when I was just a little kid.

PART 3:

OPERATION CELLULOID **"So why bother to try."**

In the happy-go-lucky days of yore, I had only two fundamental challenges. Foremost, was getting away with eating disgusting vegetables on my daily dinner plate. Hiding them was hard. There wasn't any dog to feed, waiting for a treat under the table. But I *could* pinch my sister's legs that dangled in the high chair. When she screamed and distracted my parents, I'd give Dad his well-deserved extra helping.

The other one concerned training for my future career as a beautician. I'd practice by playing "beauty parlor" with my vast collection of expensive dolls. I was short on equipment except for my comb and brush, as well as a pair of blunt safety scissors, and some of my mother's bobby pins. Saying the results were not professional would be an understatement.

At this time, when I massacred my clientele, my parents anticipated a new form of invader—far worse than the one forcing Dad to brownbag canned **SPAM.** It didn't come cheap every month paying *Boris Karloff*—at that *rip-off* Cuddleview Doll Hospital's "Frankenstein Laboratory"—to piece together butchered *Barbie* scalps.

Mom and Dad are always diligent guardians of my welfare. However, when operation celluloid arrived, they demonstrated frenetic strength—way beyond regular mortals. People were astonished to witness this zealous young couple warning everybody in the entire world, including those in need of sign language that: "By no controllable means" . . . would they ever permit their "impressionable child" . . . *any* exposure to the "horrendous new film" . . . about the "massive gelatinous glob" . . . ingesting "an entire helpless town."

Although the status of their current lives provided more than enough for them to handle, they imparted to their captive listeners a "personal gripe" with Hollywood. Why should upstanding citizens like them become hapless victims of undeserved "parental persecution?" How else could you explain the helpless town in this *egregious* motion picture coming to the silver screen as a crafty mockup of the innocent *bucolic* one—where their "gullible daughter" resided?

From the viewpoint of a kid, about to turn four, the more my exhausted parents went around the world touting a creature insane enough to gorge on *my* indigestible town, the more fascinating the prohibited feature became. Although I didn't understand their sophisticated vocabulary, I sure got the gist. I knew that, with entertainment critics like these, any probability of my ever watching this scary movie was zero—or less.

On the other algebraic hand, when my parents foolishly factored in my unconscious older cousin, these dismal odds went way up. Unbelievable as the calculations sound, *she* was oblivious to the urgent message they bounced off those magnetic radiation belts, orbiting around the Earth. Mom and Dad had security clearance concerning usage of the new *Explorer-1 Satellite,* which discovered these astrophysical parental-hotlines to begin with.

As in the past, and remaining up until the present-day, she's the only cousin I have. This is great when you're under pressure to sacrifice your stingy allowance to buy gifts for relatives, but it stinks if you need a steady role model. As tragic as circumstances were, this cousin continues to be comatose on a regular basis. I wasn't capable of waking her up then. So why bother to try. At this point now, I still find dealing with her impossible.

Owing to her obvious lack of credentials, other than being my father's niece and dumb enough to accept their paltry **15¢** an hour, my parents made a disastrous error. On a dull, overcast Saturday afternoon, with predictions of a slight chance of showers, they left *me* alone with *her* so they could "live it up" and celebrate their mushy wedding anniversary. Their plans included driving to the next town for a "sophisticated lunch," along with a new movie about some *Ben Hur* guy.

The moment my parents left the premises, instead of my cousin whipping out the tattered *Old Maid* card game that she carried around like a religion, she said there was a fantastic surprise in store. Without question, my parents would be "grateful" if she gave me a "special treat" and we went to see **The Blob**—replete with a double feature *Casper the Friendly Ghost* cartoon.

As they say at local rodeos, right before opening the dilapidated gate to release the terrified broncobuster—who's already bucking like mad on the towering saddle, "Come a ti yi yippy, come a ti yi yea."

PART 4:

NOT SO GOOD AND PLENTY OF IT "Hooray!"

As soon as the extensive breeze settled—the one caused by Mom's new herringbone cape coat, swirling around like a whirlpool during her hasty exit—my cousin jumped up to the ceiling, like a pogo stick on speed. Then faster than that slammed front door, she told me to fetch my jacket and galoshes. She also told me to bring my "Mr. Bluster" umbrella; the one she ordered for me as a gift from the *Howdy Doody* television show the prior Christmas.

Nothing much has changed; she still annoys me on a recurring basis. But back in those days, she had me madder than usual. I couldn't understand why my most adored *Doodyville* character, the breathtaking *Princess Summerfall Winterspring,* wasn't under the tree instead of that cantankerous *Phineus T. Bluster* puppet. What *was* she thinking!

On this dreary babysitting Saturday though, she more than made up for her Howdy Doody miscalculation. She planned to take me to the fabulous horror show my parents crusaded against. I must say she demonstrated a certain responsibility about the crime. When we left in the sudden ferocious wind and rain, she held my hand tight as we scooted several slippery blocks to the bus stop. We had to arrive before show time.

By the stormy way, this unexpected nasty weather gave Mr. Bluster a real run for his ensuing brief life, and also gave the radio's weather forecaster—Mr. Prate Wright—a perfect score for always being wrong.

We were sopping-wet mischief-makers, when we stepped on that sacrificial doorstep of horror. Despite a dire need for huge towels, my "dependable" adolescent relative, with chalky-white zit medication streaking down her soggy cheeks, acted more than eager to buy our tickets. She said the warm theatre would soon dry us off. I went through a chilly panic several minutes before, concerning the possibility that they might not even have enough seats left for us to *get* inside and *see* the scary feature. We were waiting in the middle of a long line, winding around the block.

She also acted sharper than I ever thought, when the lady behind the ticket booth asked if I might be too "impressionable" for a horror show. With a straight face, she accused the soon to be embarrassed worker of being prejudiced against an innocent teen with dwarfism.

Her kindness knew no bounds, when she convinced her dubious group of fellow crusty-faced—pimply-pubescent-pals—already congregating in the theatre's lobby, how they shouldn't give my presence a "second thought." Raising both her hands with a thumbs-up, she reassured them how her "sweet little cousin" wouldn't even *think* about causing them "a bit of trouble."

Hooray! The supportive remarks worked. She put her wet thumbs back into her purse and zoomed to the pricey concession stand, where she bought her dear and darling tag-a-long that super jumbo box of cavity-provoking *Good and Plenty* candy.

Later on, disastrous developments proved my parents more than correct. For weeks and weeks after seeing such a **Grade-B**—true-to-life ingestion of my immediate environment—I suffered a drawn out recovery from post-movie bronchitis. I also had sequential screaming night terrors. Every hour—like clockwork—I'd jolt up in my bed and howl like a bungling werewolf, jumping on a spiky porcupine. How could I help behaving this way? How would *you* react, if an innocent freckle on top of *your* nose kept turning into a fat baby-blob? This once tiny brown speckle just grew and grew, and yes *grew.* My chronological nightmares gave new meaning to the insufferable term people loved to direct at me, namely, "obnoxious . . . freckled-face kid."

Bad news got plenty of publicity, after everybody witnessed how such an ongoing scarcity of sleep mutates once flexible people into cement zombies—with a dreadful new attitude. Compounding my parents' misery, their other child wouldn't sleep either. Both kids engaged in a competitive insomnia marathon. My baby sister's molars developed much bigger than her gums. Painful teething caused a nighttime temperature.

Even back in her earliest years, she choreographed calamity better than Bob Fosse ever could. When I dozed off for a brief period—without the baby-blob as my pillow—that sibling of mine woke up hollering complete bloody murder. Later, while I screamed in sheer blob-terror, *she* snored so loud that the wheels on her crib fell off.

Other than experiencing the personal misery of my nightmares, I didn't comprehend how they debilitated an entire community. Hearing my dad stumbling around the house while he babbled about, "Respect for the Founding Fathers of birth control," added to the confusion.

Thinking back now, wasn't this kind of an oxymoron. But whatever he meant at the time, concerning these hypocritical *Founding Fathers,* I had no idea. I suspected my mother must have. She kept telling him in a pleading voice to, "Hurry up and implement their wisdom." I guess he did, because as soon as the crises subsided, the charitable Goodwill organization came by to pick up my sister's secondhand crib. They also took boxes and boxes of unused baby clothes, and assorted infant paraphernalia, which had also once been mine.

Watching them load all of my things into the huge truck made me even cockier about the traitors having no idea how I already stashed my favorite ones up in the forgotten attic, guaranteeing nobody would ever get their dirty hands on any more of *my* stuff. Sometimes children don't have a say in situations like this. Parents just cart off everything, and a kid never sees their possessions again. But this Nazi tactic wouldn't wipe *me* out. My preemptive voice rang out loud and clear from way up in that attic, a place where, according to an aware man like my father—who hadn't ventured that climb in over two years—"only a *fool* dared to tread."

Too bad I didn't have one of those *court jester* hats available.

PART 5:

GOODWILL?

"I tried *bouillon* once."

Trouble always hitches a free ride on my shoulder, so after everybody *finally* snored in peace throughout the night again, a clumsy roofer came across those hidden toys and stuff went, if you can believe it, *more* bonkers than before. An older man, the spitting image of the current president, came to inspect rafters in the attic before installation of new shingles.

I had just seen the morning newspaper's huge front-page picture of Dwight David Eisenhower. Even though my sister spit up her breakfast all over him, nobody could convince me *he* wasn't upstairs in *my* attic. Working with the **FBI** must have taught him to poke around big-time. The phenomenal stash came crashing down on him—straight from that wild blue yonder playland in the sky.

I thought, at this skydive moment, how *Ike* sure had a dangerous second job. Also, for someone of *his* stature, he said real bad words. I know this, because my mother kept blushing and putting her hands over my ears. The blasphemous, number one commander-in-chief in the entire world continued to wear his smashed hardhat, as he swayed around clutching his chest. His face turned a scary purple, but he continued hollering at the top of his lungs anyhow, about wanting my parents' documentation for "Workmen's Compensation Insurance."

We were lucky enough then to have any insurance on the house at all, so when I watched Mom racing over to look in Dad's desk, I knew she had a better chance of finding the *Hope Diamond* in his pencil drawer, than coming across this compensation stuff. She continued fishing around for show, just to keep this man quiet. Her move didn't work. The old White House roofer turned out to be pretty tough. He continued yelling, no matter how often my mother looked in that desk or how many cups of fresh ground coffee, and those yummy baked-on-the-spot cinnamon buns, she foisted on him.

Things calmed down after my father excused himself from a "critical" business meeting about "South African bullion" at the bank where he works. He arrived back home lickety-split, just to hand the distraught contractor, whose name just *happened* to be Ike Eisenheimer, something called **25-Year-Old Chivas Regal.** Mom told Dad he acted very impolite, by screaming at us about leaving such an "important meeting." Losing his chance for a considerable end of the year bonus wasn't any excuse to go ape.

How could it be such an important meeting? I tried *bouillon* once. Why did he make soup into such a big deal? This particular broth had no special flavor, except for the excessive salt. I felt sure the *critics* at this meeting agreed with me. I couldn't understand that ridiculous overreaction when both of his eyes twitched and sweat dissolved his *starched* white shirt into a limp dishrag. My mother knows him real good, and the reason why she keeps a bunch of fresh, ready to go ones in his closet.

Later on, with my father in a spiffy new shirt, he witnessed his generous gift of this magical Chivas stuff going to a new home. A now smiling Ike carried off his prize inside of his *former* hardhat. Maybe he did qualify as a nice fellow, at the conclusion of the massive mess. Or maybe he experienced a cinnamon-high.

Hold on. *Could* the roofer's change of attitude be due to my father signing that last minute revised contract? I'm referring to his sudden willingness to purchase those top of the line *authentic* cedar shingles that my mother wanted from the outset. The month before, when the roofer first brought over the classy samples, she couldn't coax their exorbitant cost out of her stingy husband. But boy, did she ever try. Instead, she had to settle for the cheap imitation variety.

Due to his sudden, expensive change of heart, a second mortgage loomed on the horizon—*along* with the new roof. At least my grandmother expressed this opinion. I heard her whisper those exact words to my grandfather, when they rushed over to calm him down.

I mean my *father*, not the roofer!

By the tense way, while he held the shaking pen, to put *his* fatherly *John Hancock* on the dotted line of the new agreement, *he* scared me by hollering even louder than the roofer did. He complained at the top of his lungs, about his arm being in a "painful twist." The yelling even surpassed the instance when my uncle whacked Dad's arm with a five-iron. Dangerous things happen on golf courses, if you don't pay attention.

Before returning to his office, to sip more of the dumb bouillon, he almost cried. His discomfort had to be from the *new* excruciating pain in his arm. This time the suffering popped up out of nowhere. He also kept telling my mother how giving away "that booze" killed him.

With even more of a furious look, he pointed at *me* and said, *"First,* we have the vat of noxious **Jell-O** that *you* made me swallow. I speak, Ginger, of the wicked cinematic version of this cheap dessert, transforming me into a zombie—an accountable zombie, but a zombie no less. Now, *also* do to *you,* I've had to adopt a regal approach to smooth over those decapitating toys from a lethal heaven."

Why he singled *me* out, to vent his wrath over the high cost of home maintenance, *I* will never know. This is when he said I should think twice in the future, before engaging in any more supernatural hijinks. So here I am, *all* of this while later, doing what he told me to do—for once. Getting serious though, reflecting about what is going on with me now, might force me to think ten times, just to be certain.

Let's get back now to *Goodwill,* the charity with the inappropriate name, that is. As the huge packed truck pulled out of our driveway, I protested like mad. Some of my things were still topnotch, just like those new shingles. Adding to my rage, he also hauled off the entire collection of sentimental stuff that almost eliminated the sitting president of the United States.

As usual, my parents ignored me. They didn't care at all when the charity's driver gave me such a dirty look, since they both sneered—right along with him. I have no need for interjecting any "trust me" here because, owing to my parents and the way *they* behave, such a remark isn't necessary.

This applies to my father more than ever, after he pigged out on cheap dessert. Who knew, how giving away booze could kill him. And then have Jell-O turn him into an accountable zombie, without any taste buds, addicted to salt, having big, bulging eyes protruding out of its head, while the stiff beast shuffled all over town with an extreme case of high blood pressure.

Not me, *that's* for sure.

PART 6:

SPEAKING OF THE ZOMBIE "Well—should it!"

Since then, when dalliance with esoteric forces caused major toxic waste, I have a distinct memory of my zonked dad waging war against dyspepsia. A stiff zombie soldier, wound up tight, and fueled by heartburn, belched its way throughout the entire community to protest "dual gastronomic elements from hell." We all felt sorry for the poor man. Along with a lingering wedding anniversary digestive upset, he had to stomach a household infested with *The Blob.*

Despite his new horrific stance from lack of sleep—one evocative of the scariest Voodoo's hollow-eyed living-dead—he never had trouble getting an audience to pay rapt attention to his tirade. Just one look at *his* haggard demeanor, alerted people in the assembly that if they didn't string him along by pretending to care, no prayer in the world—or beyond, could ever help them. This is why *I* listened to him, at least thirty times.

Here is what he said:

Who is hell-bent on sabotaging a civic-minded fellow like me, for being thoughtful enough to arrange a romantic Italian rendezvous? A *rendezvous*—I might add—with my *own* gorgeous wife.

I trusted my niece to babysit, so my spouse and I could dine at an exclusive bistro, where we would enjoy authentic *Venetian* cuisine.

Is this a crime worthy of capital punishment?

Should this be why I have not slept more than two hours a night for the past month?

Well—should it!

I also anticipated pouring our exquisite cut crystal carafe, filled to the brim with Tuscan wine. We planned to savor 'nectar from the gods' from exquisite antique signature goblets, while we basked in the sentimental ambiance of a cultured strolling violinist from sunny *Napoli,* at this phony Italian bistro.

Folks—I will not hesitate to tell you that this place is a dump, protected by gangsters. Their glorified violinist was *cultured* all right, just because he was *sloshed* and nothing more than a stumbling fiddler from Naples, *Florida.*

This inept musician kept dropping his bow, while he nipped at their *Tuscan* wine. I refer to the disgusting acerbic vino, in that chipped brown-glass jug, imported from some lousy moonshiner—whose *vineyard* sits atop those abundant, *green rolling hills* of Tuscany, *Nevada.*

By the by, in my own kitchen cupboard, you will find plenty of the same antique signature goblets, but my sensible wife washed out the *Skippy* peanut butter remains.

Furthermore—this eatery uses canned spaghetti. Believe me; *I* am more than familiar with *that* wallpaper paste.

Likewise—as for any of their other authentic *Venetian* cuisine, this bistro's halfway-thawed supermarket variety *frozen* eggplant parmesan, sure took the heat out of *my* anniversary tryst.

Hence—I will admit, to anybody here listening to me, how good old P. T. Barnum knew his business. There *is* a sucker born every minute. Take a careful look. One of them is standing here now, speaking to *you.*

PART 7:

DIAPER FALLOUT "I have my doubts."

Watching my father's face contort, over his obvious distress on the subject of the way gangsters had the nerve to treat him, bothered the hijacked crowd. Remember, he suggested the bistro had "protection" but people knew what he meant. This *mob* predicament, coupled with his cinematic dessert, continued to incite this already stupefied man, conveying him straight to P. T. Barnum's point of no return.

Due to his deplorable condition, a bigger dilemma soon presented itself to the listeners. How could they nod their heads in polite agreement with him, without indicating they looked at a newborn sucker? I sure found such a concept hard to handle. In addition to my anxiety over a teething baby sister, fostering my visit to a child psychologist, I now had an infant dad—with a fontanel as big and soft as an overripe cantaloupe.

I'm going to ask for your candid opinion about something. Although he had no cause to do so, might you agree with me that when my father staggered on *his* overworked soapbox, rallying against the rip-off bistro, he implicated *me* as his saboteur?

Besides finding out my father is in his infancy, who knew how such a staunch Republican like him was a clandestine lover boy. I bet my mother didn't have a clue.

Learning how my unconscious cousin is telepathic also came as a major shock. She very well may be one of those savants. Although she's obviously the kind of person who, on the surface, operates on permanent autopilot, she often ends up surprising the entire world with astounding spurts of genius.

Since she's gifted in this bizarre area, I should think about getting her on the *Jeopardy* TV quiz show. Later on, we can split the winnings fifty-fifty.

After Don Pardo announces her as all-time winner in the show's history, I'd go backstage and have my picture taken with its host, Art Fleming.

Returning to even more important questioning would I, or anybody else on the planet, ever have guessed *her* hidden talent? I have my doubts. I ask you, though, what other way could explain my cousin's ability to predict the exact amount of trouble I'd cause? She must be a gifted clairvoyant, because when she said I wouldn't cause them "a bit of trouble," she was right. I caused them a lot of trouble.

In case you're caring enough to think of the cranky sibling, who then leaked from every orifice in her body, there's no need. On that memorable Blob-excursion afternoon, my grandparents mopped her up at *their* house. If you're wondering how my grandparents fared, I think that due to the prior rigorous experience of raising my father they had no lasting repercussions from their granddaughter. I'm the only one this little smelly mess pushed toward psychoanalysis—in my *own* old baby carriage.

Still, when a family is prone toward insanity, you really do *never* know.

PART 8:

BRICK-A-BRAC

"Get out of *Dodge,* you varmint."

The most serious casualty, concerning the mass hysteria, turned out to be my obtuse cousin herself. Seeing the pathetic thing, staggering around town, caused Alcoholics Anonymous to put a flier in her mailbox. When she kept raising her hands to the sky in an apparent *Halleluiah* gesture, due to creepy super shock, she induced an astounding revival experience. I'm telling you right now, a fire-and-brimstone *Elmer Gantry* happening rolled out right in front of me, as well as everybody else in town.

Her ability to "see the light" appeared the very instant her furious parents withdrew their mummified daughter's generous stipend. They handed her this cash every week, just because the mirror fogged when they held it up to her nose. She wouldn't see her usual spending money—for the ensuing two months.

After suffering wakeup shocks, from numinous lightening bolts, my shaky cousin made a flaming vow, all over town, how she'd never again be "stupid enough" to share any of her cash with "that little brat." She based this ardent oath on her trendy new gray-felt skirt. The expensive one, embroidered with a life-size black-chenille French poodle, wearing an orange rhinestone collar.

Upping the anti of her considerable rage, we have the skirts twirling hem—trimmed with the jingling hot-pink bric-a-brac—along with her esteemed drafty hoop, swishing underneath. She got a bad case of painful chilblains from parading around in this getup, but it didn't stop her. I hope you understand how my cousin's usage of such prized swearing-collateral, demonstrated her direct admonition to me concerning the extent of her fury. This trendy outfit acted as an ironclad contract for a dueling pistol.

High Noon had arrived. Get out of *Dodge,* you varmint.

In this uncertain life, mine in particular, one should be aware of signing any contract before analyzing the fine print—a lesson my cousin should also learn. Concerning *this* relative aspect, your trust in me will compound by the minute.

Eliminating The Blob wasn't an easy task for my parents or my cousin. Most of her friends also suffered one consequence or another. Plus, if you ever saw this movie, you understand the challenge Steve McQueen had, bowing down to pick up the shattered pieces of his horrified budding career.

All of this agonizing pre-preparation has shown me that I must be a detective first and analyze every aspect of my environment—including what went on before. Any chance I have to pierce the uncanny mask *now* blobbing my life, will involve intensive scrutiny.

Without even swaying in a hula skirt, I'll use the sleuthing tactics of TV's Jack Lord, playing Steve McGarrett on *Hawaii Five-O.* I alone, will be more than capable of dissecting its ghostlike presence. Just little *unarmed* me will make the specter tremble. I will terrify it, until it cowers at my feet. I will torture it, until it begs for mercy.

After that, I will . . .

Without a second thought, I'm *sure* I will . . .

Um . . .

Journal, if you think I'm courageous—I'm not. So due to recent dire circumstances, I'm thinking about inventing a new classification of martial arts black belt in the unexplored area of *pseudo* bravery—one with bright yellow stripes.

Although I do have this newfound standing in self-defense, I must admit something to you while I still have the strength. My impending fate forces me to disintegrate a large brick, using only my bare right hand. The brick will be fine. It's red. Blood won't even show on it. Only my hand, and its former five fingers, will travel on a one-way trip to smithereens.

As a fractured result—judging from the abrupt termination of the sentence concerning my determination to slay the beast—I need a lot more practice with my unusual version of Bruce Lee, along with laying my jammed-up egg. All the same, I *will* say that the only suitable term for describing me, centering on the word brave, has to be—*bravado.*

PART 9:

GINGER, WHO?

"Humpty Dumpty sat on a wall."

Journal, I'm thinking of a no-nonsense way of presenting myself to you, since you're destined to become a clandestine exposé and all. Or maybe I should worry more about the preordained innocent reader, whom I hope will comprehend this account in the future.

I know. I'll begin by informing you *both* that my name is Ginger Autry, and I'm seventeen. I also have a formal middle name, starting with the letter **P.** I absolutely hate it. I never use this gross miscarriage of justice. This goes for its initial. In a technical way, I *am* Ginger P. Autry, but please just call me, *Ginger.* This sounds like a sensible way to start.

Next—I'll let slip about my precarious Humpty-Dumpty-like existence, plunging to those itty-bitty pieces . . .

Humpty Dumpty sat on a wall
Humpty Dumpty had a great fall
All the King's horses and all the King's men
Couldn't put Humpty together again

I, too, like little wobbly Humpty, am now in the throws of an extreme case of high anxiety myself. I'll take a break to obsess about those sorry Humpty chips, scattered across the mud-spattered dirt, at the bottom of that monumental rock wall. Worrying over his broken relationship to the imposing King *is* a valid concern of mine. By the disjointed way, *this* monarch is one I wouldn't even *think* about kidnapping. Rotund Humpty also had major weight with this King's entire entourage. Their collective incompetence, at not being able to do a darn thing for sweet, influential Humpty, is *not* a good sign. As a poor plebian, what chance do *I* have?

I'm thinking now, if there *is* an easy way to clue you in with regard to my recent lack of common sense.

Should I dare admit to you that whatever marbles still occupy my brain, are vacating their drafty location on the double?

Can I ever explain the painful wrench of that tight seatbelt, strapping me in on a surging emotional roller coaster?

Am I safe to confess how I'm no longer sure which way is *up*—on this whizzing ride? And recognizing *down*—is speeding toward problematic.

Wow, I realize you haven't told me to shove it yet. This is amazing. I'm guessing you liked the concise clarification I whipped up for you, with nary a single whine in sight. I was serious. I was even, well, *mature.* I won't waste any more energy worrying about this ridiculous stuff.

If you'll overlook my self-praise, on any rare occasion when I might gloat, I proved more than capable of verbalizing the catch-22 behind each of the nasty troubles. Although taking thirty minutes to get everything straight may have detracted from my brilliance. I should also tell you now about the subsequent waste of ten sheets of paper, and plenty of typewriter ribbon. Honest *is* honest, no matter how much you alter the word.

Speaking of honesty, the concept behind *truth* is hard to grasp. I'm sure you understand what happens when you're at the mall and see somebody you're desperate to avoid. You try ducking, but soon they'll spot you. You flinch, waiting for the inevitable, "Hi, how yuh doin'?" You reply with the perfunctory "Fine," although you want to scream.

Except—hey, I'd never be at *any* mall now. Hysterical at home, up in the bathroom, while yanking out precious tuffs of my already challenged hair, is more like it. As I watch those pathetic strands gliding down to the floor, I'd be consoling myself with the notion I'll save money on shampoo, setting lotion, and hairspray. A "Mr. Clean" look is very economical. I'll ask the *King of Siam* for non-styling tips. *He* is as bald as a bean, and still looks great. I think his regular name is Yul Brynner.

Yet bald *or* not, if you take the sentiments I've outlined, and magnify them a thousand times, you'll still have just a small idea about my current situation. Explaining details to my family is impossible unless I savor *Elmer J. Fudd's* rendition of Sigmund Freud, carrying his dilapidated analysis couch—to my equally dilapidated front porch. He might be ringing that warbling Dixie doorbell right now.

PART 10:

MORRIS

"Remember, I *am* a writer."

Contemplating dilemmas is easier for me, when I put them down on paper. Writing is my best problem solving solution. I have a habit of observing things. I get creative input from life itself. I carry around a large copybook, along with a pen, in my roomy shoulder bag—the color of an overripe plum—taking the abused satchel with me everyday for years. My faithful companion resembles a smashed eggplant now, but *Tonto* still gets the job done.

This efficient practice will continue making things easy for me to keep an accurate handwritten account of these private circumstances, as they unfold. Later on, I'll transcribe the notes so they make sense as to time and place. When the journal's finished, I'm taking the typewritten contents and making a single set of miniaturized copies of everything.

Have *you* seen the new unbelievable **Xerox** machine, which reduces print to a smaller size? They have one of them at a local post office, where they charge **5¢** per copy. Yes, I do realize I'm paying a lot. But no matter how much things wind up costing, I must reduce the paper size of my journal, to secure my final text, by rolling the substantial document up and stuffing the entire thing into an empty canister.

This twelve-inch-long cylinder—made of sturdy tin—reeks of vitamins. Just last week, the stinky thing was full of potent treats for malnourished cats. A picture of *Morris,* the tabby tomcat, starring in all those new **9Lives** cat food commercials on TV, decorates the front. The strong smell doesn't matter since I'm burying it right in Central Park Zoo, and this zoo is already a hangout for some pretty funky aromas.

Journal, I'm now giving you, and your forthcoming reader, an apology if an odor remains in the future. I've been trying my best, except I can't track down anything else strong enough to stand the ultimate test of the elements. I guess you *could* say that concealing my journal in a manner like this is my version of an oddball time capsule. Remember, I *am* a writer.

After I've done a good job of hiding everything and brush dirt from my hands, paying special attention to my chipped nails, I'll resist the urge to go splurge on a manicure. Instead, I'll visit all the animals imploring them to guard my secrets.

I will never return.

What will be, will definitely *be.*

PART 11:

PSYCHIATRIC REFRESHMENTS "He *is* a smooth operator."

In less than two measly months, I'll be eighteen. As of yesterday, acting gung-ho about celebrating my *legal* liberation with a big blowout, consumed most of my energy. I agonized over finding people who'd attend my celebration with *real* gifts, and not cheap prizes from empty boxes of *Crackerjacks.*

Anticipating this milestone, and the sanctioned autonomy attached to the title of *adult,* used to be the foremost thing in my world—until this afternoon. Now, I'm wondering if they have birthday cake inside a funny farm. Wasting precious resources, to commemorate special occasions in a place where people hallucinate, is stupid. Any worthy resident of a psychiatric ward can conjure up her *own* birthday bash.

An insane party-planning patient like this could never resist *that* suave apparition of a caterer, checking her out. He *is* a smooth operator. He tells her, while using his trademark seductive whisper, splattering her ear with remnants of *Sen-Sen,* that his name is Chef Randolph Lothario, but his friends just call him *Randy.* She salivates at the thought of how *he* above *all* will bake—exclusively for her—a more than spectacular quadruple-decker, mocha-fudge, butter cream creation—laced, by the intoxicating way, with champagne from Napoleon Bonaparte's private stock.

This chef knows where the exclusive catacomb wine cellar exists. He's used the place for various activities many times. With an animated wink-wink, he snitches about the laissez-faire nature of Napoleon's new corset-loose and fancy-free wife. Her future bridegroom didn't like her long name of Marie Josephe Rose Tascher and insisted she change it to plain old "Josephine" before they married. He wanted to wipe that itch out of her roving eyes prior to her starting a clean slate with him. He should have bought dozens of erasers to keep up the illusion. She didn't change at all after the nuptials. This is the real reason why she gave Randy the sole key for the corroding catacomb lock.

Before the whacked-out birthday girl even has a chance to question how he'll pull everything off, concerning the situation where *she* is, he mentions he needs no oven or ingredients to accomplish the immense culinary task. All he has to do is flick his left wrist and ***voila.***

She believes him, because this chef isn't shy. He shows off his diamond-laden Rolex on this left wrist, by waving the tony timepiece in front of her face. The bulky thing glows brighter than an infrared beam, on top of a remote lighthouse, causing her to blink a mile a minute.

To top off this all-around validation, we have this chef's professional hat. He bleaches this tall culinary badge-of-honor to a blinding bright white, and then he starches it stiff as a board. When he swaggers around the place, this smokestack converges with the ceiling.

In flavorful addition, he'll whip up his famous escargot—the casserole smothered in shallots and butter—by utilizing his celebrated *Lothario's Banquet Hall,* the one hovering in the sky right over the top of the Eiffel Tower. So why doubt *his* expert culinary credentials. Of course, she has no idea that "escargot" means snails, but the dish sure sounds tasty.

Later, when *The Beach Boys* drop by to enhance her apparition, Brian Wilson motions for her to come and sit on his talented knees. From *this* cozy vantage point, she'll blow out her eighteen glowing candles decorating the top of this cake. But the most beautiful candle of all is the four-inch-tall rotund one that alights in the center of this fabulous cake, just for her special good luck.

Almost as if she's hearing a record playing—The Beach Boys sing the traditional *Happy Birthday* refrain. Their superb soft tones resonate throughout the cold, institutional space. Therapy from Brian and the boys harmonizes triteness to a crescendo, where even her notorious fellow inmate, Dr. Strangelove himself, collapses from sentiment. When attendants rush over to revive him, he jumps around the ward in reaction to the huge colony of ants in those baggy britches he stole from Friar Tuck.

The legendary corpulent cleric was an easy target for Strangelove. As usual, this fan of crusty loaves of bread, washed down with a barrel of his favorite ale, slept it off under a gigantic redwood tree in Sherwood Forest—where ants become stout on droplets of alcohol and scattered breadcrumbs. After the selfish doctor steals the underwear of his dreams, he lands right next to her, ants and all, on Brian's already overburdened lap.

The additional candle on the cake now performs an incredible array of dazzling flip-flops, while circling around in the air. In her vain attempts to blow out the floating light, this delusional patient's feeble head wobbles with the skill of a ventriloquist's dummy. As a lopsided result, in addition to her obvious cerebral malfunction, she's suffering from a painful stiff neck.

She need not worry though; several incarcerated chiropractors are with her at the celebration, and with this kind of far-out party-trip—who'd ever want the real thing instead?

Not me, *that's* for sure.

PART 12:

LOONY TRUTH

"I do have *one* fault."

To be fair, I should reassure you right now I'm not an actual lunatic. Although I'll confess, some people do call me a kook. Oops, we should pause a minute. After typing only a few pages of this epic, the notorious penchant I have for *fabricating* is taking over. "Fabricating" is the polite word people often use to suggest I'm a liar. I never intend to deceive people on purpose, but I do have an innate tendency toward embellishment.

In my defense, I'll say preparing to become a creative writer *does* take groundwork. This time, though, my ingenuity is popping up in areas where I shouldn't distort the essentials. I have no excuse. I've had plenty of chances to think about being honest. Perhaps, I didn't ponder things enough.

I took a seminar last year about the art of keeping a journal. I learned that if you're serious about recording any sort of *diary,* as I'm planning to do, you must tell the complete truth. There's to be no shirking around. Integrity with a journal is important to the author. Since I'm counting on a person like you to read this *someday,* I have a double reason for being straightforward.

Trying to locate my typewriter afforded me an opportunity to give myself a necessary pep talk about candor. Unlike me, my fortunate typewriter can hide from sight. Throughout fifteen minutes of searching, I found the pitiable machine. It struggled for air, devoid of an inserted ribbon, while cringing at the bottom of the huge box I'm using for a temporary closet. This moving carton bursts at the seams. I hold the thing together with packing tape, but always manage to shove one more item inside of it.

I also discovered a new Remington ribbon, stored underneath the typewriter's cover. This put me ahead in the financial department, while giving me another fifteen-minute chance to mull over specifics about being candid.

As usual, it took me this long to perform what people think is the *simple* task of inserting a ribbon into a typewriter. I won't deny my inadequacy any longer. I do have *one* fault. I'm a complete klutz, when changing a typewriter ribbon. I can never accomplish this cumbersome task, without the spool unwinding—all the way down to the floor.

Are you also of the opinion how exasperating things can get when you're handling a fresh ribbon? Without fail, the smudgy thing wraps itself a way too tight around its skimpy wheel. You can't escape the miserable task, no matter what. Having to align the cumbersome ribbon, through those two tight narrow slots, jutting out of a typewriter, will be the end of me one day. In my inept opinion, whoever designed this frustrating system did so on purpose to persecute me.

As you will now see, they have succeeded.

PART 13:

HAZARDOUS MATERIAL

"It's all about the *ribbon.*"

You may think I'm a superior typist. You're right. All the same, there's a miserable caveat. I know how typing faster than *anybody* wouldn't get you squat. I flunked that professed "Typing and Preparation for the Business World" elective for only one reason. The *skill* of typing is not about speed or accuracy. It's all about the *ribbon.*

Those puritanical rules concerning *decorum,* when typing in any kind of office environment, are enough to make Nathaniel Hawthorne's novel *The Scarlet Letter,* a modern commentary on liberal thinking.

I'm speaking about no skirts shorter than one-inch below the knee, no bare legs, no sandals, no spike heels or faddish boots, no dangling earrings, no tight sweaters, *no* cleavage under *any* circumstances, no denims or slacks, limited makeup, no perfume, short manicured fingernails with clear polish only—and if you're not a nun, don't even bother to apply.

Imagine, whether in or out of the convent, the awful quandary of being an honor student unable to master a ridiculous thing like *typing?* My ancient instructor, Mrs. Hermione Hazard—the exact likeness of the portrait of *Whistler's Mother*—told me she wasn't impressed with how fast and accurate I type. What "good" is my "questionable" skill, if I can't keep a typewriter *functional?* Her continual message harped on my learning how to change its ribbon with "expediency"—or suffer the "ultimate" consequence.

I'll never forget the haughty parody she stood up to rhyme, on the stormy afternoon of the last official day of school in my junior year. Bad weather or not, all the girls in the dumb room sure acted cozy *inside.* For those worthless classmates, watching *her* let *me* have it tasted better than the school cafeteria's special of the day. I'm referring to my unparalleled favorite, the fantastic bologna hoagie, including the usual side portion of creamy mashed potatoes, smothered in rich brown gravy.

"Miss Autry, I must make you realize how a typewriter, and a typewriter ribbon, goes together like a horse and carriage. It's an institute you can't disparage. You can't have *one,* without the *other.* You *can* try *and* try to separate them, but it's an illusion. So now—you've come to *this* conclusion."

With that sardonic look on her face, one lined heaver than a road map, she handed me the hilarious **F–,** accompanied by thunderous applause from my fellow students. She had great difficulty doing the job, while clapping louder than anyone else did.

Wait a minute. In thinking this over, stodgy Mrs. Hazard could never come up with anything so inventive. She ripped-off her comparative dialogue direct from *Ole Blue Eyes.* I sure heard the "original lyrics" of her cribbed jingle often enough. I recall its popularity almost ten years ago. My mother loved singing Frank Sinatra's hit *Love and Marriage.* Everybody noticed her fondness for the catchy song, while she puttered around the house. And believe me mother could putter.

More to the clawing point, I know *why* Mrs. Hazard tried to tear me down and embarrass me, but too bad for her. She had no idea about *my* thick skin. I'm sure her miserable attempt to break me, stemmed from the influence of other students in my class taking turns, running up to her desk every five minutes. They put pressure on her with their continual nagging on the subject of my "inadequacy," and waste of any *new* ribbons inside of the dented metal cabinet containing typing supplies. Just like me, this rusting mess sat at the back of the unventilated room where we *both* eroded.

My usual "trust me" would be too mild for this one, although, keeping in line with truth, they *were* right about the lack of any intact ribbons.

But did they have to be so catty about it?

PART 14:

GREETINGS FROM WOODSTOCK "He won't."

During my personal war with Mrs. Hazard, along with every contorted typewriter ribbon in the junkyard, summer school shouted my name. The approaching vacation would be a total bummer. I didn't want to swelter inside a classroom without any type of air-conditioning or efficient fans, just to end up flunking the typing part *again.*

Such a miserable thought grew more exasperating by the minute, because of the travel brochures scattered around the house. The rest of my family planned on two glorious weeks in Bermuda.

My father lives, sleeps, and breathes golf, so this exciting vacation involved, as usual, one of his dumb golf tournaments, but so what. When he goofed-off like a cartoon version of Arnold Palmer, I'd enjoy the gorgeous beach while splashing around in my animal-print bathing suit. I couldn't wear this wild two-piece one at the chilly end of the previous year, after purchasing my bargain on sale for a song.

Except—no more singing or ocean breezes waited for me. Sulking at home alone, I'd raid a packed pantry on a daily basis. My mother's guilt for abandoning me ensured a gain of at least five pounds. I wouldn't fit into the bathing suit anyhow. How much safer could I ever be than under those crumpled chocolate bar wrappers up in my room.

Naturally, local relatives volunteered to spy on me, and I had to keep up with credits for graduation the coming year. Someone of *my* superior intellect not graduating was unthinkable. The gates of summer school incarceration would slam shut, while I wilted inside, trying for a breath of fresh air with my nose sticking out between bars on the window.

Regarding Bermuda, my sister told me not to worry about missing "a thing" since she'd bring me back a great souvenir *if* Daddy gave her the money for it, that is.

He won't.

The moment they placed those handcuffs on my irritated wrists, I never expected to get such an awesome prison break. My new typing teacher turned out to be a young substitute, roving through my sweltering town. She embodied a beautiful vagabond—a free spirit—picking up spare bread, traveling across America.

What's even more smoking hot, the year before she ended up standing in front of a classroom full of junky typewriters, these travels escorted her to *Woodstock.* I mean she really *went.* There are actual pictures of her, up on the stage with a forlorn John Sebastian. He missed his former group the *Lovin' Spoonful.* While she comforted him with hugs and kisses, everybody witnessed how they *both* believed in magic.

Over the blistering weeks, rumors also flew that we had a real life *flower child* for a teacher. This conclusion wasn't just because of the perky sub's multi-tiered, ankle length, handmade, tie-dyed skirts. Everybody really flipped over her abundant collection of those neon-colored, off the shoulder peasant blouses, as well as her marvelous thirty-inch-long, triple strands of *Yin &Yang* symbols, strung on authentic *hemp* rope. And she *did* stem from San Francisco's infamous *Haight-Asbury*—a street even more strung-out than the necklace.

Gossip, however, soon became truth, when students admired the offbeat jewelry one afternoon. She told us how this *trinket* ranked right up there as a "special gift," among several *other* "way out things" from her mentor, Dr. Timothy Leary.

Yes, I'm talking about *him.*

Daily Woodstock Festival chatter like this circulated right along with the sultry air in the school hallways and wasn't the *only* buzz about *wraithlike,* Abigail Fairweather. The clamor over her "expertise" at arranging **Love-Ins** shook the very foundation of the building. Such an *earth-moving* "immoral skill" sure added to her fame among the school's male population—including teachers. This is why *boys,* of any age or status, eyeballed her like a juicy Big Mac.

Unlike Mrs. Hazard's class, intended just for girls, the summer school version excluded puritanical office rules. Hermione could no longer be available for the convent gig. She rushed out of town to sit for another one of those true-to-life granny portraits, so lots of drooling guys decided to explore the art of *typing.*

Ever since that day, beautiful Abigail came as close to a celebrity as I could ever get in my dinky town. Therefore, none of this "hippie talk" fazed me one bit. Why should it, when streetwise Miss Fairweather set her channel to a nonconformist philosophy about the sacrosanct typewriter, predicting the "contraptions" would eventually disappear like dinosaurs. So don't sweat the small stuff. She gave me an **A+.**

I doubt that her typewriter prophecy will ever come true. These tortuous devices can't become extinct. People and industry need an official form of written communication. I checked in the library the other day. Up until now, we've been relying on them for a hundred years. What could ever take their place? How do *you* feel about the eventual fate of typewriters?

I'll resume now, with the current messy-ribbon chore. While scouring all the yucky black ink off my fingers, I vowed to tell you stuff for real—no matter what. This includes fessing up about "out of it" Abigail. As I progress, please don't forget how the brief summation of my pathetic screwed-up life doesn't take into consideration the almost eighteen years I've been around. Allowing ancient hang-ups to compromise the fundamentals of this important documentation, will lead to self-defeat.

I won't write another word about my urgent situation until I take that deep cleansing breath, along with my supreme idol, Jack La Lanne.

PART 15:

SHAPING UP

"I did say this with a whine."

Every Sunday evening after dinner, I catch Mr. La Lanne's fitness show on TV, even if I'm smart enough not to copy any of the contortions he demonstrates. During *his* workout, I eat apple-crumb pie. While Jack is sweating up his steam room, I smother large chunks of English Double Gloucester all over my liberal portion of this freshly baked, *real* butter-crust creation. This imported cheese is kind of like Cheddar, except a lot, lot better.

Often, I take my slice of gourmet pie and add two scoops of first-class vanilla ice cream. The creamy one with those tiny flecks of vanilla bean that signal my taste buds how they're in for a delicacy. *This* connoisseur's favorite dream comes to fulfillment, while the ice cream melts on top of those sweet, crunchy crumbs.

Of course, I realize this extravagant dessert is costing me my arms and legs in more ways than the monetary price. But I *am* a hard worker from Monday to Friday, so on the weekends I'm entitled to a quality treat. *Moreover,* along these tape measure lines, I convince myself how the word "dessert" is a derivative of the word *deserved.* This rationale, in heaping addition to the pie, does leave a good taste in my mouth.

Say—I ought to quit goofing off here, and come clean about the liberal use of these delectable dessert frills, I just pointed out. I often indulge myself by putting both of them on at once, in a supreme attempt at topping off what I'm fond of calling my "exercise pie." However, I'm sensible—in the *talkative* "end" of things. Whenever I do use both toppings together, I make sure the pie slice is smaller. Instead of my usual wedge, consisting of half of the pie, when I do have seconds of the toppings, I cut my treat into just a quarter of the pie that remains. Don't you agree this is a very satisfying approach?

You don't have to answer. I know you're too polite to call me a hog. So let's just put aside this full-bodied attempt at rationale right now. I realize you're thinking about what kind of a dope is keen on watching an exercise show while she's sitting on her ample derriere, and wolfing down at least two slices of this kind of fattening dessert.

Okay, I know.

I . . . *know.*

I *do* know.

Yes, as usual, *you* are correct. I did say this with a whine. I realize how unrealistic I am to believe a person benefits from exercising by osmosis—although they *do* stuff their crumb-filled face in perfect synch to the workout music. Expecting an immediate drop of two dress sizes might be overoptimistic, but there could be a rare case of success. What do *you* think?

Don't even bother responding to such a dumb question. I've been trying the method for years without success, except for the element of hope, along with hardy Jack, since for now they *both* spring eternal. I bet he'll be very active in his old age, due to the sacrifices he makes to keep in shape. I do admire his resolve. More power to him, I say. As for me, I'll stick to being a couch potato with a muscular brain.

Getting back to the dessert Jack would never eat, I'm smacking my lips now, because I've been eating the pie tonight. I'm balancing the plate on top of my typewriter, while I hunt and peck with my left hand. With my stomach expanding like an overinflated balloon, and noticing tons of those greasy crumbs all over the necessary typewriter keys, I do need to remind myself of the coming imperative *deep* cleansing breath. I'll get the vacuum cleaner, before I pay strict attention to what Mr. La Lanne is doing. I think I'll dust him off too.

Everything's clean now, including Jack, so I'll return to the worthless television I use. This 13-inch black and white relic gets burning hot to the touch and makes strange crackling sounds. At times, when I'm watching an important thing, smoke comes out of its back. Due to some demonic electrical force, I'm always expecting an expensive tube to blow up. I hope it doesn't quit on me tonight, before the show finishes.

So far, so good. The usual commercial for *Pepto-Bismol* ended without any static. After my pie feast, I often think they're aiming the vile pink antacid straight at me. They're right you know. Pardon me while I get some from the medicine cabinet.

Back in a minute.

PART 16:

SWADDLING CLOTHES

"Waste not, want not."

After Jack plugs the magical rectifier of all overindulgences and I take a generous swig, the regular moment has come for him to sit down on that thick floor mat in preparation for something he calls the "lotus position." This tactic is part of each show. His back becomes as straight as a ramrod, while he crisscrosses his legs—drawing them up until they form a tight "X". Then he struggles to tuck this **X** into his lap.

Right now, I'm witnessing a new angle concerning the strangled lotus. He's doing something I haven't seen before. Do you believe, since locking himself into this floral position, my idol has found the power to bobble himself up and down. He's gaining enough frantic momentum to boost him three-inches off the floor. He looks like a hyper yoyo.

Oh no, here comes *another* first. He *is* still up in the air, but turning into a big blur from whirling himself around like a spinning top—decked out in gymnastic swaddling clothes. I'm sure you'll agree that it's not customary for an exercise guru pushing sixty—or a sane human being of *any* age—to twist like a pretzel into such scary poltergeist postures.

He's returning now to his regular solid position of anchoring on the floor and twisting his neck by turning the pulsating thing around and around like a rubber corkscrew. Such an entire new "possessed person" routine of his should be in some kind of spooky *exorcism* movie. It would scare the wits out of anybody watching except for my sister, as she doesn't have any to start with. This remark may have been cruel, but it *is* true.

Non-the-possessed-less, at present I'm watching a dizzy Jack uncross his legs and get up off the floor to stand straight and flex his bulky biceps. I recognize *this* movement. He's warming up for the crucial deep cleansing breath part that I've been anticipating.

I'll organize myself to follow along with him, before he starts inflating his massive chest. He'll accomplish this by puckering his mouth, prior to opening it so wide you can see his tonsils jump. While trying to gulp up vats of air, he resembles a panicky dry-docked fish, flopping on the sand. Don't worry; with the kind of superior lungs Jack has, the fish is safe.

Now we're coming to the point where his eyes will pop out, right before he propels himself forward. He's approaching my favorite part, when he exhales all the air he just sucked in, and reverberates like a rhinoceros—with an impacted nose.

Whenever I hear him make this nasal explosion, the reverberations remind me of the embarrassing sound, whooping without a hint of shame, from a sat-upon joke cushion. I find myself laughing each occasion he does it. I'm succumbing now, to his inadvertent bathroom humor. I'm yucking it up, in spite of being depressed and wanting to cry. My lips *do* taste wet and salty. Perhaps tears are already trickling down my cheeks—from a combination of laughing and crying at the same time.

I'll admit here, although I did take a cleansing breath, the inhalation wasn't that deep one. Why tire myself out by breathing in stale air, when I don't have a massive chest to inflate. I'm flatter than leftover pancakes from Saturday's breakfast, moping inside the fridge on Sunday. There are two of them on the top shelf right now. I'll throw them out later.

No. Wait. How about all those starving children, my mother used to tell me about. Later on, if I heat the cardboard disks up in butter, and smother them with maple syrup, I'll eat them for a snack. "Waste not, want not."

Somebody told me once that Benjamin Franklin takes credit for coining this expression. What do *you* think?

He *is* the one who said this first! Now I'm thinking my very own *mother* should check into this honesty stuff.

Putting aside my charitable donation to underprivileged kids, summing up the personal courage to admit such a paltry physiological detail like *pancake girls* encourages me to let loose with *everything*. Thanks to Jack and his exhalation skills, brace yourself for the whole truth and nothing but the truth—so help me, *me*.

PART 17:

BESPECTACLED HISTORIANS

"Hey, that's not bragging."

To say that only some people think I'm *kooky,* as I told you before, isn't exactly accurate. I fudged with this point at other times, and probably could continue getting away with this description as borderline truth. However, since I've been writing this journal, the more I force myself to tell the truth—the easier things get.

Concerning my purported status about being "so way out she's gone," I admit this frequent observation is the opinion of almost everybody I meet. I also agree with my crowd of detractors. For instance, take right now.

You're asking me why, aren't you?

Please brace yourself for my reply.

You may find the answer peculiar.

As I formulate this anthology here tonight, you're making contact with a girl who's an aberration on wheels. This "weirdo" hangs out in the forgotten past, where, at the very moment you read these words, she's spilling her guts to a secret journal. The sad girl has fervent hopes how somewhere in the very distant future—long after she's buried the journal—an unknown person will come across the unmarked grave, one way or another.

She's also very confident that when this stranger unearths her decaying epic, instead of pitching her hard work into the nearest rubbish container, they'll dust off a mound of dirt to read her heartfelt words.

Better yet—this person will be so wild about the mildewed jumble, they'll have a publishing company include some cool italics plus other classy touches. They also may want to bind this journal, adding a creative illustration on the cover. Of course, the altruistic stranger will keep strict adherence to the unabridged, original context, warts, and all. Maybe you're reading this upgraded version now. I sure wish that I could see my own "flight of fancy" in print.

Since my transportation just landed—skidding on the tarmac as usual—I'll return to the girl who, while you're reading this, exists inside the past. She has a weird notion how, with the help of a magical space-born microscope, the benevolent hoped upon stranger is in sync with her, intent upon checking out the journal they discovered under serendipitous circumstances.

Whoever the person may be, they'll devour the unearthed thing word by word, at the exact moment when she's spoon-feeding it to them—no matter *what* the design. Permeating through everything, this reader will find the mystical power to coordinate with this girl at the "beyond place" where *she* is now typing—what *you* are now reading.

Due to the success of this amazing contact, they'll soon be engaging in a metaphysical co-meeting of the minds. As an astonishing outcome of this esoteric heart to heart, the reader will somehow become capable of entering the realm of this girl's *present,* yet *previous* existence—the one an ever-evolving universe relegated to bespectacled historians years ago.

To complicate matters further, as far as the girl from the past is concerned, this unknown individual, whom she counts on to become her best friend, is—in accordance with *her* reality—floating on a *Tomorrow-Land* cloud.

At this dizzying point, I'll leave you to decide whether the kooky allegation is overblown or not. I'll also let you ponder the superior intelligence behind my capability to articulate the preceding heavy duty—blast-out-your-mind—brain-twister. In my opinion, this feat places me on the level of Einstein.

Hey, that's not bragging. You above all know how a person like me refrains from haughtiness. However, nobody could argue the truth about my similarity to Albert.

This is Einstein's first name—in case you didn't know.

PART 18:

AZIMUTH CIRCLE "*What* is wrong with me?"

Staring now at the new piece of typing paper I just inserted, I'm imagining who my future reader is. I'm also thinking hard, about where you might exist in a hip dimension that has yet to be. If I were a gypsy, I'd use those divining skills I inherited from my grandfather and see your face in tealeaves.

I guess I also inherited them from my cousin. Sorry to say though, tea gives me itchy hives, and the prospect of morphing into a clairvoyant like her, with even more of those oozy, splotchy-blotches on *my* face this time, won't be a glamorous sight. Therefore, I'll just scratch this idea.

Oh no, did I just use such a ridiculous play on words? *What* is wrong with me? I bet I already slipped up, more than once. I did, didn't I? I shouldn't be surprised. In recent months, I've been succumbing to puns on a regular basis. I'm sorry, but I do have a valid excuse. I live my life under the blight of "grammatical harassment" and can't even report the crime. When I tried, authorities only laughed like mad after they said, "Commies might want to use this *skill* as a cold-war tactic."

How do I explain the quirky situation to you, other than saying I grew up with someone driving me insane with incessant puns. *He* represented my social equivalent of a medieval plague, the bubonic kind of scourge, where a just hatched flea suckles blood from an infected rat. Then, after passing its first pediatric checkup, the slimy insect hops on you for a regular meal ticket.

To complicate matters more, this *person* lived across from me in a house with identical structural design. During construction, our rambling community of homes typified many of those cost-effective tract-developments—proliferating across the nation.

Seven is the address of his dwelling on good old *Azimuth Circle.* Can you guess the number of mine? I refer to the house of doom on this dusty, narrow cul-de-sac that's full of handy pebbles for slingshots. This cursed sacrificial abode, horseshoeing around the bend, ends up facing its bizarre mirror image nose to nose.

I'll be fair here and give you a hint. Think about my house with a number that *if* this double-digit falls on a Friday, you do *not* want to come across a black cat, step on a crack, break a mirror, open an umbrella inside of a building or dare to stoop under a ladder. You may not even want to get out of bed.

In the early days of living in such close proximity, our young moms strolled along together with their prized babies. Of course, they pushed them in cute *matching* prams. The little boy accompanying me arrived in the month of October. I didn't come along until the following July, so my long-awaited appearance became the perfect opportunity for this homely nine-month-old to reach out of his identical carriage, to wave and squeal incessant mumbo-jumbo at his unfortunate new playmate. After time enabled me to sit up in *my* pram, I'd reach out for *him.*

By now, he could sit in a toddler stroller. Since my pram-halter fastened me around the waist, I had freedom to giggle while stretching way over—aiming to get a good vice grip on his large, floppy ears and squeeze both of them with all of my tiny might. I hear he never cried over my antics. Instead, he goaded me to pinch him even harder. Drinking in the joy of my rage surpassed that grape juice in his new *Captain America* sippy cup. As I grew older, and found his "suffering" almost as entertaining as he did, I'd holler, "I want my little Dumbo."

Over the years, this is the story my mother used as a lame sympathy-getting ploy, whenever I'd complain to her about his unbearable presence. Because I expressed my discontentment with this pest, every ten minutes throughout my childhood, her desire to soften my hostile present-day attitude concerning him—by referencing my once naïve and tender, baby elephant analogies—doesn't work. She only makes me more determined than ever to get rid of him.

"Dumbo" also had the same schooling as me. He went to every class I took from kindergarten through senior year in high school. By some hook or crook, real ones I'm sure, he always wangled sitting right next to me, behind me or across from me. But there was one exception, when Mother Superior Hermione—and her exclusive class for girls—locked the convent gate.

He sure tried to enter that convent. He complained to the principal about their ostracizing him and threatened her with a discrimination lawsuit. She took the situation straight to the Parent-Teacher Association. My mother often tells my father how the P.T.A. stinks. They backstab people who are smart enough not to attend the unproductive meetings. Those who do attend, put getting better teachers, or additional funding for fieldtrips, at the bottom of the pile. What could be more important than who's "having a fling" or "packing on the pounds."

I guess they tried to improve their shallow reputation by helping me with my *Dumbo* problem. They gave the pest a call saying that if a kid like him could pay an expensive trial attorney to represent his claim, then give the legal route a whirl. Since he had no *means* of any kind, he decided not to spin.

Later on, as usual, he more than made up for his inability to penetrate Mrs. Hazard's postulant preparation for the business world, by taking the co-educational summer school version. I found out he could type as fast as me. While we sat there, together in the crowded classroom, with our typewriters colliding, we performed a piano duet. I'm sure I heard a rendition of *Chopsticks* more than once.

At my high school graduation ceremony, he almost pushed me off the small narrow bench we *shared.* There *we* sat, together with the other honor students, also occupying those little benches two by two—in an exclusive cordoned off area of the outdoor platform. When they announced his name to give the valedictory speech, he behaved like a bumbling out of control *jack-in-the-box,* jumping up and bolting off that small seat, before making a clumsy dash for the microphone. In so doing, he plugged one of his bony, razor-sharp elbows into a socket under my ribcage.

Did he even stop to apologize, when he saw me double-over gasping for air? The answer is not really, although he *did* say a tiny "sorry" in passing, but only because the principal stared daggers at him from across the platform. And things only got worse from that moment on.

PART 19:

PUN GEYSER

"He deserves some credit though."

My infamous high school graduation occurred almost a year ago. The debacle still feels like yesterday. There I stood, with my lifelong dream of emancipation from academic constraints coming to fulfillment right in the palm of my sweaty hand—the one holding that live grenade.

The ceremony sure included **pomp** but with dire **circumstance.** I didn't need the help of my perpetual classmate to detonate the occasion. Things were about to explode with my own family's support, thank you very much. I'll explain in more detail later on.

Although I should be immune to him by now, I'm not. All of my life, I've been one of those Sherwood Forest ants with the miserable job of crawling across the hostile ground, while carrying a huge crumb on its aching back. Whenever an opportunity rears its linguistic head, this annoying *punster* spews out stupid one-liners like those regular volcanic eruptions from Old Faithful, in Yellowstone National Park. Because *he* is also *faithful*—at driving me nuts that is—I refer to him as "Pun Geyser." Dumbo and his huge ears have long since flapped away.

At this exploding point, I can't help harkening back to my *first* day of school. I also had something in the palm of my hand then. I'm talking about my gullible little freckled-face, with eyes looking sideways at that traumatizing kindergarten. This place was an exact replica of the Stone Age one, enabling Fred Flintstone and Barney Rubble to become best pals with the truant officer. You'll also be hearing all about this Bedrock playgroup later on as well.

As I regress to that sweltering graduation afternoon, taking place on the first Saturday in June, I baked like an unseasoned pork chop under my heavy cap and gown. The material being heavy gold velvet—instead of logical, lightweight cotton—is just another example of hometown stupidity.

As miserable as I felt, I was actually grateful for my typewriter ribbon nemeses. Otherwise, to everyone's perverse amusement, people would've seen Pun Geyser, as well as me, stooping over in the center of the platform. The *Bobbsey Twin* salutatorians were at hand again, with a determined *Flossie* and a conniving *Freddie*—together as usual—playing fierce tug of war with the acoustics.

Non-the-accolades-less, while we didn't split top honors fifty-fifty, I did receive a large plaque engraved with *my* studious endeavors—sans typing, of course. Now please don't let me be remiss and forget to bring up the advantageous scholarship I received—along with the impressive *genuine* sterling silver medal. The gleaming one, attached to a wide, four-inch long, blue satin ribbon.

Then again, I won't boast to you about such matters. Bragging is totally out of my character. I'm a way too humble. I avoid tooting my own horn—except if I don't toot it, who will? I'll refrain from mentioning my accomplishments any further. I'll totally disregard how the distinctive pecuniary award exemplified summa-cum-laude excellence, in the prestigious area of *fine arts.*

Oops.

Journal *and* reader please don't think I expounded my erudition glories on purpose, no matter how suspicious things look. So being the unassuming person, you know that I am I'll return to loquacious Pun Geyser.

Throughout my entire existence, almost all of those insufferable "Old Faithful puns" he spews into the air—ended up trickling down on me. He behaved the same way at graduation. But as the Valedictorian, he surpassed himself in the compulsive pun-jinks area by espousing to *everybody,* "If you're stupid enough to be a doormat—don't complain when people step on you."

Along with, "Life is a daily gift—so every morning unwrap your tremendous *present,* and show appreciation for what you're given."

Followed by, "If life hands you a lemon, just make lemonade."

Gee, if this clichéd-dilly about the lemonade is true, *I* ought to be drowning in the stuff. He deserves some credit though. Our former teachers took out their frustration on the rest of us. They could never compete with this geek's lingual frivolities. They weren't too thrilled about a twerp like him, trampling on their doctorates. Here you may trust me from an obvious academic standpoint.

In any bothersome event, I also encountered him at church every Sunday. As a youngster, I endured Sunday school with him sitting, where else, but next to me. Of course, whether I felt like dropping verbal bombs or not, I could never curse at him in this staid environment. Besides, I didn't know any cuss words then, other than remnants of the almost inaudible ones—courtesy of the *Oval Office,* especially the one that sounded like "puck."

If I *had* been able to swear up a Ship of Life *drunken-sailor* storm, you can sure bet that I'd carry the honor of being the first kid, and probably the last, they would ever expel from pious studies due to a "ranch-hand mentality."

My goofy picture with those oatmeal cookie crumbs, clinging to the gluey apple juice on my chin, would forever hang on the famous **Bible Villains' Hoosegow** bulletin board, suspended in front of the classroom. You could look for me there, posing between Judas and Jezebel.

On this one, since biblical truth takes precedence, there's no doubt you'll trust me.

Right?

PART 20:

DANCE MACABRE "Yes you do!"

Speaking of Sunday school, and life-lasting impressions, how strange, yet maybe not, that surviving the Christmas season without a burning pain at the back of my throat gets harder each year. The doctor calls the symptom a "phantom manifestation," because he never finds anything *wrong*—at least according to the powerful light, he shoves into my sore mouth. He makes me gag for nothing.

I do believe I've now traced the source of this *phantom* to the annual enactment of the manger scene. Standing center stage, with my feet deep in the straw, represented the most glorious moment in my young life. I flung off my usual potato sack shepherd's robe to become a superstar in the town of Bethlehem.

Pun Geyser also *happened* to be an understudy. I'm talking about the Christmas pageant *standby*—who was eager to wait backstage, during those temper-tantrum rehearsals. He stayed above the fray, by memorizing lines inside the safety zone of the papier-mâché stable, where he shared his endless supply of caramel corn with the cute donkey.

Of course, later on, he denied having anything to do with *Bongo's* extreme case of constipation or the expensive veterinary bill for its resultant tooth extractions. He felt comfortable in glutinous seclusion, inside the colorful shelter, while he anticipated the absence of the no-show "carpenter" destined to come down with a bad case of the measles, hours before the play.

I often wondered about this measles *coincidence,* when Pun Geyser, himself, had a bout with this childhood right of passage—just a week before the performance. The fierce red spots popped out in the classroom. At least he spread the patriotic American variety. As a feverish result, our gorgeous young teacher—Miss Trisha Cyprian—with a face and shape making the breathtaking actress Hedy Lamarr look like "a dog," and whose attitude centered around the word *whatever,* sent him flying home faster than Superman's speeding bullet.

I'm afraid she wasn't quick enough on the contaminated trigger. *He* had already managed to spew his loathsome germs all over a future incubating time bomb, with the name of "Joseph".

You guessed it. Pun Geyser made a recovery so rapid that a movement started to have his cure certified as a miracle, so he got to play an extremely dedicated *Joseph*—to my furious *Mary.*

I also came down with a severe case of these measles that coming New Year's Eve. My excursion to the hospital, for a tonsillectomy the following week, equated with a belated chunk of coal in my stocking. As this is also another story, I won't tell you details about the incident when my measles-induced smoldering throat resembled a charred marshmallow, which, as usual, fell off its stick—straight into the roaring campfire.

Okay, since you really *do* want to know everything now, stuff happened when a two-faced hospital orderly, wheeling me into the operating room, told me how the imminent surgery wouldn't hurt me, "one little iota." All of the while he lied like a medical version of Pinocchio, dressed in green scrubs, I heard *Dance Macabre* playing on a radio somewhere. I refer to that overpowering part, with those loud **dom-da-da-doms**—heralding your arrival to the undertaker.

In perfect slow rhythm to this morbid music, the orderly wheeling in another child, also having a tonsillectomy, gave the same garbage to *him.* Do you recognize this other kid? Yes you do! You even know that after we survived the operation, he recovered in the little steel bed next to mine. His "miracle" only went so far.

We were relieved to go home, after healing from our mutual surgery. Recovery took us longer than usual due to our constant fighting over which one of us received the largest portion of *medicinal* ice cream from the *nice* nurse. We still sounded like bullfrogs, when we left the clinical ice cream parlor.

I'll now croak my way back to Sunday school.

Every week, as soon as what we learned flew out the window, along with assorted spitballs, this forty-five minute communicable class let out. We all dragged our feet toward the church building. Due to a collective short-circuit we became a group of once rowdy kids, winding down into dutiful robots. More than once, I saw Miss Cyprian push the classroom clock ahead several minutes to speed up this dismissal. After knocking on the closed church door too early, she played dumb telling the usher, "That cheap clock keeps breaking."

As soon as he swung open those heavy wood doors, whether early or on time, we separated to join our families waiting for us inside. The regular moment had come, when I expected the wrath of damnation to chop off my head for being bored stiff.

During the monotonous service, my mind darted around the sizeable space, along with my distracted eyes. When the strident sermon reared its frightful head, a frantic Nomad, searching for his misplaced caravan, looked like he just popped a Valium compared to me. Without fail, the droning of those repetitive hymns eventually transported me to the land of *Winkin' Blinkin' and Nod.*

I remember mentioning to you before, about this Sunday school dismissal procedure leading us to church. I didn't say then how Pun Geyser sat with his own parents in pew located far from mine. These mandatory seating arrangements helped foster sincere prayers of gratitude over the years, at least on my part.

Compounding matters about tolerating him at any kind of *school,* my sister adored him. They were picture perfect best buds. *He* hung around my house more than the mess in my room. Thinking about our nail-biting relationship now, I did have Lady Luck on my side concerning a change of seating arrangements in the Sunday school classroom. My angst ceased right after that huge—and I do mean *huge*—scandal, concerning our teacher that conniving Miss Cyprian. *She* ran off with the church organist.

I refer to the married father of five children, all under the age of seven, creep, who everybody said had "bedroom eyes" like Rudolph Valentino. Or maybe he carried her off to his tent like the *Sheik of Araby.* We never knew for sure. No matter how seductive Rudy behaved, whatever happened to all of the "free will" she kept pointing out, when we tried to blame our "unholy spitballs" on the devil?

Since you could not have religious education without a teacher, and nobody volunteered to follow the red-hot spiked heels of *Trisha,* seventy-year-old, Mrs. Blossom Biddle, with all of all her pain, bravely came out of retirement. She had those arthritic hips and needed crutches, but managed to keep us in line. She also said I was to be her "right leg" and sit next to her desk. I'd help her out by walking around the classroom with the snacks and anything else she told me to do.

This hands-on lesson about *miracles* qualifies as the best *I* ever learned in those days, even beating out Pun Geyser's extraordinary recovery from the measles, and topping how the organist's wife had her mother watch the kids so she'd be free to catch up with the shameful-duo.

How incredible when she found them in Texarkana, Arkansas where they set up housekeeping in a rented doublewide. While she kicked in the front door, the thrifty couple benefited from a shower together sharing soap and hot water. The scorned wife tried drying them *both* off for good, with Stonewall Jackson's *LeMet* pistol. She nabbed the historic firearm the Sunday before, right out of the cabinet holding the church pastor's collection of historic Confederate memorabilia. This antique weapon, which she transported inside of her tattered diaper bag, wasn't loaded.

When the local sheriff arrived, he didn't prosecute. Instead, he offered to go find ammunition. *The Great Valentino* once held the position of organist at this peace officer's church. Those *bedroom eyes* caused the bitter sheriff's divorce twelve years before. I bet you don't trust me on this one, although you should. Even I couldn't fabricate something like this.

If you're thinking that maybe the organist's ex-wife hooked up with the divorced Sheriff, as usual, you're right. What a beautiful wedding. Together they added two more kids to the new family and were real happy.

PART 21:

COCKEYED POD "See what I mean."

My life is full of mysteries. One primary one, other than being born in an outlandish place, is how dumb Pun Geyser and my little sister hit it off from the moment they knew the other existed. Until this day, I don't understand their attraction for each other. They must be two perpetual jerks in a cockeyed pod. Our parents are still good friends, continuing to socialize with each other. I often heard how during the lifetime of our grandparents, *they* were also the closest of friends.

Due to my failure of never being able to tune him out—over these long, arduous years—I realize he did manage to brainwash me after all. The evidence is I now find myself gravitating toward metaphors. In the sentence structure department, I'm a big old grizzly bear—heading straight for the honeycomb.

See what I mean.

Otherwise, I'm using puns and double entendres. Maybe I do all three of them at once. Who knows? Call my grammatical idiosyncrasies what you will, but nowadays, in spite of myself, I'm transposing into my writing and speech all the idiomatic distortions this fool uses as relentless instruments of my persecution. I'm evolving into his syntagma twin.

Symptoms of my new maladaptive syntax condition have hit me at an awful point. In addition to the other paranormal weirdness going on with me, all of a sudden this menace has arranged for my possession by a vindictive Webster's Thesaurus. The uncanny lexicon is having a picnic—running amuck around the left hemisphere of my brain. Believe me when I tell you, I won't employ puns in the future. But don't be surprised when I give them an interview.

Do you now begin to understand why I've been stressing out over this exasperating grammarian? He's been a continual pain in my backside since the primal moment when the doctor swung me upside-down, before giving my round rump a resounding smack.

This abusive initiation to life ceremony was the way to go, when *I* squished out. They may have a different approach now, but the procedure still can't be pleasant. Punitive birthing practices or not, you can sure bet how after I finished smarting from such a stinging greeting, a happy Pun Geyser took up the slack.

Circumstances dictate it's not necessary for me to care about his presence any longer. So why do I? Why does his pun-essence continue to surround me? In any grammatical event, as you witness the evolvement of this journal, you'll grasp how figuring out how to handle him, and *what* he symbolizes, isn't the only million-dollar question in *my* life right now.

PART 22:

FABRIC SOFTENER

"Time will tell."

I may not yet grasp how to handle Pun Geyser, also known as Dumbo or Freddie Bobbsey and other choice expletives—but I do know how to manage my last link to sanity. *You,* Secret Journal, together with your attentive reader, are going to be a great pair of "existential" psychotherapists. Both of you will help me on my journey to search for the core of myself, within the framework of my isolated existence.

Gee—what a heavy thing to say. I get all this stuff while waiting at Dandy Boy's Laundromat for their slow machines to finish the job. I sit there on an old beach chair that this establishment holds together with duct tape and read the works of gifted Jean-Paul Sartre. My once favorite *Seventeen Magazine* doesn't do it for me anymore. This sort of new "fabric softener" Sartre-therapy suits me. In case you don't know, he pioneered the *existentialist* belief that from the moment we're born, we rattle on alone for the duration, no matter how many nannies we have.

An existentialist also deems everything in life is an *illusion.* For this reason, I hope the philosophy prepares me to comprehend the significance of the thick paranormal haze surrounding me. If everything *does* turn out to be an "illusion", I'll gladly send the whole lot off to join the French baker and his harem. I'll return his Rolex too. He needs a good watch with *his* busy schedule.

More importantly, a journal is a *probono* analyst. In legal jargon, this means *free.* I still don't believe any kind of shrink won't charge me the usual—mortgage the farm for an hour session. Time will tell.

As I've mentioned before, as soon as my homemade psychoanalysis is complete, I intend to bury the cathartic results in the ground. The hole where I end up stashing my anguish will be so dark and so deep not even long-tailed Beelzebub, with his professional pitchfork, can dig it up.

If my family, or anybody else connected with me in my present-day, ever sees this journal, too many people will be hurt, and *I'm* the number one *people* on the long list. Since winging life alone now is my only alternative, not that I ever had a crowd along for any of the previous calamities, I really need that reliable friend. Counting on a special person to discover my hidden secrets keeps me sane.

Not a single human being where I exist is capable of ever listening to me in general, let alone with what's going on now. If by chance, they ever *do* put their hearing aids back in for a minute, they'll attribute whatever I'm saying, concerning my current insane life, to, "typical Ginger off-the-wall."

I've been able to validate how people fail to listen to a fraction of what I'm saying. I do this by administering my scientific attention span test to significant others. I use casual conversation, backed by strategic questions with expected *appropriate* responses. I rate these "responses" on a strict gauge of one to ten, with *ten* being the highest score on Ginger's grasping notch.

At the conclusion of these experimental questions, I'm sad to say how nobody of relevance in my environment ever scores over a negative-two. This is with the exception of Pun Geyser. *He* always scores a perfect ten. Having *him* give me this ideal attention score, depresses me even more than before.

Owing to the complexities of my current problem, compounding nervous tension with such a disappointing statistic, forces me to admit I'm wrong to expect those who are important in my life to comprehend the mystical haze surrounding me nowadays, when I don't even understand it myself.

I'm confident though, as my saga unfolds, *you'll* at least be empathetic. Even if you are *not,* there's no way to hear those critical comments coming from *you.* You're out there, sleeping on a fluffy cloud, snoring up those loud claps of thunder with *Thor* and your *Rip Van Winkle* pal.

Staring at this typewriter—while preparing to dredge up juicy tidbits about my private life—is a drag. Dishing regular gossip is more fun—except for the victim of the gossip. Direct experience has made me well qualified to write a book about the detrimental aspects of tittle-tattle.

How stupid can I be?

Don't answer that.

I just realized I *am* writing such a book this very minute, and *you* are now reading what I wrote. I must finish its introduction, if I have to stay up all night. I'm having difficulty verbalizing exact circumstances as of yet, because I've maxed-out Sartre's illusion theory. When I attempt to dwell on what occurred this morning, I start shivering and my teeth chatter. Something very, very weird is *out there,* and about to devour me. I must prepare for a future confrontation.

As an introspective result, half of this journal has to be a time machine regressing back, back . . . and yes *back,* maybe all the way to the womb. Who knows? The one thing I *do* know for sure is I must assume the roll of a dedicated astrophysicist, researching the complicated data behind my own cosmological *Big Bang* hypothesis.

Organizing those innumerable notes that I jotted down throughout the entire day, regarding what went on with me from the moment I rolled out of bed this morning, hangs over me like the sword of Damocles. Whatever happened to me must be deciphered, and it's *not* normal—even for a kook.

Without the foresight of keeping a record of the current extraordinary state of affairs, I'd turn into a complete amnesiac like Sgt. Raymond Shaw, the leading character in *The Manchurian Candidate.* Unlike magnificent Laurence Harvey, playing the programmed lethal victim in this movie, I wouldn't be acting—at least not this time.

PART 23:

SHELLEY

"As usual, she just acted nice."

Are you of the opinion it's hard to concentrate sometimes, even under normal conditions? If you're answering *yes,* I ask you to imagine what I'm experiencing now with the icy breath of a nervous breakdown—panting down my clammy neck.

Recent tribulations are getting to me. As a rule, I'm a bundle of energy, but at only 9 o'clock, I'm already exhausted. On usual days, I stay up past midnight without a single yawn. So to secure the long haul, I need a substantial emergency snack; the one I'm tucking away in the kitchen.

Last week, while wandering around Park Avenue during my lunch hour, I found myself stumbling into the Epicurean Emporium. Please don't think I'm being a snob, for mentioning *Park Avenue.* I'm just keeping my promise to be truthful.

In case you've never been there, *Epicurean Emporium* is one of Manhattan's trendiest gourmet food stores, where three whole floors of palpable aromas greet you. If your mouth doesn't water when you're exploring this place, you need to check your salivary glands. Before I made my way into the store's interior, I spotted fabulous imported cashew nuts at the first counter where they sat on sale for half-price—plus an additional **20%** off at the register.

These cashews have a succulent coating of golden Greek honey and a sprinkle of Celtic sea salt. They're also stored inside of an octagon-shaped box made of a velvet-like black material. Adorning this classy package is a spectacular garland of gold and silver mesh ribbon. Later on, this decorative box will come in handy for storing some of my smaller pieces of jewelry. I can also use the trimming for lots of things.

I've already taken precautions to ensure my roommate cannot get her itchy fingers on *this* scrumptious treat. She's not just an ordinary companion in poverty. I have *her* down to a familial science. I'm sure you remember my comatose relative. You know, the one who is older than I am—and took me to witness the gluttonous Blob, eating its way to a stomach ulcer. I knew you could never forget.

I'll tell you now that her name is Shelley Cherubim. She no longer loves horror movies. She's replaced them with being a sucker for stray cats. She'll definitely try to remove the metallic trimming decorating the top of this distinctive box of cashews. Her neurotic need to fashion a chic collar, for her newest fleabag from alley-hell, will be the first thing on her agenda—after she wolfs down at least half of the contents.

Why should she have the audacity to expect me to donate my exclusive ribbon to her scabby gray ragamuffin? Although, she definitely will. I'm positive you're familiar with the phrase, "Experience is the greatest teacher." If you're not, *I* sure am. So please just call the overused slogan, *Shelley.*

This is why, in order to protect my property, I've been camouflaging these fantastic honey-roasted gems in her now empty box of faddish junk known as *Nutritious Nibble Nuggets.* This fat free, low in calories, high in sodium, preserved with strange chemicals and artificial flavors, as well as food coloring glowing in the dark like radium—is the stuff she told *me* to eat, whenever I want.

As usual, she just acted nice. She hates her snack choice and wants to get rid of the crap. Then, due to her *generosity,* she'll lay another guilt trip on me. I'll suffer from constant harping on the subject of my callous lack of appreciation and failure to pay more rent. The way *she* goes on about my strange resemblance to *Silas Marner* must have George Eliot spinning in a grave somewhere.

A woman by the name of Mary Ann Evans really authored this novel in the year **1861**. She took "George Eliot" as her pen name, not wanting publishers to overlook her serious talent due to the perceived frivolity going along with being female. I think the same way now, over a hundred years later, how stuff hasn't changed very much. I bet she also had blond hair like me, and even if hers didn't come out of a bottle, the color certainly added to her perceived *unprofessional* image.

Speaking of *frivolity,* darling Cousin Shelley should devise a better bribe than this junk for getting more cash out of *me.* Her assumption that I'm senseless enough to scarf down the whole Nibble Nuggets' package is a cheap strategy, because she needs to justify wasting her money. Now as for me—I never waste *my* money. I opt for excellence. At the outset, people *will* spend more on their purchases, but end up saving later since they won't be throwing away money on inferior groceries and almost everything else.

I tell Shelley every day, to stop her slapdash shopping. She never does pay attention. This inedible snack denotes another classic illustration of her compulsion to spend the least amount on food, every chance she gets, ending up with plain garbage. I'm not a big spender myself, although every so often I splurge on quality essentials. When I come across great items for almost nothing, you can't find more of a win-win situation. Take my pricey nuts, as an example. Now I don't mean this in a literal way. If you ever *did* purloin my snack, chances are you might not finish reading this masterpiece.

How funny, given that whenever I hear the word "purloin," I always think of the loin of pork roast my grandmother's Chihuahua, named Carmen Miranda, once managed to leap up and steal right off the buffet table. The astonishing new spring in her tiny paws caused a major commotion. The little thing devoured the entire huge roast in under a second. She stayed in the veterinary hospital for a whole week. When the surgeon removed the huge chunk of undigested meat, he took out an additional surprise.

Three very well nourished puppies!

I begged and begged to bring one of them home. My mother refused saying she already had a *hyperactive animal* in the house, and this one equaled more than enough. Wasn't this a strange thing to say, since we had no pets of any kind?

Barking back to the other nutty situation, I'm sure you understand what I mean about the price of the gourmet cashews. At first, they listed at five bucks. You don't have to remind me how much food you get for *this* kind of money. Due to my purchasing skills what originally listed as *more* did turn out to be *less.* The **$5.00** became **$2.50** after I dug into my purse to pay the cashier. She rang up the additional **20%** off the already discounted price, making the grand total only **$2.00**—a very inexpensive ticket to bon vivant paradise.

As disgusting as it is, getting back to the horrid Nibble Nuggets, you won't believe how those "nutritious" concrete pellets jammed up the bathroom plumbing. Imagine what they would have probably done to the other kind of plumbing. Ugh. I tried flushing them and found out why Shelley calls this trash her "Trail Mix." What a mess. I need strength now from authentic nourishment. I bet that one day soon experts will admit how real nuts are healthy for you. As usual, I'm way ahead of everybody—including those inexpert, *experts.*

Concerning health in general, these "pros" scare people into starvation by telling them to stop eating the "new culprit." However, what they're talking about has been a diet staple for centuries. I'll use *eggs* as a carton in point, and the current media blitz to equate them with cyanide. The next day, after telling people how evil egg yokes will pave their way to coronary thrombosis, they retract the new "scientific view" by saying how sorry they are you listened to their sage advice in the first place.

They're apologetic when announcing how they've spiced up the omelet too much and, if you can believe it, are completely *wrong.* You were okay with doing the original. Therefore, out with the tasteless new imitation liquid eggs, and back in with the natural ones that you've already put in the garbage.

As a ravenous result of their perpetual incompetence, I tell them all to scat. I do exactly what I want, striving for moderation. I think this is true about most things in life. Moderation is the key. I'm working hard on opening the door. I haven't entered the room yet, but I *am* trying.

I just felt an overpowering urge to lay my own jammed up *egg.*

Done!

I put it in the basket with all of the others. The extreme amount of pushing I've been doing so far worked. I sense true progress. I'll head for the kitchen now, and since there *is* no door, I'm free to wash down my "healthy snack" with vats of my usual curative tonic.

The one prescribed by my personal physician.

PART 24:

SOUP-TO-NUTS

"Their idea didn't work."

I came into existence via loving parents who made an unwise decision to live in a small rural town in Texas. Although my father happened to be born there, he could've ventured to much more sophisticated fields when he had the chance.

This minuscule dot on the American map has the name of *Tillagevale.* As countrified as the "dust bowl" appears, and from my standpoint *is,* there's one good point. The place is only an hour's drive from the original Dr Pepper factory, where the popular soft drink originated over seventy years ago.

This old plant still turns out the historical formulation for the timeless soda, down to the minutest detail, using initial equipment. Any Dr Pepper produced in the facility qualifies as a bona fide bygone-era prescription. I have a valid appreciation for this medicine, because management has promised never to alter anything about their pioneering formula or their notable operation. Their vow holds true, no matter what any of the other worldwide Dr Pepper franchises may choose to do in the future.

Ever since I can remember, good old **Dr P** became my physician. Managing without him during stressful times, would have been impossible. After all, he wasn't far from my front porch and this *doctor* makes house calls any minute of the day *or* night.

Although my mother refuses to equate Dr Pepper with competent medical management or to admit how he plays such an important role in the field of psychiatry, my father agrees with *me.* I can prove my theory too. More than once during our inconceivable family fiasco, concerning Dad's acquisition of that *Ford Citation,* I found crushed cans of an empty Dr Pepper 6-pack in *his* den wastebasket.

None of us, including him, could figure out what set our prolonged nightmare into motion. Everything started in such an innocent way, on a humid Saturday evening during the end of summer. We sat in the dining room and devoured the kind of chicken and dumpling dinner where you must have at least two portions. My father had four. When we finished the last scrap, Mom cleared off the table. Then she told him to get off the chair and escort his inflated paunch over to the minimart to buy us some ice cream for dessert.

She also told him to choose the flavor. Putting this kind of crucial trust in a person who thinks sludgy prune juice is an elixir from the Garden of Eden upset me. I worried about what kind of horrid bargain-sale junk he'd bring back. Tasteless as things turned out to be, I remember how dutiful he appeared, while hopping behind the wheel of our forever tried and true, black and white *Chevy Handyman Station Wagon* to drive ten minutes away.

Regardless of this earlier "normal" conduct, after what felt like at least a week, he came back home wearing a cunning look, one I had never seen before. With this visible crafty expression on his face, he steered a convertible with its top down right into our driveway. My father sat behind the wheel of a *Batmobile.*

The answer to your obvious question is *no.*

Robin decided *not* to travel with him.

We all had an unobstructed view of his tardy return. Everybody sat waiting outside while we rocked up a breeze on the wide front porch. Mom had left the messy pots and pans and dinner plates soaking in that big sink brimming with soapy water. She once hammered a big plaque on the kitchen's swinging door, dedicating the hot room to *Harry Truman.*

During this interim, when we all fixated on the driveway—in anxious anticipation of our *delectable* frozen treat—we joked and took bets on what weird flavor Dad would get. To compensate for his definite lack of taste, the big jar of rainbow colored sprinkles was already in my hands. After his being gone for so long, my mother speculated that he was, "shooting the empty breeze with his out of shape, cigar smoking cronies." She also cautioned he better not stink of fusty *stogies* when he decided to come back.

Whatever odor he had his mind on, and later we found out that cheap perfume was the culprit, he sure took his sweet time to show up after an hour—only to beam at us with those impish eyes, and that mischievous grin, staring straight at us from the wacky Batmobile.

I compared his new deportment to our resident mouse, and the way it chomps with glee on the huge chunk of *Velveeta* cheese it snatches from that new kind of humane trap. The local exterminator, Reliable Annihilation Technicians, or **RAT** for short, set up the ambush in the pantry and made an exception, promising us that after they caught this pest it will go free somewhere in the woods. We really didn't want to kill something that had become part of the family.

Things turned out to be more of a *setup* than RAT thought. Their idea didn't work. I named this mouse, **P.G.** We just couldn't get rid of this chubby escape artist no matter what we did, until one day it just took off. My mother said the scrounger waddled straight to a fat farm. I should be so lucky with the other *P.G.* pest.

By now, you must be thinking about the ice cream my father went to buy. He did get some, even if the description was only a quart of pistachio soup—spilling inside Batman's former trunk.

I, above everybody else, understood my father's depression over his old Chevy's deplorable condition. In further dilapidation, none of us—including my father—could understand why armadillos used the top of our station wagon as a boxing arena. Maybe they went at it like wrestlers owing to the gargantuan luggage rack he rigged up on impulse the month before. Who knows? All the hostile same, do you believe that when ardent armadillos duke out rivalry—on top of a black and white car—they're capable of sculpting an expert rendition of a lumbering Holstein cow with a sorry swayback. I'm referring to the exact kind of bovine, roaming with blissful freedom, all over Tillagevale's back roads.

Still—who among us ever predicted how an uptight Daddy could swerve in the direction of a ridiculous . . . conspicuous . . . glaring . . . gaudy . . . psychedelic . . . turquoise **Edsel.**

Not me, *that's* for sure.

PART 25:

FROGGY'S RIVAL

"Bingo!"

The only way to avoid a letdown on Saturday afternoon, after a fantastic morning of children's TV, was to go along with my mother to her regular gathering of the *Serpentine Ladies Auxiliary.* This club meets every weekend over at Dad's favorite place to hang out, with the exception of his den.

Where else could I be speaking of, other than Tillagevale's feral *Bullsnake Civic Lodge?* Maybe this club keeps "anointing" my father their "Chief Reptilian" for the reason that—boy is he in love with the place.

Wait. In focusing on Dad's Bullsnake Lodge obsession, I realize nobody else wants nasty hot snake oil rubbed all over his forehead during the annual installation ceremony. Responsibility for prancing around, wearing the traditional *required* Chieftain's Robe, while busting up slugfests, may not be every guy's idea of a weekly fun night out with the boys. I'm talking about the odiferous "poncho" put together from the skin of *genuine* Australopithecus-era Bullsnakes. The one my mother forces Dad to keep on a peg, outside in the remote backyard shed.

She should also include the Chieftain's ridiculous Viking-style headdress, which is composed of lightweight aluminum, with a twelve-inch-long ex-antler horn protruding out of each side of its domed or should I say *doomed,* top. But she doesn't. Instead, she leaves it on a table in the hallway, right near the front door, to remind him of its ugly presence. Otherwise, he forgets to bring this part of his uniform to the meetings. Sometimes he has more common sense than I think he does. Everybody that enters the house laughs, seeing *Leif Erickson's* hat sitting next to her collection of Capodimonte porcelain figurines. Talk about bad costumes at the opera!

Speaking about Vikings, my mother buffs these horns with clear shoe polish, before each of Dad's lodge meetings. Bingo! The puzzling reason why my father is their continual "Chief Reptilian" is that his horns glow in the dark. They facilitate lodge members finding their beer and pretzels in a blackout.

What *other* explanation could there be?

After that memorable excursion with Shelley, witnessing what my mother calls, "The movie promoting dissolution of marital relationships," Mom took me with her every Saturday. With my hair in pigtails—and pajamas replaced with a Sunday-best dress—we headed across town on the bus. She refused to drive "the monstrosity bomb" so you'll automatically trust me here.

She avoided using the Edsel since the bus stopped near enough to our house. It let us off in front of the log cabin built for this community center—where they welcomed anybody in the county to join. The obvious dedication of the local population originally had volunteer wannabe carpenters, of every affiliation, putting the lopsided thing together on weekends.

I'll never forget the exhilaration every week, getting my fix from tangy whiffs inside of this asymmetrical lodge. The closest I can come to how I felt, was the building's strange combination of odors containing a foreign mixture of:

> A damp forest, after a downpour . . .
> Lifebuoy Soap . . .
> Lucky Strike cigarette butts . . .
> Residual smoke from dubious *Cuban* cigars . . .
> Cheap whisky . . .
> Burnt coffee . . .
> Flat cola . . .
> Moldy peanuts . . .
> Mimeograph-machine fluid . . .
> And stale jelly donuts . . .

Being over there with her helped avoid a major letdown after watching *Andy's Gang* on television. With no offense to the excitement of the lodge or that unique smell, I'll admit how the typical wet-your-pants from sidesplitting laughter of this Saturday morning show for kids was awful hard to beat. Reflecting about her reasoning now, I see why my mother left me in those pajamas until lunchtime—meeting or not.

The antics of the Serpentine Ladies Auxiliary were a close second to those of outrageous *Froggy the Gremlin,* strumming the mysterious ukulele-like instrument known as a "magic twanger." This unpredictable green puppet strummed the cords when he was ready to get visitors into outrageous trouble. As soon as the show's host, the consummate grandfather, Andy Devine, gave him the authoritative command to, "Plunk your magic-twanger, Froggy" the tricks started. My favorite ones were when he'd *twang* the visiting lecturer.

As usual, this *guest* ended up stammering in a flustered state, while trying to give his tutorial, due to Froggy's insane interruptions. As a soggy result, befuddled from tip to toe, the *professor* wound up dumping whatever liquid he demonstrated, i.e. waffle batter, all over his own educated head or straight down his baggy trousers. The kids in the audience screamed with laughter, watching him crackup in front of everybody—thanks to Froggy and the wacky twanger. I'd be hysterical at home, screaming right along with them.

In accompaniment to Froggy's hilarious behavior or any of the other zany skits, there was adorable Midnight the Cat, standing straight as a crowbar on stubby back paws. For a continuous routine throughout the show, it grasped the instrument's bow with its front paws—as virtuoso on its tiny violin. Let me tell you, Midnight performed better than the tipsy violinist from "Naples" did. I know this, because my father commented on this cat's exceptional skill every week. However, he'll never admit that *he* also adored Andy's Gang.

Attending the lodge meeting with Mom provided much more *education* than staying home and being bored for the rest of the afternoon. A kid could hear some real hot stuff from *this* assembly—with plenty of delicious potluck-eats on the side. Soon after discovering the evidence of my father's hush-hush Edsel consultation in his den, with trusty Dr P, this excellent *scholastic* entertainment did *not* disappoint me.

PART 26:

SERPENTINE EDIFICATION

"It sure fooled me."

At this memorable gathering, right after the Batmobile darkened our driveway, the affiliates wore, as usual, their official maroon picture hats. Even though they acted as nothing more than sanctioned bad-hair-day disguises, as far as *I* knew then they substituted for Buck Rogers' flying saucers—hotwired by that silly auxiliary brooch.

This unforgettable eight-inch-long silver badge, in the form of a serpentine snake, had protruding yellow glass eyes the exact shade of jaundice. The women fastened them, without rhyme or reason, around the brim of each spaced-out chapeau, causing these pins to wobble with every movement of the hat. Since a nod-a-second ruled the cackling roost, I had an effervescent experience watching dazzling wild-eyed snakes—with a bad case of the hiccups—slinking around the room. If there *is* such a thing as a convention for inebriated reptiles, I attended this conference on a regular basis.

Another very exciting thing at this week's particular summit, involved being part of the hullabaloo. The ruckus started when the group made a quick motion to dismiss the "embarrassing news" about the harsh penalty from the *ridiculous* County Department of Health, concerning that disastrous cake sale *humiliation* a couple of weeks ago.

Why waste precious time finding out which one of the members had the absolute *gall* to use *rotten* eggs and leave those *putrid* eggshells, floating in the disgusting *weevil-spiked* batter. Surprisingly, they expressed a certain admiration about the way the treacherous *artistic-affiliate* finished off the mess by masking her extra long, serves up to sixty-people sheet cake, with those dexterous swirls of rancid *Dream Whip.*

Generous slivers of appetizing toasted coconut also garnished the *creamy* substance. Boy, oh boy, who'd ever think that those thin brown shavings actually came from a bar of *Kirkman's* kitchen soap? I saw this yummy looking cake on the selling table. It sure fooled me. My fingers itched to pick off a couple of pieces of that generous spread of *coconut.* My mother's angry look stopped me, just in time.

Gagging our way back to the auxiliary, the members were certain the culprit who *did* the salmonella deed had no idea *whatsoever* how the congressman's stunning new twenty-year-old *bride,* with *natural* ash blond hair, would bring herself as a tart for the bake sale. Their certainty about this newlywed staying free and clear of the lodge in general, rose from the thermometer of knowledge how she already had a *bun* in her *own* oven.

What's around six-months more, we shouldn't ignore the delicate matter of the geriatric legislator, Governor Dickinson Peckenpaw, and the way he *discovered* his "wife" when she entered a *Miss Chitlins* beauty pageant contest at the lodge last year, with *him* as the sole judge. At the lecherous time, the old geezer marveled at how fast the then finalist answered his crucial *deciding* question, "What personal value do you, *my dear*—place on swine intestines?"

"Well—ya cutie-pie *Honorable,* my momma always told me if I *evah* have any moochin' kinfolk I can't get ridda, hangin' round *my* kitchin', just nail your windas down tighter than a miser's floorboard—before ya set the revolvin' fan on high. Then, boil the free loaders a big kettle fulla them stinkin' tah total high heaven—*Chitlins.*"

Progressing further, into the not so cake-sale *bargain,* what devoted Auxiliary member could have guessed how the *new* Mrs. Peckenpaw would ever be the one to purchase the sumptuous oversized "spiced" angel-food killer? She just could not wait to tell everybody how she bought the "delightful dessert" for the well-publicized third-term victory dinner, honoring her *magnificent* husband's swearing-in. She also said the black-tie affair was taking place at the renovated Governor's Mansion on the same night of the sale.

What she did *not* say at that moment, was how taxpayers picked up the cost of this gubernatorial makeover to the tune of seventy-five grand. They allocated a good portion to the immense ballroom downstairs, and the huge master bedroom upstairs, with its en suite bathroom. I'm speaking about the opulent one, with the tall fountain-shower, next to the deep Jacuzzi tub. It sure wasn't cheap either, to import all of that marble from Spain to build the Juliet-style balcony. It has more than enough space for Romeo, and looks out over the newly landscaped garden, designed for their sole personal pleasure. Well, all of this bookkeeping slipped right out of her empty mind.

In this all-around excessive case, silence saturated the region of the dangerous makeshift bakery when the excited young bride carried off the choice *creation.* She told everybody in her wispy naïve-like voice, "In spite a everythin', you Bullsnakes did help re-elect my lambkins by that piddlin' one vote margin. I'll be charitable, like the Good Book says, and overlook how everybody had the nerve to demand the *worthless* ballot recount.

Oh lordie, I am *sure* you *do* rememba your broken ribs, barn-bustin' brawl of two months ago. I'm speakin' about the one with more black eyes than a pea patch. Y'all *also* know how the disgustin' display ended up on *nationwide* television. Everybody watched the goons from the Board of Elections puttin' my darlin' Dick, moanin stiff as all-out, completely alone, to cool off overnight inside that cold cement-poky."

She further astounded the group, as she left the sale, by balancing the big cake box on her expectant belly. She wiggled her curvy hips in a manner more reminiscent of a *Gypsy Rose Lee* than a pregnant woman should do, when she swung around and said, "You people may like to learn how they still have him taped up like a shriveled King Tut. He has to use the wobbly walker his mama left him in her will. But, and it's a big but y'all, I do have to say she was okay, except for her screwy pastor. I'm talkin' about that preachin' weasel who's obsessed with losing the Civil War, and looks like Adolph Hitler's creepy identical twin.

That louse ended up gettin' her huge Alpaca farm, includin' all a her dough! The contest-the-will lawsuit my hubby had to pay the damn lawyer a *fortune* for *losing,* are the real reasons why we married in that broken-down City Hall without the high-and-mighty *benefit-of-clergy* stuff, y'all been blabbin' about."

As soon as the awkward draft from the booty shaking subsided, there were whispers within the group, and *I* sure got an earful. On the *hush-hush*—yet *everybody* in town could hear them—they spoke of his *forsaken* ex-wife. The *poor thing* suffered through a *grueling* "way above and beyond the call of duty" forty-year marriage, only to have him *philander* and toss her to the curb. He had benefited from a long marital *holiday* while *she* worked off her *derriere.* Now, the brittle thing waited for the trash collector like a spent Christmas tree, with those sad remnants of silver tinsel—blowing without purpose in the wind.

She had also *baked* a cake for the sale.

By the urgent way, the next morning after the victory dinner, people heard about the washed-up governor running once more. He also bought a load of stock in *Kaopectate,* albeit, for some underlying cause, this potent diarrhea medicine failed to stem the tide.

Under the duress of these uncontrollable marital woes, the committee didn't have enough aspirin to spread around concerning how in the world to raise the astronomical **$200** sanitation summons, due at the County Court House by 9 o'clock the coming Monday morning. With proceedings turning out to be a hopeless mess, worse, if you can believe it, than the culpable cake, they had no choice other than opting for a different kind of gabfest.

Their animated chatter wound up crisscrossing the room where a mesmerized me sat in wide-eyed wonderment, right in the middle of it all.

PART 27:

CHEAP CHARLIE

"Now I have a question."

On this precise Saturday afternoon, the meeting turned out to be one of calamitous topics. After deciding to put soapy-cake down the drain, the more than usual psyched-up group picked apart my father's Edsel mess. Since they were all pros at hen pecking, these women had no trouble shredding the club's agenda.

To start, the members exclaimed how since the convenient minimart situates adjacent to "debauched" *Cheap Charlie's Caressed Vehicles,* what typical married man could ever resist such a raunchy sales pitch? Any husband who would perform a family errand *without* protesting became *fair game*—along with those bunny rabbits, I'd soon be learning about.

Seeing how they all blamed themselves for my Edsel crises, and cried while they apologized to my mother, surprised me. I never thought they could be so nice. Listening to them explain, I learned how the mess started as soon as this—"Sordid, lit up like an airport runway, shameless, honky-tonk, open all night, *harrumph,* used-car lot" first opened.

After the traffic-control tower gave its approval, the distaff members of the Bullsnake Lodge demonstrated against the "vile place." My ears burned for sure, when they said how Cheap Charlie's personnel consists of some of those new Playboy Bunnies or babes who could easily pass for one, with the sole aim of *moonlighting* for extra cash. The "Bunnies" do get chilly sometimes. However, according to *Charlie,* who could ever top *their* pointed selling assets. Can Cheap Charlie be a close relative of Pun Geyser? I wonder.

No matter what, the Serpentine Ladies Auxiliary, and their conscientious attempt at anarchy, failed worse than the cake sale. Charlie offered employment to three of the "stacked-gals" who jiggled while they picketed, and they all took the jobs, especially with his usual year's supply of free perfume bonus.

One of these zaftig "defectors" happened to be a youthful widow—who, out of fear for her life *and* mine, shall remain anonymous in this journal. She not only acted as director of the *protest*—she also carried out her job as current head of the group. Madam President made herself a windfall in commissions at her new job, earning enough dough to purchase a luxurious condominium penthouse on a sandy, palm-treed beach in Hawaii.

Less than one month after she moved to luau paradise, the brazen—although curvaceous ex-president—sent the Auxiliary a letter boasting about her successful organization of Cheap Charlie's Honolulu Branch. She also included a recent photo of Don Ho, wearing those exotic floral leis around his neck. His muscular arm hugged her tiny waist, attached to her tanned, ultra flat stomach. She showed off these *worldly goods* without any *dignity* in her new yellow polka-dot string-bikini, which the club called a "birthday suit."

The failure of the auxiliary to prevent Cheap Charlie from duping my father, didn't affect my mother's forgiving heart. She invited her remorseful club members over for a fondue brunch. For emergency purposes, Mom had some cans of Dr Pepper on the buffet table, making me suspect how she, herself, is a closet Dr P aficionado. Her thoughtfulness appeared more obvious than ever, when she baked her penitent pals a pineapple upside-down cake—decorated in pastel pink icing—along with the philosophical words, "Such is Life and Women's Lib."

I gobbled up several yummy slices of this insect-free, *non-sudsing* tutorial work of art. Now I have a question. Can you think of a better humanitarian lesson for a young girl than this kind of confectionary education? If so, I never heard of any. Back in those days, the Serpentine roost sure beat out Sunday school.

Oh. My mother begged my father to beg the Bullsnake Financial Officer, him, to loan the distraught ladies the summons money. After they used up a jumbo box of tissues, he accommodated their pleading. He stipulated they must pay off his munificence with a very high rate of interest. Here, concerning what the Auxiliary titled, "Blood money from that loan shark," you should trust me more than you have ever done before.

He also insisted on the county sheriff fingerprinting all the auxiliary members, before having them sign a pledge stating they'd dump *baking* for *bingo.* They were relieved when he told them they could still wear their hats. I remember crying, while they stuck their fingers into the thick black inkpad. I wanted the sheriff to take my fingerprints too. Pressing down and dirty looked like fun. My father told me not to worry. There was an excellent probability the messy process will happen to me soon enough on its own.

PART 28:

AUTRY'S ALBATROSS "I'll have to take this back."

Dad denies sexy bunny suits had anything at all to do with his automotive *bargain.* He doesn't have a clue that Charlie fleeced him. Up until this day, he says he got "a steal" since the car looked new and had "less than a hundred miles on the gauge." You can't deny that *steal* is the right word to describe the honky-tonk bomb. Believe me when I say he's not making any pun. He's too straitlaced for wisecracks.

I do worry about my father sometimes. Why doesn't the pristine condition of the Edsel tip him off that the previous owner never took the thing out of the garage? Isn't this naïve for a man who has a college education? Remember, I'm trying to be honest.

Dad did have an idyllic week to act like a proud peacock, flashing his *new* wheels around town, until the legendary Saturday morning arrived when every ambulatory person, living within a radius of five miles, gathered in *our* driveway. They were there just to stare at the clinker of all time. None of these people even made a modicum of effort to stifle laughs regarding, "Autry's albatross."

Wait a second. I'll have to take this back. Maybe Eddy Cherubim hid any true emotions. Getting his brother-in-law riled up, with their **PGA** doubles tryout coming the same afternoon, looked like more of a risk than the outrageous car. *Uncle Eddy* is married to my father's sister *Sharon,* and they're Shelley's parents.

On the morning when the enormous crowd showed up to ridicule the car, Aunt Sharon told Shelley and me that *Inspector Clouseau* {a.k.a. my father}making an attempt to play professional golf with *Mr. Magoo* {a.k.a. Shelley's father}"is the personification of an exercise in futility." I couldn't understand what my aunt meant. Shelley had problems with the words too. She went inside to check her school dictionary.

All the same, I understood my mother when she told Aunt Sharon to go and buy plenty of popcorn. Watching Daddy and his cohort, Uncle Eddy, fumbling on the snobby *Country Club* golf course later in the afternoon, could turn out funnier than any *Pink Panther* movie you'd ever see.

Later on, when Daddy's ball kept sunbathing in the sand bunkers, and Uncle Eddy's took swimming lessons, I almost choked from laughing while gulping my own unforgettable large, salty, buttery, and yummy—bag of that popcorn. Some spilled on the classy grass. Happy sparrows swooped down to vacuum my inadvertent contribution.

I'll never understand where my father ever got the nerve to drive that car to the country club, and even worse to have its chassis baptized the next day.

PART 29:

HOLY WARS

"Notice, I used the word *begin*."

There's only one consolation in my life concerning the preposterous Edsel. It occurred when Dad drove the thing to church and hit the unavoidable truth about Caesar O. Frisby. I'm speaking of the phony-baloney, blowhard of a minister, who's incapable of showing a scrap of consideration to members of his own congregation—most of all the neglected philanthropic ones.

If you suspect the **"O"** in his name stands for *Octavian,* I know that you're already acquainted with the Frisby clan, in particular his mother, Cleopatra, and his father, Nero. Perhaps you *also* know his psychotic brother, Cal—short for *Caligula.*

Since all roads *do* lead to Rome, the Freudian topic of this clan's maniacal fixation with ancient rulers—takes me straight to my father. Whenever we went to church, I tried telling him how Reverend Frisby's crooked smile is out of character for a member of the clergy. And every Sunday when this *preacher* shouts at people, his bloodshot blue eyes resemble two demonic marbles that shift and roll around in his head. They remind me of frenzied bulbs, blinking inside a ringing pinball machine, right before flashing ***TILT.***

You cannot help but notice this "man of the cloth" with his liturgical garb composed of luxuriant black Alpaca, from the tip of his greedy fingers, to the bottom of his hammertoes, squashed without mercy into white leather platform shoes. He never learned *elevators* couldn't turn Mickey Rooney into Gregory Peck. He's not relaxed at all about his calling, and always appears uptight squirming in his clerical collar.

While he stands in front of the worshippers, especially under that picture depicting Judas accepting the thirty pieces of silver, I always visualize him as the perfect villain in an old silent movie. He's using heavy ropes to tie sweet Pauline onto the railroad tracks, while a speeding train in the distance heads toward her. Her panic-stricken mother, begging him from down on her hands and knees, couldn't meet his demands to pay the huge mortgage in one lump sum and save the family shack from demolition.

Now leaving *Pauline* to her grim fate, I'll get back to "Caesar the celebrant". My father gives *him* a not too cheesy donation twice a year. These hefty checks to our church grant anybody related to the Autry family the exclusive privilege of sitting in the front pew. This prestigious long bench is in direct alignment with the base of the altar.

On the morning that the Edsel stuck out in the church's **VIP** parking spot, the only thing I saw was the throbbing sore thumb I had once. I deserved the pain back then, after sneaking off to play "construction worker" with my dad's heavy wooden hammer. However, this painful morning, I became a blameless victim of an ungrateful preacher delivering an outmoded sermon titled: **ALL THAT GLITTERS IS NOT GOLD.**

By the nefarious way, I'm talking about the very words *he* copped straight from Shakespeare's trembling hand, right along with *The Bard's,* quill pen. I know this, because *William,* this is Shakespeare's first name, wrote the famous poetic line with the word "glisters" instead of "glitters." Frisby pulled a cheap attempt at paraphrasing. He doesn't realize how I'm at least one-step ahead of *his* oration ploys.

Adding his literary insult to my mental injury, he screeched out this sermon much louder and more grating than an evangelizing baboon, at the top of its besieged lungs, already steaming with nicotine. While we're on the subject of Caesar's obvious nicotine craving, *Camels* were—as they marketed this brand of cigarettes then—the ones he *would* walk a mile for. This even holds true if he had two broken legs, with full-body plaster casts, up to his reedy-neck.

Now I ask you to visualize the additional raucous aspect of his maniacal gyrations around the altar, while he knocked down assorted vases full of flowers. We experienced a family-style baptismal ceremony, with water splashing all over us. Couple this with the frightening sight of his gymnastic chimpanzee-style somersaults down the aisles, and you'll begin to understand.

Notice, I used the word *begin.* I've yet to mention his woolly arms, flailing the whole while. He must have glued magnets on to his nicotine-stained fingertips to attract the ones he attached to the metal plaque stating **Superior Congregants,** on the pricey-pew where my relatives, including a mortified me, sat in stunned silence.

This *devout* zoological escapade was not cool. For God's sake, I never saw my father perspire like he did that Sunday. The time when he tackled the overgrown lawn, using the push mower—while the outdoor thermometer read **100°** in the shade—couldn't compare to the current flood.

My mother has a habit of stuffing a titanic-sized hanky into the pocket of Dad's jacket. I mean not only his best suit jacket for church; *any* kind of jacket gets the treatment. Her laundry efficiency saved him for sure *that* day.

PART 30:

BITTER CHARITY "No, she did not."

Reverend Frisby's "pious" attempt to alchemize Daddy into a moist fruitcake stands out as a fundamental Dr P 6-pack moment for my father and for me too—since I sat right *next* to him. On the unforgettable morning of unstoppable hounding—by a balding primate from Stratford-upon-Avon—I wasn't allowed to sit in my usual pew space. I had to switch places with my mother, owing to what my father identified as, "The Battle of Normandy."

I don't know *where* he ever scrounged up such a weird description for a plain-old fistfight, very similar to those occurring with regularity under his Saturday night watch over at the Bullsnake Lodge.

Under normal day-of-worship conditions, I'm dozing off attached to the hip of that "little" sister of mine. We *always* sit together, way over on the opposite end of our parents and other relatives, on the long *Autry* pew. On this horrible Sunday though, my sister refused to speak to me. I, likewise, wouldn't say a word to her. Our current *little* feud over "bitter charity" caused the chilly silence. At least, this is what my mother said, but I am telling you here that our behavior resulted from a blowout of mega proportions.

Now—getting back to the aspect of truth, we fought the second our eyes popped open on any given morning, except, that when hair does fly, it happens in our personal space at home and not in the front pew of the church. On this disturbing public view occasion, Mom kept the family peace by assuming her frequent "unpaid" position with the United Nations.

She donned her diplomat-hat because, without permission from me, my sister had on *my* coral-colored cashmere sweater; the one Grandma gave me. Please picture a valuable sweater with pearl-like snaps and a brown fur collar. The material *is* faux fur, but still—is this audacity or what then?

The night prior to church, my mother put together a box of clothes for their charity drive. And, since there is no other person as unselfish as me, I dropped in my beloved sweater on top of the filled carton. Just because my darling possession had a few visible snags, *some* impenetrable mustard spots, a couple of miniscule holes, a threadbare pocket, and I did sort of outgrow it, this had nothing to do with my generosity.

All the charitable same, did my squirt of a sister even have the simple courtesy to ask me if she could take my self-sacrifice out of the box and wear the donation herself?

No, she did not.

The way *she* gets on my nerves, should be an entire journal by itself. Reflecting on this observation, I'm again tempted to say trust me. I don't have to though. This time you'll agree with me—one-hundred-percent.

My sister is a *real* troublemaker.

PART 31:

REMEMBER THE ALAMO "I recognized big trouble."

After the church debacle, I took comfort in realizing my father concurs with me about *something,* even if only a mere medicinal soft drink. All the embarrassing same, I had to suffer for years while he drove us around in his tacky Edsel.

Where did a so-called "lemon" develop such muscle? How could I make tasty lemonade out of this dud, when the car wanted to get me at every turn? I'll prove my supposition too. What follows next is rock-solid evidence.

On the fateful morning of my very first day at Junior High, Dad completely ignored my imitation of Laura Ingalls. The stress of pretending to be sweet did nothing other than cause a huge pimple full of pus to erupt on my chin. Did *you* ever read *The Little House Books,* the autobiographical series written by this prairie Pollyanna?

In case you're not familiar with her work, I told him *if* Laura were me, she'd fling off Cousin Shelley's pungent hand-me-down *Ked* sneakers. After all, only a teenage battleaxe like Laura *or* Shelley would wear them without a stink in the first place. Laura also removed her mother's old-fashioned equivalent of those ugly brown *Peds,* before telling her own father the following words:

I am ready to go, *Poppa.* I will leave *now,* to scamper *barefoot* over the blistering prairie, on my way to school. The nurse will give my feet first aid, when, and if, I arrive. On the way, I will pluck wildflowers—although they are surely wilting by now—and my feet *are* burning like your temper when you trip and miss that winning putt. I will ignore my pain and search for your favorite *bluebells.* I will make a drooping bouquet of them, for *all* of my new teachers. The joyful beam on my face will follow the sun's broiling one, leading the way to school, as I scamper across this grassland inferno. Will you grant me your permission, my dearest Poppa?

A snowball stood a better chance than I did with my father, on that hot Texas Monday in mid-August. Begging the peeling white picket fence, surrounding our house, would have been more productive. I could've bashed my head on the spikes. At times, dealing with him in situations like this, I have a mental block concerning the sad outcome of tenacious Davy Crockett at the revered Alamo Mission. This ineptness of mine, regarding *fatal* aspects of American history, caused Dad to chug up to the *local* Alamo, a.k.a. Tillagevale Middle School, at the last minute.

Matters only worsened, seeing as he took forever to get any place in that car, due to all the other vehicles honking at him or trying for the thrill of cutting him off. Using a back road was much faster, except he refused. He worried about, "possible heifer damage." I wondered whether he meant to the poor heifer or his prized car.

When I arrived without too much detectable mental or physical damage, the crowd of fidgeting kids, who sure were glad they used *Safeguard* soap that morning, waited in the intense heat for academia's dramatic doors to open. I recognized big trouble. Time had come to call me, *Miss Crockett.*

As those boisterous sparkplugs jettisoned me to the curb, in front of the fortress-like building, the car backfired so loud I swore cannons at the Alamo came back to finish the job. I became all the diversion the bored gang needed. Everybody gawked at yours truly, skulking out of the flamboyant Edsel.

The radiating sun overhead bounced off my father's fixation with *Turtle Wax.* He must have rubbed a ton of the Vaseline-like polish, all over the Edsel's already garish shade of turquoise. Adding to the adroit bad news carwash, his brand new battery operated—genuine lambs' wool buffer—gave additional enhancement to the traffic-stopping glint on this car's notorious chrome trim. "Autry's albatross" had altered into a hostile automaton, refracting the sun's intense rays with results more blinding than a burst of paparazzi flash bulbs.

Then, guess what.

Yes, *you* are correct.

Later on after dinner, Dad had an emergency lodge meeting so he tried starting the thing up without success. The contrivance finally ran out of malicious steam and bit the dust. And behind our remote storage shed, where that car parked, there's plenty of dust to bite.

Within an hour later, Cheap Charlie's Caressed Vehicles sent over their wrecker to collect the broken-down contrivance, for whatever parts they could salvage. Unlike the original hot summer night visit, to his raunchy lot so long ago, my mother went together with Dad. She squashed on his lap uninvited, into the front part of the wrecker's small tow truck. Playboy Bunnies make wives very aggressive.

Upon arrival, they found Charlie sitting, as usual, inside his Quonset-hut office. His feet rested on top of his improvised desk made from empty orange crates. He puffed a Cigarillo with affectation and stared at the ceiling, while large circles of smoke evaporated into the air. He was just a shifty kid, blowing bubbles.

Within a minute, he stubbed out the Cigarillo's butt inside of an already soiled souvenir ashtray stating, "Route 66 or Bust." He couldn't stop ogling Mom, all the while during their "negotiations." He ended up giving my parents a generous trade-in deal for a brand-new *Ford Mustang*.

When they arrived home with this fabulous automobile, painted the latest silver-frost color, and Dad pulled this gem into the driveway—I cried with joy. Also realizing how my dream come true came equipped with every bell and whistle imaginable, put me on the verge of collapse. I'm positive, though, you're aware how important first impressions are, and this great transaction arrived too late. The permanent damage on that fateful paparazzi day was a done deal.

For the subsequent three years, everybody I met in the school hallway deigned me with either a bow or a curtsy, saying in the loudest way possible, "Your Royal Duchess of Edseldom." Their spiteful designation dogged me—all through Senior High. I bet the words still resound off those cement-block walls.

Nowadays, if I encounter any human-residue from this era, I'm never bothered. I prepare myself for their majestic manners. Just think about how the hoards of people watching such an interaction here, in a crowded city like New York, might be impressed and actually believe my "aristocratic" pedigree.

You *never* know.

PART 32:

SHORT STATURE

"I am not typical."

I would never make such an empty promise tonight, telling you I won't drink the entire Dr Pepper 6-pack chilling in the refrigerator. Since my exclusive hometown variety is the *only* kind I'll ever accept, sometimes Mom will ship authentic cans to New York so I'll have them handy for any psychiatric emergency. On the other greedy hand, in order for her to do this favor, Daddy charges me triple the price. I paid him plenty for those frosty cans that are waiting for me now.

At this psychological point, although equating *my* father with any constructive therapy represents a contradiction in terms, I'm thinking I might. Even though he *did* deserve criticism for buying the dumb Batmobile, at this moment I find myself sympathizing with his isolation. Even if he had different circumstances when he agonized alone in his den, I'm also alone, where I am now. And, as he did then, we both relied on a 6-pack of Dr P to help us struggle with our problems.

I'll tell you for sure, recent circumstances gave me a new-take on the word *stressful.* This impractical benign-term will never exemplify a situation where one is about to tête-à-tête with heartless *Miss Wrack,* and her conniving partner, *Mr. Ruin.*

Speaking of my occasional reliance on Dr P when a crisis hits me, I admit I sometimes am undisciplined. I'm also the first one to acknowledge how drowning my troubles in an ocean of soda pop is a literal depression in my otherwise flawless armor. Plus, adding to my tooth decay is often valid. There's no denying everybody has a weakness. Of course, I have a hundred—if you believe my annoying sister.

I remember reading somewhere how what you're obsessive to take *in* will someday escort you *out.* Once in a while, however, a girl's got to do what a girl's got to do. Right this second I want my pricey cashew nuts and therapeutic Dr Pepper.

If you think I'm stamping my feet in a fit of rage and frustration, I'll just say, "right-on." *I* had a bad day. In temperamental addition, sitting here assessing everything going on with me not only today—but also throughout my entire life—is *not* helping. This newfound insight cautions me how turbulence is turning my brain into a pinwheel.

I'm being more than honest in saying how prefacing this journal isn't just for your benefit alone. I need clarification more than you do. If I weren't me and didn't know better, *I'd* think I'm bonkers myself—except I'm not; no matter what you'll hear to the contrary.

When I alluded to those journal notes, I didn't mention they're strewing all over Shelley's shabby apartment up in *The Bronx.* Living here is somewhat like fulfilling my lifelong dream of being a New Yorker, except the truth is only *Manhattan* has the ambiance *I* deserve. Rooming with my cousin is nothing more than a cracked steppingstone, on the path to my own pad.

Shelley had one positive initiative in her life three years ago when, on a rare impulse, she brushed off all the dust and left Tillagevale for good. And, since I escaped from its mind-numbing atmosphere myself three months ago, using her pad as a city pit stop made sense. My scraps of scribbled-on notepaper, concerning the ominous events of today, are covering the entire place, including the bathroom floor.

Understandably, I prefer not to be an itchy gypsy so being clueless about tomorrow's expected manifestation is merciful. I would cinch my burnout if I had to prepare in advance to navigate another situation like the existing one. They'd be hauling me off **ASAP** to that jumping joint known as the psychiatric party-ward. You'd locate me there, stuffing all of the imaginary mocha-fudge cream cake into my mouth. I also might be having a celebratory toast with Napoleon and Josephine. Or maybe not, if she failed to stitch up her generous underwear and they are now divorced.

Speaking of Josephine, I'd like to give *her* a good lecture. Really now, what *do* women want out of life. Okay, this ruler was a shrimp. Nevertheless, being a bigger than life *Emperor* turns him into a kingfish, don't you agree. How much better can you do than that? You should see the gorgeous wedding gown he bought her. There's enough material to stretch the long train behind it—all the way from Fordham Road to The Bronx Zoo. You could never buy this creation anywhere. Even New York's popular bridal shop *Kleinfeld,* located in Bay Ridge, Brooklyn, couldn't come close to this kind of splendor.

A huge painting depicts her wearing this spectacular creation, during their imperial wedding ceremony. Napoleon stands at the altar while awaiting her. His eager, outstretched arms hold a magnificent bejeweled crown, ready to place on her chiseled head, as soon as she states her vows of fidelity. I often wonder if he took the wedding gift back later on, after he caught her playing around. I also wonder how he ever managed to set this crown on her head in the first place, since she already wore a thick circlet of diamonds in her hair.

While he acted so solicitous, he had no idea she'd break his heart in the future. I think some of the people attending the wedding knew. Even though this portrait by *David* glorifies how things actually happened, the guests still don't look too happy about the nuptials. The work of genius hangs now in a famous museum.

Yes, I *do* know the name of the museum.

It's the *Louvre* in Paris, France.

As a kid, I sort of went to *Paris* a lot.

Leaving excursions to France behind, in serious preparation to tell-all, my obvious confusion over self-worth confronts me with cruel facts. I'm certain now, more than ever, if I continue struggling throughout life convincing myself I'm an "ordinary girl" I'm being a masochist. Or worse yet, maybe I'd be a misogynist. On the other debasing hand, this *misogynist* deal could be a favorable one, then I'd be a girl who's an actual *girl-hater*—with a convenient *Seven-Eleven* type of one-stop-shop for unending self-deprecation.

I'd love to keep on pretending the trait setting me apart from everybody else is how my kind of *ordinary* has a slight edge. As I'll explain later, I've come to the realization this afternoon, whatever is going on with me must be a maze-like whodunit-map, full of disturbing twists and turns.

Classifying me with a precise term has never been easy. I don't have many friends. Even the few that like me have fun singling me out—somehow. In general, people react to me in a peculiar manner. I'm frustrated, because I know some of these *friends* distort my obvious superior intelligence to demean me on purpose.

So—I've decided on my *new* mantra:

I am not typical.
I never will be.
So just accept it.

You say that you'd like to hear my former mantra.
Are you sure?
How sweet.
I'll recite it now, before you change your mind:

Let them all drop their paddle,
When they rowboat up the raging water,
While passing under Niagara Falls . . .

If you're wondering about my change of heart, as shown in the latest mantra, this newer and kinder *introspective* stance comes about simply because I am now convinced that the logic behind what *I* am—is a conundrum for a magician.

Trying to locate a Wegi Board, to schmoose with *The Great Houdini,* is not on my agenda tonight so it will have to wait, but I'd like to try it out in the future. I want to understand how, without any key, he freed himself from all those heavyweight chains in his life.

PART 33:

PYRE FLAMES

"You have every right."

One of those *Houdini* chains I must cope with, night and day, is how people won't give up their perverse hobby of strangling any life I have left in my name. You'd think they had better stuff to do with their imagination. I'm convinced they never did see Dark Shadows.

Also, the poor choice my parents made, while filling out my birth certificate, gives the populace additional fuel for burning me at the stake. What a waste, since by now they have more than enough kindling for another historic Chicago Fire.

Are you wondering why?

You'll see.

Speaking of *pyre flames*—I've been educating myself concerning the history of *Saint Joan of Arc.* I understand why there's such great respect for her. On the apolitical surface, "Joan" is my heroine. Except, am I correct how in current gendering terms she is now my *hero?*

Concerning my above illustration of "Joan", this new gender-neutralization fad is tiresome when trying to write descriptive dialogue. Characterizations of people are either *male* or *female*—at least until further notice. Grappling with nonsense like this destroys any richness of the words a writer uses as an instinctual mode of creativity. Author's feel they're under attack by aggressive literary-cops who think aberrant *pen-to-paper-felons* deserve nothing other than the maximum-security stint, right along with *The Birdman* over at Alcatraz.

They closed the institution down, not too long ago. I think the penitentiary's warden might make an exception and reopen the vile place to accommodate me. The one thing we *all* know for sure is that *I'm* for the birds.

I did not change "Birdman" to *Birdperson* on purpose. So if or when I manage to affront your sensibilities, you have my apology. And, just like blessed Saint Joan, you will forgive me. I think.

This conflict with *bookish* snobs is very evident, if an author dares to use any of the ingrained "no longer acceptable" speech patterns they grew up with. I, conversely, am steadfast in my refusal to comply. I'm a writer who plans on soaring like a phoenix, toward an unrestricted literary horizon. I hope you'll be flying along with me, carrying your bookmark.

My pen and me are planning to reach the mythical-pinnacle. I don't care what critics say. I've had plenty of experience ignoring them, literary or otherwise. Please understand that in relaying this personal account, I'm speaking to you as though we just grabbed one of those coveted booths at the back of Bobcat Billy's Burger Barn, where we chewed the fat until the lights dimmed and they threw us out.

I'm not preparing a term paper, editing a yearbook or anything else of an academic nature. I've been doing that field of writing adnauseam, and I grew to hate the restrictions. Having to deal with any of those recent political correctness maneuvers, creeping into mainstream society, crimps my style. Even with mistakes, I write the way of my literary heart.

I am Frances Hodgson Burnett, hiding in *The Secret Garden.*

I am Jane Austen, spying on inhabitants of *Mansfield Park.*

I am Emily Bronte, listening to lamentations of the wind—howling across the moors at *Wuthering Heights.*

Did you just say I exhibited, "delusions of grandeur?"

Don't worry.

You have every right.

You *are* my shrink.

PART 34:

SHUT UP! BE QUIET! "Or so she thought."

Explaining that I've never met the singer and actor Gene Autry is important. In case you don't know, *he* is the cowboy who sings, without a care in the world, while lethal bullets and piercing arrows whiz by his untouchable ten-gallon hat. I'm sure he must be a sane person in real life, but his ridiculous on-screen behavior *could* qualify him to be a member of my family. However, he isn't—not by a long shot.

Only pure coincidence has my father's last name being Autry—Mr. *Alex* Autry. My grandfather had the name of Destrehan Autry. Everybody called him, *Destry.* Not me. I called him, *Grandpa Des.* Given that he owned a travel agency, he never crooned to any *horse.* That huge picture of him, taken at a Dude Ranch for advertisement purposes, doesn't count. Even if he had to dig ditches for a living, he'd have done the backbreaking job just to avoid singing lullabies to any four-legged creature.

Sometimes, though, I love visualizing my own dad wearing his favorite cherry-pink and apple-blossom-white Bermuda shorts, while getting down on knobby knees to serenade a stallion. If I'm ever in a funk, this depiction pulls me right out of it.

Harkening back now to *Gene Autry,* and his musical version of "shooting it out in the old corral", my mistaken familial connection to this pistol-packing vocalist is a never-ending source of aggravation. Hostile tribes have been drumming up major Tillagevale air pollution at their recent powwows.

In honest reflection though, bizarre stories about my connection to him are nothing new. I became aware of this painful fact, on the very first day of grammar school. Although they actually might go all the way back to the period of gospel truth, when I hung high in Bible Villains' Hoosegow.

When kindergarten approved my early entry, Mom had no idea what she did to me. I think she only cared about the long-awaited opportunity of dumping me in a safe place for a few hours during the week, without them charging her for the privilege.

Or so she thought.

Although she has a bachelor's degree in library science, she often entertained the dream of being a stay-at-home mother. Until she could achieve this noble aspiration, she was out in the salaried workforce. She was Chief Librarian at the local library.

This comment, about her previous employment, leads me to the historic afternoon when those bunko *wannabe* **SWAT** guys showed up at the front door. *They* sure had a scary attitude. Of course, a budding juvenile delinquent like *me,* at least without any *priors* that law enforcement knew about, grasped how you could not dismiss their bullying.

You couldn't help noticing this dedication to police work when they waved an "official injunction" in my mother's petrified face. These tough guys, sanctioned by the letter of the law, conveyed—by use of this judicial fan—how she acted like a total idiot paying seventy-five dollars in precious "cookie jar cash" for "scorching-hot" *Worldbook Encyclopedias.*

What made the crime even worse, Mom got conned by a felon with a rap sheet longer than the Colorado River. This door-to-door *salesman* had that crooked Fuller Brush Company mustache and looked exactly like the pastor of our church. When she made the *purchase,* she thanked him for, "the fabulous educational opportunity."

As a rule, I'm not into praising books of knowledge, but this gorgeous set consisted of fifty genuine leather-bound volumes, with numerals painted in real gold on the binders. They were also the rich color of that claret *Bordeaux* wine my father drinks when he has the *sniffles.* Usually, he doesn't have a thing wrong with him. He just pretends with phony sneezing and grabbing a wad of tissues from the box on his desk. He's so wasteful when he crumples them up, tossing them unused in his wastebasket just for show.

Getting back to police brutality, I tried real hard to stop those aggressive cops by telling them my mother was in the clear, since *trusted* Reverend Frisby was the pusher. But for some reason, she kept putting her hands over my mouth and wouldn't quit using the stranglehold. I even left teeth marks!

My mother started crying when they confiscated each of the hefty stolen books by yanking them from the expensive new custom-made cabinet Dad designed himself, to display these "classics" in his den. He paid one-thousand dollars. I think the high price came from those handcrafted stained-glass doors, reminiscent of the entrance to a magnificent Gothic cathedral that bathes in flickering votive lights. To keep the place company, great looking young monks, wearing hooded robes, chant all day.

In the actual scenario concerning the bookcase, however, votive lights came courtesy of overhead fluorescent bulbs. Any chanting from a robed *monk* resulted from my father's mumbling, while sitting in his ragged bathrobe at midnight, and trying to balance my mother's checkbook.

During a span of several weeks, after she went bananas over the injunction, she lived in fear that the cataclysmic shock might cause amnesia. She didn't have to worry. I tested her out and she remembered *everything,* even stuff I wished she *could* forget. All the same, are you curious how this thief-of-all-thieves managed his "educational" caper? Well, I'll tell you right now.

The "scene of the crime" library *is* quieter than a mortuary putting trained personnel, right along with the public, into a catatonic-state, so he had the smarts to don a phony uniform advertising *Trustworthy Bookbinders, Ltd.* Then, cooler than a frozen cucumber, he packed the heavy encyclopedias into a super jumbo, bright-red *Radio-Flyer* wheelbarrow, and rolled the stolen thing straight out of the library's marble-columned portico.

I'd like to interject here how amazed I am that as backward as Tillagevale is now, those antebellum town commissioners built a library with more than enough grandeur to equal the *Lincoln Memorial* in **Washington DC.**

When the dejected works of knowledge suffered the rebound contraband-treatment once again, after removal from their prohibited cathedral lodging in Dad's den, Mom thought long and hard about what kind of soothing spin she could put on the bare situation. My father would come home in the evening, ready to relax and watch *I Love Lucy.* He wasn't expecting to participate in the episode.

Later, when the result of her spin-attempt sent her beloved husband into orbit, she flopped around the house for a week—crying her head off. We thought she'd never stop explaining to everybody, including perfect strangers, how she'd be a, "forever-permanent former-librarian."

Huh?

At the rate of any overdue book penalty, when she toiled at the library, she made the most of her position of authority. She loved practicing the art of being gracious. She wrote her own manual concerning hundreds of polite ways to tell people to shut-up and be quiet. I sure understood, while growing up, how she possessed superb skill in this area.

Eventually, she dumped her elevated position. The proverbial twinkle in her eye had left for a more complicated location. The doctor confirmed my suspected existence when a laboratory injected a needle full of my mother's probable pregnancy-pee into one poor and innocent—soon to be dead—rabbit.

Filling out floral flour sacks, known to the fashion world as maternity clothes, offered the perfect opportunity for an exalted member of the staff to leave the arsenal of books behind. She only took with her those shopping bags full of lute from the staff's goodhearted baby shower—along with her overblown expectations of joyful motherhood. And that's about the only positive thing concerning her future life at home with diaper rash.

Of course, if you ask her, she'll tell you, "There never could be a *more* delightful baby than Ginger, an absolute *joy* to bring up." Please ignore the heavy accent she puts on these endearing descriptions, while swaying around with her eyes shut. But putting *Desitin* salve aside, Mom wound up getting the well-earned break she needed on the day she dropped me at the Flintstone establishment I mentioned before. The "Bedrock" antithesis of the new type of *Montessori School,* I should have been attending.

What institution of lower learning can I be referencing, except that headquarters for lamebrains? Of course, it's none other than the one, and you have to thank goodness the only, **Tillagevale Kindergarten.**

PART 35:

SCHOOL BELLS CLANG "And thus, it began."

As a child, I had one redeeming quality. I hated being a clingy type. This is why, on my first morning in such a classroom full of lamebrains, I waved a happy *bye-bye* to my lucky mother. I just couldn't wait to wiggle myself behind the pintsized *desk.* And, with the agility of a kid, ravenous for a new experience, I plopped myself on its hard bench.

Afterward, as noted earlier, I cradled my illustrious freckled-face in the palms of my hands. A desk too decrepit to burn had to be good for *something.* I got scabs on my elbows from digging into this piece of rejected firewood. I was the perfect specimen of a kid with a residual summertime tan, resembling a bronzed statue of a hopeful *Spartan Thinker,* contemplating whether snack-time came *soon.*

The way things turned out, on my first day of corruptible education, my mother had no idea what actually went on. I never told her. She still doesn't know. Even if she defended me then, things usually ended up being my fault. On the confusing morning, while I fantasized about a possible *Twinkie,* more than half of the kindergarten children exhibited something Mr. Drench, the overwrought principal, flew around dubbing "separation anxiety."

I felt sorry for this frenzied administrator. While he wrung his hands and wiped his dripping brow—by using a crumbled piece of baby-doll-pink construction paper—he kept trying to hang on to his dilapidated bullhorn. He needed the scratched up amplifier to holler over the pandemonium.

Unlike my professional mother, his unskilled wife didn't have the convenient hanky in the jacket habit. His determination to continue those futile saturated attempts, to get the attention of the flipping-out kindergartners, made him a superhero—at least to me.

Too bad, you couldn't have witnessed what went on. Some of the phobic kids in my new classroom had twisted themselves into tight balls. These budding contortionists wedged their gross scabby knees, as tight as they could, underneath their sticky chins.

Adding to the amazement of watching such an acrobatic act, they performed this nimble-feat out in the hall, where they rolled around on the hard concrete floor. I witnessed a bizarre hockey match, when Mr. Drench manipulated a yardstick in an admirable attempt to prevent children from meshing their tiny brains into a collective chunk of peanut brittle.

Some of the uncontrollable children, who had been having those good old-fashioned scream out your guts temper tantrums, got emergency fresh air outside on the grass. I watched them from the window near my desk. Others used their outdoor arena to perform like hyperactive trampoline artists, jumping up and down holding their breath, until they turned alarming shades of chartreuse.

Several of these lamebrains were upstairs in the infirmary, tossing their cookies. I overheard Mr. Drench say how the venerable school nurse, Mrs. Bettina Bulwark, was on the verge of collapse herself, and needed some serious reinforcements—*pronto.*

The remaining students gathered around my desk, while they asked me to open my mouth and show them my teeth.

And thus, it began.

PART 36:

SAY TOOTSIE

"*Ginjar's* eating number-two!"

In retrospect, I shudder to think what else could have happened to me on the morning of my introduction to academia, if my grandmother didn't drop by after breakfast. She could sniff out my turpitude, better than a veteran hound dog. She dragged me off to the bathroom where, under her watchful eye, I brushed a mound of Tootsie Roll goop out of my mouth.

I loved my grandmother the best in the world, much more than any candy, and she loved me back. She could read me like a *Nancy Drew* mystery. Plus, at this time, my sister was learning the awesome power of speech. The little squirt accrued twenty new words a day, and practiced her recent arsenal of verbal weaponry to rat and tell on me.

Let's just say that I gave her plenty of opportunity for language lessons.

If you've ever seen this candy, you understand why she confused pieces of unwrapped . . . one-inch long . . . condensed . . . tar-like . . . dark chocolate *Tootsie Rolls,* with her potty-training regime. Whoever happened to be around, while I got my chewy-fix, heard her piercing toddler voice informing them, *"Ginjar's* eating number-two!"

This comment alone helped my grandmother win the dental hygiene battle. She also removed the hoard of *poop* I scrunched in my hand. Instead of confiscating them, she put the spare Tootsie rolls into my skirt pocket—her way of giving me permission to have a treat after my lunch.

Another break came my way, when she never asked how I had access to these sweets, so early in the morning. Otherwise, I'd have to tell her I stockpiled a huge supply under my bed, camouflaging them with the mounds of dust—I told my mother I cleaned. This wasn't a total lie. When I attempted to comply with her rules, the fuzzy stuff made me sneeze like crazy, and what if this excessive sneezing led to my getting sick. Moms never want such a thing to happen, and only wish the best for you.

After everything that I experienced in school that morning, these morsels of candy, Grandma allowed me to keep, were a major consolation when I listened to the mindless rumor, circulating throughout the now giggling classroom. It concerned my abnormal infancy. My parents fed me big bowls of pabulum, but I *really* craved a rack of barbecued ribs. So wily me yanked out my first baby tooth.

Why be a *dummy* like all the other babies in the world?

Why should a little one, with diaper pins made of solid silver, have to wait six miserable years like all "regular kids" do, for the parsimonious nickel-and-dime Tooth Fairy to show up?

I had that rich "cowboy star" waiting in the wings, along with all his wealthy Hollywood-cronies. These guys were good for at least a lifetime supply of those juicy ribs.

I soon figured out that all I had to do was give the dainty tooth a little tug, make a gurgle, and spit the discolored chunk of enamel into my teensy-weensy hand. Before long, I became a total addict to superstar *Sugar Fairy* dough. Whenever another baby tooth surfaced, I'd yank out my lucrative chance to tap everybody in *Tinseltown* for more cold hard cash. I forgot about those ribs. Now I only concentrated on hoarding the big bucks.

This is what I lived with, as the structured weeks wore on. The nauseous contortionists did eventually empty all of their resources, and finally reconciled their dismal fate. After that, the entire classroom of kids went bonkers over my mini-set of false teeth. They kept asking how much my parents paid to buy them from *Dr. Norman*—the Orthodontist with a reputation for "highway robbery."

He *is* on the expensive side, but no *other* dentists of this type exist in town to compete with him, and he happens to be an expert at what he does. My father often tells parents how the manufacturer of my favorite "tar candy" aids and abets the *supposed* crime. He tried hard to stop me from eating them anymore but failed—just another battle of the wits that I was sure to win. Some fights take longer than others do, but inevitably, as you will see later, I get my way.

In any dental case, I grew suspicious of our teacher, Miss Harriet {the horrid} Heller, and her attitude concerning the kindergarten's fascination with my mouth. When the class begged me to use my "posh" dentures for

Show and Tell, Miss Heller ignored their rude behavior. She just gave me her sly simper, which pursed her lips into two dried raisins.

Also—how could I remember my first exposure to academia from a prehistoric sphere, without visualizing these pathetic ignoramuses and the vicious way they grilled me about my "fat piggybank?" The class really went *hog-wild* with the third degree over getting me to donate Valentine cards for their stupid party.

How dumb did they think I was?

The answer is that they counted on me being much dumber than they were.

I'd never get any of these coveted greetings, even if I did pay for the unfair things. I bet that *if* by some major miracle, anybody other than annoying Pun Geyser *did* put a Valentine addressed to me inside that ridiculous classroom mailbox these kids *would* have signed what *I* bought for them:

♥♥♥♥ LOVE AND KISSES FROM YOUR SECRET HATER ♥♥♥♥

Trust me.
Trust me.
Trust me.

PART 37:

THE NAME GAME

"As usual, you're right."

I doubt that you will trust me, concerning what I'm about to tell you here, but then again you might. The ancient kindergarten story, concerning my false teeth, *still* makes the rounds. Only now, they refer to an inferior dental laboratory in Mexico that uses discolored *recycled* material. They created a *mature* set of them for me on the cheap. To seal the bargain, they threw in a free lifetime supply of dental adhesive. I only have to pay the cost of shipping *Poligripó* from Tijuana.

Over the years though, I've grown to admire the creativity behind these stories. You have to admit they're pretty farfetched. If I heard about these events happening to someone else, I wouldn't believe a word. However, since I'm the actual one living the events, the sting of their truth burns me every day.

As I write this, the current yarn concerning my last name is taking on a ferocious new life of its own. Nowadays, not only must I continue tolerating the influence of those classic Gene Autry cowboy movies, which never quit feeding the voracious Tillagevale rumor mill, I must also survive his old television series. Some sadist made a very unwise decision to show the entire package again as reruns *every* Saturday morning.

Okay—you miserable TV moguls, why not hurry up and breed a whole *new* generation of boob-tubers to continue the persecution. You could air Gene Autry seven days a week, ensuring how my distress will never end, unless I get married. But *if* I ever *do* say, "I do," I won't be looking into the eyes of any guy with the last name of "Rogers". He could be a James Dean clone, for all *I* care.

I'll never consent to become any *Ginger Rogers,* even if the fellow popping the question is filthy rich, and so handsome that he causes more swooning than James Bond did in the movie, *You Only Live Twice.* I'll tell him to shove off. He can take his traffic stopping, 5-karat, and pear-shaped *perfect* blue-white diamond, right back to where he purchased the rock. This, of course, is nowhere other than the bastion of upscale baubles on Manhattan's Fifth Avenue, *Van Cleef and Arpels.*

Of course, it *is* possible that I'll reconsider my stance if this dream man happens to be so head over heels in love with me that changing *his* surname to something *I'd* pick wouldn't be a problem. I think "Mrs. Ginger Rockefeller" sounds good. I won't have any trouble getting a credit card with such a title. My flawless diamond will blind them into giving me an endless limit on expenses.

Also, while we're on the crucial question-topic, let's not forget about the impressive matching wedding band he'll buy me; the thick, wide platinum one—adorned with a ton of diamond baguettes—equal to, or greater than, the engagement ring itself.

In hopeful addition, since I do expect to meet my dream man *someday,* the "Autry" issue will resolve itself. As of late, I've been thinking when I do turn eighteen, I'll find one of those lawyers who specialize in name change. I'll dump the "Ginger", and the dumb middle name with the *P,* when the law allows.

Setting this prime Prince Charming fantasy aside, guess who is ecstatic to inform me about the recent "Autry" misrepresentation—now buzzing around my visage.

Did you say my sister?

Wow, you're almost as smart as I am.

As usual, you're right.

And you'll see why in a second.

PART 38:

STATUE OF LIBERTY "He doesn't like me."

If my sister didn't take constant pleasure in repeating the latest Autry rumors to me, I'd lead a boring and dull life. She's able to be my daily social director, while they compound on a twenty-four-hour schedule like **Greenwich Mean Time.** Some of these latest deformations are hitting home better than Babe Ruth, since they center on the funny farm I might be using for my birthday bash.

According to *her,* as of yesterday afternoon, I'm incoherent and babbling in a padded cell inside some mental hospital. I'm there due to my recent brain injury. What's even more insane, the cause of this "brain injury" is while visiting my "relative" Gene Autry—at his palatial home in Beverly Hills last week—my usual moronic-self clicked into overdrive.

Under the impetuous influence of Hollywood, I went off the track by confiscating *Champion*—his taller than the Statue of Liberty stallion. Possessed with the fervor of Paul Revere, I grabbed the gardener's ladder, and climbed up onto this horse's bare back. I'm referring to the horse with an airborne tail, propelled by a lightening bolt, which gallops through the sound barrier in every Gene Autry Western, as well as the sappy TV show, I've just been trashing.

Adding to his stratospheric speed, Champion's the equine equivalent of a movie star brat. He doesn't like me. My inability to sing his owner's most famous ballad—*Back in the Saddle Again* put me on his hate list. Although I tried hard to belt it out, I insulted him by being off-key and forgetting most of the words. Out of pure spite, he threw me headfirst into the empty swimming pool.

You never saw such a tragedy. The most competent brain surgeon in the world or the most juiced-up shock treatments the hospital has to offer, can't help me recover from diving headfirst into a huge dry basin of mosaic tiles.

Although people in town *are* familiar with me as a less than competent kook, they'll soon be doing a double take. Watch their reaction, when they see the steel helmet on my head—the one protecting my smashed brains from oozing out of the substantial crack in my cranium.

Now, thanks to Champion, my status as "kooky village idiot" has been upped a notch. Everybody, from this moment on, will refer to me as the kook who is a *certifiable* village idiot with a gaping hole in her head. Certainly, this represents nothing more than a load of complete claptrap. I'll now list the four primary reasons why. I needn't tell you, though, to trust me concerning *their* authenticity. Every one of them is renowned in the *Guinness Book of World Records.*

Well—they should be!

In the 1st place:

I happen to be a genius with a noggin much thicker and harder than those dynamic presidential rock heads—carved in South Dakota's *Mount Rushmore National Memorial.*

In the 2nd place:

I have an enviable voice. I realize this every morning when I take a shower, and sing *Wakeup Little Susie.* The Everly Brothers fear my competition.

In the 3rd place:

I have an astonishing photographic memory—as you must have realized by now.

In the 4th place:

Don't you think Gene Autry is affluent enough to keep his swimming pool filled?

Well I do!

If you're perplexed about what happens to my sister for sharing the identical last name, I'll be glad to tell you. *She* only hears that dimwitted justification for why she's "movie star gorgeous" and I'm so far out of her league, the one positive thing in life I look forward to is my future job with a freak show.

The popular rationale among the masses verifies how my sister inherited the "Goddess of Venus" genes, and spiteful genetics zapped me with a mutant strain that was the missing link—once lying dormant in a fetid cave with Cro-Magnon Man. Thus, I say to you, if the stench of this kind of logic doesn't make you barf—you're a better passenger on the Ship of Life, than I'll ever be.

The time has arrived for me to top off the incompetence of the horsemanship rumors. I wish to inform you, and everybody else in the world right now, how the very same people who are gullible enough to think I'd ever get on *any* stallion, above all Champion, are clueless about my legendary equestrian status.

I'll never go within a mile's radius of another live horse, after the horror that took place three weeks before *my* fourth birthday.

PART 39:

MISADVENTURES OF ZORRO

"And I mean *shout.*"

Several years ago, the American Council on Pandemonium made an emergency decision to recognize a manifestation they had never encountered before. They wound up calling the phenomenon "Kiddy Chaos Syndrome" or **KCS.** This new psychiatric classification resulted from my sitting down on that packed *pony-cart* ride. In circus lore, things are never as plugged. There wasn't any *pony* or *cart.* I became the victim of a gargantuan white Clydesdale horse, pulling a matching gargantuan hayride wagon.

Before continuing, I'd like to state for the record that *if* you hear any reports about the Kolinsky Brothers Traveling Circus, with a special focus on any of those *clowns,* coming anywhere *near* the vicinity of Tillagevale ever again, you've been sadly misinformed.

Also, regarding this circus troupe, and their constant habit of badmouthing *me,* I want to recap all the details right now as part of my defense. As far as *I'm* concerned, I only acted like a courageous kid with the guts to warn her good buddies, riding along with her in the self-appointed "cart", how the mean phony-baloney-pony was changing into the *boogeyman.*

This notion sounds irrational now, but I actually thought the horse was prancing right into monster-mode. I got the nutty idea from the antics of that short and scrawny clown, dressing up like a down-and-out *Zorro* on welfare. His awkward attempts to steer the immense wagon led me to this misconception, which could have turned out to be Dance Macabre personified.

For your further information, they *chose* me to squat in the small compartment of loose hay—right next to this "Zorro" driver's makeshift bench. I didn't ask them for the honor.

What a mistake this clown made when he picked me up and put *me* in this seat. I saw stuff the other kids couldn't. The thin slab of discarded lumber, which they used to fashion this small "bench", bore the vivid imprint of a huge skull and crossbones foretelling an early *Halloween.*

Owing to my supposed *esteemed* position in the wagon, I assumed leadership of the bursting at the seams kiddy-pack. Everybody else squashed behind me, atop compact bales of hay, in its main section.

Witnessing this shabby clown's continual frustration—at bungling attempts to change the horse's direction—caused him, with every breath he took, to holler the word "boogie" at the colossal, uncooperative Clydesdale. Later on, I found out the horse had the *name* of Boogie—like in the *dance.*

For me, dancing at the age of four just meant good old *musical chairs.* I could never even win the dumb game. I got black and blue from trying every time. The boogie-woogie didn't jive with my lifestyle.

Even at this point, when I'm almost eighteen—*The Twist* is a trial. Everybody says I look like I'm having a seizure, while I'm gyrating to Chuck Berry. But lack of dancing skill aside, I sure knew all about the boogeyman then. I still think there might be some truth to him.

Now—twisting back to the circus, there I sat, staring at the perturbed driver, as he tugged like a maniac at the horse's reins. I thought he was doing some kind of a great trick, aiming to look Fourth of July patriotic, while I watched his face turn chalky white, his scrawny neck get as red as a beet, and his pulsating Adam's apple convert to a nationalistic shade of blue. I wondered about asking him later on, if he could show my father how to perform this colorful stunt. Everybody at the Bullsnake Lodge would be impressed.

Further adding to my great idea of becoming a talent agent, his unshaven mug—with stubble for stars—resembled the American Flag, while his squeaky voice turned croaky from shrieking at the immense horse. As far as I remember, Zorro commanded his obstinate steed with something along the lines of:

> Whoa—you damn Boogie.
> Man!
> Do you think its fun, working your stupid reins like the devil?
> Hey you, Boogie.
> Man!

You're one nasty critter from Satan's stable.
I'm ordering *you* to turn inside the *ring,* Boogie.
Man!
I am *no* dumb clown.
I have real power to switch *your* evil fiery-ass, *now!*

Being the recent veteran of the horror movie to end all horror movies, I realized the danger lurking behind this dialog. I did nothing other than the valiant thing. I stood up to shout my emergency bulletin. And I mean *shout.*

I paid more than one price for standing tall and balancing myself in the rocking wagon. That prickly hay, migrating up my shorts to a sensitive area, made an uncomfortable situation worse. However, my determination to save the day gave me the equilibrium I needed. I turned around and faced the gang. I funneled my petite hands around my big mouth, right before expanding my not so petite lungs. With a deafening sound, shrill enough to shatter a window, I called out:

"Listen up, you guys! *Zorro* is not just a *dumb* clown. Zorro is *evil.* He works for the *devil's* ring. Our horse is really a *nasty* critter—straight from *hell's* fire. For *fun,* Zorro is *switching* this stupid ass because *Satan* ordered *him* to turn *it* into the *boogeyman* right *now!*"

I went on to educate my compatriots about those reliable stories *I* heard, concerning the boogeyman's penchant for running away with as many naughty children as he could gather at once. Since we *already* sat as his captives inside the cart, we made the boogeyman's task very easy to accomplish.

My accounting about the boogeyman's desire to collect *naughty* children hit those guilty and impressionable minds like a ton of those dreaded holiday *cement* cookies, from the kind, elderly lady next-door. I'm also certain that one-hundred-percent of the kids on this overfed ride fell into the "naughty" category.

When Zorro heard those earsplitting howls of unbridled panic, erupting inside the screwy rig, the startling upheaval traumatized him to the point where he passed out cold. He was now a lifeless marionette, slumping over in his driver's seat. His shoddy Zorro mask became even more askew than before, after one of his big, pointy ears poked out of a ripped eye slot on this flimsy disguise.

At first, this corny Zorro-on-the-skids costume represented nothing I'd ever waste precious film on. However, later on during the mayhem—with my new *Brownie-Hawkeye* camera in my hands—Zorro provided plenty of photo ops. Stuff got wild.

My grandparents also gave me a convenient carrying case for this great camera, to slip around my neck. Throughout all of the commotion, this loaded to the hilt dream rode along for the ride of my life, at least as far as I knew then. The entire Hawkeye kit, including a spare bag of flashbulbs, came as an early birthday present and added to the excitement of heading off with my parents to the circus

What a photograph I took of Zorro's black "cape", as the moth-eaten rag fluttered in the wind. Boogie, having excellent peripheral vision, saw the fabric's dark silhouette looming over its head. The already spooked Clydesdale mistook this cloth for a black cloud of doom, about to snag it. As a further crazed reaction, the animal, along with the trailing wagon, picked up more turbulent speed. Everything flew by us in a blur.

And—as soon as Zorro's flat sombrero, the dilapidated black one with those several missing red tassels, joined the breeze, I took another great snapshot of the cape. The thing now covered his poor conked-out head and tied itself into a tight knot, under the stubble on his chin. Zorro wore a peasant's babushka!

While I quit beautician school to develop a new career as *Life Magazine's* youngest photographer, my frantic parents consulted with the sheriff. I also know those deputies, and I think the fire brigade too, had their own ears ringing.

The flamboyant mayor of Tillagevale, Wolfgang Sleazerman, also came to the circus. He used those two complimentary passes for first-row, deluxe center-seats. Everybody asked him what caused those nasty chapped lips. He told them the crusty mess came from his recent campaign for a fourth-term and having to kiss hundreds of damp babies, while he traipsed all over the county. As my mother relayed to everybody later, she wondered out-loud why "Mrs. Mayor" wasn't with him at the circus.

Reporters from the local newspaper rushed over to take an official picture of the mayor. The editor came along too, for an authoritative firsthand quote concerning Sleazerman's "bird's eye view" of the bedlam. *This* important mayoral commentary would be a hot off the presses feature and a prominent part of The Gazette's Editorial Page the next morning.

The formal name of this paper is—**The Tillagevale Gazette.** Somehow, everybody in town simplifies their hometown daily to just *The Gazette.* Formal name, nickname or no name, the esteemed mayor refused to talk. Instead, he tried to hide his new secretary.

How ridiculous for *him* to think he could camouflage such a gorgeous and statuesque strawberry-blond, pageboy-coiffed Rita Hayworth look-alike—by shoving *her* behind *his* back. This stubborn maneuver could never work. The then mayor of Tillagevale made the emaciated actor Don Knotts look like the *Incredible Hulk.*

The reporters acted surprised too and started scribbling on their pads faster than ever, because getting rid of his bombshell "employee" appeared far more urgent to this politician than commenting to the local newspaper about the dire situation.

I can't leave out the medical staff inside the ambulance. My parents said how telling them what happened was difficult. My father shouted in competition with their deafening siren, while the podgy lawyer wheezed from doing pushups in preparation to chase it.

PART 40:

CLOWNING AROUND

"Zorro remained out like a light."

A cool, calm, and collected me, rode along in the wagon on that revolutionary night at the circus. Maybe taking all those pictures distracted me. Or perhaps having recent nocturnal encounters, with a voracious creature made from wicked Jell-O dessert—that slobbered across my face while planning to devour me like a bag of Fritos Corn Chips—put the whole thing in perspective. There's no doubt I documented some riotous goings on with my camera.

Zorro remained out like a light. However, the *other* clowns zipped around underneath the huge three-ring circus tent, trying without success to keep up with the runaway cart. They dripped with perspiration. You'd swear they just came from one of those saunas over at *Shrink Your Gut Health Club.* My father joined six months ago and paid up for a full year. What a waste of money. He never leaves the couch to go out and use any of their exercise equipment. My osmosis fitness-thing must be hereditary.

I'll leave the smelly gym now, and jog back to all of these saturated comics who trailed us. The stress of running so hard caused them all to trip on their wet and now *deglued* red-rubber schnozolas that flew off one by one and started bouncing around the circus tent. This mass of Spalding balls went way . . . way . . . way . . . *up* into the air, before landing right smack down under the clowns, by then, disintegrating cardboard shoes.

Under its own weird supersonic power, the spooked *pony,* and the beyond comprehension out of control wagon—filled to the brim with panic-stricken kids—kept circling like an uncanny rocket, impelled by hell. These dynamics convinced me, along with all of the other kids, how my emergency bulletin was indeed accurate.

The madcap performers in the tinfoil Martian costumes made admirable efforts to chase us too, while they wobbled on those tremulous stilts. They had the absolute worst experience. Yowling poodles followed them, and these dogs kept gnawing at the plastic space-boots attached to the base of these stilts.

These *Martians* could have all fractured their legs, due to poodle-fury. By some miracle, just one of them toppled off headfirst. The unfortunate *launched* alien, from the big red planet, broke his fall on a hefty pile of elephant dung. *He* only needed immediate resuscitation and a quick shower.

People were amazed how the circus band could concentrate in the midst of something like this and continue to play *Stars and Stripes Forever* nonstop. Their peppy rendition of the patriotic march boomed over those chilling screeches from kids in the wagon, as well as horrifying proclamations of terror coming from everybody else, sitting in the bleachers of the outdoor arena.

This screaming-competition—up against continual patriotic oompah —escalated into bloodcurdling when *The Great Frantz Kolinsky*—billed as "The Bravest Wild Animal Tamer on Planet Earth"—came bounding after the flying wagon. As usual, he wore his leopard-skin tights. He cracked his whip with zeal when one of the vicious foaming tigers escaped from its cage, and dragged the dented wire-thing on its back. The angry tiger chased *Frantz,* while Frantz chased the wagon!

I'll tell you for sure that a tiger with a deceptive name like "Sweetie"—in hot pursuit of its trainer—makes for a gruesome spectacle. Now imagine if the ferocious thing disgorges raw meat, through razor-sharp daggers, inside of its mammoth trapdoor mouth. The gory sight doesn't help a horse calm down one bit. It has the opposite effect. I doubt even the venerable *King Kong* could match the ferocity of an amuck beast like *Sweetie.*

If you don't trust me on this one, *when* will you?

PART 41:

BUTCH

"The description rides on its own merit."

After such an alarming situation, you must be wondering *how* the rescue took place. I can say that I'm alive, and writing this now, due to "The Great Vladimir Kolinsky" and his airborne exploits. When they bill him as **The Most Daring Trapeze Artist in the World,** they are not kidding.

While parents alternated between sweats and chills from panic attacks, with their fibrillating hearts performing their *own* trapeze acts, *he* teamed up with the *Whirling Dervish Jugglers* and the *Topsy-turvy Tumbling Triplets.* In synchronization, these skillful performers managed to stop the horse in its crazed tracks.

What a shame many of the panic-stricken parents never observed the dramatic rescue. While everything occurred, they were storming the ambulance and rocking that white truck up and down like a seesaw. However, there are pictures of the rescue. A comprehensive photographic account, of these heroic details, is now part of Kolinsky Brothers circus history—the part they all want to forget.

Concerning the KCS phenomenon, a mental health professional wrote about the entire fiasco in a pediatric publication, full of psychobabble about this new condition. A photo I took of a disheveled Zorro, enjoying his prolonged nap, made the cover.

Although there appeared to be no serious injuries, as a precaution *everybody* went to the hospital for checkups. As I like to say, you *never* know. Since these extreme circumstances involved a stampeding horse, you do not *need* to trust me. The description rides on its own merit.

I think the emergency room experienced major shock too, along with the hyperventilating multitude. I ask you now, *who* at this tiny rural medical facility ever imagined that on a quiet cricket-chirping Saturday evening, three days before the Forth of July, almost the entire population of Tillagevale would explode at the facility's doorstep, and tow along a three-ring circus. And that bushed horse, Boogie, as well as a prostrate Zorro, really sent them over the big top.

The hand-painted hospital door, known for its prominence, displayed a large red cross—along with a realistic portrait of Florence Nightingale—wearing her trademark cape. She proclaimed their solemn dedication to the community. Owing to their Hippocratic training, the staff could never lock this door. But from the look on their faces, with eyebrows raised to the ceiling, and jaws dropping to the floor, they sure wanted to.

The Kolinsky Brothers pulled up stakes within a few hours, as soon as *all* the parents, *all* those clowns, the Whirling Dervish Jugglers, the exhausted Tumbling Triplets, the *revived* Zorro clown, and of course, unsteady Boogie—the *former* stampeding horse—were given medicine to calm their collective frazzled nerves.

Franz the animal tamer dodged a grisly fate. During the chase—within only *seconds* of nabbing *her* prey—Sweetie, the foaming tiger, collapsed from exhaustion. No further medical attention was necessary. After sleeping under her blankie for two days, she woke up with more energy than ever.

Vladimir had to have both his armpits strapped-up in a sling. You see, while he soared with valor on the trapeze—attempting to swing down on to the fugitive horse—there was a complication. The pumped-up Tumbling Triplet, anchoring Vladimir's legs, won an Olympic Gold Medal for weight lifting the week before.

Ouch.

While his legs dangled halfway out of their sockets, and his disjointed arms didn't function the way they should be, the excruciating pain didn't stop *Vladdy.* He landed on the horse and grabbed the reins. Boogie, smart enough not to mess around with his new *driver,* stopped short with only one tug of those, by now, shredded *reins.*

At this Herculean point, if common sense leads you to question why the sheriff didn't immobilize Boogie with a harmless tranquilizer gun, saving Vladimir and Tillagevale Hospital all the future agony, I have the answer. The Sheriff *did* contemplate using those temporary knockout darts. He hesitated, only because the insane horse was in the perfect environment to go, as he said, "further round the bend."

Aiming straight for Boogie was *dicey,* and this about-to-retire officer had seen more than his share of backfired crap games. However, confident enough to ignore the obvious risk, one of the deputies by the name of Butch Brawnmeister, a sharpshooter with a legendary record for subduing maverick steers on the rodeo circuit, volunteered. He earned this trust-worthy reputation, due to constant practice on a herd of these unfortunate males.

You may disagree, but I'm from Texas, and I'm telling you for sure that steers *are* bovinity. This is true, even *though* they are "minus" those high-flying, all-boy badges they once displayed with pride—before some callous surgeon paid them a visit. The consequence for this very sore snipped-group is their inability to control testiness.

I have to give Butch a lot of credit because, out of ten attempts at subduing Boogie, he only missed twice. Gosh, you should have seen those two poor clowns. They both buckled in unison, for their brief siesta, faster than you could say *tidily-wink.*

Are you now thinking about those other eight darts? Well, they just wedged like Medals of Honor, into the horse's tough hide, without doing a darn thing. A competent veterinarian had to rush over to the emergency room and she took them out. She told everybody how Boogie, that rugged old-boy, was just fine. She placed some numbing medicine, along with several jumbo Band-Aids, on all of those prickly spots the darts left on his backside.

By the sore way, these wide adhesive strips are the best boo-boo consolers *I* had ever seen. How could you not love those assorted big and colorful pictures of cute monkeys engaging in various poses of their see-no-evil . . . hear-no-evil . . . and speak-no-evil schemes, in complete denial of reality.

She *also* informed the crowd how those flying-tranquilizers proved ineffective with Boogie since they were the *human* variety. Those two former zapped-clowns, although still groggy enough for their quivering necks to mimic a pair of those Slinky toys, nodded in vigorous agreement with the good doctor's analysis.

PART 42:

OBSCENE POLYESTER "It's *so* good on waffles."

In further discussing the ramifications of tough hides, there's no way how willful old Boogie could ever outdo the Polish Rock-of-Gibraltar, Vladimir. By tremendous coincidence, one of the hospital's young emergency technicians had the night off and went to the circus. Owing to her extreme dedication, she jumped out of her seat to run across the ring and volunteer her medical skills to the brave trapeze artist. Later on, the hospital gave her permission to continue helping him in her civilian clothes.

Thanks to the extensive cultivation of eavesdropping skills—over at the Serpentine Ladies Auxiliary—a pro like me overheard mothers in the emergency room murmur about this medical technician's "fabulous tan." They wondered where she went, and somewhat reminiscent of former Madam President, what she might have *done* to buy all that *Coppertone.*

The perturbed moms continued their amazement, talking about how she dared to flaunt her excessive use of tanning lotion by wearing a vulgar new "miniskirt" sewn with flimsy red, white, and blue "obscene polyester."

They also hated her blouse, with the American Flag motif. How could *anyone* call this kind of *getup* "hospital attire?" These physicians must have saved all that "gall" from their expensive bladder surgeries to allow a braless *endowed* nurse, wearing *nothing* except a loose-fitting spandex tube top, to hover over a *conscious* male trauma victim—lying flat on his back on an official gurney. This sort of *brazen* behavior was certainly not *medicinal.*

These women were also irked because this "nurse" had the *nerve* not to fetch an *official* cap to conceal her *burnished* black hair showing off the snazzy new "poodle-cut."

Also, along these fuddy-duddy lines, they said, "Oh heavens!" And "Oh my goodness!" And, "Hey, girls, take a gander at those *earrings."* They all questioned why so-called "doctors" didn't order that *vamp* to remove her large dangling gold-hoops. These heavy earrings had etchings that resembled laurel-wreaths of *victory.* They couldn't get over how her earlobes—just like the rest of her—had absolutely no *sag.* Besides, no kind of qualified *medical* attendant wore *this* sort of *dangerous* jewelry.

The verging on hysterical moms, also wondered about the disposition of this attendant's regulation clodhoppers, and this sure became a hot-topic. They were a glee club of magpies, lined up on a wire, squawking over her, "new-fangled *Winkle Picker* stilettos"—along with the *glitzy* gold ankle bracelet.

"You know," they said, while holding their heads haughty-high, *"she* should never wear any kind of ankle decoration, and she's too *mature* for one with sparkly rhinestone-hearts." They also criticized her for flaunting "Betty Grable-gams"—in a manner going, "way beyond the call of clinical obligation."

And—she had "the absolute impudence" not to wear any *stockings.*

Later on, when we arrived home exhausted, but still in one piece, Mom and Aunt Sharon scooted to the fridge to retrieve some of what they call "remedial refreshments." This is the code for *Pabst Blue Ribbon.* While I waited for my usual glass of lemonade, I recall Uncle Eddy telling Daddy "the poor gal" who those jealous moms called "tramp of the century" also had an official name—"Miss Roxanne Roma, EMT." He winked when saying how "Roxie" sure gave "lucky dog Vladdy" a lot of *TLC.*

My uncle *also* mentioned how when Vladimir left with the rest of the circus—so did Roxanne. With one of her compassionate hands, she pushed him in that whopping baby carriage the clowns use in their act. And with the other hand, she caressed his hair.

Further stating how her departure from town resulted from "wanderlust," they used the sneaky laugh they always bring into play, when sticking those golf tees *not* so deep into the green.

Listening to both of them, I wondered what the heck is so crafty about leaving home to join the circus. Kids often threaten their parents about doing the very same thing Roxie just did. I know this, because when my mother told me how a baby macaque, wearing tiny overalls and sucking on the cherry-flavored licorice stick it snatched out of my hand, could never make a good pet—I threatened to join the circus myself. The

Kolinsky group sure cured me of this *wanderlust* stuff on *that* day. Besides, the way this circus operates, they *need* an excellent nurse.

On the other three-ring hand, please remember that at this tender stage of my life—in spite of growing up in the midst of a *hillbilly* version of *Peyton Place*—my knowledge about the birds and the bees had the following limitations:

1} Winning a church raffle may bring home the colorful parakeet you saw in the window of Harriman's Exotic Bird World, but the colorful thing won't automatically talk. *Petey* must hear the phrase hundreds of times before opening that sharp beak to say, "Big butt," and sometimes even enjoy taking a nasty sliver out of your finger.

2} Any pet bird, including a sweet and chirpy finch, ends up being a lot more work than you thought, while you begged night and day to bring cute little *Berry* home after that nasty parakeet went back to Harriman's.

3} All bees sting like there's no tomorrow. You must avoid them—except for honey in a jar. It's *so* good on waffles.

And—when on a *Cinco de Mayo* picnic, if you ever stumble into a bunch of bees, I warn you to toss your prized corn tortilla, stuffed with jumbo Mexican shrimp, floating in your aunt's special Tex-Mex sweet sauce, right onto the sandy ground—without any Jack Benny hesitation.

Otherwise, while swarms of bees jacket your head like a hairnet, you must dive into the muddy cold lake. You can't even take a second to worry about the eventual ruination of your best Donald Duck sweatshirt with the disloyal *runny* decal—and those "bargain" dungarees that will shrink to fit an anorexic-pixy.

On this one, trusting me isn't necessary. I have the newspaper clipping. But you might not recognize me with all of the *Calamine Lotion* masking my face.

PART 43:

TUMMY-TROUBLE

"Nah, there's no way."

Dragging shivering me out of the cold lake, and heading back to Vladimir's warm, strapping charms, you can't overlook this major hero. Ignoring his piercing pain, during the rescue stint, he did end up on the horse's back and gain control of those reins.

The Dervish Juggler's mistake could have put Vladimir six-feet under, when he missed catching the lasso aimed for the horse, and instead the rope landed right around Vladimir's *neck*. Good luck followed him around even before he collapsed into Roxie's toned arms. The tiger did well in the lucky department too. After she woke up, her only punishment was no raw steak for a week.

Frantz thought the incorrigible beast also deserved a spanking. Every worker in the Kolinsky animal-taming department agreed with Franz's disciplinary philosophy. Franz wasn't up to the task, due to a terrible headache. He said his generous offer of a month's pay as a bonus, for anyone who volunteered, landed on *deaf* ears. Do you think that maybe all of the hollering caused this problem? I'm wondering now, if perhaps *you* would have shown that ferocious tiger who *really* possess the clout.

Nah, there's no way.

At least the Kolinsky Circus troupe didn't hold any grudges. All the performers acted kind to the children. They at least pretended to be cheerful coming over to the hospital cafeteria with a huge barrel filled with assorted jelly apples, and sticks of colorful swirls of cotton candy. All of us kids ate as much of this junk as we could stuff in, especially me. I got a big bellyache to prove it.

In reliving the instance, if one must come down with tummy-trouble, there's no safer place to writhe on in pain than a sterile hospital floor. In general, I'm leery of speaking about "bellyaches" because when I do, I get one. Although right now, my belly's not involved. My brain is acting up. I might be experiencing one of those *eureka-moments.* They're rare, yet not impossible.

After an extended eclipse, the brilliant full moon illuminates my mind. Light shines once again, upon the dark day in the middle of that month of August so long ago, when I spent my memorable first day in kindergarten—just a month *after* the circus fiasco.

Recollecting about this stuff now, I realize most, if not all, of the kids from my legendary-class had huddled with me inside of this circus wagon, and later on they were part of the emergency room mayhem. This includes the teacher's favorite nephew, Harry Heller. In those days, though, he had the nickname of "Hairy Heller."

I'm now experiencing a vivid recollection of watching his stark transformation in the hospital that night. A children's magic show couldn't have done a better job. Who knew how extreme fright could cause a little fellow's bushy black eyebrows and his wiry, spider-like eyelashes to fall out—in one huge heap—all over the white tile floor. You'd swear a doctor had lathered him up with a strong depilatory or something. And what about Harry's thick and black Eddie Munster-like mane, with a hairline so low that it once meshed with his former unibrow. Until then, nobody realized what a big cone head he had, hiding underneath his **1313 Mockingbird Lane** bush.

Up until the present, Harry's hair didn't grow back too much—other than the Mohawk-like clump, nesting on the peak of his pointy-head. He's lucky for having any hair at all, is what I say. It's pure white, but so what. This is why everybody in town knows him now as *Pappy Heller.*

Another good thing is how his eyebrows grew back. They're very thin now and arch high up in a semicircle—way over the brow bone. You'd swear he draws them in with a black pencil. But he claims they're natural ones, like Gloria Swanson's are.

I also remember seeing Zorro in the emergency room. He had regained consciousness. Our eyes met for a brief moment. In a slow and menacing tone he said, "Geese, the name meant no more than the *boogie,* man." My mother trembled while grabbing my hand and rushing me out of the crowded room.

I guess I'll get back to talking about my name tribulations now. Dwelling on this pony-cart episode, gives me a cranium-pain, and this isn't too good for a certifiable idiot in a steel helmet or a person having a memory-quake.

PART 44:

LAMAZE

"Do not *ever* go there."

As you already know, answering to the name of "Ginger" causes me grief. I remember being in the womb and hearing my mother make cracks about my being "too spicy." People say it's impossible to remember what happened then, but I have hearing like a hawk. Or is that vision? I tend to confuse the two.

She always says severe pregnancy heartburn gave her the idea to call me what she did. I rolled around and kicked her with such force, "twenty-four hours a day," that she believed me to be a massive Mexican jumping bean—taking up permanent residence inside of her. Is this not a shameful excuse, for destroying a child's entire life?

I'll never learn what kind of malicious force prevented my mother from being a normal pregnant woman. She refuses to tell me why she just didn't tap her husband's *Alka-Seltzer.* He keeps a separate cabinet full of the fizzy substance up in the bathroom. Maybe if she'd burped more, I'd carry a noble identity—like, *Victoria.* And my middle name would be none other than, *Regina.*

When I ask my dad why he didn't stop Mom from burdening his sweet and innocent first baby girl with a moniker like, *Ginger,* can you guess what his answer is? He tells me that picking out my name was none of his business. He could never be such a *scoundrel,* when his dear wife agonized in the delivery room for over thirty-six hours. According to him, he feasted on those fabulous meals his own mother brought over to the hospital cafeteria or he took advantage of "pain-free naps" on a cot as comfortable as a lounge chair, inside of the expectant fathers' waiting room.

In those days, after accomplishing the more pleasant aspects of conception, dads didn't play too much of a role in the birthing process.

The year my mother gave birth to me, *Lamaze* existed as a cheap French restaurant, on the outskirts of Tillagevale's Chinatown.

Therefore—Mom tells me how my dad *not* cut my umbilical cord.

Nor, did he massage her contorted brow.

He did *not* tell her to exhale with frequent steady puffs, which are purported to guarantee relief from excruciating pain. The type of *pain,* that in order to be relieved in the real world, necessitated his socking her in the jaw, and knocking her unconscious for the duration.

He did *not* tell her to "push" while he had fun counting to ten or encourage her to use those visualization techniques, like walking along a mountain stream on a warm and sunny day.

He also escaped hearing her scream until the walls shook—and didn't witness her damn the day she married him.

By the laborious way, *I* ate at this "Lamaze" restaurant once. I bit into my "meal" and found a large and still-squirming cockroach, in my supposed *truffle-filled* crepe flambé.

Do not *ever* go there. Comparing to this place, my dad's Italian Bistro experience looks like dining at the exclusive *Rainbow Room,* on top of 30 Rockefeller Plaza in New York City, which just happens to be the building my dream fiancé owns.

Dreams seldom come true—non-nightmare ones anyway. Therefore, the all-around agonizing situation concerning my birth encourages me to be arm in arm with the current fired up *Women's Liberation Movement*—although I'd surely waste energy and money participating in any "march" and burning *my* brassiere.

Who would notice the smoke?

PART 45:

DUMB WILLY

"What *hole* did he crawl out of?"

If you think things could never get worse for me concerning my nomenclature, you're wrong. When I turned nine, a ludicrous television series appeared, and my existence took an even greater sadistic turn.

Did you ever watch a brainless guy with the name of *Gilligan?* If so, I ask you, why does he always wear that smashed-up floppy hat? Why does he want to persecute me? What *hole* did he crawl out of? Why is he so ecstatic about living on a primitive island?

Although you might know about him, many people are unaware that "Gilligan" is this beanpole's surname. His given name is *Willy.* I'm speaking about pathetic, dimwitted, Willy Gilligan, another major plague in my life—after Pun Geyser, Gene Autry, my father, and my sister. Do I really need any more additions to my menagerie of aggravation?

To start with, the closest I ever came to a tropical island is a pineapple-coconut fruit drink. Also, how could *I* find an island so remote nobody even knows about the place? My sense of direction is so bad that if I didn't smell pizza rotting under the bed, I'd need a compass to find my own room.

I *never* had any friend with the name of *Mary Ann,* and the only *Skipper* I know is Uncle Eddy's mangy dog. I'm also not mingling with any guy who's a millionaire. And—if by chance I ever do get to hobnob with one, I doubt he'd ever invite *me* over to meet his wife named, *Lovey.*

When it comes to *The Elite,* I'm not what you'd call an expert—although I'd sure like to be. This is why I'm asking you to think about why any kind of millionaire ever sailed on a chunk of floating debris dubbed, *Minnow.* Shouldn't a millionaire and his wife sightsee on their private forty-foot luxury yacht; let's say a gleaming white yacht with a regal appellation. How does the name *Piranha,* strike you?

Can you believe that people have the insolence to compare somebody of my caliber to this kind of television plot? But they do. I will say, though, I *have* encountered a few odd professors in my lifetime, and not one of them qualifies as good-looking. The only thing factual, relating to Gilligan's "Ginger", is I, too, am capable of being a television actress. When you hear people saying that *I* have ability to dramatize—better than Bette Davis does—they're not kidding.

If we're ever to become best friends, I'm thanking you in advance for refraining from any of the Gene Autry and Gilligan's Island analogies. I know them all. I hear these trite-quips every day. Would you like to hear my favorite, way-out wacky-one?

I'll tell you anyhow.

Gene Autry's on a special government assignment to rescue his beloved—albeit "daffy" relative—*me,* off Gilligan's Island. In addition to being a superior singing cowboy, who's immune to bullets and arrows, he's also capable of riding on Champion while swimming the lengthy *English Channel.* Its equestrian four-legged backstrokes, on the way to *get* me, put the big screen's swimming star, Ester Williams, to such humiliation that she quit showbiz.

Now—I know what you're thinking, so I'll answer your thought.

No, Gene Autry did *not* drown, whatever you may hear.

He wore his lifejacket.

Champion inflated it for him.

What *else* could you expect?

PART 46:

WHERE ARE WE, SCOTTY?

"But I bet I could."

I'm not telling you yet, what year I live in. I don't want to jinx the imaginative technique I'll be using, to insure we both make a smooth connection. Maybe you've already figured out where I suspend in the galaxy, because you're a genius like me. On the other eager hand, I bet you gave in and skipped ahead to check. Don't worry; I forgive you. I'd do the same thing.

I get sad thinking about never knowing your name or anything else about your life. You may not even be in the same *century* as me. I'd give anything to see how different things are, where *you* hang out.

As of this minute, I don't have any Wegi Board. And since my savant cousin isn't here, I've figured out that in order to make any kind of headway in the area of clairvoyance, I must slouch over this typewriter and concentrate using telepathy—the only sure way to make contact with extraterrestrial vibes.

For years, I've been watching *Captain Kirk* do this sort of cosmological communiqué. As a result, there's a strong possibility I'll be able to match his *Enterprise* power. My superiority to him, in every way, will be a walk in the space-park. I do thank the stars though, how there's no need for me to compete with *his* masculine physique.

But I bet I could.

Now, as we continue to discuss the magnificent captain's physiology, I'm sure you've noticed how his defined-abs rock-and-roll underneath the clingy spaceship uniform he wears.

Um—excuse me for pausing here. That Captain Kirk is something else. I'll need a second or two to regain concentration. I won't be long. In only the bat of a watery and bloodshot eye, I promise to reactivate my advanced deep-space mental probes. I plan on pointing them toward the huge cerebral void that's out there in the vast cosmos, occupying the *unexplored* "final frontier" of my brain. Although astronauts—also known as friends and family—try hard to send me into space every day without success, I'll now attempt to accomplish the exploit on my own.

Thanks for your universal patience.

I'm back, ready to launch, without another second of hesitation.

In order to spin inside this metagalactic whirlpool, I'll use cerebral technology.

Whir... here I go, tapping into telepathic future cyclonic wavelengths. I'm revolving into a mental version of cute little Dorothy in *The Wizard of Oz.* Before you know it, I'll tumble through a rogue heliocentric-frequency where the sun *does* move around the earth, no matter *what* smarty-pants *Copernicus* said. The incredible force of this sun will act as a galactic Bunsen burner, propelling me over immeasurable light-years.

Oh gosh, I'm *now* heading toward a stellar-orb. The vast thing is in dangerous proximity to an astral-wormhole. Keep your fingers crossed that the hot exploding gamma rays, spewing out of this *wormhole,* won't fry my brains like a Saturday night *Colonel Sanders* extra crispy special—with half-a-pint of free coleslaw and two bonus biscuits. *If* this occurs, I won't get to finish my journal. And, after my working so hard, what a shame if you can't find out what happens.

Hey, if my brains *do* turn into fried chicken, *I* won't find out what happens either. That is, unless I steer clear of those gamma rays and plunge through cerebral inner space, only to tumble through a huge black synapse-hole. I'll spin and spin downward, until the sinister void dumps me into a parallel universe, where I'll confront my doppelganger.

The confused Universe will need several crucial minutes to decide which of us must terminate, as even the vast scope of infinite outer space can't handle the two. When I'm sure I can preserve the "real me", I'll navigate past the fiery solar flare and circumvent the wormhole to reach the safety of a friendly galaxy.

By the fiery way, in comparison to the roaring flames spewing out of *this* solar flare, any prior depictions of people "burning in hell" now appear to be nothing more than sunbathers, basking themselves on a tranquil beach—like the one in Bermuda I didn't get to visit!

Upon arriving in one uncharbroilded piece, I'll hook up with a Supernova. Then, by use of its smoldering ring of exploding neuron light, this simmering star will beam constant magnetic signals to me, from its wavelength that's a hundred light-years away. It also has the capacity to synchronize *your* physical vibration—from wherever *you* are, with an exact match to my physical vibration—here at the place in the universe, where *I* exist. When it comes to bending time-and-space, I sure am a *cerebral* astrophysicist.

Uh, oh, I need *Dramamine* pills. The ones for motion sickness.

Too late.

These pulsating signals are now churning my stomach worse than ever, by rocking me back and forth—while they zap glaring lazars at me. They're frantic to synchronize with me *here,* at the exact moment they'll channel an electromagnetic hologram of *you,* aiming straight for my typewriter.

Now is the moment for another exclamation of fear.

Yikes!

Things are real serious. The crucial signal is fading fast. I think a hostile alien astrocyte is blocking the frequency. I'll self-destruct in the flow of dark energy, if I don't circumvent the enemy *now.* I must prepare to fire an infrasonic cerebral neutron, which will then evaporate into an impenetrable blood-brain barricade. Only this kind of gray matter fortress will stop the astrocyte from interfering with my extrasensory perception.

Phew, what a rough telekinetic balancing act I just pulled off. As far as the glitches go, please remember how our noble Captain Kirk lost *his* equilibrium on an occasion or two. His attempt to decode the "time-continuum puzzle" failed miserably. The crew had a crestfallen commander behind the controls during this episode. All the same, I did get rid of that alien cerebral life force and I think in so doing, *I* penetrated that illusive puzzle for him. He hasn't thanked me yet, but he will.

You know what, the enigma was nothing more than the bright star, hovering very low over *your* house—right this second. Look outside now, and see if you spot its brilliance. Don't worry if daylight remains where you are, you can check stuff out later—after dark.

Did you find the special star? I hope so. If you saw the celestial signal, this means our friendship has made a quantum leap—at least according to *Scotty.*

PART 47:

THE TWILIGHT ZONE "My sister never did."

I guess, at this stellar point, you're wondering how I speak such excellent space-lingo. I can do so because, while the *Star Trek* television show lasted, I paid strict attention. I remember being eleven when it first aired. After three skimpy years, the network said adults found the plot *stupid* so ratings tanked. Keeping an expensive show of this sort on TV, just for the amusement of kids, wasn't profitable. Consequently, the series imploded within itself as the sun will do someday.

Relax, I don't mean to frighten you. Accredited scientists predict *this* won't happen for billions of years. But are they truly trustworthy? I often wonder how many of them cheated on their physics' tests.

I ask you though, as we get back to television science, do media people really *know* the huge about of money kids spend. I don't think so. It's too bad that they didn't call my father first. It would have made his day, giving them an authoritative earful about this matter. And they shouldn't dismiss the monetary power of a certain group of peewees who know the wisdom of the glorious words, "I love you, Grandma and Grandpa." As they say in New York's borough of Brooklyn, Nonna isn't stuffing all those celebratory cards with chopped liver.

My parents did watch this program from time to time. My sister never did. The storyline didn't hinge on a popular comic book. For me, I made viewing the show a priority and I saw every episode. I still do, although, just like Gene Autry, and his cowboy hat escaping bullet holes, the show's now in reruns.

The premise of science fiction, concerning outer space, gets me philosophizing about what happens within our own *Milky Way Galaxy.* This turned out truer than ever, when I witnessed courageous Neil

Armstrong walk on the moon. Live space exploration transpired on *my* 15th birthday. All eyes in the Universe watched Star Trek happening for real on their own TV sets *that* spectacular day. Even my sister's uncharacteristic excitement forced her to put down her comic book for a few minutes. *Iron Man* had the strength to wait.

I hope they'll be a series of awesome Star Trek feature films in the future—with all the same television actors—since I'm sure billions of people worldwide will pay good money for a ticket to *these* movies. Perhaps, by some small miracle, those TV corporate-bigwigs will smarten up and Star Trek gets a chance to entertain dedicated fans on an international level. Only the cosmos will create the power to produce this picture later on.

I'll now extend my concern about the future of all inter-galactic situations, to my own life. There's desolation here where I am *now.* Chill and fog are wrapping a heavy blanket around this dimension. Today, I found myself thinking about another great old sci-fi television series, analogous to my current situation. Did *you* ever experience *The Twilight Zone?* If not, try to find the channel. Sometimes they revive this original old series, so check out television listings in your area.

I've been finding out lately that Rod Sterling, the show's creator, was right. Thinking how a higher authority initiates everything happening in our lives—including those things we believe to be insignificant—isn't that far-out. This may also translate to what we call "luck."

It's truer-than-true, and not just a simple cliché to avoid. "There *are* no coincidences." Don't dismiss any event in your life, because you think it was just happenstance. It conveys an important message you should not ignore. For example, this journal exceeds simple curiosity or something to read on a rainy day. The motivation for its durability pertains to your present life, as much as to mine, and to the dear journal itself.

How do I know this?

You will be the first to find out.

Along these fated lines, I also know for sure, there's a significant reason *why* my secret journal continues to survive in *your* safe hands. I think you were leery about trusting me, whenever I told you to do so before. Please get over your mental block and start *now.*

I'll try to trust myself more too.

PART 48:

PRACTICAL PLANNING "Dadgumit!"

Three months ago, the ingenious method of persuasion *I* invented worked at last, by catapulting me over malleable meadows—to New York concrete. My father says don't be so arrogant. He remembers a time when, what I'm now proud to term, "practical planning," *his* father labeled, "testing a saint's patience." I didn't invent *practical planning* to escape Tillagevale due to hating the place or anything. I just feel that nothing special is there for me.

Switching back to television—did you ever see *Green Acres,* where farm living surpasses life in New York City by a country mile? In this zany rural town, nobody cares about gourmet shops on Park Avenue. After all, the residents use Mr. Drucker's general store. And there's always doddering Mr. Haney, wheeling and dealing his underhanded merchandise from his broken-down truck behind the barn.

I'm sure you're familiar with *The Andy Griffith Show,* and Opie Taylor's idyllic life in *Mayberry.* Here, in this easygoing place, problems are nothing worse than a summer thunderstorm, felling a windswept tree, blocking *traffic* across a rustic road. In Mayberry, Opie's father—trusted Sheriff Andy—will solve the worst tight spots in thirty minutes. In bucolic addition, if an occasional "to be continued" tribulation ever does stumble upon this cozy hamlet you could spend the interim salivating over Aunt Bea's upcoming scratch biscuits, topped with her fresh-churned butter. And don't forget her collection of Mason jars, containing assorted batches of homemade preserves. I'm sure my mother gave her the strawberry-rhubarb recipe.

Do you know about those antics in *Petticoat Junction?* This rural community's big thrill every day is waiting by the railroad tracks for the

Hooterville Cannonball to chug through the area, and old ironsides doesn't chug alone. There's more than enough dense steam pouring out of this historic locomotive—to pollute the entire Western world. The townsfolk don't mind. *This* sooty train has the vital daily mission of dropping off Turkish Taffy at the *Shady Rest Hotel.*

After the smoke clears, dearest Minnie Pearl materializes on the *Hee Haw* show, and has that perpetual price tag—dangling off her flowery straw hat. Do you wonder why she never clips off the store's ticket? Dadgumit! Where is *she* ever fixin' to go, anyhow? This brings me to Hee Haw's famous nightlife. Perhaps you're interested in those wild Saturday night disco-dance moves. If so, what kind of club could you swing at where they'd attempt outdoing Roy Clark, plinking up a shindig on the old banjo?

At this rural juncture, please combine all of the *down-home* genres that I just illustrated. When you do, you'll be gazing at the place where I débuted. This is also the perfect opportunity to catch you up on the here and now concerning my new life in *The Big Apple,* and the daily ingenuity I use to polish the round, red fruit. Although my existence is still crazy here in New York, it now represents a more sophisticated kind of madness.

On this one, don't worry about trusting me.

You'll be finding out for yourself—starting with the next few pages.

Chapter 4

Polishing the Apple

PART 1:

<u>IRT NUMBER 4</u> **"I don't wear *any* kind of wig."**

Survival in life hinges on asking the *why* question. It's the same as the air you breathe. That's all there is to it. Never accept things at face value. I don't. My attempts at being a sleuth often backfire—louder than the old Edsel did. But I don't care. I'm stubborn when searching for answers. Every time sparks fly, I learn how to use common sense as a fire extinguisher.

I know that within every aspect of life, no matter how benign any events appear on the surface, unseen forces lurk underneath—ready to pounce. I'm always leery of this happening. This trait influences almost every decision I make, right, or wrong, and causes me mega stress. Yet, as irksome as my dogged nature happens to be, it contributes to being an exceptional writer. Before you slam me for arrogance, please remember I have a gorgeous blue satin ribbon to back up this egotistical observation.

If you pair these characteristics with my insatiable love of snooping, you'll be in complete agreement how I'm a natural for a career in investigative journalism. I always knew that someday, in order to make this dream come true, I'd hear the loud lure of New York City's ever-present traffic jams—honking in my ears.

Since I've arrived, with my feet firmly planted in the asphalt like those ubiquitous **TOW AWAY ZONE** signs are, I realize having an editor discover me won't be so easy, but I'm resourceful. Instead of being discouraged day-after-day, I resort to my trusty imagination to spur me on *if* I feel overwhelmed with despondency. Although I don't visit the dumps too often, every now and then I drop by to take an inventory.

For the most part, I rely on *daydreams* about my eventual success during various discouraging phases of commuting back and forth to work from The Bronx. You may be thinking while reading this that I've been capitalizing the "The" in error. I'm not. This is the real name of the borough itself, *The Bronx.*

Every weekday—around 7:30 in the chilly morning—I wait outside at the elevated *Fordham Road Station* where I catch the **IRT Number 4**. And, when the train pulls into the stop, I become what New Yorkers call a, "straphanger." I accomplish this miserable feat by standing up and grasping the train's overhead safety rigging. In spite of this, I still sway like mad and lose my balance. I do a regular rush-hour *rumba,* while my hips swerve in a teeming subway car.

The only view, during this literal stomach churning trip, is the train's grungy interior full of nonsensical graffiti. The dizzying swirls of gaudy color splash across its walls and doors. Or I'll see those threatening messages using derogatory terms against cops. And when the train is rushing by on outdoor tracks, any potential sights to relieve the boredom hide behind windows smeared with paint. Although I'd prefer reading a newspaper or a magazine, it's impossible while standing and losing my balance. I must also tolerate droves of rude people, shoving into the train and squashing me.

What makes matters even worse is how these fellow commuters often lack basic hygiene—like deodorant and mouthwash. As you will understand later, there's a good reason for my being oversensitive to human odors on transportation.

Speaking further, concerning negative aspects of commuting on the subway, I'd like to caution you now how you must never, and I repeat *never,* focus on a fellow passenger—no matter how bored stiff you may be. Once, when I found a rare seat, a derelict-individual stood straphanging in front of me. In her free hand, she held a long black umbrella that had a large wooden handle, chiseled into the shape of a white duck's head. Forget the concept of a cute and adorable duck, and substitute *Donald* with a gruesome clone, sporting a sharp, six-inch-long sinister beak. She also had a large brown shopping bag full of torn newspapers and piles of rags, tucked between her legs.

Within a minute, this woman shrieked at the elderly man sitting next to me. With slurred speech, she accused him of *staring* at her. Soon after her aggressive remark, this *bag lady* lashed out at the hapless guy. Thrusting the duck umbrella's pointed beak, she dug the spiky thing right into his skull.

He wore a thick toupee so the matted mess cushioned the blow. The *rug,* disheveled from the whack, slid off his head and flew across the train's ceiling. At first, we all gaped in shocked silence, until everybody realized the poor guy looked okay. In a second, people stifled giggles. Within a minute, many of the standing passengers doubled-over with laughter. As soon as the fluffy-toupe wound up spinning around and around in the compartment's overhead ceiling fan, we were *all* hysterical.

This hair-raising situation gave Froggy's old antics on Andy's Gang some strong competition. I gave *that* particular subway car the bum's-rush at the next stop. I didn't care how changing trains might make me late for work. I don't have the protection of a hairpiece-helmet. I don't wear *any* kind of wig. I wanted to once, but found out they're uncomfortable when I tried one on. I thought the itchy thing looked like a botched-up Cuddleview Doll Hospital Barbie-hair repair job, popping out of my irritated scalp.

Traveling back to the scene of the crime train, the next day I read the conductor held it up until the cops hauled her off, minus the umbrella. They took the bloodstained thing for evidence.

On this hair-raising episode, how could you *not* trust me?

PART 2:

CAST OF THOUSANDS "What an ingrate!"

If you live in Manhattan, escaping the subway is impossible. As a hectic result, in order to get home in the evening, I must catch this same Number 4 subway after I finish work. I'm a busy office-temp at various New York City job locations, with a clear-cut focus on Manhattan. I know its transit system very well. I'm on a city train or bus more than I'd like.

Taxis are out of the question, because if you don't come up with the expensive fare, the driver will threaten to confiscate the equivalent.

On my lunch hour last week, when rushing back to work from shopping, I had just enough money left in my wallet to pay for the cab I took. Otherwise, handing the taxi driver my new imported Italian, hotter-than-hot—cotton jersey shirtdress—by the beautiful new designer, **Diane von Furstenberg,** was a probability.

That morning, I saw her posing in a magazine ad, while she wore this innovative style, and held a sign that said, "Feel like a woman, wear a dress!" I'm sure she has a great future in the world of fashion and design, with more variations of this popular dress to come soon, plus a myriad of other things.

I braved multitudes of wild women to purchase one for a fraction of their soon to be price. Gimbals had a promotional sale for two hours only, between **12** and **2** in the afternoon. Macy's across the street looked empty. They always say, "Does Macy's tell Gimbals?" But this time—Gimbals sure didn't tell their archrival, Macy's.

Cecil B. DeMille directed the mob scene, and didn't even have to bring along his usual "cast of thousands." Crowds of bargain hunting *wacky* ladies—with *their* lethal umbrellas—replaced them. They stepped on my ingrown toenail, and my shins had a few bruises, but totally worth my suffering.

In this workday situation, I needed an expensive taxi. My jobs are strict about punching in on schedule. Everything still turned out to be a fantastic lunch hour. I had a once in a lifetime chance to buy something I'd never be able to afford. On balance, including the cost of the taxi, the gorgeous dress equaled the bargain of the century. Now, I'm really equipped to become the cosmopolitan woman of my dreams.

Getting back to the cost of cabs, their prices are uniform in all of New York's five boroughs. No doubt, you'll trust me on this one, since I learned the hard way. The first occasion when I took a taxi, here in the city, that hack's meter ticked like a financial time bomb. It happened during a heavy traffic jam on congested **FDR Drive.** I almost fainted when the gyp's neon gauge flashed **. . . $8.00 . . . $8.00 . . . $8.00 . . .** in obnoxious red, when I reached my destination.

If you're thinking about why I just didn't stop the cab, pay up what I owed at that moment, and walk to a bus or train—whether late for work or not—I'll tell you now. There's no safe way to exit a vehicle on this insane Eastside thruway, unless I want the 6 o'clock evening news showing up at the local hospital to televise me later on. The camera crew will hone in on the "deranged pedestrian" with her legs in traction, while she moans about suing the city's Taxi and Limousine Commission for all they've got.

Judging from the *taxes* New York City collects on everything—including transportation—"tax" is part of the word **taxi** no matter what some linguists might protest. As a profitable result, chickenfeed won't dump into my newfound bank account if I win the lawsuit, which I won't since I'm *nuts.*

Furthermore, concerning these exorbitant *cabs,* their drivers expect you to hand over a *tip.* After making my safe exit near my destination and standing at the street's curb, I paid him the eight dollars and still felt obligated to include a generous *gratuity* along with the fare. Instead of saying thanks, the creep opened a window, flung those five pennies back at me, and took off.

What an ingrate! I had to bend down to pick them up. I did get four back. I'm sorry to say that one fell down the sidewalk's subway-grid. Marilyn Monroe's hot scene from *The Seven-Year Itch* movie, played out again on Manhattan asphalt when gushes of wind irrupted out of *this* grid and blew up *my* dress. I almost didn't wear those black cotton tights that morning because they had snags, but they saved me from even more embarrassment.

This stupid **X-RATED** taxi splurge, necessitated using Shelley's crappy peanut butter and artificial jelly she hides in the vegetable bin, along with the stale bread. I had to eat these yucky sandwiches for breakfast, lunch, and dinner for two days. There was no other way to make up for my initial naiveté, concerning loss of prized cash over superfluous use of New York's legendary yellow taxicabs. However, literally never the less, I won't rule out this expensive transportation in an emergency.

PART 3:

DREAMS OF GLORY "Maybe next time."

Due to the dangerous ramifications of boredom on the subway, I'll let you in now on my favorite career-saving fantasy. I use this daydream to prevent my eyes from wandering while I ride the vile thing.

This musing starts, with me sitting in a premium box seat situated on a high balcony. My lavish new shade of light blond hair piles up like a mountain on top of my regal head. In the center of this coiffure, a genuine platinum tiara basks in the glory of it all. This million-dollar chunk of precious metal, festoons with a hundred tiny diamonds. The brightness of the spotlight makes these diamonds appear like little moist snowflakes, floating in the sunshine.

I also gaze down on a crowded auditorium. I hear the crucial announcement. I feign surprise, even though I totally expected to win. *Who* could ever beat *me?*

You didn't have to answer this question with that snide remark, and interrupt my fantasy, but you did—so I'll take your comment and put it in the basket with those eggs. I will now continue without *any* interruptions, I hope.

You are now with me again inside of the balcony, where I prepare to stand. I'm careful about mussing up my expensive *haute couture.* The moment I've been working so hard for has arrived. Taking all the Tillagevale complications to start with, and continuing with more of the same later on here in Manhattan, has led me to this grand instance.

As I lift my firm tushie off the plush French-Provincial chair, all prior aggravation has been worth my mental and physical pain. I sort of damaged this dark blue velvet antique, which once belonged to *Marie Antoinette,* by spilling some perfume on it—just minutes before I stood up.

Yes, I *know* what happened concerning her troubles of going from riches to those bloodstained rags that held her former head. But this gruesome episode in history won't apply to me. Unless, of course, the gendarmes find out about the perfume mishap. If they do, I can handle it. After all, I have a lot of experience with affairs of French Aristocracy, including what happens in their cellars, do I not.

Why should I worry about anything having to do with Marie Antoinette? I love eating cake too, but I don't *command* other people to do it. If they want to gain weight, they can decide by themselves. I'm also a very sanitary fantasy participant. I always scrub my neck extra hard on the morning of the daydream. I don't know whether she prepared for the guillotine like this or not. It's none of my business, although it *might* be, if I had more time to investigate hygienic practices that went on in the year of **1793.** But I don't. Maybe next time.

Right this minute though, I must tell you about my dreams of French *fashion* and its potential for unlimited accessories. To keep up with the trends, I'm obligated to mention how I, along with the tushie, am swathed as tight as Josephine never was, in my aubergine silk *genuine* Givenchy ball gown. I'm not referring here to any prior chintzy creation, which I've previously worn from that redneck *Sears-Roebuck* catalog.

Now, that I'm standing in the box seat, I wonder whether I should take that risky bow. What happens if I split my Givenchy wide-open? And, heaven forbid, what if my authentic stole, made from true *Persian* mink, slides right off my shoulders. I wouldn't even attempt to bend over and pick the luxurious heap up off the floor.

Instead of bowing, I simply nod my head in acknowledgement of their applause, and looking as regal as the "literary queen" I now represent, I descend the balcony's marble staircase. I hustle down the aisle as if somebody just yelled, "FIRE." My tripping at that moment, while wearing my Adolfo white satin sling-back stilettos, would be a major embarrassment. Arriving intact, at the polished wooden stage, is more important to me than Queen Elizabeth's coming invitation to Buckingham Palace for brunch tomorrow.

I climb the steps to this imposing platform. During this imperial ascension, I'm aware of the seductive scent of my *Channel No.5* trailing behind me. Standing on this stage, I'm very smug while I wear a supple pair of creamy white, elbow length, kidskin gloves. I speak now of those priceless gloves given to me by that tall, dark, and very handsome Ricardo Montalban look-alike bullfighter in Toledo, Spain—*after* he conquered the bull, of course. *He's* the one the crystal ball reader, with those hideous nicotine-stained fingers, told me about at the county fair. Let's face it, a ten-year-old girl has complete faith in a woman who wears more makeup than the drugstore could ever stock.

She *also* told me how instead of the long-stemmed red rose—full of perilous thorns, clenching between a bullfighter's teeth—the matador visible in *her* smoggy crystal ball, substituted this traditional flower with a small bunch of pansies. What she said about the "pansies" just *has* to be accurate. That *never-fail* fortuneteller cost me an entire week's allowance. Yet picturing the historic Spanish artist, Francisco de Goya, painting a macho matador in a scene like this would never work.

Did I just hear you say that *you* think this kind of painting would be avant-garde? Maybe so, but this is *my* fantasy so I'm leaving it out.

Fighting our way back to much clearer prophetic air, I'll be ever so demure while removing the kidskin glove on my *right* hand. I must prepare to be courteous. Very soon, I'll extend this bare hand that cost me a whopping twenty bucks to show off. I had to use shiny cherry-red false nails to give some pizzazz to those pathetic, bitten-down stumps on *both* of my hands. Please understand how I'm accepting my televised award in front of millions. If I pinch any of those usual pennies, I'll smear my new manicure.

While my glamorized nails, although artificial as the day is long, blink like that rip-off taxi's neon gauge, no one can miss my middle finger. How *could* they, when I wave around that dazzling silver marquisate band—with a center-garnet as big as a boulder. *You* are right. Anybody looking at it does need shades.

Hey, how did you know that *shades* are what they call sunglasses in Tinseltown? I'd love to pursue your extraordinary knowledge about the fashionable habits of superstars who gather at *Grauman's Chinese Theatre* on Hollywood Boulevard. But any further distractions will have my fantasy slipping away, so I can't elaborate. I can though, tell you now, all about another trinket on a different finger.

This excellent gift came from a German baron with bulging biceps. He showed up on his own. Don't let me forget to mention how this devotee rules, with all of the majesty befitting him, from his cliffside citadel overlooking the River Rhine. I plan to visit him there very soon.

As I stand on this stage, I am a definite ingénue thanks to the strict influence of Weight Watchers and those embarrassing weigh-in meetings—along with *Twiggy's* apocalyptic quest to popularize a dress size of double-zero. My pencil-thin—designer-garbed body—uses every *ounce* of its recent status. I cannot let myself revert to acting like a former chubby plebian. How uncouth to grapple the **Pulitzer Prize** on primitive impulse, from the hands of that sophisticated presenter.

Gee—this dude has a manicure better than mine, and he acts more conceited than I do in *my* fantastic couture, while *he* struts around in his custom-made pinstripe tuxedo.

Soon, my big head starts swelling even more, as dignitaries give me a standing ovation. Thunderous applause validates my abundant talent. I sure waited long enough. At this triumphant interlude, I'm careful not to drop my mink, the precious glove—or my prestigious award—while they bestow me with a huge bouquet of fragrant tea roses. These gorgeous roses, despite their botanical classification, will not spoil the illusion and give me hives.

≈≈≈

DREAM OVER
SNAP OUT OF IT

Just like my memorable childhood modeling clay, I landed back to reality with a resounding thud, in spite of all the weight I lost through osmosis.

I'll get up off the floor now and resume my focus on "apple" polishing.

PART 4:

LOVE ME TENDER

"Everybody calls her, *Sister Gracie.*"

Each instance when I travel to the *Dreams of Glory* fantasyland I just imparted, I jolt myself free of this nonsense. What chance is there to become world renowned, if you work for a dumb **RFD** newspaper? You're awful quiet. You don't have any idea, right. I thought so. I guess you're forcing me to answer my own question.

This just isn't going to happen where typical front-page news centers on a cute mule named, *Little King*. Do you realize the talented fellow brays himself giddy, while swaying in his adorable blue-suede booties, keeping perfect time to an instrumental of, what other than, *Love Me Tender.*

There's also *another* folksy-side to this headline. I'm talking about the real hot exclusive, centering on the best shortcake over at the annual Strawberry Festival. Everybody in town wants to read the winning details about Sister Gracella Spinster. Who wouldn't? *She* is in charge of the old folks' home.

This geriatric facility is in the large converted barn down near the railroad tracks. What *is* the name of this place again? Oh, yes, I remember now—Last Roundup Habitat. Some charitable peanut farmer from Georgia helped her build the place a few years ago. You can't deny that the nursing home helps a lot of people in Tillagevale, where longevity statistics are the highest in the nation.

I guess there's a bright side to boring stuff after all. Blood pressure stays very low for every resident, not just seniors, unless they're addicted to salty bouillon. When people sit on picnic tables in Town Square Park—to play an *exciting* game of what local teens call, "Madame Tussauds Wax Museum rendition of a Tillagevale checkers competition," a single game takes them an entire day to complete.

The director of this nursing home has plenty of pep though. Everybody calls her, *Sister Gracie.* She jumped out of bed at 4 o'clock, on Strawberry Festival morning, to milk the nursing home's cow. How *else* could she whip up such tantalizingly fresh, first prize sweet cream? Adding to her abiding virtues, we have the readerships' overwhelming interest in her lineage. *Sister* descends from a long line of early rising and talented *Spinsters.*

In *this* kind of *Fourth Estate* environment, the actuality of getting a Pulitzer Prize stays forever frozen, shivering up on the North Pole with Santa and his frostbitten elves. The doddering population of Tillagevale has no interest in anything thrilling, other than a possible rise in the bulk price of turnips. I'm with it, concerning weird happenings, but never heard about any parapsychologists investigating a haunted patch of rutabagas. Have you ever seen them digging around?

You did! Now I wish more than ever that we could talk to each other. Haunted vegetables on the table or not, any kind of intriguing story involving the slightest thing metaphysical, and worthy of *my* expert investigative talent, will result in the editor of a rural newspaper chalking stuff up to "Halloween shenanigans"—no matter *what* day of the year.

This "editor" will then pitch my noteworthy effort into his *dead file,* which is newspaper jargon for "garbage pail" where creativity cuddles up with the rotting remains of his favorite daily salami sandwich—slapped together on dark pumpernickel—and do *not* hold the horseradish. This is the regular mile-high-hoagie that causes said *belching* editor a perpetual digestive upset.

As a matter of heartburn course, he orders the food from that world famous Armadillo Family Pharmacy and Luncheonette. This establishment has the nerve to advertise authentic "New York Delicatessen." I don't want *you* to believe *their* bogus claim for one minute.

What's plenty of antacid more, whenever he eats the gross sandwich he guzzles that effervescent *lime-ricky* to wash down the stale bread. In order to preserve this drink's exceptional *fizz,* their "soda-jerk" brings the bubbling stuff over. He wears his usual speedy roller skates, but stumbles and spills some of the bubbling liquid on a daily basis. I ask you, why should cleaning up this kind of sticky mess, in the editor's backroom office every day, be part of the job description of a talented writer like me?

Everybody's got dues to pay, you say. If this is true, I sure am forking over plenty.

Now I *know* what you're thinking concerning the suitable "title" of this dedicated delivery boy. There's no need for my adding a mocking comment concerning this. You've already done my job for me.

PART 5:

BIG WAMPUM

"All I need is a nickel for the ferry."

Getting back to non-fizzing creativity, New York is the complete opposite of Tillagevale. For artistic people, including writers like me, a phantom heart thumps within New York's shadowy skyline, and every vibration is an inspiring lifeline. In Manhattan, whatever floats your investigation boat is fine—as long as your pocket is full of subway tokens and you're carrying a map of the transit system in your briefcase.

There's a golden potential to work for a famed newspaper or magazine, here in New York City. If I manage to pull off this employment, my Pulitzer fantasy will experience a rescue from extreme cold on the remote frozen tundra where Santa lives. With the right connections, the opportunity for recognition of my investigative skills will bounce the Pulitzer toward the ultimate urban tundra—The Borough of Richmond, also known as *Staten Island.* This wilderness is much more accessible to me. I don't need to hitch a ride with any *Iditarod.* I'm able to get there from Manhattan whenever I want. All I need is a nickel for the ferry.

Otherwise, I'll get to Staten Island by driving over the somewhat recent double deckered Verrazano Bridge from the Fort Hamilton, southwest-Brooklyn side. Opening day impressed the world by affixing a huge American flag, flapping up to the sky, on to the steel spirals of this bridge. I have a picture showing this rendition of *Old Glory,* taken early in the morning, before wind shredded it to pieces later in the afternoon.

As of this writing, New York has the longest suspension bridge of this type. The toll for cars is pricey though, at **75¢.** You can also take a city bus over it for the regular fare, or cross free on foot or by riding a bike.

I bet since the erection of this Narrows-Strait overpass, the now accessible area—no longer having to rely on a small ferryboat—will become less and less rustic. Before you know it—Richmond will be on a par with the other four boroughs. As usual, we'll see if I'm right. If somebody wants to invest in a house there, do it now.

Also, while I'm on my New York soapbox, please don't ever believe those exaggerated accounts claiming that the heart of a New Yorker is made of metal and stone, just like all of their bridges and skyscrapers. These stories are *not* true. There's no shortage of compassion here.

On the other abrasive hand, when a person is born in *any* of the boroughs of New York City, including Staten Island, they must start survival training in their playpens. Sure, everybody in Manhattan *is* as tough as nails, but only out of necessity. The city hums with activity day and night, and sirens are its backup band. As a congested result, anyone attempting to live *here* will need, just like much of this sometimes-impenetrable city, an outlook made of mortar.

While we're on the buttressing subject, I suggest if people are serious about succeeding in a mega metropolis like New York City—with a population of millions—they better go back "many moons" to its locale of days gone by and observe *Miss Hohum* marrying *Mr. Humdrum.* How romantic to watch the happy couple, after they tie the lasso. These newlyweds embrace each other and hold hands, right before paying big wampum—to split town with the Pony Express.

Speaking of Mr. and Mrs. Humdrum, I'm convinced, as sure as the crow flies, this lackluster couple hightailed themselves to Tillagevale—where their ancestors have hung on ever since.

Now—if you don't trust me here, all you need do one day is stroll down Tillagevale's *Main Street.* Yes, this *is* the actual name of the town's central thoroughfare. Be sure to count your yawns while you're checking things out. Unless, of course, there's a parade going on—with all of the usual marching livestock.

In *this* odiferous case, just count something *else.*

PART 6:

A TRIP TO NATHAN'S "I guess so."

I'd like to give you an illustration here, concerning what I've told you about New Yorkers, and their uncanny ability to survive. Often, since being in the metropolitan area, I hear the strange word *chutzpa*—pronounced something like "hutzpah." I learned it's a succinct Yiddish expression describing, "Nerves made of granite." In Texas, we have another way of saying the same thing, but you'll need to ask Butch Brawnmeister about that.

I get the feeling "chutzpa" has the most relevance to people from Brooklyn. This incident, coming from real life, substantiates my theory. I often envision the bizarre circumstances I'm about to describe, as they foster my resolve to succeed in an environment where, at any given moment, a hostile duck might smash out my brains. I also rely on them more than ever, when I tire of my Pulitzer Prize fantasy.

The story I'm referencing, concerns an elderly lifelong resident of Coney Island. In early April, this woman had the hard luck of stumbling into a cavernous ditch near *Stillwell Avenue.*

Right before the accident, she headed straight for *Nathan's Famous.* As usual, she could not wait to put her elbows on their counter, her ritualistic way of signaling her chafed tummy—squashed underneath a sweaty rubber *Playtex* girdle and a ton of *Ammens* medicated powder—how its refreshment-stand lunch waited just seconds away.

To her—the tempting anticipation of the day's choice of a ten-inch-long grilled hotdog, hidden under a ton of greasy fried onions, topped off with melted American cheese and dill pickle relish, was more than her grumbling stomach could wait to have her swallow.

In caloric addition to her lunchtime passions, there's always her favorite frothy root beer. The usual one, with a foamy six-inch head, served in a tall frosty mug, complete with a fancy handle made from beaded glass. She had a daily thrill wiping off *that* mustache.

She also debated whether to pay for a jumbo size of fries or settle for the skimpy senior-discount portion and the real reason *why* she missed the huge sign, with the flashing assorted lights, posted by the City Marshal. The thing blinked brighter than the annual Christmas tree at Rockefeller Center, and warned pedestrians how the perilous construction site had ceased building due to the builder's bankruptcy.

Pondering her doctor's recent admonition, concerning the alarming result of her cholesterol test, also contributed to her distraction. He had the nerve to blame the **529** outcome, on her frequent consumption of Nathan's French fries, their supersized hamburgers, those extra large frankfurters—hot off their grill—and their exclusive pastrami on rye, with two fried eggs on top.

"What's the big deal?" she said. "Why should an educated woman like me, pay any attention to such a *dummkopf* doctor? He just got off the boat from Yugoslavia; he looks like a regular baby, and his English ain't nothin' to brag about neither. What could *he* possibly know about Nathan's swell nutrition?"

This woman happens to be Mrs. Fanny Faller. Television reporters cracked up, trying to explain a situation where a person with this sort of name wound up falling bottom-down into a ditch. New Yorker's are very open about these things, and everything hangs out here.

Oops!

Pun or not, the idiom about letting stuff "hang out" *is* a popular expression in New York City and part of a true Manhattan dweller's vernacular—so I'll leave the term in.

Don't give Mrs. Faller's possible hurt feelings another thought. She doesn't care. She's been hearing this sort of talk plenty, echoing back to her from behind the Berlin Wall—thanks to Johnny Carson. I think his cohort, Ed McMahon, played some part in it too. That *Tonight Show* on TV sure is popular.

Despite sky-high television ratings, poor Fanny remained down in the city's cold and dark ditch for almost an entire week. Wearing her trench coat and the clunky combat boots that morning probably saved her life. She got them from the new army surplus outlet—over near the *Parachute*

Jump ride. In further snug addition, the muskrat earmuffs, and matching set of mittens that she won the week before, playing skeet ball at the *Steeplechase Arcade,* sure came in handy.

Her husband, known to all as "Feisty Fritz" laughed with regularity about her overflowing hobo bag. It always contains, *Lydia E. Pinkham's Herb Tablets,* some aspirin, tubes of *Bengay,* a bottle of multiple vitamins, a large box of *Cheerios,* several of her favorite *Heath* candy bars, a large can of *Planters* mixed nuts, some *Saltine* crackers, and two triple-packs of *Milk Duds.* She had all of that muddy rainwater too, courtesy of the ditch.

Is ingesting muddy water *good* for you? I guess so. Maybe it has healthy minerals or something. Thinking back to the birds and the bees, *I* swallowed a glug of the stuff and I'm still around.

Returning now to her ever-loving hubby, Fritz, and the way he ridiculed Fanny's "portable supermarket," he was embarrassed. After all, the hoard helped save her life. He took that library advice and shut up. Yet, before he zipped his lips, he informed the *Daily News*—a local newspaper—that even after being married to her for so long, he still felt a thrill when his Fanny returned. He wasn't functioning very well without her "constant nagging."

Too bad for him that Fanny heard about his remarks the night she came home. She put on a clean girdle, picked Fritz up by his ankles, and carried *him* over to the ditch. He dangled there while she threatened to give him "a spectacular vacation" like the one he promised her when they married fifty years ago. She let him know how she never imagined smooching for half-a-century on Coney Island's boardwalk.

Anyway, while *she* had her turn vacationing in the ditch, everybody in the neighborhood, including a desperate Fritz, searched like bloodhounds for this missing senior citizen. When the police found her, some anxious rescue workers argued at the top of their professional lungs, about the safest way to manipulate their crane. Extracting a fragile victim like *her* wouldn't be simple. All of a sudden, the crew was stunned into silence by a steely voice—vaulting out of the abyss—telling them to, "Knock it off and quit ya damn bickerin'!"

By this apprehensive stage, television cameras broadcasted at full speed while the mechanical hoist labored with loud creaks and groans, as cables pulled her out of the deep ditch. She sat up straight in the shaky thing and stared right into the camera. She wasn't shy about blowing kisses and laughing her head off.

This woman shouts louder than my father does. She *has* to be a distant relative. I must say, however, that she got her *Andy Warhol* "fifteen minutes of fame" *that* night. Her sonic-boom voice so startled the evening news reporter that he jumped back and dropped the microphone. If Wolfie, the German shepherd rescue dog on the scene, didn't sink its teeth into the seat of this guy's pants, to drag him away from the ditch, who knows what could have happened.

I saw the same reporter again on TV three days later. He sat in a special chair, equipped with one of those big donut cushions, when he presented Wolfie with a plaque and access to a lifetime supply of *White Castle* hamburgers.

As for the crowd of obnoxious pedestrians watching the rescue—waving like maniacs into the network's camera—when Fanny informed them how her entire fiasco was, "a thick piece of chocolate babka with streusel topping" they all cheered louder than those *Brooklyn Dodger* fans once did, back at good old *Ebbets Field.*

This elderly lady swung in that lift, like a regular Tarzan-in-drag. She kept ordering the rescue crew to wheel the thing around the corner to an open-all-night Greek diner, the only place in town to get a "decent toasted bagel with a heap of Nova lox." And—she let them know, in a commanding tone, worthy of a Five-Star Army General, how she wanted it "heavy on the cream cheese."

She also insisted the diner put her whipped cream garnished hot chocolate, with those cute mini-marshmallows, into one of their cardboard cups decorated with a picture of the *Parthenon.* When the reporter asked her why she demanded this sort of cup for her beverage, she said with authority, "Did *your* brain fly to Miami? Don't you realize my drink will taste better?"

Furthermore—she notified the crew she needed a "black and white" to go along *with* the hot chocolate. She'd accept no substitutes. Might there be a translation needed here? Fanny just wanted a local dessert-staple made of a sweet, large, round, moist, and flat cake-like disk. There's a skillful dividing line of glazed frosting on each side. One side has icing in chocolate, and the other has icing in vanilla. I wish that I had one in front of me right now.

Make that *two.*

I'm sure that you wouldn't mind having one or more of them. Are you *now* pouring yourself a glass of milk in anticipation of eating this specialized dessert?

You're not.

Oh, I understand.

You're okay with taking the tea route.

See, as usual, I'm correct. You'd be nuts not to want a black and white. These cookies are *so* yummy.

Mrs. Faller is indeed a real tough specimen—even for Brooklyn. The very next day after the *rescue,* she went back to her job over at the **VFW** hall, around the block from the *Cyclone Roller Coaster.* As usual, without the use of any microphone, she still did a great job of announcing those bingo-card numbers.

And—as a reward for giving them so much free publicity, Nathan's graced her with a gift certificate for a year's supply of hotdogs and fries with "the works." Fritz went on that popular Tonight Show to thank her for, "pulling off the caper." Fanny refused to be on camera with him, since television will add *ten pounds.*

Doctor Dummkopf heard the worldwide news about Mrs. Faller's dim view of his medical proficiency, from his family overseas. He told Fanny that if she ever calls him for *anything* in the future, his office had orders to disconnect her the moment they heard her exasperating voice.

By the remote way, all of his informative relatives live in a mountainous section of Yugoslavia. Any visitors, who locate the place, will need oxygen tanks, roadside assistance flares, and an emergency parachute.

Well—what more do I say other than this story screams, "That's *Brooklyn* for you."

On this one, trust me *indubitably.*

This is such a cool and succinct word for, "No doubt about it."

PART 7:

HAUTE CUISINE

"Her initials are, S.M.C."

In reflecting on the plight of Fanny Faller, I downright understand how people flip over Nathan's fries. How *do* they cook these succulent, tantalizing potatoes so crisp on the outside and so moist on the inside? I can't believe I'm still hungry after eating all those cashew nuts. Stress is the cause. I devoured the entire box.

I think I'll go and make one of those towering *Dagwood Bumstead* sandwiches. I'll use lettuce and tomatoes, along with the nitrite-free Canadian bacon I buy at an organic supermarket.

The only bread I ever eat is wholegrain, which I bake myself. At times, the loaf turns out dry so I goop on lots of my creamy homemade mayonnaise. I fry the bacon very crisp, and drain any excess grease on a paper towel, before I stuff this multilayered sandwich into my mouth.

For the past three months, since I'm here in New York's metropolitan area, I caught on fast how eating in restaurants is an expensive deal. So I'm learning to cook by watching Graham Kerr, the *Galloping Gourmet.* If, like me, you're diligent about trying some of those extensive recipes he demonstrates on his television show, one cannot avoid making an appalling mess.

Even though *Graham* makes using an electric mixer look so easy, inevitably this handheld appliance causes a humungous kitchen disaster. I purchased my apron at a restaurant supply store in bustling *Times Square,* and even this professional one can't stand up to a budding cook covered with batter-spatter from a whirlybird. This is more than true, if the cook is an adventurous one like me, who plunges without fear into slimy strings of stick on the wall pie dough.

Now—I'll give *you* a great tip concerning kitchen maintenance. I've found out all one needs to excel in "haute cuisine" is a good imagination, coupled with some convenient pigeon to hustle and clean up the bombed-out place afterward. You need *hours* to pick calcified stuff out of those heating elements on top of a gas stove.

Following that laborious chore, we have the encrusted oven problem. I'm telling you, the caked-on mess sneaks up out of nowhere from those trial and error canapés and gets real bad. The caustic fumes that come from a spray can of oven cleaner, will broil your lungs. I make sure never to be anywhere *near* the stuff while it's dissolving all that disgusting gook. *Gross* is the word when black slime from inside the oven seeps out onto the floor, and misses the newspaper that's *supposed* to catch the residue.

Believe me—scrubbing the kitchen's old floor tiles, trying to get out the oozing mess from its numerous cracks, is a real hard job for somebody. This is why I disappear whenever the frequent process occurs. I use the opportunity to visit Macy's, and get some free makeup samples to try at home later. The best part about escaping from this nasty chore is having those salesgirls spritz expensive perfume on me. Their main job is to scurry around on the first floor and douse any gal they find.

Once, by mistake, several of them ambushed a passing *Green Beret* soldier in his trademark fatigues. His less than positive reaction to smelling like a botanic garden—in full bloom—had security guards escorting *him* to the door. When I return to the apartment, smelling like a floral bouquet myself, the result of the zealous salesgirls causes each of the cats to sneeze nonstop. I never worry about them, since they come from New York City alleyways, and this makes them much tougher than me.

Sniffing back to a good aroma again, Kerr's popular original culinary-series galloped itself off the air last year, but I'm happy to practice with the numerous reruns. And, owing to *my* frequent "flying" meal experiments, I could never function in the kitchen without that very necessary *pigeon.*

Her initials are, S.M.C.

Sorry.

I forgot to say Shelley's middle name is, *Marie.*

PART 8:

HUSBANDRY **"I'm not a happy camper."**

Now that I've ensured a future cholesterol crisis myself, I'll tell you about this morning's dutiful spring sun squirting blossom-power all around where I live on Fordham Road. When I finally left for the day, I witnessed the grandeur of this magnificent sunup. No noble effort could ever help *my* mood though. I can't be cheered up as of late, because elevating from landing in the bowels of The Bronx, to my real heart's desire of fabulous Manhattan, turns out to be almost impossible. I'm not a happy camper.

Before dawn had the chance to crack, but *I* sure was about to, my predictive clock radio blasted *A Hard Day's Night.* The vibration of the music sent my expensive new Emerson plummeting to the floor—right along with me. Without my alarm clock, I'd sleep the morning away. No matter how miserable early rising is, I must get a necessary jump on apartment hunting.

At the same time when I had this brain fog, for some reason the wakeup song invoked strong visualizations of Tillagevale and my tenth birthday. I'm being more than truthful when I say that with the strange exception of this morning, I almost never think about Tillagevale since living in New York. As you'll learn later, more than enough happens here to occupy my time.

But this morning things were different. While the sun competed with me for gumption to rise, listening to this old Beatles hit, playing on a local radio station, transported *me* to pastimes. Why? The answer is I don't have a clue.

I'm thinking, though, perhaps their coincidental selection of music for early birds forced me to recall—in vivid detail—how my family succeeded in pulling off a surprise party for me. My entire Girl Scout junior-pack came over, on that amazing Friday morning so long ago. And they all wore their uniforms.

Catching me unawares is no easy task. However, when the doorbell rang, I had no idea about every scout in my troop congregating on the front porch. This includes the members I knew for sure hated my guts. I opened the front door at Azimuth Circle and gasped from shock.

Mom had the foresight to dig *my* uniform out of my room days before the surprise, even though she never goes in there. She says I deserve to live in my own filth and wants nothing to do with the contagion. If she weren't so enthusiastic about planning the perfect birthday for me, she would have continued teaching me "the lesson I never learn" and wouldn't have rescued my smelly uniform. The crumpled mess sat quarantined for an entire month before my July birthday, ever since the local **4-H Club** sponsored my troop's last meeting of the school year. They also hosted every scout troop in the county, including the Boy Scouts, because we all tried out for the *Husbandry Medal.*

Guess the name of the Girl Scout who milked the *abnormal* goat by accident.

You're right again.

How *do* you know these things?

In the confusion, the poor animal broke away from its tether on a fence near the back of the farm. This ailing goat had *St. Vitas* dance. And with my miserable luck—out of all the kids who were there—the scrawny thing ran right over to *me.* I should've been suspicious in the beginning, when I looked at the tag on the rope it dragged from behind, and saw the name *Frisbee*—like the round plastic spinning thing you throw and chase, while the airborne disk flies all over the park.

In case you're not into veterinary diseases, this creepy condition causes an animal to kick and fidget like there's no tomorrow. The poor inflicted thing also jumps around and twitches better than a wet hose—far worse than the other "Frisby creature", I told you about. This squirming goat almost stopped me from getting the important scout ranking. Naturally, I wanted to display this coveted badge on my uniform, so no matter *what* gymnastic moves I had to perform, I saw things through. And yes, after they pinned the colorful badge on me, I felt proud. Troop leaders were astounded over the bucket full of milk I got out of that wiggler.

Before I forget, you wouldn't think that a little itty-bitty goat has a very weird smell. The odor lingers way after you wrestle with it. The stink rubs all over you.

Afterward—there's all of that funky goat milk inside of the overflowing bucket. Carrying this heavy thing to the judging table made a big mess too, since the liquid splashed all over me.

This milk doesn't resemble the sweet smelling, prizewinning variety from *Mademoiselle Goliath,* the old-folk's cow that Sister Gracie relies on. But if circumstances grew more "biblical" and she tapped that colossal cow of hers for the Strawberry Festival, while it reacted to St. Vitas dance, the hot **EXTRA-EXTRA READ ALL ABOUT IT** headline would have been about Sister's *own* last roundup.

Double trust me on this one.

While we're on this stinking subject, my mother found out firsthand how the already funky smell of a goat turns really gross, when its splashed milk ferments and gets crusty on a neglected Girl Scout uniform.

Such an odiferous observation turns into a supreme nostril-buster when the filthy uniform parks for the month I mentioned, while it festers at the bottom of a hamper. A hamper already bursting with assorted *other* sweaty clothes in an unventilated closet. You can't enter the room unless you sneak some of your mom's perfume, pour the expensive stuff on cotton balls, and shove them up your nose.

Later on, I more or less apologized to my mother for overlooking the rotting uniform. I was astonished when she said how washing the smelly thing didn't bother her. That prior experience with my constant toddler failure—sitting down on the little wooden potty in the center of my nursery, right *after* the malodorous evidence occupied whatever I dressed in—desensitized her. I never could get the connection of making my deposit in the removable enamel basin first.

Say, I *heard* that remark you just made. I assure you, I've long since mastered the skill.

Trust me.

PART 9:

PHILIP MORRIS

"I avoided this one activity."

I guess we'll leave that bad smell, and replace the disgusting scent with the appetizing aroma of movie theatre popcorn. Waking up to relive my historic tenth birthday, caused so much stuff about this party from the past to whip through my head. This included the greater surprise waiting for me.

Although I saw a *Hertz* minibus parking in front of the house the night before, I had no idea Mom was the renter. She planned to take all of us downtown to Tillagevale's new state of the art, stereo-capable, *Wingding Theatre.*

What a good thing this modern curved screen wasn't around when I saw The Blob.

If I had watched that horror movie on an enveloping Cinemascope one, with its accompanying thunderous acoustics, I'm sure Daddy wouldn't have survived. He'd never be around to tell Mom how he wouldn't join the "giggling-pack" for any premiere of *A Hard Day's Night,* even if she agreed to "stop spending money like water going through a sieve." He felt this poor-sport way, although this was the first movie the *Beatles* ever made and the best Beatles' movie too—in my opinion.

We had such a great experience that day, standing up on the seats and screaming down the aisles. I knew at that moment, how the booming sound system told me I'd write about exciting events like this in the future. *I'll* be exploring the very important who, what, when, where, and why. One of those bullets whizzing by Gene Autry struck *me* when I heard the *boing-boing* of an unraveling spring, popping out of the abused theatre seat I jumped on that afternoon.

When I grow up—I'll be a reporter. What's very exciting to me, sitting here now writing about this, is I'm right here in New York City preparing to make this dream come true. I'm turning this childhood ambition into reality. In the interim, though, I'll settle for reporting to *you* concerning all the Girl Scout mayhem at the "shaking to the rafters" Wingding Theatre.

The distraught teenage usher, dressed in a bellhop outfit just like the *Philip Morris* cigarette-kid wore in TV commercials of the era, kept coming over at five-minute intervals and told us to, "Pipe down." For some reason, he blushed a lot while he used that flashlight to inspect the seats for any damage while we jumped on them. *His* dedication to duty sure makes a great thing to write about.

To my surprise, Mom didn't act real annoyed by our behavior. She made squawks, just to prove a parent came with us, until I heard a few screams of adoration slip out of *her* mouth. I saw how a mother could also be a *friend*. She sat there, right along with everybody, joining in with the comradery.

This is, of course, with the exception of girls who threw the expensive jumbo boxes of popcorn at the usher. I avoided this one activity. I realize my friends *do* think I'm crazy. However, even *they* know I'm not stupid enough to waste money like this in front of Mom.

If I were there by myself, though, I couldn't guarantee *any* behavior having to do with this exciting afternoon at the Wingding.

PART 10:

NUTCRACKER SUITE

"You're not convinced."

Reminiscing about everything that happened on my tenth birthday, I'm gaining insight into what makes my mother tick. Her uncharacteristic *bobbysoxer* fervor at the Hard Day's Night premier, is because she's nuts about Paul McCartney. If she ever catches him on television, she gets a dopy, faraway look in her eyes. Before long, she's glancing at my father or his picture on the mantle, if he isn't around.

Then, she mentions how her once collegiate boyfriend—also known with fondness as *Ally-Pop*—did bear a striking resemblance to *Paul.* According to her, no one could have missed the similarity, especially when Dad pranced around as the *gorgeous* twenty-year-old "superstar" of Tillagevale University's *Drumline Band.* After the show is over, and Paul exits the airwaves, she sighs while plumping up the pillows on the sofa before saying, "It really *is* impossible to resist a man in uniform."

I don't know *where* my mother's brain jitterbugged during the Jurassic epoch, regarding her adamant opinion about her handsome "main-squeeze" in college resembling any present-day Beatle whatsoever. Back in that primitive era, my father's lips blew up like a bulbous balloon—on the bassoon.

Wearing his goofy *Nutcracker Suite* getup didn't help him out in the McCartney department either. I've seen a photo of my father, parading like a stiff wooden solider in this band's comical uniform. Believe me, that "Paul" resemblance, if any ever existed, faded right along with old Ally-pop and the historic picture.

Also—concerning this pictorial relic—I tried hard to locate the negative before I left for New York. I wanted to make a great wall-sized picture for his office, inviting everybody in town to his workplace. I'd have one of those unveilings as a big surprise. A classy kind of affair, where you serve tiny sandwiches made from wilting watercress. No luck though. The negative marched in reverse, straight back to the primordial soup, right along with the ancient band and its brachiosaurus mascot.

I'm disappointed about not finding that picture. He would have loved me even more at the time for doing such a wonderful thing for him, don't you think.

You're not convinced.

Why is that?

So—to revisit my cherished birthday party, I'll now march in reverse myself to that hot, late afternoon of **July 20th** in **1964.** After the movie and the Wingding hadn't collapsed, instead of dropping kids off at their homes, Mom drove the comfortable minibus back to my house so we could all enjoy a barbecue and a birthday cake.

When we did a great job of attacking the corndogs and burgers—faster than my grandfather could sling them off the grill—another surprise waited in the offing, when my grandmother popped out of the storage shed. She carried a huge box. Everybody had chipped in to give me that latest *portable* stereophonic phonograph. And tucking inside this gift, on the **45-rpm** section of its adjustable turntable, I saw the Beatles Gold Record named for the movie we had seen earlier.

As soon as I opened this great gift, we devoured, of course, the beautiful *homemade* birthday cake. A fantasy in the dusk took place, while we all watched the cake aglow with candles, as they flickered in unison with the fireflies above. Under the light of the beautiful paper lanterns, strung around the trees in the yard, I bet we played this single fifty times, making the stereo's needle wear out. This is a special pain, because whenever I change them I drop these miniscule, almost invisible mechanisms, and never see them again.

Plus—I often distort these needles trying to insert them into the phonograph's tone arm and they don't come cheap, do they. I waste a lot of time and money handling the awkward things.

Are you clumsy like me, when changing *your* phonograph needles?

PART 11:

PLUTO "Let them all give up now."

When I think back to the thrill of realizing the fantastic modern record player, sitting in the birthday gift box, belonged to me alone, I know this initial elation never did leave me. This is why, over all the years, I took great care of my wonderful gift, even bringing it with me to New York.

This morning, as outlined, Beatles' music played on my radio. In general, however, most often in the evenings—I listen to my personal collection of fantastic singles and albums from a lot of bands and recording artists. I still get a thrill playing all of them on my sentimental stereo, right here in The Bronx.

The next-door neighbors in *this* tenement, including wigged-out cranks on the floors above and below, grumble to Shelley every chance they get about my *ear shattering* high-fidelity system. They also shout at her while they say, "That bleached-blonde, self-absorbed boarder of yours, has one hell of a nerve keeping her volume up to Planet Pluto."

I do respect their opinion, I guess. But must these party-poopers use their dumb brooms to bang on shared walls and ceilings. They use this form of exercise most often when I listen to the song "I'm a Believer" by **The Monkees.** In direct response to these overzealous janitors, I'll now quote the famous words of my simpatico buddy, Alfred E. Neuman, as they appear on every cover of my favorite *Mad Magazine:*

"What, Me Worry?"

Who cares what these people say about my hair, or my supposed "self-absorption."

And what *else* do you do with a super-duper record player like mine, if you don't blast away?

Hello! I do work every day. They should allow me to enjoy hassle-free entertainment, when *I* come home. Let them all give up now. They'll *never* hear me play Shelley's favorite singer, the ever jolly, coochie-cooing, Doris Day. This is the reason why I don't let crabby neighbors, swinging chipped and dented broomsticks, interfere with *my* selection of music.

In bugging addition, if you critique the roaches and other corpulent creepy-crawlies here inside of the building—doing their insect version of that new Floridian *Walt Disney World*—I'm just being a Good Samaritan. All things considered, I justify the money these people wasted in the first place, on the cleaning function of their pristine brooms. Honorable sounds occur when I blast music. I'm performing a very charitable act, don't you think?

Well, *I* do!

Shelley though—unlike the cantankerous neighbors—acts like a complete fanatic about cleaning up *her* personal space every day. She buys a lot of the insecticide **RAID.** I often advise her how, owing to some weird aberration, the poisonous stuff definitely doesn't "Kill Bugs Dead" in *her* kitchen. Isn't this lack of efficacy peculiar? I wonder what could explain it. My dad used the exact pesticide once in the backyard shed, and those unwanted scorpions, spinning webs in his poncho, sure went belly-up fast.

As usual, she's not one bit appreciative when I try keeping her up-to-date on effective annihilation practices. She rushes into her room and slams the door. Then I hear *her* screaming, like the gang of bugs *ought* to be.

Once I informed her—with, as usual, the best of intentions—that she enabled the drug abuse of insect addicts. The partygoers in the kitchen just limp away on a high and return with friends, *after* they recover from her expensive waste of fumigation. She had her fingers in her ears. But I *knew* she heard my expert opinion, when she threatened to spray the crap on me. Do you believe that!

Leaving those indestructible Bronx bugs to their nutritional supplement, I'll get back to rocking with the fabulous Monkees. By some strange fate the original *I'm a Believer* single I bought, when the fantastic megahit first came out, met with a mysterious tragic end. I'll tell you right now, more than a few tears flowed. I missed playing this record so much. But my much-maligned sweet tooth wound up saving the day, because, by chance, several years later, I won a duplicate copy at my sister's birthday party.

PART 12:

MICKEY VERSUS RINGO "I *am* a believer!"

Preparing to speak further, on the curious topic of my sister and a grotty groundhog sharing such common ground, I must first admit to a crucial oversight. My parents jumped on my back, about buying her a gift for her forthcoming party at the Bullsnake Lodge, for at least the entire month before.

After this extensive haranguing, which only verified my belief how they took me for a kid whose comprehension level was on par with that of a toad, would you believe that when the special day arrived—along with *Punxsutawney Phil*—I had forgotten the gift part. Croak! Croak!

Well—in spite of what you think, it really *could* have been "subconscious" on my part, instead of your theory of *unconscious.* But, as a miserable result of either theory, since I didn't bring any present for her, and if I didn't produce one—just as fast as my grandfather once did his puzzling beret—I'd never stop hearing about my selfish attitude. They'd carry on until her next birthday. Then, I heard my name announced as winner of the raffle, and the prize was my precious record!

Making a halfhearted motion for my sister to come up on the stage with me, when I received this record for winning the raffle, sounded like a great idea. I would, right there in the Bullsnake spotlight, become noteworthy for my altruism. I thought, wow, how tear jerking for the audience, as they watch me place my fantastic gift directly into my sister's birthday loot bag.

Tears on my part, in any recorded case.

My heart broke letting this prize slip out of my hands, since I wasn't able to play my original sentimental edition of the **1967** hit. Back then, I saved a portion of my allowance each week to buy this chart-topper. In retrospect though, if I didn't use half of the money for those Drake's *Ring Ding* cakes, I wouldn't have gained a nasty pound—and could have played the then hot single a lot sooner.

After a month, I accumulated—along with the stubborn weight—enough money to get the record of my dreams. I got soaked in the pouring rain on the night I hoofed that long and wet mile over to the Tillagevale Record Shack. It's a good thing I did brave the weather, even with that bad cold I caught. I snatched their last one off the rack. I *am* a believer! Now—I found myself getting soaked once more at the Bullsnake Lodge.

While everybody clapped during the transfer of this coveted prize, I must have looked like a glum philanthropist. I couldn't hide my pain, dwelling on my long-lost original edition, and now, having to part with its replacement, gave new meaning to the absolute pits.

Then, out of nowhere, a lodge member rushed up onto the stage. He stood there to announce the winner of an additional raffle prize and called my name. I had guessed the exact amount of **3,326** jellybeans jammed inside the large clear glass jar. He handed me the filled container, brimming over—by the scrumptious way—with my favorite black licorice variety.

I wrapped myself around that colorful jar, holding on to it so tight that my arms turned blue. I knew for sure, she'd give me her sweet baby sister anticipatory look in front of the crowd and did she ever. The big and heavy jar could never fit in her loot bag anyhow, so common sense saved me on this one. I wasn't completely bad. Later on—from the strict goodness of my heart—I'd pick out all the green ones from the mix and give *them* to her. I hate this flavor.

"Waste not, want not."

Hey, good old Ben Franklin would be proud of me.

Now leaving jellybeans to nostalgia, I'll return to the original single I once cherished above all others. Wondering about its fate bothered me in those days, and it still does. I'm usually so careful with my record collection. I never got a handle on where that old **45-rpm** went until my mother cracked the mystery. One Monday morning, she discovered how *The Monkees,* instead of spinning around on the usual phonograph turntable, made a strange decision to forsake their regular residence for her clothes dryer—set on ultra hot.

In view of resultant warping on that lethal washday, my former possession is now nothing more than a forlorn black vinyl taco, sitting on top of the dresser between the dormer windows in what is now my old room.

Don't you think it's very suspicious how the load of wash my mother dried that afternoon, consisted of my sister's camp clothes? Strange accidents often happen in families, mine above all, where people know absolutely nothing about a single shady thing in their own environment, but concerning my fried recording I never proved any *malfeasance.* This is a fancy legal word for when you suspect a deliberate violation of your trust. I asked the TV detective *Peter Gunn* to help me out. He couldn't. When his movie flopped a few years ago, he quit gumshoeing to play trumpet in Henry Mancini's orchestra.

Oh well.

I'll now spin back to a viable version of this record.

When the birthday-girl bounced home from the lodge later in the day, after a vindictive groundhog predicted prolonged lousy weather, instead of thanking me for being a magnanimous sister—she had the nerve to insult my gift. She just could *not* wait to comment how, on the recording I sacrificed to give her, *Mickey Dolenz* sounds like he's drumming on a set of tinny pots and pans, if you compare him to *Ringo Starr.* Of course, after her nasty remark, I had no other choice than to snatch the record back—right out of her grubby hands. After that, with typical fury, my sister screamed, "You're a big fat traitor."

I retaliated by screaming back even louder, "You're a pea-brained ingrate."

The sworn truth is, she'd damage this great single if I *had* let her keep the prize. My clumsy sister never figures out how to place the tone arm on the record's grooves *before* she starts playing it. Are *you* able to avoid scratching *your* records? When a nicked one starts to skip and repeat the sound is awful and drives you mad.

I'm very good at never marring any of mine. I keep them like new. I care about my recordings—unlike *some* people, I know. I'm so glad, that here in New York now, I still possess all these records in great condition. I have no idea whatsoever where *hers* wound up.

Do *you* think they're still around?

PART 13:

THE DISNEY GANG "I sure don't!"

I never reference my record collection without talking about Karen Carpenter. I adore her voice, and all the lyrics to the *Carpenter* songs. I bet you like them too. Their latest hit single—*It's Going to Take Some Time*—seems apropos now, as this is how I feel about my assumed liberated life here in New York.

Sharing this claustrophobic shoebox in The Bronx with my comatose cousin is bad enough. So is waiting everyday for that primitive 13-inch black and white TV of hers to blow up. I'm sure I told you about this erratic television before.

I can barely afford tickets for movies once a week at this point, so relying on my stereo or radio, and a decent television, is basically all I have for entertainment. Too bad people can't rent old movies cheap, together with current ones, including musical soundtracks, and somehow play them on their televisions at home—whenever they choose.

As usual, this idea is only dreaming.

Dreaming . . . dreaming . . . dreaming.

Visiting again with reality, also termed Cousin Shelly, she never suffers from watching this old TV. She has a 21-inch color one with a cool remote control. I never see this new model that's locked up in her Fort Knox bedroom. However, she'll expect me to repair her old broken-down one when the thing finally peters out. Or nag me until I replace the piece of junk with a newer and better one.

In annoying addition, this small television with that bent rabbit-ears antenna, tortures me with static. It's in cahoots with those lethal weapons, known as *broomsticks,* forever trying to bust through the flimsy ceilings and walls. Their entire reason for existence is eradication of my stereo and me along with it.

Now—doesn't *that* remark label a person who is unhinged, and blathering about wild conspiracies, as they head straight down the road toward paranoia? Remember, though, TV's *Dr. Marcus Welby* says all paranoia stems from seeds of truth. This man is *so* trustworthy. He has the best bedside manner of any physician *I* ever encountered, including the kind and familiar one practicing in my hometown.

The most irritating thing about living in this environment is that I never know when another one of her feline waifs will drag in an army of fleas. These parasites, by the itchy way, are delighted to join the Disney gang. Believe me when I tell you how, just like all the other assorted bugs in this abode, these fleas are safe here too.

One entire cabinet, in the already crowded kitchen, overflows with assorted *ineffective* veterinary supplies—including gallons of so-called flea bath. Shelly should just save money, and use plain old tap water. Judging from the bites all over my legs, these pesticides don't work. In my humble, and totally disregarded opinion, she's giving this undeserving Disney gang a relaxing spa treatment like my mom gave the tarnish, only this one includes a hot tub. She spends a fortune on all this junk, in hopes of helping her stinking bunch of stray cats. She believes "nothing is too good for these sweet little kitties." She feels *sorry* for them.

I sure don't!

Do you remember the orphaned gray kitten I mentioned to you before? I wake up each morning to this cat staring at me better than *Svengali* could, with those round spooky eyes of hers, almost the same color as her dark fur. Shelley says this cat might have some *Burmese,* but I don't care where the annoying animal originates. She has the name of *Daisy,* but I call her, "that furry pest." The veterinarian says the "poor little thing" means no harm and is only *teething.* I, however, think this dust mop sleeps and drools on my chest all night long just to irritate me, even though she has a bib of white fur around her neck.

Shelley says I should be *flattered* seeing as the kitten, "loves me." Oh, yes, this must be right, because my cousin the *cat expert* says so. She's forgetting how, when recognizing a con artist, I'm much more of an expert than *she* can ever be. The little creep of hers just wants me to bribe it with a handful of those gross vitamin treats so it'll take off. I, on the contrary, refuse to cave—concerning that slobbery purring. Crashing at the insane asylum, they're rumoring me to be in, is preferable to coming back here for even one more night.

I ask you, what am I paying for in this dump?

The answer is—a lumpy sofa bed, insects jazzed on RAID-juice, five obnoxious alley cats, and all of their stinky—and I do mean *stinky*—litter boxes.

Or if I do decide to acquiesce, my life could turn out worse than ever. I'd have to retreat home to wearisome Tillagevale, where I'll suffer the humiliation of defeat. I'll have a genuine Ship of Life upchuck then, listening to everyone's haughty, "See, I *told* you so."

Speaking of *everyone,* I'll stop stalling and give you some verbal snapshots, taken from my own family album. I *will* get to all the paranormal junk soon enough. I'm just not ready yet. Although, from all of the stuff I've told you about my zany life, you may think I already have.

Chapter 5

Family Album

PART 1:

COVER GIRL

"She doesn't *need* makeup."

I mentioned my kid sister a few times, but refrained from illustrating specifics about her. She's fifteen. Her name's Vivienne. It couldn't be just plain old *Vivian.* Instead, everybody pronounces it *Viv . . . i . . . e n n e,* and it means some nauseating thing like, "joy of life."

Why *she* got such a sophisticated first name I will never know, since we both took the same route. My parents gave her a classy middle name too—*Alicia.* And, adding to the nausea, this one means *truth.*

When I ask my mother why she favored my sister with such a great name, the only reply I ever get is the old jumping bean rationale she uses. If a third daughter had come her way, the name would reach the epitome of spectacular. I'm betting on *Sabrina,* after her favorite Audrey Hepburn movie. Then, I'd be a permanent resident of the bottom of the nomenclature barrel. As things stand now, I have an extended lease.

Getting back to the reality of the only sister I *do* lug around, what I know for sure about Miss Vivienne Alicia Autry is how she mastered the art of harassment even better than I did, and I'm the worldwide titleholder who taught her the skill.

I must caution you here how she speaks with such an intense nasal pitch, it surpasses the irritating sound of chalk grating against a blackboard. If you ever need to drive somebody to the brink, forget that *drip-drip* water-torture stuff. Just find Vivienne. *Her* voice is custom-made for professional nitpicking. Husbands around the world could hire her to get back at their wives. I bet Fritz would put her on the payroll.

What really peeves me is the way she harped on me from the moment I made my decision to leave home. Her sermonizing *still* echoes in my ears:

Ginger, you're not being rational. Ever since graduation, you're lucky to be working for a *real* salary at the *only* newspaper Tillagevale has. Daddy says they are *Socialists* and the lack of competition is definite proof. However, he gives you a free room, including the ton of food you eat. He buys all of your clothes too. I may not be very good in history, but this sounds *Marxist* to me. Mom also acts like a commune member, when she toils to make your lunch to carry, and irons all your outfits for work.

Since you live at home, your savings account is *humongous.* That once cute and chubby polka-dot pig of yours has changed into a bank account passbook—with an extreme case of obesity. I know Mom and Dad do all of this for you, hoping that you'll save for college instead of skipping town, but you mooch off of them just to get out of here fast.

I'm sure your miserly lifestyle is the cause of you *not* paying attention to a very important lesson, taught to us in Sunday school. Did you *completely* forget how it is easier for a rich man to fit through the eye of a needle, than for a camel to enter the Kingdom of Heaven?

Also—what seems so great about New York City, anyhow? Mommy agrees with *me,* and Daddy says you are quite immature for a girl who has finagled herself a *real* job.

Okay, now that you've heard Vivienne's holier than thou tone, and tasted a sampling of her *philosophical* words, I know you realize what I'm up against concerning her. Dwelling on a possible mix-up at the hospital is something I do every day. *She* doesn't resemble me, in any way *whatsoever.*

At **5'8",** she's already three-inches taller than I am and a full **36-C.** She never has any interest in borrowing my bras. On the contrary, I do have to worry about her returning everything else she helps herself to.

I am learning the hard way concerning the sibling "lack of equanimity with genes" hypothesis. After her illuminating camel remark, I'm thankful that this also includes brainpower distribution. I'm miles ahead of her in the cerebral department.

To continue with honesty, Vivienne could pass for a gorgeous model. Who'd ever doubt she has cover girl status? This runway observation is apparent, after looking at her rich ivory-cream complexion, which resembles flawless alabaster. She doesn't *need* makeup. I never see her buy or use any and this is why she snatches my lipstick, whenever I forget to hide my latest color.

She also has perfect sculpted legs, which match her long explanations, because they extend on and on without end. Also, in stunning addition, her sweet and fawn-like *Bambi* eyes remind people of velvety cocoa, swirling around in a steamy cup. Then, there's the matter of her natural dark auburn hair, shimmering across her shoulders. Everybody says Vivienne resembles the current *Breck Shampoo Girl,* whose beauty shows up in full glory on color TV. I'm sure you've seen her.

Um . . . what *is* her name?

Oh, I remember now. It's—Jaclyn Smith. She's the famous model who has what I call, "sassy hair." When my sister struts around, people hear an undeniable come-hither *whoosh* while her hair swings. Thick tresses sashay behind her like a luxurious fan for her shoulders, in the same way that *Jaclyn's* does.

Some of us *do* have it to flaunt, don't you think.

PART 2:

BOOP-BOOP-A-DOO! "Ginger has Huns' blood."

By now, you may be thinking what *does* Ginger look like comparing to Vivienne or to anybody in the world. Well, *I* am more of a *Betty Boop.* I do have a small waist, although I often overhear petty comments about my *generous* hips. More to the point, what my critics call, "big below the belt" is also that coveted *hourglass* shape.

I do see guys staring at me at times, almost as if they think I'm hot. But they're probably just taking a good look at the perpetual stale breakfast I carry around on my chest.

Somehow, as far as *my* long legs are concerned, they ran off to somebody else. Nevertheless—and I do give literal meaning to this word—I often overhear people referring to my thighs as *big* or "burly as a tree trunk." Either way, you get the message. Yet please don't let people's insensitive comments mislead you. These thighs of mine are solid. They're all bone. Thick bone, but *bone* no matter what.

I remember back in high school, during a swimming meet, how a boy at the gym pool pointed me out to everybody. My formfitting team bathing suit acted like a second skin, enabling me to clock those winning laps in record time. His gruff public statement echoed off the gymnasium walls, for all to hear, when he said, "Look people! Ginger has Huns' blood." I'm sure whatever he meant, qualifies as an affront of mega proportion.

I do like what's behind me though. I actually got one break in the anatomy department. My bottom is very high up and tight. All the same, I often wish how a beautiful superstar, with a similar build to the one I have, will popularize my unique feature. She'd make "junk in the trunk" something to envy. Maybe I'll see her in the future, and watch this hottie ignite my carbon-copy caboose on the big screen. You *never* know.

Concerning the crowning glory department, mine is not at all sassy. Far from it. In reality, *Mother Nature* ran out of verve on the miserable day when she fell asleep under the hair dryer and forgot about me. The stuff on top of my head looks like curly fuzz, seeping out of a discarded feather pillow.

On the other hand—full of strands of hair from excessive teasing—I'm showing her. I bet you've heard the expression, "Only your hairdresser knows for sure." This doesn't apply to me, because visiting any beauty parlor here in New York is out of the question. Tillagevale's no different. Appointments over at Mildred's Beauty Circle were a definite risk. I'm not talking about the price. I'm talking about the malicious beauticians who'd all gossip about my tresses or lack thereof. And having a showy Manhattan salon work on my substandard hair will be my ultimate humiliation.

So—instead, I consult with a discreet *Miss Clairol.* For a mere pittance, *she* enables the gracious perpetuation of my lackluster—very mousy-brown and baby-fine strands—to come into view as sweet petite locks, kissed with tenderness by magical rays of sunshine. Pretty good, huh!

I have a belief that what sociologists call, "The peer group" symbolizes a snobbish sorority. In order to compete, everybody has pressure to develop some kind of exceptional feature. Any girl, whether young or old, finds survival without a major effort impossible—unless you're like Vivienne. All *she* has to do is wake up and comb her thick hair.

Oh, she also has to brush her sparkling white teeth, which, *unlike* those in my mouth, are not mottled and didn't need any straightening. Gosh, those metal braces I wore were gross. They made my gums bloody and sore too. My dad spent a fortune on them. Now my teeth look better than they did when I was a kid, but hers are still much nicer. I'm resigning myself that my teeth won't ever be a clear and clean looking *white* like my sister's are—unless I undergo an expensive and painful procedure to cap them.

As a toddler, on summer vacation with my mother, I came down with something. She gave me a new type of medicine, prescribed by an unfamiliar pediatrician in the area we visited. The side effect manifested later on, how this medicine causes permanent teeth to grow in mottled. She feels guilty to this day, although she shouldn't. She only followed doctor's orders.

Even if mine escaped with only a slight discoloration, I'm still ashamed of them. Although most people don't indicate they notice, *I* notice and this is worse. I'm very disappointed in the pharmaceutical company responsible.

Before approving medicine for anybody, growing children for sure, they should realize what they're doing. This is why I trust Dr Pepper, but I still give my teeth a good brushing, as soon as feasible, after I drink any.

I do wish occasionally, how popping over to the dentist for a few painless sessions, under a magic light, could make my teeth look *better* than normal—like bright and dazzling.

Or a little porcelain cover, resembling a piece of original white *Chicklet* gum, could slip right over them—like a change of socks for your teeth. I'd buy instant *toothy-glamour,* badda-bing—badda-boom! This is what people in Brooklyn, and I guess Hoboken, New Jersey too, say when something happens very fast. Perhaps I *can* have stuff like this done *someday.*

There I go *again* with the daydreaming. I think I'm obsessed with this habit even worse than chocolate.

Getting back to that run-of-the rumor-mill *me,* I'm ahead of the banal-game in *one* area—my complexion. Of course, my coloring can't compete with the level of Vivienne's, but I do okay. My skin has a natural rosy glow. I almost never get a blemish, unless, as mentioned, I drink any tea or battle with my father at the revived Alamo.

I do suffer from the obnoxious smattering of russet-freckles, sprinkling across the bridge of my nose, and along the tops of my cheeks. They set me apart in many aspects, although not in the way I want. My mother says these freckles are *precious,* but I abhor them. The lingering effects of posttraumatic stress from the baby-Blob episode, makes me want to scrape them off.

I'm old enough now to use pancake-makeup, so things aren't as bad. Except *Revlon* and the often disappointing—overpriced cosmetic-ilk—never stop me from hoping I'll find a treatment to fade this disfigurement to whatever beauty I have. Maybe there will also be a magic light for permanent freckle removal someday. Do you think this might be possible in the future?

You do! That's great. I'm doing it as soon as I hear them offering the procedure, no matter the cost. I don't think I've ever told you before, but you make me feel better. You give me hope. Thanks.

There's one inheritance, though, that I never want to disguise. I'm talking about my father's deep dimples. I've got them too. I also received a cleft like his, in the middle of *my* chin, although mine's a slight one. His is much deeper. My grandmother often mentioned how I resemble him when he was young. I guess I sort of see what she means. Yet because of my eyes, we're opposites. By some miracle, my round azure-peepers came from an ancestor somewhere down the line. I'm the only one in the family now that has such large eyes, plus nobody else, other than me, shares this rare color of blue.

After summing up my assets and liabilities, I tell people to take me or leave me.

Now, I'm going to say something to you that I've never told another living being. Very often, it's a hard job to take myself, and I would like to leave me. I can't though. Wherever I journey—just like that goldfish tail—*I* am swimming right along behind me. Still—for some unknown explanation, this is how I'm turning out. What shall I do, other than try and make the best of my lousy situation.

PART 3:

HELLO, DAD

"Don't knock it, because the pay is good."

I remember mentioning before, how my dad doesn't look like a thing like Gene Autry. He's not close by a long shot. Jack Lemmon is more on target. *He* is a ringer for Felix Unger in *The Odd Couple* movie a few years back. I'll now attempt to portray him to you. Doing so won't be easy.

As I start trying to paint a portrait of him with words, you'll soon understand why it's a strange concept to think of my father giving—as he loves to say—"a hoot" about any kind of antique goblets, signature or otherwise.

What's even more out of character, is to envision him waving his pinky in the air, while he drinks imported Tuscan Wine, and synchronizes his dainty sips, with wiping away sentimental tears—evoked by a Neapolitan Violinist. Knowing him, as I do, this facet of his personality goes way over *my* head. I'm willing to try though.

Let me see.

At **5'11",** you really can't say Dad qualifies as short, but his dad stood taller at **6'2".** He isn't thin due to a small potbelly. Yet you could never call him fat. Just like practical *Felix,* he blends into the crowd like an average no-frills kind of fellow. If there *is* a category for an unremarkable neurotic, put my father in the slot.

His 10 o'clock Saturday morning—rain or shine—twice a month trip, to good old Gus the barber, keeps Dad's graying nondescript brown hair cropped to his head. Mom calls it the *whiskbroom* look. In my opinion, Gus gets a bit scissor-happy sometimes, and, when he does, Daddy resembles *Sgt. Orville C. King* in the hilarious movie *No Time for Sergeants.* This look suits him. There's isn't a boot camp in any branch of the service where *he* wouldn't fit right in.

With the exception of still going to the same barbershop—he's not at all, like Grandpa Des once was. I know I told you about his memorable Old Spice, but Dad refuses to use any stuff of this sort, including common aftershave. Taking a fun trip to the drugstore as a child, to buy him a little toiletry gift on his birthday or for Father's Day, could never happen. What *do* you do when he tells you not to bother wasting *his* hard-earned money on useless "smelly items?"

I'll tell you what you do.

At the desperate last minute, you're stupid enough to ask—disregarding *everything* you know about his aversion to grooming-gifts—whether he's forsaken the *Wall Street Journal* for *Gentlemen's Quarterly,* and had some sort of a fragrant epiphany. You *then* mouth along with him, the exact words he'll say to you, "What's wrong with first-rate *Ivory;* the pure soap that floats?"

This surgical attitude of his, leads me to mention my father's penetrating dark brown eyes, probing *eyes* that dissect the environment around him. They display intense frustration due to his habit of engaging in futile efforts to fit perfect matter, into an imperfect world. He'll stay up all night to balance his checkbook, even if the total's only a penny off—in *his* favor.

And referring to that hodgepodge checkbook of my mother's, that sends him off to Gregorian chant-land, it's a sore topic. I guess this accounting proclivity of his, explains why he works for United Cornpone Bank.

Okay, he *is* Treasurer of this dippy bank, but so what. My mother says, "Don't knock it, because the pay is good." She's right. There are times, however, when I wish Dad did have a famous movie star for a relative—a popular one, like his Jack Lemmon counterpart or remarkable, John Wayne.

Here I am again, with the daydreaming.

What a bad habit.

Since there's not very much more to say about my father except that this is the way he goes, I suppose you should meet *Mom.*

PART 4:

LIFE WITH MOTHER **"Don't you worry, *darling*."**

If you're speculating now about my mother's reaction, not only to academic strife within the family structure, but also to every other dysfunctional aspect of being in charge of the Autry household—she handles stuff okay. I bet she has an even tougher hide than good old Boogie's impenetrable posterior.

I think Mom is such a relentless pro at homemaking, because everybody tells her she looks like *Beaver Cleaver's* mother. And although my mother can be less unreasonable to deal with than Dad tends to be, she's still capable of being a regular pain—although she cared enough to tip me off about that charitable Miss Clairol. She's the gal Mom discovered while hunting for a peroxide replacement. She taught her how to become a bombshell blonde. As of my graduation day, her hair's top of the line platinum pale, teased way up, with no visible roots. I'm talking a big *beehive,* here.

Mom does benefit from a tiny waist like mine, except she's not hippy like me; she's a chiseled-willowy. People often call her a, "mature Barbie doll." Daddy gets jealous when any fellow Reptilians at the Bullsnake Lodge pay obvious attention to her. I guess the guys can't help gaping. She *is* attractive *for* her age.

While Dad steams about men admiring his wife, he never shows the emotion. In a way, I think he's proud. However, just like Shelley's ancient TV, he'd blow a fuse for sure if he ever knew what happened on the afternoon Mom stopped at the minimart, to buy several containers of his favorite *unflavored* yogurt. *He* told her to go, since they advertised the junk on sale.

Before she even put the sour stuff in her cart, she spotted pudgy, out of breath Cheap Charlie, tailing her inside. He panted more than usual, while whispering to her about the new bunny costume with *her* name on the cottontail. Furthermore, or should I say *furtherless,* he also said the "getup" pined away next-door—right along with *him.*

My father never worries. If there's one thing we know for sure around here, it's how Mary Autry loves her husband. You can't help noticing this devotion when she uses her cuddly-voice, most often while I box with my sister. Mom gives Daddy those baby-pats on the shoulder while telling him drivel like, "Don't you worry, *darling.* Time is on our side."

I have no idea why, but when he hears mushy junk like this, he'll calm right down. She's been sweet-talking him more than usual, even though I called a truce with my sister. We haven't stepped in the ring for days. If I didn't know better, I'd think she's one of those *Stepford Wives.* I read this scary new book last week, and finished it within an hour. I'm certain a movie will be out soon, concerning *this* recent bestselling thriller.

Given how Mom loves those frilly aprons, the type an "upstairs maid" wears, she is never without one. As a tidy result, visualizing her walking around the house like a stiff Stepford wife—with a domestic lobotomy—would *not* be a stretch of the imagination. On the plus side, buying her a Mother's Day gift is never a problem—or any gift for that matter. I think she has about fifty of these fluffy domestic-girdles—in all shapes, colors, and styles.

Mom's been living in Tillagevale for over twenty years, but still has one of those New England accents. She grew up in urbane Massachusetts, on the beautiful outskirts of Boston. People know she's not a native Texan, especially when she says words like *hahba*—the place where a boat *pahks.* Daddy tells us not to make fun of her because she's, "an adorable innocent from Beantown." We do it anyway. So does he, just ask her. I *know* you can't, but if you *could* talk with her, you'd find out I haven't fabricated one itty-bit.

Now and then, he jokes around, telling her to add the suffix *Jo* after her name, in order to create a southland "Mary-Jo." It gives a more "Texan impression." His aim to help her fit in better, only sets off the famous smoke alarm. She tells him how she doesn't appreciate his, "branding me like livestock," followed by—"Alex, *why* are you so fixated on destroying the dear song about *Mary* being the grand-old-name that existed, long before the fashions came?"

Other than rare occasions like this, I never hear them argue—at least not in front of me.

PART 5:

AUNT ADELE

"Would *they* have loved me?"

My mother's parents died in an auto accident only three weeks after her birth. An intoxicated driver, coming straight at them on the wrong side of the road, caused the fatal crash. A maiden-aunt, by the name of *Adele,* baby-sat for the evening. Keeping her much younger sister's fussy infant long-term never entered her mind, until the knock on her door at midnight.

At first, she acted reluctant to adopt her niece. This strict—and set in her ways dowdy aunt—had to take on the responsibility, if she didn't want the baby placed in an orphanage. No other available relatives existed except Mom's uncle, her father's younger brother, who took off in search of lucrative Alaskan oil many years before the tragedy. While my mother was helpless in her bassinette, nobody could locate him. I guess he's still up there with the caribou. Anyway, I never heard otherwise.

Mom keeps a small picture of her parents, set into an old scrimshaw frame, on top of the dresser in her bedroom. Around any of the holidays, she places this on our fireplace mantle. As a youngster, I'd step on a stool, take the frame off the shelf, and spend several minutes a day observing the strangers in the photo. They looked healthy and full of life.

How did this attractive young couple sound?

Were they like me at all?

Would *they* have loved me?

Every Christmas morning, while growing up, I so much wanted to find a present from them under the tree. I still wish for that connection now. I can't imagine how my mother has no recollection of her parents, but she doesn't. This is her only picture of them.

I never saw a picture of Aunt Adele, so I felt sure she resembled the face on the Old Maid cards. I guess she wasn't a total washout. I won every one of these games that I ever played with Shelley. All of this curiosity makes me luckier than ever that my dad's parents lived so close to me.

Right after her aunt died, my mother turned twenty. She left her a small inheritance, to finish college. For some weird motive, Mom wound up switching from a local junior college in Boston, to Tillagevale University's library science program. She says the idea came to her in a dream, and that's about all. When I ask her if she didn't really have a nightmare, she just laughs. How did she even *know* about the place, when the small town of Tillagevale wasn't even on the map then? Even now, you have a hard time finding it.

Upon arriving, I'm sure she made a lot of adjustments—like going to wild rodeos and stuff. When the university's accounting majors, shared orientation sessions with the library group, she bumped into Dad. The rest, as they say, is encyclopedic history—wrapped up tight in aprons.

Speaking of Mom's *apron* collection, I know *why* she loves them. They represent the personification of the nurturing mother she never knew. She deserves as many of these frumpy-doodads as she wants.

If you think *I'm* turning into some kind of psychoanalyst, you're wrong. Grandma pointed out the real significance of the aprons to me, when I went through a stage of ridiculing my mother for never being without these household-shackles around her waist. All of a television-land-sudden, I no longer addressed my mother by the usual title of *Mommy.* I started calling her, "June Cleaver."

In order to point out how stupid I sounded, Mom and Grandma called me *Beaver* and Vivienne became a ridiculous *Wally.* Of course, my father made a perfect *Ward.* Later on, we all sat down at the kitchen table and laughed over a glass of hot cocoa and some of Mom's great, what else but—backed from scratch molasses cookies.

This is the way of the prairie home front, and forever will be.

I think after reminiscing about this little "Beaver" misunderstanding, I should ask if you're ready for an accounting of—as Ed Sullivan always said—the really *big* show. Since I'm doing great with the honesty aspect, why should I let a few knock-down-drag-outs stop me now?

You want the nitty-gritty, don't you? Dirty laundry flapping on the line is what sells all those tabloids we *both* love to read. So enjoy the juiciest one ever, starting now.

Chapter 6

Combat Zone

PART 1:

ALLEMANDE LEFT — "*He* didn't."

You must realize by now that the town of Tillagevale won't ever be my favorite place to languish. Since experiencing the "boinging" on the Wingding Theatre seat, this girl's been steadfast to embark on an exciting career in Journalism, *before* engaging in *any* kind of higher education—other than what life's experience has to offer.

For clarification, I'm not saying I'll never attend college, as in forever and no way, or even if you bribe me with a million dollars. I only want postponement for now. Owing to this growing Autry tradition how the moment Tillagevale High spits you out, Tillagevale University sucks you right back into the fold, I'm finding my goal difficult. Sometimes I feel a little bad about this, not that I really should.

As academics turns out, I'm Daddy's last hope for continuing the Alma Mater he holds so dear. You should've seen the expression on his face during Thanksgiving dinner last year. He looked like the turkey came back to life and gobbled at him or something, when airhead Vivienne told him how the moment she turns eighteen, *she* is joining the Peace Corps. She plans on teaching *Pygmies* in the jungle how to square dance.

Nothing could have been more priceless than witnessing my father's mouth drop open from shock. He looked as if *Mount Vesuvius* had just re-erupted in our dining room, while all of this slimy, gushed-up cranberry-walnut stuffing, resembling Pompeii lava, poured down the front of his favorite yellow-plaid lumberjack shirt.

Oh, please do *not* let me forget my mother's overwhelmed look concerning the almost impossible removal of the gross stains on her latest wheedling-project. That luxurious crème colored wall-to-wall carpet turned into rubbish before any of her friends could even admire her stylish new decor. Daddy finally agreed to buy it two weeks before. He paid full price, because she told him that he never had to buy her another anniversary gift, of any kind in the future, even if they made it to the fiftieth. As a guilty and later on deprived result, she felt helpless about the damage.

She wanted that impractical in vogue light color. *He* didn't. Now she could only display a destroyed marital feather in her depleted cap, and couldn't ask her husband about calling in an expensive cleaning service. He'd just make everything worse by doing the chore himself or put the task on the "honey do" list, which never gets read. So she just stared at the messed up carpet and cried while my father acted more upset about the damaged shirt. The one she calls, "that Johnny Appleseed reject."

Let's twirl back to square dancing in the bush. My sister just couldn't contain her excitement over reading an article in *National Geographic* about the extraordinary agility of *Rain Forest Pygmies.* Due to this awesome aspect of native skill, as a patriotic service via the Peace Corps, she plans on designing an exclusive line of Lilliputian cowboy hats and batons—*after* she starts her dancing school in the *Belgian Congo.* A happy future of instructing these innocent tribesmen is her *only* aim in life.

What a quirk of fate for Daddy. He's the one who *forced* her to read National Geographic in the first place. The commotion started last year, when he flipped and tore up her entire *Soap Opera Digest* collection—subsequent to signing her dismal report card. Her history teacher demanded he stop by one afternoon so she could show him the essay his daughter wrote about *Helen of Troy.* It read that Helen's face *sank* a thousand ships after her mean and poisonous pet snake bit her gorgeous boyfriend, *Marco Polo.*

See what I mean.

With astounding predictability, while we sat alone at the dinner table, Vivienne exploded *worse* than Pompeii—right after Dad ran upstairs to shower and change his shirt. We also heard Mom rummaging down in the basement, in frantic search of a potent cleaning emulsion.

On this regurgitated holiday afternoon, my sister didn't appreciate the hysterical reaction I could no longer contain concerning her "Pygmy" plans. What else could she expect of me, other than my being in a prostrate fit of uncontrollable laughter, while rolling underneath the dining room table—further adding to the already damaged carpet.

Gee—during chokes of hilarity, I only expressed interest in her career choice by asking if she planned to show these Pygmies how to *allemande left.* Of course, they must do this while twirling their partners—along with their flaming batons.

After they master this part of the act, she must train them to throw these tiny burning sticks up into the air. The biggest challenge she faces, will be having the Pygmies catch the fiery things without burning their hands—while they swing their partners to *allemande right* at the same time.

Now I ask you, what's so bad about this choreographic concept? The moves sound awesome to me. She could take an act like this to Broadway. This flattering view of her potential success just caused Vivienne to claim I'm not *supportive* of her. I say she doesn't appreciate me. How could I ever be a better sister than I already am?

You say that you can think of a few ways.

Well—try living with her, then get back to me.

PART 2:

SHOW AND SHOCK

"Relax—no harm done."

Now that you understand what my family situation is all about, let's get back to the topic of my *own* college rebellion. Knowing me, as you do by this time, you realize I'm humble to the point of being stoic. The plain truth is, in the area of literary prowess, *I'm* outstanding. There's no other way to say it, and Tillagevale U isn't the place to cultivate my large amount of natural talent.

My parents took me in for some kind of intellect testing when I was four. They worried about my being below average. I didn't act like other kids. I marched to an off-key drummer that only I heard. To their surprise, Dr. Clayton Mendel, our trusted family physician said, "She's bored out of her gourd." He told them my **IQ** of **150** verified my need for "special educational consideration." He advised them to send me to school a year in advance. However, his astute observation wasn't banking on the likes of Miss Harriet Heller.

I did prove the dear doctor right though, with wisdom way beyond my years, when justice prevailed and I resolved the false teeth rumor. What a stroke of genius, getting an emergency pass to the bathroom right before the regular Wednesday afternoon *Show and Tell* session. I had already hidden those grotesque mechanical *Godzilla* teeth in my sweater pocket, along with a small packet of ketchup from the lunchroom.

My jaws *are* bigger than big, so the monster-sized choppers fit me perfect. After I smeared the slippery red condiment over them, they slipped right into my mouth and didn't taste bad either. I pulled off my preparation for the fiendish plot, thanks to the privacy of the toilet stall. When my turn came, as soon as I stood in front of the class, I switched on the chatter-sound as loud as it could go.

Next, jutting my chin forward, I wrenched the "bloody" artificial teeth out of their hiding place. The ketchup, having mixed with a pint of saliva, poured out of my mouth and spewed all over the classroom like a bursting dam of anemic blood.

Miss Heller sat at her desk right behind me, so she, as usual, had no true idea of the situation. But she caught on fast when the screams started and she saw kids fainting one by one, like a stack of dominos in an earthquake. This astounding sight made carnage from the recent circus episode look like nothing more than a childish game of hide-and-seek.

Relax—no harm done. Mrs. Bulwark, the poor stressed-out school nurse, kept an unprecedented supply of smelling salts up in the infirmary. Boy, oh boy, she used all of her hoard *that* day.

She continued this precautionary stockpiling practice until the following month, when she left for an enforced early retirement. The whole building whispered about the reliable nurse's sudden strange behavior. Mr. Drench paid a visit to the infirmary, late one afternoon, and found her alone. She rested on her own emergency stretcher, while staring at the ceiling and talking about *kangaroos.*

I'll be the first to admit how, for her, solitude on the job didn't exist. You'd swear the crowed infirmary gave out free toys to kids on a daily basis. That day, however, school let out early. When he bent down to talk with her, she grabbed his necktie and yanked the thing with the fury of a dog, having its bone snatched from its mouth. She ignored how his face turned blue, as she begged him to transport her to any mental hospital he could locate in the outback of *Australia.*

What a baffling tragedy, until I overheard Mr. Drench telling teachers how "dear Bettina" suffered from "shell shock." The affliction sounded like a terrible curse, where harmless seashells could drive a person to the bottom of the world. I thought about what would happen to her if *she* ever sits next to Zorro. Not enough kangaroos or those cute koalas *Down Under* could ever help the tragic thing—*then.*

All those long scholastic years ago, moved at the pace of a snail with an exceptional lack of ambition until my compulsory education ended. At still sixteen, I relished being the youngest graduate in the bunch. This achievement alone, ordains me the intellectual sibling. Vivienne did earn her famous nickname of *Ditzy* without doing much hard work. The Pygmy Follies, along with that rich man playing second fiddle to a camel at the Pearly Gates, and the human torpedo named Helen of Troy, are only a few small examples. Please understand how on the totem pole of intelligence, Vivienne is the stake that anchors it under the ground.

I'll now return to my most recent bout with academic dilemmas.

While high school graduation waited around the corner, *Lady Luck* headed to my side of the street. She knew I needed a worthwhile career-promoting job *fast.* So wonders of wonders, in the middle of last June—just a scant four days before donning my cap and gown, a miracle occurred. The Tillagevale Gazette offered me a paid position as a trainee in their *Obituary Section.*

Okay, I'll admit what really happened. I *did* take the bus downtown to fill out the tedious application. The job's not what you'd ever call *glamorous,* but it will give me a definite head start. I think *Lois Lane* got *her* chance in investigative reporting this way. Or was *Jimmy Olsen* the one?

At this melodramatic stage, without a moment of pause, candor obliges me to state how I do deserve my title of *Drama Queen.* Everybody knows I'm the sole person in the world who's perfected the intricate art of whining down to an absolute science. Not even my protégé, Vivienne, beats me in circumstances like this—although she comes close. Even so, my *Oscar* caliber fits of begging and pleading, at least twenty-times a day, could not get Daddy to waiver and give me permission to take this job.

What's the big deal about directing me toward the obituaries?

PART 3:

LIVE WIRES

"*You* are what *they* deserve."

Earlier on, I mentioned snippets about commencement in relation to Pun Geyser. Now I'd like to explain in depth how the actual volatile events of the momentous afternoon, eventually wound up detonating my way to New York.

Preparing for this graduation day exhausted me. I didn't have a moment to spare. With the threat of the newspaper withdrawing the desirable job offer, if I didn't accept soon, that pressure cooker with its wobbling gauge—also known as my life—would explode worse than when I used the one kept in the kitchen. I wanted to surprise my mother with a delicious dinner. I cooked corned beef and cabbage in the thing. Tillagevale's water is so full of chlorine that I used seltzer instead.

Yeah, it *was* a big, bad mess, but even after taking hours to clean it up, I couldn't convince my father concerning this potential journalism job—no matter how much I tried. I didn't need the momentum of my tireless campaign interrupted by his taking that long trip out of town to the Mayo Clinic. He had to suffer through all those painful tests, with live wires poking out of his head, just so their big-shot neurologist could tell my parents that Dad's recent excruciating pain resulted from "severe idiopathic migraines."

Such medical-gobbledygook scared the life out of my mother. She grabbed the hospital's telephone without even asking them for permission, so she could call me. When I first heard her say he had something called *idiopathic,* I thought she said, "idiot-pathic" so how could I even be one-bit shocked. After all, for the past few weeks, he sure acted like one. Then, she contacted Dr. Mendel for a translation.

He told her that in simple English the medical term of "idiopathic" means, "mysterious origin." She wasn't to worry. He heard directly from the clinic that her husband tested in better general physical condition than a hippopotamus.

Placing clinical terms back on the examining table, I ask you now, how did *my* father ever come down with this kind of wacky symptom in a laidback place like Tillagevale? Sure is a puzzle to me.

Due to his baffling new manifestation, worsening more than ever on his daughter's long-anticipated commencement day, all hell broke loose. During the three-hour outdoor procedure, under the roasting sun, he had to sit in a rented portable wheelchair.

When Armadillo Family Pharmacy dropped the necessary transportation off the night before, this chair festered like a busy outhouse. Somebody tried masking the strong odor with pine disinfectant before delivery. Believe me the combination of pee and pine does *not* work in your olfactory favor. "Get that damn thing out of here," Dad said, while he turned green. However, with no more wheelchairs in stock, he couldn't see me graduate without one.

Mom took toxic matters into her own hands. She wore rubber gloves, as well as the mask my father uses to strip furniture, and wiped down the health hazard with rags saturated in rubbing alcohol. Her brave attempt only made the stinking situation worse, and after the rolling health violation sat outside in the **100-degree** heat the next day, along with my father, Mrs. Bulwark's smelling salts sure would have come in handy.

Right before we loaded the wheelchair into the car, my father said he needed a new *bridge* from biting so many bullets. That's pretty strange, huh. Why did he need *any* kind of bridge to cross when my high school is only a mile from the house, without a drop of water in sight? Plus—he couldn't even drive due to his blinding headaches. And *I* never saw any bullets in *his* mouth, unless they masqueraded as *Jimmy Dean* sausages.

After we all managed to arrive at the ceremony without puking, he was in exile a few feet away from us in the jalopy wheelchair. Mom parked it right next to his immense red metal cooler with the big ***Coca-Cola*** logo that also read ***Delicious and Refreshing.*** The one he uses for fishing trips.

On this jaunt, however, the thing filled up to the rim with huge gauze icepacks smelling of ripe trout. Dad had to bend down often during the ceremony, in order to replenish the soaked bunch of those once frozen *fishy* ice cubes, melting on his hot and throbbing head. These gauze bundles kept thawing, causing water to drip down his cheeks. As a wet consequence, he overheard people buzzing like busy bumblebees throughout the large crowd saying how Alex Autry, "that tough banker with the skin of a leathery alligator," just could not stop crying from sentiment over his daughter's graduation.

There I sat, along with my sweaty pride, on the outdoor platform—under that sun's blistering rays—in front of my peers, my family, and any of my so-called *friends.* When he jumped up right before the ceremony concluded, and flung his current icepack to the ground, everybody in the assembly, including me, thought he intended to take photos with the fabulous new slide camera he bragged about—from the moment of arrival.

Instead—he made a tight fist with both of his dripping hands. Next, in unison, he thrust these pulsating clenches forward. And in a clear act, reminiscent of a boxer's defiance, he proclaimed to all:

Ginger—I quit!

I no longer give a hoot about the paltry college scholarship this dysfunctional high school just awarded you. I also no longer care whether or not you go to college at all. Anyway, they would probably throw you out within the first semester for destroying the campus.

Leave the stage right now, and go work your kiester off for that *libertarian-rag,* calling itself The Tillagevale Gazette. *You* are what *they* deserve. Every person in town knows how they are the *only* Chamber of Commerce member crying poor, and reneging at the last minute *every* year, about supporting United Cornpone Bank's golf symposium every summer. For this very cheap *raison d'être,* we are forced to carry out our annual tournament at those debasing *public* courses.

After his embarrassing outburst, Mom stood up too. She said, "Please excuse my husband's *French,* but the word *is* in the American dictionary." With everybody staring in shocked silence, she took Dad by the collar of his soaking wet shirt and shoved him back into the wheelchair using a move *Wonder Woman* would love to copy.

With a look of determination on her perspiring face, reminiscent of Custer at his last stand, she made a mad dash in her best two-inch heels—heading straight for their car. My father held his arms down, outside of the wheelchair, almost like he tried putting on the breaks. He looked terrified while she pushed the rickety-thing at lightening speed, over that rocky and bumpy turf.

She managed to get home, even though he kept hollering out of the window about *red journalism.* My mother ran in the house to call our doctor's private hotline number while in a state of hysteria herself.

My father refused to get out of the car, unless she put him in his wheelchair. He kept growling and dribbling all over the dashboard and acting like a rabid Rottweiler, with frightening bubbles blowing out of its frothy mouth. Since everything happened on a Sunday, the county dogcatcher went duck hunting. Otherwise, he'd haul him off to get those painful shots, ensuring that Dad wouldn't drink all of the water in the local reservoir and howl at the moon.

I'd like to add here that this entire graduation fiasco is only a small sample of the weird things that happen to my father, without any obvious cause, and qualifies as a someday book too. I have plenty of writing material for the future, if I can survive until then.

Of course, competent Dr. Mendel arrived in a flash along with his little black bag—loaded with the stock medical gadgets—including his usual cold to the touch stethoscope. He suspected a mild case of heatstroke.

The physician also cared enough to help Mom get spaced-out-Dad from the car, and put him back into the abused wheelchair. I bet he gave himself a hernia to treat, from lifting my father's dead weight, now slumped in this heavy contraption. Somehow, he single-handedly pulled that weight way up those steep steps to the front porch. As soon as he pushed the load into the living room, the good huffing-and-puffing doctor collapsed on the couch.

After a few minutes of sitting down, the man was still breathless with a face as red as a ripe tomato. He placed poor Daddy on strict bed rest for the next two weeks. In a manner reminiscent of endearing *Dr. Steve Hardy,* on Mom's venerated soap opera, *General Hospital,* he reassured her concerning the excellent prognosis of her husband.

When my mother told him she had more aches and pains from this crisis with my father, than she did from running the Boston Marathon, he said she needed help. He would send over a hefty home attendant right away who sported prominent whiskers.

Her name was Hildagard.

Only *she* could wrench Daddy from his security wheels.

Only *she* could lift my father out of this, by now, dented chunk of smelly scrap metal. For beefy Hilda, his heavy, rigid body felt as light as a feather.

Acting like a *Luftwaffe* tank, Hilda also carried him upstairs and around the bend, down the long hallway—right into my parent's bedroom. And, once there, she used her body like a slingshot. He became one of those convenient Azimuth Circle cul-de-sac pebbles, when she flung him straight onto the bed.

She also came every day to give him a *thorough* sponge bath, and pour talcum powder in areas he never knew he had. When she spoon-fed him maple-flavored Farina cereal, she let him play *airplane* so he would open his mouth.

By some huge miracle, my father made a speedy recovery. My mother, though, in her unbelievable wisdom, keeps a supply of those migraine pills in the medicine cabinet, because, after all—you do *never* know

PART 4:

PASS THE CAP

"Do *you* know about that?"

Eight frustrating months after this June graduation last year, and Dad's meltdown under the blazing Texas sun, I completed the almost impossible task of programming Shelley. She turned out to be tougher than those steaks my father barbecues. Why do you think she acted so reluctant to share her new life with me?

I had to subject her to every strategy in my personal handbook of brainwashing techniques. I'm proud to say that the size of this instruction manual makes a thick Manhattan telephone directory resemble a postage stamp.

Months of pain awaited me, because of everything *I* had to suffer, until her bombardment ended in February. Cease and desist time arrived, when she agreed to convince *compassionate* Uncle Alex to do her a tremendous *favor,* by allowing *me* to become her *roommate* in New York.

All the exhausting same, at last I accomplished this admirable feat and pulled off the rest with ease. Just like me, my father has only one sibling to contend with and this is Aunt Sharon, a.k.a. Shelley's mother. Now this really could have been a definite liability, on the widespread plus-or-minus persuasion-scale of life.

Unlike me, however, when *his* baby sister bats her eyes, my father melts like the fat bar of butter that Mom left sitting on a hot stove when a telephone call from her best friend distracted her. He always says how Fiona Natter represents the, "height of a busybody." I never understood how a person needed to be of a certain size in order to stab somebody in the back. Do *you* know about that?

Anyway, while butter coated the stove, she told Mom about a *friend,* their exact age of forty-five at the time, with two children in college.

The "poor thing" just found out she's having triplets resulting from a romantic vacation with her husband. This *foolish* woman *succumbed* to an expensive hotel in Hawaii, complete with a luau. The entire extravagant trip attempted to save their rocky marriage, which the stork had now turned into a granite quarry.

My mother reminded Fiona about Madam President and that Hawaiian *Adonis,* Don Ho, who corrupted this once responsible woman. Later, they heard she gave birth to a *bouncing* baby boy whose father remains a mystery, but the kid played the ukulele and sang "Tiny Bubbles" before he could even talk.

The situation they *discussed* just exemplified another sad lesson learned, concerning the salacious aspect of *any* type of Aloha-intimacy. The long and distracting chat ended with a vow they'd *both* shun vacationing in Hawaii, as you would a leprosy camp.

I guess the juicy aspects of their conversation led to my own sidetracking, so now I'll deposit *poi* on a plate for another day and continue explaining all the difficulties concerning my cousin becoming an escape-hatch from Tillagevale

Shelley's my father's favorite niece, only since there aren't any other ones to compare her with. He couldn't dispute how she's the responsible *marital-age* of twenty-six and a definite bonus in getting his approval.

Please don't mention this sensitive point when she's around. *I* only gave her my opinion regarding the fortune she spent on those six hideous bridal-attendant dresses, especially that tacky bright-orange ball gown. The stiff linen-thing crumpled like a concertina—the moment she slipped the waste of money over her head.

What's so wrong with saying, "Always a bridesmaid, never a bride?" Gosh, it's just an old saying and stuff. You'd think the dermatologist notified her she had a terminal case of acne and he knew a good attorney to put her affairs in order.

At any defensive rate, continuing with the awesome Shelley perks, she's also an employed *librarian* with an established "residence" in New York. Her place sits way up in the boonies of the city but it still counts. She wound up there from the start. *The Bronx Public Library* offered her the job.

Even expert, practical planning me, couldn't set up collateral any better than *this,* concerning my father. Her list of exemplary qualifications became more relevant than ever, when I told him how she's *treasurer* for her local chapter of *The Young Republicans.* As a positive result, when these superb character references boxed him in, he had no other choice than to give his vital, albeit halfhearted permission.

In anticipation of this inevitable outcome, my high-end, white Samsonite luggage ensemble waited packed and ready for my eager hands. I hid it months before, wrapped tight and tucked away in my secret nook in the basement of 13 Azimuth Circle, where those Texas-sized palmetto bugs could never hitch a ride.

This classy-set includes a deluxe cosmetic carrier with battery-operated lights surrounding a large magnifying mirror, and holds an entire department store of beauty supplies. Like me, this luggage had amazing patience while waiting for Dad's eventual acquiescence to his no-win dilemma.

On the antsy contrary, the *impatient* one-way, prepaid *Greyhound* bus ticket—straining at its leash in my wallet—could not wait for its chance to take off and deliver me to Shelley's downtrodden lobby. I had also arranged to send those two huge moving-cartons to her address by freight, when the exact day came.

In any transportable case—getting back to the bus part—in reality, no one could call that old dog "quick." The overworked Greyhound made every hole-in-the-wall stop to pick up even more scruffy passengers. I sat for five tortuous days next to a fat guy who wore a huge white tee shirt, smeared with an assorted menu of stains, along with a bold black advertisement promoting, "Lose the Flab. Live Longer."

No way could I change my seat. Who'd ever switch with me, and there weren't any empty ones available to confiscate. Let's say this individual had a definite air about him. He perspired from the moment he sat down.

To make profuse matters worse, he ate nothing except olive oil, infused with huge chunks of garlic. He carried the stuff in a tall thermos, and poured this foul concoction over endless chunks of assorted stale bread he grabbed from a large paper bag—the kind of bread old ladies feed to squirrels in the park.

Each of the countless times I tried handing this health-risk a mint he'd tell me, "Don't you see I'm on a diet?" followed by a king-sized fart. He spread such a pernicious odor throughout the bus, the passengers kept complaining about not having overhead oxygen masks. That is, until the driver went ballistic and pulled off the highway.

Who could ever anticipate how a professional Greyhound Transport employee would ever stand in front of the vehicle and gesticulate with his hands about strangling everybody. He also bellowed for the riders to get off the bus, explaining how he didn't have a license to pilot any *jetliner.* And, he further roared, if *we*, the paying passengers, weren't so "damn cheap in the first place," we'd all be *on* one.

The driver cooled off after five minutes of ranting, when he gave us the offer we couldn't refuse. He handed his cavernous cap, emblazoned with the famous racing dog logo, to the rider who sat in the first seat—way up in the front of the huge, packed bus—telling her to pass it around without missing *anybody.* He put a major emphasis on the "body" part of this word.

This driver's likeness to an individual to whom one must kowtow, under penalty of disappearing on a trip to nowhere, popped right out of the big screen as he ordered us to fill the gross, sweat-stained thing with enough money for his meals—including beverages and snacks—for the duration of his shift. He looked and sounded like Marlon Brando in *The Godfather* movie. I saw this blockbuster at the Wingding, the day before I split Tillagevale.

I'm sure the great cop, *Lieutenant Columbo,* could prove this driver guilty of "double indemnity." I bet Greyhound picks up the tab for these necessities, while an employee is driving *their* bus on the job. Unlike the actor Peter Faulk or the characters on the hit show, I did not obtain witness protection in the form of a fictitious television series. The captive group may as well have stared into the deep barrel of a gun, while we looked down into the menacing *cap.*

While we gave to him with one reluctant hand, he took from the petrified other. He skulked around the bus while he waved around a big plastic cup advertising *Sands Casino and Hotel,* making it very plain he required, "moolah to spare." With a sneer so crooked, Novocain poured out of his mouth, he told the hostages how our "future generosity" aided his anticipatory trip to *Vegas.* With a long walk looming on the bunion-interstate, we had no choice other than to *contribute.*

At the conclusion of the threatening travel days, I had no complaints about the ten bucks fellow passengers got out of me. I had finagled myself, after all of the cumulative torture, to what former Madam President called, "The Big Kahuna."

Against all odds—including *Don Vito Corleone*—I arrived alive to New York.

Yes!

PART 5:

NEW YORK MINUTES

"Well—almost never."

I found out quick that *wild* is the word for New York. There's some sort of battle going on every minute. No provocation is necessary to meet your opponents. You can count on them bumping into you. The popular euphemism for New York City is, "The Big Apple" and means you must learn how to tackle and play the local game or they'll soon slice you up for my famous Jack La Lanne exercise pie.

After playing the game here on a daily basis, I know the score. Doing temporary office work, throughout the entire City of New York, places me in demanding situations. Traveling to various jobs every weekday never rattles me. You get staying power, once you've milked a goat with a terrible affliction like Saint Vitas dance.

I'm forever hoping that one of these days the agency I work for will send me to a place like *Newsweek.* And, while I'm there, a great by-line will unravel and fall into my lap like the typewriter ribbon, I'll soon be attempting to change. Don't smirk. It *can* happen, with both that future by-line *and* having eventual success with changing the ribbon. Besides, putting my high hopes of fame aside, office-hopscotch gives you a cool way to meet interesting people.

Yes, I'm talking about guys. My job had this real cute one sitting there the other day, working the teletype machine, and he looked exactly like . . .

Do you know if Troy Donohue has a twin brother?

Love-connections aside, at least I have great job security. No matter what or where—there's no other temp around daring to outdo this *Kelly Girl* on a typewriter. I'm a lightening **90**-words-per-minute, and never need the *White*Out* goop.

Well—almost never. Although I *do* carry a bottle around, in case of an emergency.

I looked into learning shorthand once. You make more money when you're in the stenography-pool, as well as the typing-pool. I checked out both the *Pitman* and the *Gregg* steno-methods. Although I am a genius, I failed to catch on to either of them. My mind kept drifting around the night school classes. I passed by a narrow margin. Thank goodness, stenography wasn't part of Mrs. Hazard's syllabus.

While I tried learning these *hieroglyphics,* which are supposed to correspond with the English language, I thought that I was doodling from boredom. I'd imagine how my stenography books illustrated those psychological tests, where you decipher squiggly-pictures and tell the shrink what you *think* they represent.

Now if I ever tell a psychiatrist, one like Elmer to be specific, what the symbols for the word "exnihitonihilfit" represent—in Pitman *or* Gregg—pick me out a get-well card. Just imagine Dr. Fudd trying to pronounce this word in the first place. They require shorthand students to practice with this mouthful. Any idea what the word means?

Well—according to Webster, the dictionary translation states, "You cannot make something out of nothing." If this doesn't sum up shorthand, what does?

Other than failure to master glyphs, my main snag, since arriving here in New York, is the *pad.* I stagger out of bed every weekend, often while still dark, to get an early jump on finding a decent place to call my own. It's just me against the competitive world of realty. The salary I get here in Manhattan doubles what I earned at the stingy Gazette. If *The Fates* allow, I can pay for my own place. Come hell or high water, I won't quit until I do.

But, because there's never a clear choice between the two, with *water* constantly drowning *hell,* I stagnate and do nothing, other than *thinking* about doing *something.*

Has this quagmire ever happened to you?

PART 6:

MR. PIG

"She gives me the shivers."

The other night, Shelley scooted around in an unusual rush before she bolted out of her unfortunate Bronx hole. She made an impulsive decision, after her regular Friday evening Yoga class, to attend a week's retreat at some kind of austere ashram. The place is somewhat distant, but still accessible, in Northeastern Pennsylvania's Pocono Mountains.

A bunch of her fellow *Yogis* had rented a van, and they had one seat left to ascend the summit. Before this offer, she was planning to "try and relax by staying home" for her scheduled vacation week. I have no idea *why* she changed her mind at the last minute. Do *you* know of a good reason?

A *million* of them, you say. What could they be? But since there's no chance to list them, and how could I read them all in this lifetime, I'll just get back to her impulsive vacation planning, as well as her never-ending habit of making hasty decisions. This time, her last minute swap of The Bronx, for mountain climbing, gives me refreshing privacy for seven-whole-days. The unanticipated trip is just more evidence how she's totally flipped, even surpassing Miss Fairweather and her pal, Timothy.

The proof is, I've been noticing over the past few weeks the way that Shelley talks to herself—more than she does to the cats—and she babbles to them a mile a minute. I talk to myself too, when there's nobody else around to annoy. But now, she's answering herself back. She looks in the mirror, and argues with that enraged image reflecting back at her. Some awful unilateral tussles go on in front of her dresser. *She* gives me the shivers.

Within the past few days, I've been imagining how she might be one of those insane relatives who the author *Edgar Allan Poe* shackles in chains. His plot keeps her secured and hidden in the ancestral mansion's windowless tower.

The situation is always goose-bump-eerie, when plaintive-wails persistently echo throughout the manor's tapestry-laden dark hallways. The recent bewildered guest can't figure out where those chilling moans come from and is now on a hunt for the wailer. He shakes from nerves while carrying that flickering candle, which will soon topple and cause said tapestries to catch fire, burning the entire place down to the ground.

In a way, I'm like that perplexed guest—wandering around like a lost soul in Poe's manor hallways. I'm also in the dark about *my* cousin's sudden, outlandish new habits. The worst behavioral change though, is how she's become obsessed with primitive grunting noises, interspersed with gravelly snorts. We have frightening business going on when Shelley makes hog-like sounds, since she already looks like a carbon copy of *Mr. Pig.*

Do *you* know Mr. Pig? If not, he's the symbol for *Piggly Wiggly* supermarkets. Back home in Tillagevale, there are at least four of these Piggly Wiggly places. Everybody there knows this cartoon depiction of a flat-nosed, chubby-cheeked pig with a goofy round face. He smiles on billboards, all over Texas. This chain of grocery stores is most popular in southern areas of the **USA,** and they use the little guy as an advertising gimmick.

At this hog-like point, since you're my friend, I'm cautioning you not to ever remind Shelley about her famous "porky-double". Last week *I* lost my last scrap of patience, along with an entire carton of orange juice, after she drank the whole thing and claimed an innocent *oversight.*

Oh really now, since *when* does *she* buy classy juice like *Tropicana?*

The answer happens to be *never.*

The empty juice carton made me so furious that I pasted a huge poster of Mr. Pig on the bathroom mirror, before Shelley went in to slather on her makeup. I'll tell you right now, since the past three months I've lived here, this is the closest I ever came toward bouncing back to the Greyhound terminal.

Despite all the problems she causes me, there's no need now to worry about Shelley for the coming week. Also lucky for me, she is, right this minute, practicing "non-violent resistance" while meditating with gaunt *Mahatma Gandhi* clones on a foggy mountaintop. Disrupting her beauty sleep *this* Sunday morning is a problem for them, not for me.

I'll confess here, that my cousin is correct when she complains about my hairdryer sounding like a screechy cement mixer, but I have no plans to stop laying the foundation. I'm not buying another one, and she has hers well out of sight

So she thinks.

I, however, know where to look.

When she's not around, I help myself to it. Hers has a diffuser attachment and gives my hair wonderful body. She really needs to buy a new one too, because if you put the red-hot doohickey down, even for a second, it hops all over the vanity.

Despite mutual unruly technology in the grooming area, I need to make a good impression every day. She has a tendency to be quick-tempered, with regard to my extensive beauty regimen. And on the weekends, "quick-tempered" turns into savage warfare.

I don't let this kind of stuff get to me. In general, Shelley takes a lot longer than *I* do to put on a public-face every morning—owing to her regrettable *oink-oink* mascot plight, and all.

Poor little piglet.

PART 7:

CHOCK FULL "*She* wasn't an original blonde either."

Getting up with a still visible moon on weekends, in order to accomplish this apartment hunting, sure gets me depressed. To help make such early rising tolerable, I treat myself to a delicious Sunday breakfast at this fabulous coffee shop chain known as *Chock Full o' Nuts.*

Without much effort, you'll find these "Chock Full" places all over New York City.

Hiking up my skirt, even the mini-kind, while crossing my legs to pose on one of their high counter stools, makes me look ever so sophisticated. Hollywood discovered a famous actress somewhere, while she did this counter posture. I don't recall her name. Wait, I remember now. Lana Turner is the one! *She* wasn't an original blonde either.

I never worry though. This search for a future superstar could still happen to me someday soon. Besides, I enjoy watching the waitresses at Chock Full scurry around, while they wear their hairnet-hats. These women carry clear glass Pyrex-pots, filled to the brim with steaming coffee, and it's a dangerous job.

If you're wise, and take my advice to go there, be sure to try their famous cream cheese sandwich made with special date-nut bread. They're fantastic. In yummy addition, if, like me, you enjoy good donuts, they bake a great variety. The best one is cinnamon. I ate two of them, in addition to the cream cheese sandwich. I needed fuel for the long day ahead.

I wound up spending the entire morning traipsing my feet off on the Eastside of the city. As an excruciating result, of this fruitless excursion into territory of the affluent, the newest huge blister on the back of my ankle cries out for me to give *you* the benefit of my painful experience.

Please remember this. If you *ever* read about any "cheap" uptown rentals near the *Guggenheim Museum,* these are blatant figments of a realtor's imagination, no matter *what* the conflicting advertisements may imply.

The necessary background information is now complete. Well, as complete as I'm able to accomplish under pressure to finish stuff and still get some sleep. Regardless of how exhausted I feel, I finally sorted through all of those handwritten notes. With the usual help of Dr Pepper, along with a jumbo bag of *Lay's* potato chips, and—since I never eat "just one," I will, without further stalling, divulge the shattering circumstances of today.

I'll switch my narrative into the format of official entries, informing you verbatim on any current events, starting with what went on with me since early this morning. I'll continue by following up with what goes on tomorrow and every day thereafter, as long as the situation continues.

I'll also include any more frightening new **SOS** bleeps coming my way, including those looming whitecaps, so intent on sinking me.

Here we go.

Be prepared.

My Ship of Life is about to hit that paranormal storm.

Do you have *your* life preserver handy?

Chapter 7

THE DAILY ENTRIES
SUNDAY NIGHT, MAY 28TH

Journal *and* reader:

Time is **11 PM.** Before I begin these **Chapter** 7 entries, please know how everything in this binder thus far—including the following sensitive information—is top secret, and also true. At least, I *think* everything's true. The way things are going lately, I'm beginning to have my doubts.

Also, please remember that I'm a new writer you've just discovered—and a friend you never knew existed before. Right now, I reside inside the past. I don't know where I'll be when you read this.

You are about to become a tangible part of my life, as I cope with it now. Come along with me as these astounding events unfold in the year of:

1972

Events of 5/28/72

ENTRY 1:

SOUPY AND WHITE FANG "It's impossible!"

The caloric donut-adrenalin pumping me up this morning—in anticipation of finding my dream place to live—took its own hike. Having to tear down the long block, toward the cross-town bus stop on **86th Street and First Avenue** exhausted me and aggravated my backache.

Wearing those impractical new boots, with the narrow high heels, didn't help hunting matters. If you ever have a perverse need to end everything, I recommend participating in the wild goose chase—also known as "searching for an apartment in Manhattan."

When I saw my bus coming in the distance, the simple exertion of sprinting to catch it sent me spiraling inside a funnel—with a vast array of city sights, smells, and sounds amplifying around me. How I squashed into the crowded bus at all was a fluke, and spotting an empty seat was a one-in-a-million occurrence. The dizziness I felt made me nauseous. I lunged toward this seat, and landed much faster than any baseball team shortstop ever could.

Getting a chance to sit down and close my eyes helped the belching. Hanging on to the second cinnamon donut got mighty iffy. I feared my shoulder bag was about to serve a dual-purpose. As the bus started moving, I made an anxious wish for a calmer stomach, as well as a soon to be valid real estate offer on the Westside, when out of nowhere I heard, "Hot digity, it's Ginger baby!"

My heart stopped beating while this—sorry to say—familiar voice rumbled like seismic activity inside my eardrums. No way could that *be* the singsong-sound of Tillagevale's most infamous nerd, *Bertrand A. Norman.* It's impossible! *He* is incapable of plaguing me, or anybody else, ever again. And the likelihood of his current appearance on New York

City public transportation was more out there than *Soupy Sales* boarding the bus with *White Fang* and throwing pies at everybody.

Turning to check the person sitting right next to me, I almost passed out, before I choked out, *"Bertie* is it really *you?"*

The extreme shock of seeing him caused me to tremble like a leaf, desperate to hang on to its branch during a tsunami. My once steady knees, attached to my famous tree trunk thighs, knocked together and whittled away with the gusto of an avaricious woodpecker. As my entire being went awash in this tempestuous *Arbor Day* scenario, something crucial occurred to me.

I forgot how to swim.

Events of 5/28/72

ENTRY 2:

NIGHTMARE LANE

"Oh heavens, heavens me!"

Not too many hours prior to turning into a tree, and drowning on the tsunami-bus this morning, Vivienne made a frantic sunrise phone call to me. How weird, because she never gets up so early on the weekends. Why she knew I was already awake is a real mystery. I'm famous for sleeping until noon—when I can get away with the laziness. If you wake me up before I'm ready, I get nastier than a disturbed nest of hornets.

Putting sleeping habits back to bed, I won't be referring here to my quirky sibling's occasional, although I will admit laudable, bouts with histrionics. During this nerve-racking, break-of-day discussion, she blubbered in a way I'd never seen before. She was in shock over the sudden death of Bertie Norman. She told me the tragedy happened on Friday, May 26th. His formal name may be *Bertrand* but everybody, with the exception of his mother, always called him, "Bertie."

Vivienne led me to believe she only heard about his demise last night. My mother happened to read a brief mention of his passing in the late edition of Saturday's newspaper. My stunned parents phoned his parents at once. Nobody answered. They ran across the cul-de-sac and rang their bell. They pounded on their door. Just like the phone call, no response.

Calling us with the news was a no-go. We weren't around. My usual Saturday night chick-flick with colleagues from work had me occupied, and due to her Yoga class on Friday night, Shelley already started mountain climbing.

My sister went on to inform me about the callous lack of any funeral or memorial service, prior to his strange and hasty cremation. According to her, Bertie's death is the biggest mystery ever to hit Tillagevale—if not the whole United States of America. Do you now get a sense of why I left?

Through choking sobs, she persecuted me with stories regarding him and his moronic pranks. I thought she'd carry on all day, with an endless rendition of her hackneyed account of those puns and sick humor-bombs he dropped on me—as well as an innocent public. Sometimes in life, when a sibling's in distress, scrounging up miniscule compassion is necessary. She wasn't crying her usual crocodile tears, and she hurt for real. Therefore, I let her ramble, for as long as I could tolerate, concerning that Bertie Norman imbecile.

Here is what she said:

Ginger—I bet you remember when he called up every grocery store in the county, including the Piggly Wiggly markets, inquiring if they keep tuna canned in water. So when, as expected, they said *yes,* he sang to them in his phony operatic-voice:

How cruel can you guys be?
Oh heavens, heavens me!
Those poor, dear darling cramped-up fish,
Throw them right back in the sea.

That's a real good one, Ginger. Right?

Next—remember when he took all of us to get the notorious greasy tempura from Samurai Fuji's Japanese Takeout. Bertie demanded to talk with Samurai Fuji in person about their lousy cooking. When they told him that 'Samurai Fuji' didn't exist, and besides, they weren't even Japanese—they were Korean—Bertie threatened to sue them for false advertising. As soon as the cook heard the word *lawyer,* he screamed in Korean. That's when Bertie made up those jumbled words imitating him, pretending to answer him back.

Where did Bertie ever conjure up the real Korean expression for 'sallow bastard'? It was lucky for him, how he babbled-out a politer version of the insult. The sushi chef, brandishing the giant knife at Bertie's chest, was not kidding.

I think his usual ton of hair-grooming goop saved him from getting a bad burn, when the furious waiter tossed that wok full of hot tempura at him. The steaming vegetables landed right on Bertie's forehead. Also, what the heck were the odds of the flying wok bouncing off of Bertie's forehead, and landing right back onto the traumatized waiter's *own* head. Looking at it upside-down, you'd swear one of those sampan-hats roosted on him.

Wasn't it real lucky how the poor waiter wore a protective kerchief—the big one, covering his head with pictures of those immense *Sumo* wrestlers. Otherwise, if he had a bare head, gee, I hate to think about *those* ramifications.

Or here's the best one of all, at Tillagevale High's Senior Class bowling playoff last year. You know, the night when Bertie used his wildlife safari hat. Remember how he paid a fortune for this authentic *Zimbabwe* hunting gear, since he ordered it from your favorite Sunday night *Wild Kingdom* television show. He never missed an episode either. Bertie acted so sneaky when he positioned the thing on the real, full-sized skull with the moveable jaw. It fit that skull like custom-made.

I'm sure you recall this skull, the one with those big, brown monstrous teeth. Whoever the thing once was, obviously never heard the words to those catchy new *Ipana* toothpaste commercials—with the jingle . . . *brusha . . . brusha . . . brusha.* Bertie always said that when his dad trained in dental college, the future Dr. Norman practiced stuff by telling the revolting thing to, 'Please open wide.'

Could there ever be a better humdinger than Bertie?

Ginger—I'm sure you remember how Bertie lit up this skull's cavernous eyesockets by using those tiny flashlights with blinking infrared-bulbs. And right after that, he fastened the skull, and its makeshift menacing eyes, onto a long pole. He also had that realistic-looking zebra-material to make a cloak for the skeleton,

And—what about when he shackled the big sign saying, **Doctor Livingstone I Presume,** right around the skeleton's scrawny pole-neck!

Wasn't Bertie a regular practical-joke mastermind or what then?

I'm sure you remember how Bertie crawled on the ground, so nobody could see him, while he waved the grisly smiling bone-face around.

When Brad Patterson looked up and spotted the ghastly skull, dressed in its jungle-getup, the sickening sight shook him up to the point where he lost all his concentration during the rest of the match.

Did you ever think *Brad* could throw so many gutter balls?

I'm sure you recall *everything* Ginger, since *you* were there.

Events of 5/28/72

ENTRY 3:

ORTHOPEDIC BOWLING "And the wok that flew with it."

I give you permission to applaud me. With painstaking attention, putting special emphasis on the *pain* part of that word, I listened to my sister reminisce about Bertie—also known to me as *Pun Geyser.* He's the only other person in the world, who drives me to the brink of insanity. Not even my father or Vivienne can compete with him.

Concerning my sister and her eulogizing about this idiot, enough *was* enough. Sucking in my breath, much deeper than Jack La Lanne ever did his, I screamed back my answer about those gutter balls:

Do you really think I'd ever forget any of the Bertie junk that you just sobbed? Bringing up the bowling-bomb wasn't such a good idea. If *you* recall, I played on that stupid Senior Class bowling team with that unfortunate name of *Unstoppables,* and Brad was its captain. He was an exceptional bowler, who, until Doctor Livingstone showed up, never rolled less than what bowling-speak calls a *Turkey.* This tasty term means he could knock down every single pin, in every single frame, for a perfect competitive score.

Now referencing that turkey, I'm going to ask you—with every *slice* of offense intended—do you recall Brad's pitiful nervous 'ally' breakdown where he dropped the bowling ball and rolled himself down the lane and we lost the dumb tournament!

Screaming at her gave me the sensation of my tongue boiling, while rage percolated in my mouth. Spitting out this hot fury didn't come easy, but I still managed to continue with my tirade.

"*You* above all, dear sister, know how much I wanted the First Place award, donated by Dr. Walker Schlep, the chiropodist. I'm speaking, of course, about the neat two-foot-tall, gold-plated trophy. The gleaming one, with an embellishment of a bowlegged American bald eagle, wearing its orthopedic bowling shoes. So right now I'm going to ask you, do *you* remember *that* one?"

"Uh, oh, you sure got me there, Ginger."

You bet I got her *there,* I thought, before continuing to scream, "Hey, Vivienne, now I'm going to tell *you* something about Bertie. *I* really hoped that the Korean restaurant guys would brand him for life with a big fat zero, right in the middle of his obnoxious square head, courtesy of that searing fried onion ring.

And the wok that flew with it."

Events of 5/28/72

ENTRY 4:

DEAD MAN PESTERING "What a gasser!"

No more than a few minutes passed since encountering Bertie on the bus, and the residual garbage from Vivienne's earlier hysteria trudged its way through my stunned brain. Focusing on him became impossible, while the bus kept rocking and hitting potholes. People sitting nearby gave us dirty looks, while trying to concentrate and read their newspapers. I couldn't blame them.

How could they accomplish this commuter-task over the din of Bertie's gibberish, while he addressed my natural disbelief about his presence?

Of course, it's *me.* Maybe you thought you were sitting next to David Cassidy. I *have* tried losing some weight with that new lip-smacking chocolate-shake diet powder that you use in place of three meals and a snack. It buffed me *out,* instead of *up,* and tasted so darn dreamy, because I mixed the stuff with heavy cream, instead of using that watery skim milk. Anyhow, I don't think I could have changed too much since Vivienne sent me that invite to your bon voyage party.

What a gasser!

Please do remember how I was the guest at that bash giving you the best goodbye gift of *anybody*—the fabulous 14-inches-long *real* 10-karat gold chain, from that new *Wal-Mart* place. I can't help noticing how you are not wearing this fabulous fashion accessory. Gads, how soon we forget.

I could hardly hear him insulting me about the dumb chain, because my stunned heart pounded louder than a jackhammer. Overruling the noise, I mustered a loud but shaky voice to inform him:

"Bertie—for once in your useless life, clam up and listen. This is real serious business. Vivienne told me early this morning, how *you* are now . . . nothing more than a heap of charcoal!"

Events of 5/28/72

ENTRY 5:

THE SNAFU

"Robust *is* the word for me."

Bertie didn't act one bit surprised by the rumor that he was among the dear departed. On the contrary, his response to my startling description of his supposed extinction was to stare at me like the simpleton he is, acting like I just told him to expect rain tomorrow.

He acted nonchalant as ever when he said, "Oh—*you're* talking about *that* pesky little snafu. They had a very unprofessional mix-up in The Gazette obits on Saturday evening, one of those transpositions concerning names. In reality, an elderly Mr. Norman A. Bertrand gave the bucket a kick. He lived to be over ninety-years-old, so the codger had a long life."

I stared at him in disbelief before he continued with, "I'm sorry for the maudlin situation. I had no control over the matter. As you can see for yourself, *I'm* still on the planet. How touching that Vivienne is crying over me. I'll surmise she talked with you *before* seeing the correction in today's paper. And if she disturbed you with wrong details, it's the fault of *your* old job, so don't go blaming your sister."

Who does he think he is, I thought, bossing me around and telling me how to handle my sister. But before I could let him know how I felt, he said, "There's probably just been *another* slipup and those incompetents where you once worked forgot to *publish* the revised obituary for poor Mr. Bertrand. People should rise up in arms about their mishandling of such a sensitive issue. They are indeed falling to pieces, without efficient *Ginger P. Autry.*"

As usual—his flattery did *not* impress me. And hearing Bertie throw in my **P** initial, further infuriated me. What an egotistical dork he was, presuming Vivienne cried over *him.*

"Maybe Vivienne *is* upset Bertie. As of this morning, she thinks you're no longer around. She told me how she's been overwhelmed since finding out about your *demise.* She was on the phone, all of last night, trying to get some kids from high school to help her arrange a memorial service for you, even when your own family doesn't seem to care."

Wiggling his long, bony fingers with a conjurer's gesture, using *his* brand of sorcery, Bertie spoofed Reverend Frisby doing the bogus solemn look. I only find him amusing when he impersonates a maniacal chimp. Flailing his arms, while scrunching up his brow into the evangelical primate manifestation, he moralized, "Ginger—I am certain Viv *is* overwhelmed, concerning my lack of proper commemorative accoutrements. Everybody knows she seldom lies, and if you compare her to you, she is Mother Teresa. So she's correct. I *am* no longer around. I'm now in Manhattan, on a bus with her sister."

Laughing nonstop, and superseding my hostile-self, I said, "Yep, you're right. Viv and *Goody Two Shoes* share so much in common, it's frightening. And, since *you* are looking about as robust as I've ever seen, everything she's done so far concerning your *croaking* has been an apparent waste of her already limited organizational aptitude. Since she *is* so upset, maybe you should give her a call and explain, just to be sure she knows about the mix-up stuff."

In typical Bertie fashion, he didn't address my concern about reassuring Vivienne.

Instead, he stood up and started flexing his serious non-muscles. He had to make a big show to verify my comment about what good shape he's in.

His stupid imitation of the current *Mr. Olympia*—bodybuilder Arnold Schwarzenegger—lasted until the stocky straphanger standing over him thought Bertie got up to leave the bus. As any seasoned New Yorker would do, this passenger slid-in for the supposed vacated seat. He never expected to be, shall we say, the victim of a slight scuffle. To my amazement—Bertie wrestled back his coveted position. I supposed "heavy cream" fostered his newfound bulk and his stint on TV's *Partridge Family.*

"See *that* my Ginger! As usual, your adjectives are right-on. Robust *is* the word for me. My superior physical condition renders me more than ready to take a huge bite out of what you guys here in New York call, *The Big Apple.*"

Scrutinizing him, from head to toe, his healthy appearance was undeniable. "Yeah, looks like you *are* ready for your usual obnoxious bite. I hope you choke."

When I made this quick comeback, I heard the still-miffed straphanger laughing like the madman Bertie had caused him to become. That is, until Bertie mimicked those weird *kah-kah-kah* choking sounds, which even alarmed *me.* Forget about the rest of the passengers.

After he shrieked at the top of his healthy lungs, not to stop the already shaking bus and call any paramedics, I said, "Bertie, why are *you* in Manhattan on a Sunday afternoon. Did you move here or something?"

He answered in a split-second, almost like he'd been versed in a reply. "Such an idea would *not* be a further stretch of your already overinflated imagination. You're right to say that I did make a recent *permanent* relocation."

My biggest fear had come true. He'll be moving into Shelley's building. I bet he rented the apartment next-door. I heard yesterday how the original tenant left the other night due to some weird mental issue over a hearing loss. An eager new tenant—who popped up out of nowhere—already took the place, sight unseen. Locating a permanent pad became more urgent than ever. I had to find out right away, the real reason why he came to Manhattan:

Bertie—aren't you that voice of doom who told me a thousand times what a jerk I am to trade my safe and welcoming hometown nest, for coldhearted New York. When I did succeed with leaving Tillagevale this past February, in spite of negative people like *you,* you're the one who came to the Greyhound Bus terminal for a final dig.

I left in a bus, not an ambulance. You acted like a life or death emergency took place, and cried like a baby while the thing pulled out of the gate. You kept saying I'm not ready to be *Midnight Cowboy*—and without any *Ratso Rizzo* to protect me—I'd never get out of 'uninhabitable' New York in one *recognizable* piece.

I'd like to know what's going on with your unexpected decision to live here, and why you're screwing up this bus too. Is there no bus I am foolish enough to ride on that's safe from you? {Other than a Don Corleone protected one, I thought to myself.}

He brushed over my legitimate question by cocking his head and saying, "Ginger, my pet, since you are staring at me with such intensity, I can only surmise how much you miss me." My entire body went rigid with fury, as those years and years of pent-up rage erupted.

In a moment, his own geyser would smack *him* in the face.

Events of 5/28/72

ENTRY 6:

CHIPMUNK TALES

***"I* crashed fast."**

When I heard Bertie say I *missed* him, the emotional rubber band, which had secured a lifetime of suppressed emotions from dealing with his lunacy, had overstretched to the max. I heard my ears pop as it snapped. Hoover Dam, bursting all over Nevada, couldn't compare to me as my tirade flowed, and he didn't even have the security of the same water wings he's been using since the age of three.

You can't imagine how many times I thought about the moment when I'd tell him how I really felt. Or maybe you can. Over the years, I just learned to swallow the anger. He always existed in my life, on a par with my mottled teeth, my freckles, lousy hair, and daily pancake breakfast. I dreamt about the day when I'd be free of him for good. Now, on the New York City bus, with him appearing out of nowhere, he became the straw that broke the back of the frustrated camel waiting at the Pearly Gates. At long last, I was ready to drown *him:*

Run this junk by me again, Bertie. Did I hear you say how much I miss you? Well, you are right in a way, because I do miss you. For example, I miss *you* as much as the bad case of mumps I had at the age of eight. You, above all, remember the very big swelling under my jaw that didn't subside for two-whole-months. How could you ever forget it since you're the one who kept telling me I looked like a greedy, stuffed to the gills pelican? My having to dress up like dumb *Alvin the Chipmunk,* at that Bullsnake Lodge Halloween Party, became the personification of my social season.

Later on, I experienced the particular pleasure of witnessing my mother pack up the original Annette Funicello **Mouseketeer Club** costume I had planned to wear. I cried myself sicker, realizing she put adorable Annette in storage for Vivienne, since by next Halloween I'd surely outgrow the *cute* size.

Do you recall, Bertie, when those terrorizing bats bred inside the dormer over my bedroom window? For weeks and weeks after the exterminator came, I still couldn't sleep. I knew, without a doubt, I expected the real Count Dracula to drop by one night and bite off half of my huge, still-swollen neck. His bat breath was definitely in the air.

So—Bertie, if you tell people I miss you as much as I do a ravenous vampire—who, at the time, did not act one bit *compassionate*—you will *not* be exaggerating.

Bertie—I'm capable of staying here all day, citing typical reasons why I miss you so much. However, if you must know, I'm staring at you now since I'm wondering why you don't straighten out those abominable buckteeth. Your very own father is Tillagevale's big-shot Orthodontist. I realize Dr. Norman is expensive, but how much could he charge *you?*

Plus—beyond allowing you to hog the dental insecurities, you're well aware of how I hate *my* botched-up teeth. When you say nothing is *wrong* with them, I'm convinced, more than ever, that they're in dire need of emergency treatment. If I had a dentist for dad, I'd take advantage of his generous services, so there!

I'm not too sure about how much of my chiding speech he absorbed, because Bertie's voice spanned a few more octaves. "Ginger dear—are you suggesting I change my trademark? Why should I? These teeth of mine are part of a unique persona."

He followed this statement, concerning that glorified version of his mouth, with a flash of his painful jack-o-lantern smile, causing an unbearable whistling sound to escape between his jumbled teeth, as he said, "Who'd recognize *me* without these protruding renditions of *your* favorite presidential noggins, carved on South Dakota's Mount Rushmore?"

In this split-second, I stood on top of *Mt. Rushmore* myself, ready to jump off the tip of Thomas Jefferson's projecting nose. I tried pulling the unyielding cord on my malfunctioning parachute. As usual, the thing refused to open. *I* crashed fast.

Events of 5/28/72

ENTRY 7:

TIGHT END

"What a familiar cry."

While all the bus-junk went down, I knew I sat crammed into New York City public transportation and had actually grabbed a seat. At first glance, everything appeared secure with no perceptible smell of garlic and no threats of eviction. I had dreams. I had plans. Now these aspirations slipped out of my reach, when ferocious mountain wind wrapped my typical deflated parachute around my legs like a tourniquet and also whooshed in my face, *and* exploded in my ears.

They say at times like this, how your life flashes before your eyes. Mine did. The worst parts of it ganged up on me. I began reliving the experience of Bertie escorting me to our Senior Prom last June. This horrific recollection, as I tumbled toward infinity, caused an ocean of perspiration to collect under my arms.

I was glad that after speaking to Vivienne in the morning, I took a long thirty-minute shower—even if I used up every drop of hot water in the building. I'm also glad I helped myself to Shelley's exclusive *Arpege* spray deodorant, instead of using *Mum,* my usual bargain one. I believe that hers saved me from a potentially embarrassing situation. She hides a can inside the deep crevice behind the medicine cabinet. As usual, I know where to look.

I also know for sure that I rode along with Bertie this afternoon. Nobody else in the world could even pretend to be him. Except today, we weren't on a Manhattan bus. Instead, we traveled backwards in time. With an abruptness reminiscent of The Good Fairy and her magical pumpkin, the bus changed into the backseat of a luxury limo, where Bertie tried to kiss me. Visualizing his squishy lips, closing in for the kill, put that expensive deodorant to the ultimate test.

Prom night will be one-year-ago, as of the fifth of next month. This is when I watched him puckering his mouth, and removing his eyeglasses, with gestures very similar to those of the busy French chef. On this evening from the past, though, Bertie acted more like a hot-to-trot Bucky Beaver, about to suck on its juiciest log. But *this* goofy beaver wore its grandfather's ratty black *Zoot Suit,* while its fireman-uncle's bright red suspenders, shored up its baggy pants.

I heard, once again, the celebratory sound of clinking glasses emanating from the exclusive Tumbleweed Ballroom, over at Tillagevale's Majestic Hoedown Hotel. My eyes squinted, just as they did before, while I passed under those magnificent spinning lights. These inexhaustible stroboscopes, still whirled around and around, over the center of this ballroom's reflective dance floor. I remembered again, *why* the palace-sized ballroom floor blinded people. Seeing energetic young guests dance a *Lindy,* on just waxed marble, was not a pretty sight and fodder for lawsuits.

A dislocated shoulder must be very painful. The captain of the Senior Class Tennis Team screamed when he hit the floor. He sounded like a furious banshee, when its older sibling took a jumbo lollypop out of its mouth, and flushed the favorite hard to find pineapple flavor, right down the toilet. What a familiar cry.

In any medical case, after twirling through that revived horror, I closed my eyes and relived another optometric nightmare. Bertie's shocking-pink poodle-tie still jiggled, without shame, on his dingy white shirt.

I also shuddered again from the same chill, as I extended my toned arms—the ones attached to my chic bare shoulders—to help stabilize Bertie without laughing in his face. I watched the repeat of an amusing movie, as he continued with his struggle to walk straight in those black patent-leather shoes. They reflected everything around them, like he just polished them with shellac. When I tried stifling a guffaw, my lipstick-stained fingers covered my mouth. Not smearing any of that new "long-lasting" *Purple Passion* shade on my *own* formal attire was pure dexterity.

Trundling back to the outlandish shoes, those narrow white stripes continue to enhance them. Imagine trying to help a chubby beaver that's wearing horn rim glasses, while tripping on feet transplanted from a hobbling Zebra—if you dare. Never would I have suffered the gross humiliation of going to the prom with Bertie in the first place, if my then hot-date, Tillagevale High's famous All-Star tight end, wasn't rushing away in an ambulance for an emergency appendectomy—fifteen minutes before the scheduled arrival with the chauffeur.

That's what I get for saying "yes" when the hunkiest high school football stud in America asked if I'd be his date for the Senior Prom. What a shock, when he came right out with the gruff invitation in the lunchroom and said, "I assume you'll go to the prom with me." I looked around to check and see if he wasn't talking to somebody else. I nodded my head *yes,* although I *knew* he had a crush on Vivienne.

My father was sure to say Vivienne's too young for this popular eighteen-year-old jock. I, on the other available hand—being almost seventeen and his equal as a fellow candidate for graduation—made getting in good with the family easy. Also, having the most adored athlete in town escort me to something I'd been dreaming about for so long, had me planning where to place the eight-inch-high rhinestone **Prom Queen** crown without messing up my hair.

I paced around the living room, on the most important night of my life. *Waterproof* midnight blue mascara streamed down my cheeks when my father said, "Too bad you're all dressed up, with no place to go. Don't worry; I can drop you off. Even better, I can escort you."

He turned to my mother, standing next to him, and said, "I've still got the tux from our wedding."

Patting his protruding stomach, she said, "Don't be ridiculous. That old thing will never fit you now and besides, it stinks of mothballs."

Vivienne was in the room too and heard everything. She looked at me with sympathy and started shaking her head with a firm no-way don't even go there.

If you're guessing that my frantic state welcomed her to get involved, you *are* getting to know me. In retrospect, I'm sure my new *Wonder Bra,* designed for such an occasion, influenced my desperation in ways I shouldn't have allowed. It really added that necessary generous *oomph* to my slinky satin strapless sheath with the high side-slits. Besides, I spent plenty to dye my stilettos, and the evening bag with the real *Swarovski* crystal clasp, to match the exquisite burgundy color of this gown.

To embellish the occasion even further, my mother finally caved and said I could borrow those dangling diamond earrings my father gave her the year before. Dad went for broke in honor of her turning forty-six. He reserved the exclusive reception room at the brand new Howard Johnson's

Restaurant. Everybody said Dad owed Mom this surprise, after his stupid blunder at dinner one night.

Whatever possessed him, when he burst out with, "I realize Mary, looking at you tonight—here under our *sparkling* dining room chandelier—how *you* sure are well-preserved for a woman now technically exceeding the point of middle-age."

If you think she cried over the contraband encyclopedias, too bad you didn't see the waterworks concerning her pending *Grandma Moses* status. I think her attitude stems from being older than Dad is. She's oversensitive about this slight difference.

My *tactful* father did not help critical matters at all, when he further said, "I only meant it as a compliment, honey."

Concerning this foot-in-the-mouth episode, we watched him inch further and further into the doghouse with stupid apologies on a daily basis.

Back at the birthday party, all of the family and guests witnessed Mom opening the obvious *Tiffany* gift. Dad looked real sheepish when he handed her the unique box on bended knee. I don't even think he even went this far on the day he proposed, and her engagement ring didn't come from a place like this. She once told me he bought the tiny, but genuine symbol of betrothal, from *J.C. Penny* on the layaway plan.

As soon as Mom lifted up the dangling diamond earrings, at least a dazzling half-karat each I'd say, everybody in the restaurant exclaimed in unison, very reminiscent of a harmonious choir, "What in blazes did that man do now?"

Each person in the place, including those who weren't even invited guests, ran outside to check the restaurant's parking lot. Cooks and servers too. All were happy to see that the dear Mustang hadn't done any presto-change-o yet.

Returning to the circumstances leading up to that disastrous prom night, I knew no matter what departure from the norm waited in store for me later, the entire future prom would center on my beautiful diamond-laden pierced ears, with my mother's *Heaven Sent* perfume dabbed behind them.

I also couldn't forget about the special order for a double black-orchid wrist corsage, with glitzy burgundy ribbon. The color matched my gown. I designed this spectacular creation, along with the florist, for the important wow-factor. What had now turned into my puking-it-up—appendix-zonked ex-escort—had already forked over the dough two weeks before.

He balked at the price, until Vivienne happened to walk by the store. Her new short and tight knit dress, displayed her long legs—and every single one of her curves—with **3-D** visibility, as she passed in front of the huge picture window of Leonardo da Vinci's Floral Creations. The jock followed her with his eyes until she disappeared around the corner. Then, the strangest thing happened after Lenny told him to, "Check your family jewels." He took out his wallet, placed the cash on the counter, and ran right out of the shop.

What was *that* all about?

Plus—the expensive white stretch limousine, with the full-sized overhead mirror, was parking outside of my house. The jock already paid for this too. I'm sure his parents diverted the chauffeur over, since their son had a different kind of date waiting for him in the operating room.

Not enough mascara in the entire world could save me—waterproof or not, be it blue, brown, black or otherwise. Trusting me here, concerning *this* setback will be a given *if* you happen to be a woman.

Events of 5/28/72

ENTRY 8:

ALFALFA **"Working at a comedy club, are we?"**

Only a couple of minutes lapsed before the authenticity of Bertie's *Aqua Velva* jolted me back to the bus. Owing to the overpowering smell of this aftershave that he plasters all over his styptic-stick spots, I sneezed myself out of the pumpkin stupor. A little bit of the scent is okay I guess, but he goes haywire. After I finished *achooing* for about a minute straight, everybody on the bus shouted, "Triple gazoonhite."

Everything happening on the bus gave me a splitting headache, but not an idiopathic one. The cause called *Bertie* sat right next to me. He made the pain worse by sneaking peeks at the newspaper on my lap, before he pried, "I see you're looking for an apartment."

"Why do you assume that?" I asked.

"Hmm," he said, "now let me think this answer over. Could there be a remote chance that since you're holding the entire *New York Times* real estate section—with everything circled in red—another change of residence *might* be in your future? The paper looks like a pathetic chickenpox victim."

"How droll, Bertie. Working here at a comedy club, are we?"

When I asked if he worked in Manhattan now as a comedian, I didn't stray too far off his theatrical-base. One look at those immense Arnold Stang frogeye-spectacles—still slipping down his nose—will convince the most skeptical of people to buy a ticket for his show. He's been wearing these slapstick black glasses since we started high school. He never changes them, and I don't think he ever even cleans them. The usual fingerprint marks still spread all over the thick lenses.

Now—let's discuss the matter of his preposterous Bazooka-gum-pink turtleneck with those long sleeves. You'd think the worn-out thing would be in shreds by now, but somehow it still looked as good as new. He must own a collection of these blinding shirts, in various psychedelic colors. I think he chooses them on purpose to clash with his usual multicolored, and way too short, plaid bellbottoms. Even today, these pants exposed his huge feet, swimming around as usual, in those stretched-out white cotton tube socks.

Why doesn't Bertie ever improve his embarrassing appearance? These perpetual grubby socks were still overflowing inside those juvenile black leather loafers. Two unfamiliar bronze-like coins, with obvious rectangular holes in the middle of them, popped out of the now wider slots that center on top of these tatty shoes. In the past, he had used them to hold traditional bright copper pennies, and this strange change of coinage was the only thing new about him.

As per usual, the ton of Brylcreem continues to paste carrot-red hair to his scalp. He never understood this styling aid's advertisement—"A little dab will do ya." He buys the gluey substance by the gallon.

I get what's going on now. He's here to work as an "Alfalfa" impersonator. I had the strong urge to take out my eyeliner and dab classic *Our Gang* brown-dots across Bertie's usual oily nose as I said, "Hey, *Alfalfa,* wanna borrow my powder puff?"

In the past, he'd ignore me when I zapped him. However, this time he said, *"Ginger*—I must say that for a cute girl who's *intelligent,* you're quite snippy."

How interesting, I thought. Girls who are intelligent—and cute too—shouldn't be snippy. I wondered what lovable little *Darla* would have thought about *this* Alfalfa remark. Who knows? Perhaps he means that girls who are cute, and *happen* to be intelligent, should not be snippy. You're never really sure with Bertie. He speaks a language nobody ever understands, except for affronted Korean restaurateurs.

At least he didn't bring up my foray into lacquered hair-flips and upper torso enhancement. I think my getup on Prom Night shocked Bertie. I'm positive he mumbled *something* about my appearance, while he maneuvered me across the just dewaxed dance floor.

You never saw hotel porters swing mops so fast in your life!

Even with the now safe ballroom, although he swung me around and around, Bertie failed at teaching me the sensuous fandango. His exhausting efforts included pumping my arms up and down, like trying to get crucial lifesaving water out of a deep stone well. His hard work was a washout. I couldn't get the rhythm *or* the steps. Ever since then, I often wonder where a guy like him picked up *those* Latin moves.

After thoughts of the seesawing fandango, I danced back to the current reality of the joggling bus and awareness of Bertie's high-pitched tone taking on a deeper, more paternal authority.

"My dear girl, I do realize it's a ludicrous thing to expect that *you* will ever listen to me. You're so irascible! Now if you could just get a grip for a second, I know this fabulous real estate guy down in Greenwich Village. I'm not exaggerating when I tell you that he has friends in high places."

Okay, I thought, now what am I supposed to do. I know, I'll just placate him. The strategy has worked before in similar situations. I'll extricate myself from this atrocious atmosphere as fast as possible, even if the creep did call me an assumed derogatory name like *irascible.* I'm not exactly sure what this word means, but I'm positive you won't find the sentiment on any greeting card.

Holding my temper, I said, "Wow, Bertie, how lucky can this cute and intelligent girl get. Write down the information on the edge of the classified."

At this stressed-out moment, I ripped off a wedge of the newspaper and handed the dog-eared corner to him, along with a pen. He couldn't just settle for writing down the useless information. Instead, he *had* to say, "*Ginger*—I do comprehend how much you loathe my puns. As you'll now see, however, this forthcoming one is much too good to pass up."

After this warning about the imminent pun-eruption, he paused and gaped at me. He looked like his *P.G.* namesake—the gleeful old mouse I once told you about—the clever one that snatched Velveeta cheese from the *professional* trap, and ran off munching like mad.

Within a few seconds though, he told me with vintage Bertie arrogance, "Ginger, my *adorable* petulant one, I completely assure you that accepting advice from me, about getting a grand apartment, will turn out to be a very smart move on your part."

I paid no attention while he scrawled something. I just let this typical pun-zinger fly past me, pretending I didn't hear him. "Thanks for writing things down, Bertie. *Er* . . . gee whiz, how about that. My stop's already here. I'll get off now."

I made my hasty exit, snatching back the scrap of paper and pen from fingers that were freezing cold. I noticed his icy touch, a few minutes before, when he grabbed my hand and squeezed it for dear life. I thought excessive air-conditioning on the bus was responsible. I had goose bumps from the draft myself, even with wearing a sweater.

Bertie looked chilly, dressed in his lightweight shirt. I wondered what happened to his usual denim jacket, featuring the face of old-time baseball player *Ty Cobb,* along with the expression, "Baseball is a red-blooded sport for red-blooded man. It's no pink tea, and mollycoddles had better stay out. It's a struggle for supremacy, survival of the fittest."

I guess he wore the stupid jacket so much it disintegrated. Yet—chilly or not—I had no idea where I ejected myself. As the bus started leaving, and I stood on the street, I made a halfhearted attempt at waving goodbye to him. All the same, I don't think he even saw my feeble effort due to that bright halo of golden sunbeams, streaming in from the window behind his head.

Events of 5/28/72

ENTRY 9:

SCRIBBLE BEFORE SCRABBLE "And nobody else!"

I found myself standing on a busy thoroughfare called *Amsterdam Avenue.* I hoped for some new hunting territory. But everything remained the predictable wild goose chase, with no luck around there. What else is new? Everywhere I searched, in the area where I dumped myself, fell way short of its newspaper advertisements and a complete waste of two hours.

When I did see something close to my expectations and wallet, they said I'd need "key money" for the building superintendent. You'll never convince me that the Godfather—with his sweaty cap—wasn't on *my* ample tail. The *supers,* as they call them here in Manhattan, make the final decision as to who gets the competitive places, depending on how much bribery money the prospective tenant is willing to cough up.

Let's just say that since I made no plans to catch a cold, I felt like *giving* up. My life with odiferous kitty litter, and stepping on the menagerie's regurgitated fur balls, remained my punishment for brainwashing Shelley—even though I performed the espionage better than any **CIA** operative ever could. No good deed shall go unpunished.

You will trust me here, if you already know how "The road to hell is paved with good intentions." I have several free tickets to ride on this road. I utilized three of them so far. The first was on Boogey's cart, and the second was on the nutty Greyhound Bus. Today became the third instance for me on Manhattan Transit.

With my headache worsening, I asked nobody in particular, "Where *to,* where to?" The woman standing next to me with the baby carriage said she had no idea, and moved away fast.

I didn't expect to receive an immediate answer to my question from the cracked curb I tripped on. Funny—but when I bent over to check the heels on my boots for any damage, I heard a persistent voice inside my head urging me to check what Bertie wrote on the scrap of newspaper that I previously stuffed into my sweater pocket.

Except the voice did *not* remind me how I had used Bertie's scribble-paper several minutes before to wrap up a big wad of chewed spearmint gum. Unraveling the spongy mess, in an attempt to read the note, took a few minutes.

> Ginger, if you can manage to get over yourself, even for a brief period, find O'Flanagan's Real Estate Agency, downtown in Greenwich Village—number 46-A on Carmine Street.
>
> Go up to the second floor. Talk to a Mr. O'Flanagan. And nobody else!

Gee, I thought, first—I'm snippy. Then—I'm irascible. Now—I'm grimy, with gobs of unsanitary gum on my fingers. I'm a snippy . . . irascible . . . sticky bonehead. This *must* be my lucky day.

Although furious, I thought he hasn't made an impossible suggestion. What do I have to lose? I'm not sure, but I have my suspicious why Bertie knows a real estate agent in Manhattan. I bet this realtor is the one responsible for renting him the apartment in Shelley's building. The only way to be sure is check out the place he recommended.

The Village, as New Yorker's refer to this area of Manhattan, might prove interesting today. I have the time. I'll show that Ratso Rizzo pun-machine a thing or two.

Or three!

Events of 5/28/72

ENTRY 10:

RAW UMBER "Or can it?"

Washington Square Park is fascinating. New York University students hang out there with guitars and bongos. This recreational section is the only part of Greenwich Village I'm familiar with. I've never been anywhere else in the area. Today the **NYU** kids performed Peter Paul and Mary classics. When I heard them singing my favorite *Puff the Magic Dragon,* I decided to hang around for a few minutes.

Following along with the music, some grungy hippy-types sprayed fire hoses up in the air and they soaked the entire recreational area, including the bandstand. I avoided getting too close. My hair has a sparse look when it's dry, so forget about seeing it wet. A sudden breeze kicked up, and charred remains of pictures of President Richard Millhouse Nixon scattered all across the grass.

Over the next few days, there's an organized Memorial Day Weekend peace rally, planning to go on everywhere in the city, in protest of the Viet Nam *conflict.* What Washington-spin proclaims is a "conflict" sure looks like a huge war to those demonstrators, and I agree with them. In step with this protest-movement, I stood in the noisy part of the park where activists handed everybody assorted paper-poppies. They also paraded around holding posters depicting Nixon dressed up like a magician. Going along with this characterization, he held a magic wand, but instead of a magician's black top hat, the president wore a pointy wizard's cap imprinted with the words **Tricky Dick.**

"Tricky Dick" is going to be re-elected president again by a landslide this November. The way I figure, Nixon's current campaign is impervious to rebellious college students, marching around dispersing vats of water. When his envisioned second-term arrives, some new protests, putting *him* under even more water in the future, will be far worse than the one going on in this park today. If anything does go down in flames later on, Nixon's picture won't be the only target. Nixon, himself, had better carry a fire extinguisher. I have an uncanny ability to predict future political situations and their outcomes with a hundred-percent accuracy, and don't understand why.

I observed the goings on for a few minutes, until the mayhem inside the park got even more worrisome. I focused on checking perimeters outside the park, but still had no concept about this **Carmine Street**. Other than myself, there wasn't a thing holding me back from finding the address. I *could* stroll by the place. I've seen a lot of real estate dives in recent days. This one can't be any worse. Or can it?

Yes, it's true that Bertrand A. Norman is a real pain, but growing up together must count for something. We shared crayons in kindergarten. Okay, we did have those notorious hair pulling battles over the *raw umber* color. Well, in essence, I pulled *his* hair. His bawling kept him too busy to pull mine. Great for me, but not so great for him, how he had a thick and tufty cowlick. I grabbed and maneuvered the frizzled thing like the stick shift on one of those wild county fair bumper cars. The ones where I'd stand with added secret padding in my shoes, while waiting on line to qualify for the height requirement.

Gee—I really had fun manipulating that carrot-red cowlick of his. I'm sorry, but yanking this protruding clump tempted me more than sneaking down to the living room on Christmas Eve and hiding underneath the stairwell. My dad always wolfed down the warm chocolate chip cookies, my mother took out of the oven for *Santa.* She wouldn't allow my sister or me within sniffing distance, telling us the portly fellow deserved them more.

She *also* said that in order to wash down these cookies, he needed the full Brandy decanter—instead of the usual quart of milk—due to recent late nights and frigid weather. But those bunches of carrots she left for the reindeer weren't so popular. We always had cream of carrot soup as the first course with Christmas dinner, and several nights thereafter.

And *I* fell for the age-old ruse. Was I ever stupid or what! You didn't have to answer so fast. But nibbling back now, to the good old Bertie *carrots,* I acted like a real sweetheart in the way I made up with him *after* the bloodshed. I broke our favorite crayon in two pieces and shared the smaller part with him.

Miss Heller always had two masterful rules to control us in situations such as my militant driving lessons and the crayon massacre, for me—no peace, no snacks, and for bawling Bertie—no peace, no Band-Aid. Although a lot went down with us over the years, I'm positive he'd never put me in harm's way.

I think.

Events of 5/28/72

ENTRY 11:

TAKE-NO-PRISONERS

"Not even you."

Ever since the moment I met Bertie on the bus, I wrestled with an overpowering compulsion to locate the nearest phone booth. I could never trust that Bertie called my sister and relieved her angst. After all, how many gorgeous girls ever cry over him? From him, yes, over him, no.

There's a strong probability he liked all the attention. I wanted to place an immediate call to my sister and say, "Vivienne dear, guess what? Turn off the Niagara Falls' tap. Poor, poor Bertie is far from dead. *He* is now plumper than ever, and just as much of a dork."

Still—I didn't have enough change for such a long distance call. I'm a sibling-expert when I tell you that Vivienne will talk for an hour over this particular Bertie foolhardiness. And even if I ever am dumb enough to use a phone booth to place an expensive collect-call—for anything short of murder—you can bet your boots I'll not only be read the riot-act, I'll be forced to pay my father back every penny.

I can't bet *my* boots though. They're premium Italian black-leather and soft as silk. I won't tell anybody how much I paid for these magnificent knee-highs.

Not even you.

I won't worry another second concerning anything about Bertie. I'm sure my family knows the real situation by now. During times like this, however, I think it's too bad there's no such thing as a wireless miniature telephone that fits in the palm of your hand. I'd keep this tiny portable phone in my purse or a pocket, taking it everywhere. I'd never be out of touch. I'd buy an inexpensive model in my favorite color.

How a miracle phone like this can ever come to be, you ask. Simply speaking, my innovative communication-fantasy dictates how everybody in the household will need their own private phone number, and an easy on the pocketbook family-plan would be available.

In my talkative case—Shelley could pay. I already picked out the color of my mini-phone—lavender. Maybe I'd customize mine with a goofy ring. The *Gilligan's Island Song* is perfect. Not only could this be amusing when the phone rings, but also a cool example of turning something you hate, into something that you like.

Better yet, there could be an indicator on this phone showing you the name of the person calling—say like Bertie! The nuisance you want to avoid could just record you a message and never get a reply. Or in the cool case of a new tight end—one with a healthy appendix—they'd get an immediate, "Hey, how are yuh?"

Along these wireless lines, I'll now visualize chatting with people anywhere in the entire world—whenever I want. I'd enhance the dream phone further, by adding a miniature camera that could take fabulous pictures without negatives to develop. And how about if I was able to transmit these photos to anybody, anywhere in the world.

I'll go even further, by imagining that the little phone could also be a teeny-television. I'd never again miss my favorite program, *Mary Tyler Moore.* Her character, Mary Richards, is my inspiration for successful independence. I like to envision now that you are as good of a friend to me, as Rhoda Morgenstern is to her.

I'd also watch my favorite baseball team, televised on this mini-phone. No, it's not those new **Texas Rangers.** They're okay, and I am kind of proud of them, but I'm a legitimate New Yorker now so—*Go Yankees.* Except, my dear, you better dream on. A phone like this is pure science fiction, stashed in Captain Kirk's duffle bag. Yet as tiny as my dream phone is, there's no way it will fit into *his* formfitting space-suit pocket.

I'm glad I wore my watch this morning, and no surprise after my telephone fantasy that the day was slipping away. I hated admitting this, but Bertie's tip—no matter how asinine—might be my last frustrating hope.

I know I told you before how cabs are a financial ruin. Today, however, feeling so exhausted, I took the risk. I saw one cruising right near me. I stepped out into the street, raised my hand, and signaled a ride.

The driver of this taxi looked exactly like *Elvis.* I thought, could this really be him? "The King" *is* starring here at Manhattan's famous Radio City Music Hall this week. Nah, Elvis doesn't need to drive any cab. Yet—there *is* such a thing as a publicity stunt. I blinked my eyes in disbelief about what I imagined, telling myself to get real. I'd never be so lucky. Even so, I'll still use my throaty, sexy voice.

"If I won't take you *too* far out of your way *driver*—please drop me off at **46-A** Carmine Street?"

No reaction there, until a familiar—take-no-prisoners Bronx accent—informs me,

"Missy—numba 46 fah certin' exists. I *know* this old buildin' between Sixth and Seventh Avenyas, but there ain't no such thing as *46-A* on any Carmine Street *this* cabby ever hoid about."

Events of 5/28/72

ENTRY 12:

FATHER DEMO **"Three obvious choices confronted me."**

I had no other recourse, after hearing the driver's unresponsive reaction to my enticing efforts, than to suppose the address logistics represented nothing more than another classic Bertie blunder. "Elvis" is a professional driver. *He* should know the city, better than a hound dog does.

Does that Bertie-creep ever *not* exasperate me. Why should things be any different now, while I'm sitting in an expensive taxi? I didn't want to waste any more valuable time *or* money. "Okay, driver, let me off as soon as possible *near* Carmine Street. I'll find the address on my own."

When the taxi came to a screeching halt, I was unloaded in front of a large triangular square, which sat smack in the middle of a busy intersection named **Avenue of the Americas**—also known as *Sixth Avenue.*

Occupied park benches formed a circle around this weird segregated chunk of concrete, and trees bloomed inside this spiritual green oasis in the middle of chaos. But where was I? In answer to my curiosity, while I looked up and tried hard to read that fading name plaque—affixed to the top of this strange park's tall light pole—my neck hurt more than my head. This weather-beaten signpost identified the floating park as **Father Demo Square.**

Somehow, while I scrutinized this almost illegible sign, I spotted illusive Carmine Street. It popped up, right out of nowhere. Just like magic, it situated itself catty-cornered to the northwest of me. I assumed a kind priest, by the name of Father Demo, led the way, and didn't even pass around a collection plate.

The stupid cab wound up costing me two bucks—plus a dime tip. Ever since learning my lesson about the *racy* aspect of tipping New York City cab drivers with pennies, I keep gratuities simple. With this kind of taxi and tip money, I should've bought a juicy slice of New York pizza—instead of fantasizing about hooking up with Elvis. A Nedicks orange drink would've been good too, and maybe getting one of those big and salty hot pretzels to go along with it, came to mind. Strolling across Washington Square Park, and *asking* somebody for directions, was another overlooked intelligent solution.

The lure of the old one-armed meter-bandit, wearing a yellow medallion for a mask, accosted me again. My temper punted so high, I thought I'd have a stroke. I don't know who made me the maddest, Bertie or myself. I'm amazed how a person with my high IQ can manifest signs of cerebral impairment. Low blood sugar from starvation, I'm sure. That huge breakfast, and resultant heartburn, wore off long ago. "This aggravation had better be worth it," I said to the overflowing trashcan that I bumped into.

Good things in my life, though, never do come easy. I went through extreme frustration to be living in New York City to begin with, and now I couldn't even find a street in Greenwich Village. The sound of my own strident voice reflected this exasperation. Shaking my painful head I said, "Well—*here* you are people; the infamous *Texan* village-idiot has landed on *Greenwich Village* concrete."

The reaction to my insane comment, from the people sitting on these benches and reading their newspapers, was only to turn the pages and never look up. *They* sure exemplified the consummate New Yorker that I longed to emulate someday. There I was, talking like some kind of nut job, standing alone on a cutoff chunk of asphalt, in the center of this unusual floating plaza, angry and lost on a street with two functional names, while traffic swarmed around me. And from this perilous vantage point, I planned to look for an obscure address, coming from the most annoying *dead person* I know.

Three obvious choices confronted me:

1} Retreat back to the cats and give them the food I forgot to feed them before I left.

2} Stand there like an idiot and start blubbering.

3} Act like the detective I always say that I am.

Which one do you think I picked?

Events of 5/28/72

ENTRY 13:

BRIGADOON

"What do you think caused this?"

Plowing up and down both sides of Carmine Street *twice* made my legs start aching too. I should have worn sneakers. Crowds of sightseers strolled along with me on this temperate Sunday of a long holiday weekend. Exploring Greenwich Village *is* a popular attraction.

Since you're very familiar with those great eavesdropping skills of mine, you won't be surprised how I overheard tourists reading a guidebook. They talked about being able to locate visible imprints of wooden wheels, from once horse-drawn conveyances. Those hardy wagoners of days gone by had etched their hard labor into telling cobblestones.

You can still see some of these worn antique-pavers on many of the quaint blocks in the area. Now, however, they intersperse with modern asphalt. Since I couldn't resist finding them myself, it only took a second to bend my throbbing head and spot some of these poetic cobblestones.

While romanticizing about them, I heard the distinct *clickity-clack* of those bygone wooden wheels. All at once, I blinked my eyes in disbelief. Did I perceive the vaporous apparition of a stately Victorian carriage? Yet, in retrospect, the faint image of this *carriage* might have been due to that smoky-haze, bouncing off this now historic pavement on a humid afternoon. What do you think caused this? Please don't say my imagination took over. I could've reached out and touched this coach. The stately thing was there—right in front of me.

Or was it?

Adding to the Victorian ambiance of this remarkable block, towering, multihued umbrellas sheltered tables scintillating under bright sunshine—in front of numerous outdoor cafés. Out of the literal blue, of the sky above, I stood inside an enchanted art gallery. Or perhaps the movie *Brigadoon* came to life.

Did I step into an actual picturesque village from the past?

Was I destined not to return to the present?

Was I to stay in this charming resurrected place, forever?

Soon—out of nowhere—an answer to my Brigadoon questions came from a strange breeze nudging my ear. Don't think I'm foolish when I tell you how this refreshing breath of air declared that meandering along this charismatic path wove me into a wistful sketch, which had once been an integral part of my ancestry.

Will you concur that this ethereal communiqué *may* have only been a fantasy, encouraged by swooshes of hissing steam—floating off the char-grill cart—when that silent hobo-mime sold roasted chestnuts to passersby.

While pondering my metaphysical feeling of déjà vu, I did, by some fluke, spot 46-A. The fading numbers are almost invisible on the building's worn red bricks. I missed it the first go-round. The conceited narrow-edifice stands two-stories high and insinuates itself between the structures numbered **46** and **44.**

Although he drove off long ago, I still said a "so there" to that gruff, but great looking, uninformed cabby.

Events of 5/28/72

ENTRY 14:

OPEN FOR BUSINESS? **"At least Shelley's not involved."**

An iron filigree gate, in the shape of large shamrocks, fortifies the front entrance of the 46-A building—where a large buzzer beckons. Although my hunger pains growled louder than the traffic, my mouth had dried out from thirst. Even though I needed a bathroom, I hesitated going any further. That is, until the sardonic cat-pee smell wafted by from an alley somewhere. This odiferous manipulation tickled my nose informing me, "Ginger—total trust for Bertie—now or never."

The buzzer's quick response reassured me as the rusty gate made a laborious effort to creep open. A musty chill in the hall gave me goose bumps. Soot, covering an already dim light bulb, caused me to trip while climbing the dark tapering staircase toward the second-floor landing.

The swaying **Open for Business** sign, on the thick green-steel door, invited me in. Finding a spacious sapphire-blue room—filled with diffused light, relieved my angst. I gazed up at realistic white clouds floating on a vaulted ceiling, painted to resemble the sky on a sunny spring day. Only a true artist painted this space. I've never seen anything like this before and it could have really been the beautiful sky outside.

The room's vivid walls jump out at you, with their bold geometric sketches done in charcoal featuring weird hexagrams and zigzagging lines. Yet nothing looked out of the ordinary to me, because—here in New York—if there's any business that should be into mazes and puzzles, it's a real estate agency.

An urge to hop on the glossy linoleum floor, due to its bold black and red checkerboard design, found me acting like one of those Spalding-ball clown-noses. With a childlike kind of glee, I hopped and skipped around the place. At a point during the bunny-hop, a huge desk caught my eye. So I quit being *Peter Rabbit* for a second. My mother loves this kind of antique maple furniture, with its carved tambour doors that roll on a track.

I wondered why somebody decorated this beautiful traditional desk with such a dilapidated linen cloth, in the bright color of Kelly green. The fraying thing appeared very similar in shade to the football uniforms worn by Notre Dame's *Fighting Irish.* After sizing up the place in general, I surmised how this O'Flanagan guy went way beyond the universal "wearing of the green" on Saint Patrick's Day. Maybe he would have liked my corned beef and cabbage explosion. He must be as Irish as *Patty's Pig.*

There I go again with pig-stuff.

At least Shelley's not involved

Getting back to the imposing desk, Mom tried hard to negotiate a similar one at an antiques' fair last year at the prohibitive price of **$400.** She knows my father, better than she does the dress floor at Neiman Marcus, so she never told him about even considering such a purchase. Regarding furniture in general, my mother has very little leeway since the cathedral bookcase botch-up. She made sense of her humiliation by telling Dad not to worry. He could fill the whole thing up later, with all of his future golf trophies.

Yes, the thing remains practically empty—except for those cheap little trophies he *always* wins—at any of those United Cornpone Bank golf symposiums. Where there's life there's hope, you say. Funny—this is what my mother mumbles, whenever she's dusting the thing like her life depended on it.

A fluffy feather pen—nesting in a granite inkwell—was content perching itself on the corner of this antique desk, here in the unusual office. And keeping in line with the era of the desk, this quill-type pen is not unlike the one Reverend Frisby stole from Shakespeare.

There's also an art-deco type of telephone, acting like a proud sentinel, standing next to the Bard's traveling pen. Its long black receiver naps in a safe brass cradle. Wondering if this old phone worked, I took a gamble by lifting the cold receiver from this cradle. There was no dial tone. I might need a special code number or something for an outside connection. Or the outdated thing just acted as a motif of the era like I thought.

Whatever the lousy user-friendly service of this wacky telephone represented, my prior instinct, about the place being an ultimate waste of effort, was correct. In spite of this pessimism, I will say that plenty of intriguing things exist in this office. One of them is a portable manual typewriter, ensconced in a wide-open buckskin travel case. The forlorn looking little machine, sitting there slumped on the desk, told me nobody cared enough to touch it for years and years.

I use a portable manual typewriter too that's much bigger and more modern than this compact office model—and without that classy cover. I bought mine used, in good condition and dirt cheap, at a garage sale last year. The lady wanted ten bucks. I bargained her down to seven. Concerning the one here, Ernest Hemingway relied on this office version. I saw a picture of him in a magazine once and he typed with something very similar.

This look-alike one is still in excellent condition and works great. A piece of blank paper was ready and waiting, enticing me to try it out, so I typed . . . **Does anybody work here?** Hoping they wouldn't be annoyed at my sort of trespassing, I left the message inside. However, as for me, I'd never want this typewriter—functional or not. I'm hooked on the kind you plug in. I'm talking about the efficient **IBM Selectric** invention. In the future, even if they're still expensive, I'm buying myself a *Selectric.*

These innovative typewriters use interchangeable wheel-fonts for different kinds of type settings. I'm sure you've seen them. They *are* great, except when you want, or need, to change the print. If you've ever used one, you'll agree how it's a real pain to snap these fonts in and out. Otherwise—how much more contemporary can you get, other than getting rid of the messy typewriter ribbon. The technical name for this cool new font-component of an electric typewriter is *Daisy Wheel.* Now how could I ever forget that!

Despite everything, no matter what, I'll stick with my up-to-date manual kind for the moment. I can't afford any sort of electric typewriter now. Saving money for future living arrangements is my number-one priority.

When I imagine my dream pad, I see cool Swedish-Modern stuff like I've been noticing while browsing in uptown furniture stores. Those colorful new vinyl beanbag-chairs are wonderful too, and the latest craze in *House and Garden* magazine. I hope my beautiful new digs will appear in this domestic publication in the future, if I ever find an apartment worthy enough.

Speaking about walking around, searching this funny place for clues to a realtor who doesn't even extend enough ambition to show up at his office, or own an accessible telephone, affirmed how Bertie's prospect of fabulous digs faded by the minute. Was I surprised? No, not one bit. Owing to all of the stuff that I've told you about him, would *you* be surprised at winding up in real-estate badlands?

You *would* be.

I should put more effort into developing my descriptive writing skills.

Events of 5/28/72

ENTRY 15:

RIPLEY'S EXHIBIT **"I found the place fascinating."**

My legs now hurt, along with the worsening headache, so checking out a place to sit was next on the agenda. Waiting for a realtor to earn a living is never boring, but sure fatiguing. Somebody answered the buzzer before. They must be in here *somewhere.* I also thought, after all the trouble I had finding this so-called place of business, wasn't there a reception area bench—or some kind of accommodation—for a person to sit down and relax on while they're waiting.

I walked around checking the place out pretty good. Those two *thrones* I saw were very intimidating and put me off. These stately pieces of velvet furniture, the succulent color of a ripe honeydew melon, wore silver upholstery-studs like medals of valor. They glinted with pride under the opulent lighted crystal chandelier, hanging from the ceiling above them.

One of these *chairs* positions itself behind that regal desk my mother wanted to own, and holds court. So does the matching one, across from the desk. I asked them in a haughty tone, "Where are the king and queen now?" Resembling the chariot's attitude, I didn't get a reply. I lack the skill to communicate with furniture. Since I'm used to answering my own questions anyhow, I surmised that they're wearing their crowns now while enjoying crumpets at *High Tea,* with the work-shy Mr. O'Flanagan person.

The arrogant air of these ceremonial seats put me off. They sure looked comfortable though. With a seat here and a seat there, but no place for me to relax, I stood in partial sunlight. The persistent rays seeped through the broken and chipped slats of a blind made from cherry wood, adhering with desperation to the halfway-open window, centered in the wall on the left side of this coveted desk. Although the natural light felt delightful, the condition of the blind was in sharp contrast to the imperial chairs.

Raising the slats all the way up, to get a better look outside, didn't cause them to disintegrate. Instead, a flood of sun poured into the room encouraging me to open the window as far as possible. I leaned over the wide wooden-sill, and took a much-needed breath of effervescent spring air.

Looking up from my position, of hanging out of this window like the old TV show character *Molly Goldberg,* I had a great view of the magnificent three-tiered bell tower of the large white marble church, which situated across the street at the beginning of the block. I saw Father Demo Square when I stretched way out. I remembered passing this beautiful church before, taking note of the address—number **25** on my Carmine Street quest to prove the taxi driver wrong.

While tramping around, I guess preoccupation took over. I failed to notice that huge printed banner, wrapping itself around this magnificent tower. But now I saw its white silken-material, blowing in the spring breeze. Acting like a ceremonious cradle, swinging in perfect harmony with the joyful caroling of the bells, they proclaimed in unison:

BLESSINGS ON OUR SECOND ANNIVERSARY AND UPCOMING DEDICATION

After hearing these bells, I stood up—back on my feet inside—and at the same moment, I watched a ballet of energetic light pirouetting across the windowsill. The talented display tiptoed in concert on this wooden stage, while an intoxicating floral fragrance imbued the space around me. I started to inhale this aroma, by taking in deep breaths of an imaginary meadow, forgetting for a minute where I ended up—and how I got there.

Standing alone in this strange room, and sniffing this incense-like air, didn't worry me. I found the place fascinating. Maybe things were too fascinating, because this "office" is a regular *Ripley's Exhibit* and, even with free admission, I grew annoyed. I had no more patience with, *believing It or Not.* I let loose with one of my vivacious, and I might add high caliber ex-cheerleader yells:

Anybody *here!*
Anybody *here!*
Anybody *here—here—here!*

Events of 5/28/72

ENTRY 16:

THE ORIENT EXPRESS "I heard his faint breathing."

After I finished my loud cheer, I heard the floor creaking behind me. My idea worked; they heard me! Turning around, I came face to face with a tall and realistic copper statue. This wax museum individual had magnetic hazel eyes, radiating piercing beams of light. This *mannequin* wore a thick tufted-turban, made from purple satin, which did a skillful balancing act on top of his head.

I'm a respected connoisseur of any type of jewelry, so I recognized how his exotic headdress exhibited *genuine* incandescent deep-green emeralds of various sizes. You *could* say he showed off at least a six-figure chapeau. And these precious stones covered his turban like the fiery poison-ivy-rash my mother says I gave Vivienne for spite. But this is *also* another story.

I had difficulty not staring at the baubles, but noticing his crisp-cotton Nehru-style shirt, along with those coordinating pantaloons, helped me to focus. They were the poufy kind of trousers a genie wears. And, not by coincidence, they reflected the exact color of the vibrant emeralds that sparkled on his audacious turban. A long and thick unadorned purple sash complemented the turban's material. It wrapped around his firm midsection, very much like Captain Kirk's toned 6-pack abs. While taking my eyes off the abs, I looked up at a chestnut-brown goatee that was trimmed, manicured, and discrete. Yet telltale tints of gray remained visible, while the goatee did a good job of covering this man's protruding chin.

Standing there, gawking at this exotic *person,* made me think I had teleported to Bombay on the Orient Express, and upon a jolting arrival, I confronted an exotic bronze statue. He looked mechanical, although I knew he was alive. I heard his faint breathing.

After a lapse of a minute or two, his nose—with classic characteristics of the actor Clint Eastwood's chiseled one—began moving. With a subsequent loud sniffle, the *statue* came to life. I was in absolute awe of him. I trembled from the shock of his deep and rhythmic voice resonating, "Welcome. Welcome."

At this literal *Kasbah* point, marveling at his eccentric appearance and everything else about the colorful real estate *bazaar,* he didn't scare me. His transparent eyes put me at ease and recreated the experience I had in Tillagevale once, when alone in the house during an early-evening thunderstorm, a countywide power outage plunged the town into darkness. When I located a functional flashlight, I felt immense relief.

Due to this reassuring recollection, I entered that radiant stream of light emanating from his eyes, and its extraordinary presence equaled ten-times the brightness of my remembered flashlight, in the frightening storm.

I felt secure enough to ask him, "Do you know Mr. O'Flanagan?"

Events of 5/28/72

ENTRY 17:

SOOTHSAYING **"Ginger isn't skinny."**

Almost like watching one of my old Play-Dou creations begin to melt, as soon as my new effigy acquaintance heard me inquire about Mr. O'Flanagan his unique physique took on a more pliable, human-like presence. "Well, *yes,* most certainly I know him. Indeed—yes *I* do. I know everything about Mr. O'Flanagan. I even know what he is thinking and doing, *Ginger.*"

How creepy, to hear him say my name. I heard my voice set off like a firecracker as I interrogated him with, "How do *you* know who I am?" After my direct question, he ambled toward the magnificent desk. Somebody or something had wound him up like the stiff mechanical toy I thought him to be. He arrived at his destination just a second after the battery died. He adjusted his turban, before sitting down on that beautiful green velvet chair. And from this comfortable position, he replied:

I speak of no other than your underappreciated friend, Bertrand A. Norman. He told me that a teenage girl, who is wearing much too much makeup, would visit here this afternoon and that her name is Ginger P. Autry. My, oh my, this young man is so perspicacious. He described you with near picture-perfect accuracy. Now let me use his exact words:

Ginger is five-foot-five, although today, with those overpriced high-heeled black boots, she's a very wobbly five-foot-seven.

She has short and curly enhanced blond hair. I don't know why she dumps those chemicals on her head. Her real brown color isn't mousy at all, being more inline with the fur on a cute hamster.

Her eyes are a funny color of blue, but not unattractive. Some may even say, enticing.

You can't help noticing her pug nose. The ton of makeup she plasters over the freckles on this cute snout, does little to hide them—although she thinks the thick stuff does. Let them be, I always tell her.

Ginger isn't skinny. But with all of that insulating meat on her bones, she's beguiling.

She'll be wearing a rose-colored beret, a corduroy miniskirt in her favorite lavender color, as well as a corn-yellow sweater with mauve buttons.

As usual, she'll carry her abused, smashed up shoulder bag, which usually never matches anything she wears. She breaks this fashion rule anyway.

She's wearing her Dumbo watch, although she outgrew the childish thing long ago. However, she never parts with this memento, saying the little elephant reminds her of someone she desperately wants to forget. Now who could that be?

Although the color of her lipstick is a bright orange, she won't smile much. She's ashamed of her teeth. There's not a thing wrong with them. I tell her this constantly, but she refuses to believe me.

All of a sudden, he stopped speaking. He just sat there, staring at me with his eyes wide open, looking more than ever like a mannequin. Grasping his description of me wasn't difficult. Bertie's authentic singsong-insults, right down to his speech patterns, came right out of this character's mouth.

I jumped when his frozen eyes started blinking again and he said in a booming voice, "*Ginger*—with your friend's precise rendering of your obvious charms, I would recognize you anywhere."

Hearing this remark, I stiffened up like a statue myself, thinking that when Bertie's personality stops by to play—plus everything *else* about him—there's never a positive change, no matter how much you wish for one.

That oxymoron of a mutant intellectual-ignoramus, has never quit playing the wannabe soothsayer-game. He knew I'd show up here at this senseless establishment. It freaks me out when Bertie sees straight through me, and predicts my desperation. Maybe his still being around is a good thing. He'll make an idyllic match for my sister in the future.

Wait a minute. Have I now flipped for sure? If *they* ever get married, he'll become a *legal* part of my family. I'll never get rid of him. Forget I ever said anything about him and Vivienne. This serious lapse might be due to my brain acting like that woodpecker. Now, instead of doing a job on my knees, the industrious bird whittled-away at my irascible and bony skull.

Although self-conscious, just gapping at this odd "genie" of a man, I managed asking him, "If you work here, maybe you know whether Bertie rented an apartment up in The Bronx from this real estate agency or not?" He replied with, "I did help Bertie with his recent relocation, but not to *The Bronx.* Laws of confidentiality prohibit my giving you any more details. I am sure you understand."

"Oh, that's okay," I said, with a big sigh of relief. "You've told me what I need."

Due to the headache, I couldn't question him any further concerning his general relationship to the office. I really needed a bathroom. Although it's not good manners, I squirmed when I said, "Do you have a restroom here?"

Events of 5/28/72

ENTRY 18:

EVENING IN PARIS

"This was okay with me."

The spotless toilet, locating itself in a small windowless area, is old-fashioned with a rusty pull-chain hanging from a sweaty water tank on top. Charmin's Mr. Whipple hasn't been squeezing this coarse brown paper. While nature took its course, I glanced at those strange magazines. They spread out on a shelf made of beveled-glass, hanging on the wall across from the toilet seat.

They still looked new, although they were all charming obsolete periodicals dated within the first seven months of **1928.** Staring at the front cover of one of the magazines triggered a series of those weird flashbacks again—the very kind I mentioned having lucid dreams about, reliving playtime as a kid in my grandfather's recliner.

A large picture of the signature cobalt-blue bottle of **Evening in Paris** perfume started the film rolling. An advertisement states a French perfumery with the name of *Bourjois* planned on marketing their product throughout the United States *soon*—by the spring of 1928. I doubt whether people still use this, in today's world of modern fragrances.

My father's mother wore this perfume as part of her being. Given that she had the captivating name of *Ava,* as a child I imagined how she must also be from a fascinating country like France. When we'd take a trip to replenish her supply of this alluring scent, she took me shopping at a place just as good as going to Paris itself.

The local Woolworth's sold this popular perfume. You couldn't buy it anywhere else. On occasion, they'd be out of stock. This was okay with me. I'd get to go back the next week. We had so many exciting things to see in my *Parisian* paradise. Without fail, my grandmother bought me streams of assorted hair ribbons and packets of barrettes, and stacks of coloring books and paper doll kits.

One afternoon, she paid for a small lace fan—hand painted with the picture of a little girl resembling a cute doll. She wore a bright blue kimono and held a bouquet of pink cherry blossoms. Later on, when I could read, I found out it came from Kyoto, Japan. I recall that she paid almost as much for this fan as she did for her lovely perfume. I still have this special remembrance tucked away in my old room.

I remember how this store carried a large assortment of merchandise that said *Made in Japan.* Small metal toys, those abundant fake flowers, and painted porcelain oddities, were all popular imports. My grandmother sure had a lot of those colorful figurines. She loved shopping in "Paris" too. Even with those Asian overtones, Woolworth's was my equivalent of shopping on the *Champs-Elysees.*

In my junior year of high school, I edited the student newspaper concerning famous streets of Paris. From the day of that research, I knew I'd forever envision her holding my hand in the early evening, as we strolled along under manmade stars in the *City of Lights.*

Rejoining reality in Tillagevale, Grandma referred to our sacred excursion as, "Going to the five-and-ten." As companionable experts, we'd sit at their lunch counter, which she called a soda fountain, and share a super jumbo vanilla ice cream banana split, festooned with *Nonpareils.* Did you ever eat these bittersweet tiny dark chocolate crests, covered with those bright white pin dots of hardened sugar?

I loved them at the time.

And I still love them now.

She paid **39¢** whenever we bellied up to this memorable counter for our extravagant banana blast. She never cared about the price and always let me gobble up the luscious Maraschino cherry, floating on top of the banana's splendid whipped cream peak. I asked her once why eating the cherry was my favorite part. She told me that since they put a single cherry—on top of a banana split—it makes the exclusive cherry very special, and whoever eats the cherry is very special too.

These trips to *Paris* composed only a fraction of what my mother never knew about the overindulgent aspects of her in-laws, and their *conspiracy* to make me happy as a child. Or in common terms—spoil me rotten.

Every so often, either one of my hassled parents dropped off that mini-version of me to spend the night. After depositing me on my grandparents' front porch, I'd beg whoever it was to lift me back up so I could ring the bell. As soon as the door opened, it was time to hand me over. I was a lumpy sack of self-rising flour, looking forward to transforming into a tray of scrumptious cupcakes with chocolate-fudge icing.

Whenever those public weekend rallies against the strange place my father called, "Tillagevale Tammany Hall" took place, I stayed with my grandparents for sure. These meetings, with Daddy in sole charge of thrusting the Bullsnake gavel, were always my permit to a long and magical visit.

Events of 5/28/72

ENTRY 19:

NOXZEMA

"I empathized with Howdy."

The place my father referred to as "Tammany Hall" fostered my great overnight stays with my grandparents, so I wanted to go visit and pay it homage. I did ask him, at least a couple of times, to take me there. He smiled and said, "Owing to the sad, never-ending political racket, one day I'd follow the noise emanating from its crooked path—to protest there on my own." I didn't understand what he meant, and still find that remark puzzling. But just like I did with finding Carmine Street, I won't give up. One of these days, I *will* locate the place.

My parents were among the first in town to join the emerging civil rights movement. I'm very proud of them. I remember how they would sometimes be busy on weekends organizing actions to end segregation, and grant equal opportunity to all. On their bedroom dresser, there's a large picture showing them in front of *Ebenezer Baptist Church* in Atlanta, Georgia. Dr. Martin Luther King stood on the steps with them. All three smiled and looked like their hopes and dreams had put them on top of the world. I know this picture dates back to sometime in **1960,** because when I was five, I stayed with my grandparents for an entire week. Mom and Dad went off to Atlanta with a busload of Bullsnake members for something called a *Civil Rights Caucus.* Vivienne stayed with Aunt Sharon.

Whenever I did get to stay over—short or long—Grandma Ava showed me how to use makeup. First, I'd set the scene by taking a foamy bath. The name of the fragrant bubble stuff my grandmother used was *Yardley,* and the smell reminded me of a big bunch of lilacs. She really did love lilacs.

After drying off under a warm and snuggly towel, I'd put her black-lace bed jacket over my Howdy Doody pajamas. I empathized with Howdy. He had freckles, just like mine. Further thinking back to our beauty routine, I also remember the vanilla-like scent of the tiny little sponge Grandma used, as she helped me glide her *Tussy* red-rouge across my cheeks. In spite of her expert supervision, I still resembled a Kewpie doll with a zealous makeover.

Afterwards, I'd smear on her velvety *Tangee* lipstick. I'd use my clumsy pinky to smooth the color out and watch my lips turning into the bud of a tropical flower. This happened right before I'd get her big, fluffy powder-puff, to smother my entire face under her *Coty* ivory-beige face powder.

I had twenty thumbs with Grandma's personal Max Factor wizard. He materialized in the form of black mascara—the caked black kind that you wet and put on with a small brush. Anticipating the mess, Grandpa Des put *Noxzema* on the end of a tissue, and had it waiting on the vanity. He'd laugh and say, "Since when is looking like a raccoon fashionable." Even though I'd be in a fit of laughter, he'd still wipe the excess mascara from under my eyes.

I'd also never fail to fish around in my grandmother's crocheted handbag. She had many upscale purses, but nothing could surpass my favorite roughhewn one. The lure of its gazillion pockets was more than a little gal could stand. While searching for her diminutive bottle of Evening in Paris that she carried inside, anticipating the discovery made me more excited than delving into a Christmas stocking.

What a thrill for me to dab half the bottle of this scent behind my ears, and on my wrists. Luxuriating under perfume *and* makeup, in the huge big-people-bed in their guest room, I always had the same colorful dream of being a beautiful movie star, who'd tap dance better than Shirley Temple ever could. The next morning, I'd wipe everything off with gobs of her *Pond's* Cold Cream, using almost the entire jar. I loved each delightful moment I slept over. When my parents took me home, if you gave me a real close look, you'd discern tear marks stained with cold cream on my cheeks.

One of my favorite overnight times alone with them, concerns that multipurpose Noxzema. The stuff's messy. My grandfather always had to wipe an excess of the white concoction off his own fingers. This is when he'd grin wider than ever, calling Grandma and me his personal glamour girls. After making us feel so important, he'd zoom over to wherever Grandma sat and dab a playful smear of it onto the tip of *her* nose.

Laughing with my heart and soul joining in delighted me. Of course, there's been laughter in my life since then, but never really the same kind of joyous expression from deep within.

And this sort of laughter won't ever be again.

Events of 5/28/72

ENTRY 20:

THE ROSE BUSH

"He knew what he knew."

My grandmother died almost five years ago, but the memory of that day is as vivid as hours ago. Prior to what happened, people always commented on how healthy looking and active she appeared—until the morning when the terrible phone call came. The caring next-door neighbor walked by and he noticed her lying facedown on the grass in her front garden. He couldn't rouse her. Apparently, she tried planting a small rose bush—still clasped in her arms. She'd been digging a hole and a small spade was on the ground next to her.

Rushing her to the hospital didn't help. They talked of an undetected congenital heart defect. How she went through two pregnancies without complications from this condition, and had lived as long as she did, was a mystery to the doctors. Early the next morning, my parents told me—in as simple terms as possible—that she was, "gone."

Within two days after the funeral, those darling purple African violets she kept replacing on the parlor's windowsill faded away. I guess the delicate plants couldn't withstand the neglect during the grieving. Seeing the dead plants added to my grandfather's sorrow, yet he cared enough to give me the embroidered yellow velvet doilies. Throughout all those years, the material still looked new. To preserve them, I wrapped them individually in acid-free tissue paper, along with real lavender sachets. I added the family tradition of some dried rosemary too.

They are still where I put them, in the bottom drawer of my childhood dresser, standing between the dormers in my old room back home in Tillagevale. The little lace kimono fan from Woolworth's, is keeping them company. I'll get everything retrieved one day when I set up my own home, a home that my grandmother would have been proud to visit.

The grief numbed us, but we all had to go on with the cheerless pace of living. Daddy told the family he feared his father wouldn't last long without adored Ava. He knew what he knew. Eight months later, Grandpa Des went to sleep in his beloved recliner and never woke up.

Although *I* know how he *did* wake up.

Just to a different morning than mine.

Events of 5/28/72

ENTRY 21:

A DIFFERENT 'MORN' **"And chill with early showers."**

I had the weirdest experience being in the little toilet and reflecting on *death.* Why this happened to me, I had no firm idea. I tried rationalizing the morbidity by telling myself the cause resulted from residual trauma, coming from the Bertie *demise* mix-up junk. Everything concerning *him* turned out okay though. I had meltdown scars from the bus, to testify he's very much alive and kicking. Still—memories of my deceased grandparents overwhelmed me.

So many terrible things happened, going back to when my grandmother died. And the same terrible things repeated with my grandfather, following not too long after. A radical change developed concerning my former trusting and naive childhood perspective of death, like putting that once chirpy pet bird in a shoebox, and burying it in the backyard next to fashionable Sparky.

When Mom and Dad said my grandparents "were gone" where did they go? Hearing this meant somebody had taken them away against their will. *They* would never choose to abandon *me* on their own. When family members continued answering my questions, by telling me how Grandma and Grandpa "went to their reward, "I didn't buy the propaganda. If dying is so gratifying, why do people fight so hard to live?

Others kept telling me that Ava and Destry were "in a better place." This didn't sit right with me either. What place could ever be better than being with me?

Or having people at church say, "Your grandparents are now in heaven" was an abstract idea—an empty one, proselytized by formal religious education, and screaming Reverend Frisby. What they said meant nothing to me. After all, in my world as a child, and even now as a supposed soon to be *adult,* "heaven" just meant getting whatever you want.

The perceived "atheistic" ideology hurt even more. My grandparents weren't light bulbs, and their life forces were not victims of the grim reaper, shutting them off by flicking a switch. This take on death frightens me. These loving people still have to be *somewhere.*

A total rejection of all of these hollow explanations came after my father read a short poem at my grandmother's wake, concerning the perspective of someone you love dying, but he or she will awake to a *different* kind of *morning.* I found this thought very comforting then, and still do. Thomas Hood wrote the powerful words long ago in only eight lines and titled it:

THE DEATHBED

We watch'd her breathing thro' the night,
Her breathing soft and low,
As in her breast the wave of life
Kept heaving to and fro.

For when the morn came dim and sad,
And chill with early showers,
Her quiet eyelids closed—she had
Another morn than ours.

Because of this poem, I know what happened on the rainy morning they found my grandfather's body in his recliner—with those once warm hands still grasping his dear afghan. Everything would be okay. His beloved *chariot* had carried him off to smile like I remember, with those dependable arms around his beautiful Ava. She blushed again now, from his endearing kiss.

This is what made sense to me and carried me through the sorrowful days, and continues to support me now—pure, basic, and simple philosophy. In the literal end, any religious guesswork concerning death's aftermath is without merit. Nobody ever dropped by for a chat, to explain the situation upon *departing.*

None I happen to be aware of—in any such sad situation.

Events of 5/28/72

ENTRY 22:

THE WILL LEADS THE WAY "She wears it now."

Grandpa told me lots of stuff when I was a kid. Some words caught my attention and I listened, but more often than not, I let his well-intentioned speech go in one ear and out the other, as children often do. One thing I do remember him mentioning to me is how during Grandma's pregnancy with my father, she created that familiar afghan. "She worked on both projects together," he said.

He never did tell me a thing about the recliner, although I pestered him whenever I got the chance. He'd just put his arm around me before saying, "Ancient history, Buttercup. Ancient history."

After we all expressed our sorrow, in the ways that comforted each of us, we realized a hollow ache was destined to linger for the rest of our lives. I saw a different side to my father then, when he took charge of settling the entire estate. While the lawyer read the will out-loud to the family, Dad sobbed. My mother said she had never seen him so grief-stricken. Although the lawyer spoke, we all heard my grandfather's voice fill the somber room that day. "I place this responsibility on my reliable son, Alex. For him I would be honored to give my life, if it were not already taken from me."

He also mentioned in this will, how he wanted the family to gather whatever mementos they preferred and, "Give everything else in the house to Sister Gracie. She can make good use of what belonged to Ava and me. I am an old person who has known true love. While I ride off to that last roundup, my dear family will support me on the inevitable journey. Other elderly folks are not so fortunate."

Within days, they emptied the house where my childhood memories were once so good and so real. I felt powerless, and I was. In the past, I counted on going back there often to visit Grandpa Des and reconnect with my precious memories. I still saw my grandmother in that house, via all of her things.

The Woolworth knick-knacks, the African violets, the fingerprints of her gentle touch everywhere, the reflection of her loving smile streaming through the bay window—along with the sunshine—or sensing her forever-positive attitude, even in a downpour. Her crocheted handbag remained sitting on a kitchen chair. Grandpa said she kept it there "right as rain" and he couldn't bear taking another part of her away. As long as her "treasure sack" sat there, *she* sat there.

This beloved house went up for sale within two months. The music had ceased. The lonely *contents* now consisted of hollow rooms—echoing at full volume—with the weeping of a heartbroken silence. Before the furniture and other contents piled up for donation to Sister Gracie, I looked around everywhere for the Creamsicle radio. I couldn't find it. When my father saw me turning the place upside-down, he mentioned the old model went out of commission several years before.

My mother took the afghan, along with the recliner, placing them both in Dad's den. In the beginning, I'd go into this room and just stare at the cherished relocated-duo. Little by little, over the empty days, I'd sit in the recliner and cry with my face in the afghan. I still detected the faint smell of Old Spice.

Later on, though, sitting snuggled under the afghan evoked a strange sort of happiness and sadness melded together. I realized at this painful point in time how, for all living things, death existed as nothing more than the unavoidable price we pay for life. This also held true for my beloved Grandpa Ava and Grandpa Des.

I know Shelley took some keepsakes too. So did her parents. I already had the precious doilies, and they were more than enough for me. As for the radio, its music will forever play in my heart.

Also, I must mention here that when he gave me the doilies, a traditional 14-karat yellow-gold wedding band sat on top of them. This ring looked shiny and almost brand new. I didn't recognize it. *Her* wedding ring was white platinum, pave-set with a circle of tiny diamonds. For as long as I knew her, I only saw her wearing this ring on her left hand, never any other, and my grandfather gave it to Aunt Sharon. She wears it now. Yet for some reason he gave this curious one to me.

I questioned my parents and my aunt about this unfamiliar ring. They never saw her wear this one either. However, since my grandfather wanted me to inherit it, for whatever the reason, they told me not to worry or question his purpose. I should avoid upsetting him, more than he already was, and just take good care of his bequest. I did. The surprising ring now sits in a safety deposit box at the bank where my father works.

I try not dwelling on my grandparents being gone. As a child, when I'd cry, Grandma sympathized with me. She'd tell me to save my tears for the future, when they'd really be necessary. Whenever Daddy told her that she turned me into an absolute diva, she reassured him there's nothing wrong with my being a *diva,* as long as I live up to the title.

Over the last couple of years, though, I've been better able to cope with the emptiness in my life. Yet now—being in this strange bathroom—I felt my grandparents standing next to me. Grandma Ava's presence most of all. Her soft Texan-drawl whispered, "Ginger darlin', wash your little hands."

Concerning brushing my teeth or hygiene in the lavatory, she never let me get away with stuff. She always told me that a budding diva owes her public a perfect appearance. I picked up the delightful bar of heart-shaped green soap that rested on the pedestal sink in the corner of the small bathroom. I felt guilty wetting and wrinkling the sweet towel, embroidered with dainty orange marigolds, but couldn't see anything else to use.

I admired the peculiar lamp on a miniature crimson-colored stand. Its delicate crystals flickered like the bright coral-embers I remember from long ago, back in the beginning of my scouting days as a Campfire Girl—the precious moments when Grandma went along with the young troop. Everybody loved her.

Soon enough, with tender memories of my grandparents, giving me renewed purpose, I returned to the office. I looked at my watch thinking I'd disappeared for over half-an-hour. But time seemed to have slowed down during my strange reflections in the bathroom. I was gone for only ten minutes.

The turban guy still sat like a king on that regal chair behind the desk. He didn't notice me at first, due to his intense preoccupation with thrusting the feather pen into the deep inkwell.

Events of 5/28/72

ENTRY 23:

WATERMAN'S IDEAL "See this pen!"

I had made up my mind to make the best of this *office,* so I decided not to prejudge it. I became more confident watching the odd man at least engage with office equipment, sensing he really might work there. Where did he hide after pressing the buzzer to let me in?

I bet he went to that toilet area.

As he continued pumping ink into the long metal tip of his feather pen, in a haphazard manner impervious to the black substance splashing on the sleeve of his shirt, I thought, gosh didn't he ever hear of a ballpoint.

While staring at the sloppy pen, I noticed his extravagant bronze ring on the middle finger of his busy right hand—now covered with messy spots of ink. I remembered that my grandfather had a pen that also used liquid ink, but it didn't have a bird's tail. He called it his nostalgic model of a *Waterman's Ideal* with a fabulous "iridium-tipped, hand-ground point."

I remember his description of the pen verbatim. As a kid, the strange word "iridium" reminded me of Superman and comic book kryptonite. I had no idea why this explanation made the pen special—other than being lethal to Clark Kent.

I didn't know what a "Waterman" meant then. I just knew he loved this pen. My grandmother gave it to him as a present an hour before they married. He never parted with his wedding memento. He used it on the night he died. It rested on the little table next to the chariot, along with an open bottle of ink and an unfinished grocery list, where he wrote—get some butter, some milk, some bread, some . . .

My father has the pen now and uses it for Christmas cards and special occasion correspondence. He kept the unfinished grocery list too.

Once we had a big blowout over some kind of crazy thing. The reason draws a blank, so Dad must have been the instigator. His fingers shook with anger when he grabbed the sentimental Waterman out of his desk drawer, and plopped it into a bottle of ink. He filled the thing with such force that the dark blue liquid got under his fingernails, while he said, "See this pen! I cannot *wait* for the privilege of hand addressing *all* of your wedding invitations."

Since I had just turned fourteen at the time, don't you think that was a strange thing to say? Never could figure this one out either—along with all the other parental puzzles.

Putting prognostic wedding invitations aside, I'll return to the matter of this man's prominent ring. I couldn't miss the similarity to the design of the coins I saw on the bus, those bizarre coins, popping out of the slots in Bertie's shabby penny loafers. But now I sat close enough to notice some kind of Chinese-looking characters—etched on the thick band encircling this man's finger. Seeing my eyes squinting, to closer study the sort-of familiar ring, he thought I singled out his old-style pen when he said:

I see how you are admiring my exquisite writing implement. My father received it as a gift from the British government when he had the title of *Rajah.* His affiliation with the United Kingdom was prominent, and the very reason for my introduction to the English language. As a boy of twelve, my father arranged for my further education in Britain. I returned to my former home in India, only for brief family visits, at three-year intervals.

Upon graduation from Oxford University on my twenty-first birthday, I spoke English with the proficiency of any British native, and thus found my way to America and dear Carmine Street. Some would say how odd it is that my journey led me here to this office. I now know, however, that what we call 'just a fluke' is the result of the glow of kismet's comet, etching destiny into the heavens.

You got that right I thought, because—while he explained about the Rajah and the feather pen—a small iron table, now *next* to the desk, glowed in the sunshine. I hadn't noticed it before. I should have. It displayed a large vase filled with aromatic white buds, blossoming on skinny green branches. Obviously, these are the flowers permeating the air with the exotic scent.

I bent over the vase, to smell the blissful bouquet.

Events of 5/28/72

ENTRY 24:

SCHEHERAZADE **"His magic carpet wore thin."**

My face nuzzled the vase for at least a minute or two. Up close, these flowers really made me giddy. I thought some company should bottle this scent. As expected, he commented on my tripping-out in the posies.

"I see how you are enjoying the delights of night-blooming *jasmine.* If you think that they smell heavenly now, you should someday be near this flower in the evening. As its buds open, under the direct supervision of the moon, a more glorious aroma presents itself. Do you know the story behind this intoxicating flower, and how its loveliness came here to Earth?"

My shoulders tightened, indicating I'm not in the mood to hear any fairytale. After all, at that moment, I was *living* one—just from being in that office and talking to *him.* I surmised that he must be Mr. O'Flanagan's loopy assistant, and the bait of a potential apartment opportunity still pulled me in, so I didn't want to alienate somebody associated *with* the realtor. Although, according to Bertie's note, I should only converse with the owner.

Judging from the way he itched to explain, I had little opportunity to answer his question concerning my non-familiarity with the flowers, even if I did feel like hearing more of his eccentricities. Besides, other than commenting about their fabulous smell, I had no words to offer. I only acted polite, standing there listening to him, as he went on to tell me their history whether I wanted him to or not.

With fanfare, he held a few stems of the flower in his hand, waving them high in the air, before beginning his tutorial with:

The legendary genie—*Aladdin*—rode his magic carpet all the way to the moon, to snatch a branch of this flower. He felt certain that the alluring scent of *Luna's* spectacular creation would temp the Sultan to fall in passionate love with his beautiful new wife, Scheherazade, and spare her life. As we hear the story told, this ambitious ruler had a reputation for killing all of his young brides, whether beautiful or not—as soon as he spent the wedding night with them.

Scheherazade, his newest bride, proved smarter than all the other doomed wives did.

Knowing what waited in store for her the next morning, she began, on their wedding night, to tell this Sultan the first chapter of a fascinating adventure about Aladdin. She knew how piquing the Sultan's curiosity, with a new chapter awaiting him the following night, promised to keep her alive—at least for as long as the tale continued.

Scheherazade involved Aladdin in every one of her endless stories. Therefore, he had very selfish motives for caring about her fate. He no longer wanted her to formulate any more exhausting, never-ending escapades for him to fulfill. His magic carpet wore thin.

Aladdin gave Scheherazade the branch he took from the moon, asking her to plant the seedling in the Sultan's palace garden that afternoon. Of course, she did. Upon drinking in its entrancing aroma that very night, the Sultan decided to keep dear Scheherazade as his only wife. They had a long life together, with many little Sultans and 'Sultanettes' living in harmony with them forever after.

Scheherazade's endless stories that sent Aladdin on those harrowing adventures were no longer necessary. He had freedom to fly his carpet at leisure, anywhere he wished. Still, his adventures found their way into script—entertaining all by the title of, **TALES OF THE ARABIAN NIGHTS.**

I thought about what he had just narrated, and shook my head in acknowledgement of his Aladdin legend, which, just like the illogical office, did intrigue me. He motioned with his hands directing me to position myself like royalty on the matching velvet *chair*—across from him. Since this peculiar fellow already dared to sit on the presumptuous "throne" behind the desk, I wondered what Mr. O'Flanagan would say when he shows up, *if* he ever does.

While I made my way over to the other throne, I also wondered what his boss might think about my daring to fool around with the threadbare blinds and open the office window. "Before I forget, I hope Mr. O'Flanagan won't be angry how I needed some fresh air. I've got a terrible headache."

I heard no direct reply from him, but after I sat down—and yes indeed, this cushy chair *could* be fit for a monarch—he handed me a delicate white porcelain cup, decorated with dainty green shamrocks. On its large matching saucer, he had arranged a circle of small chocolate-covered crackers.

"Ginger—I have taken the liberty of being certain that some delicious Irish biscuits, along with a serving of the popular new *Ovaltine* drink from Switzerland, will be to your liking. I have enhanced this healthy refreshment by sprinkling butter and caramel sugar on top. Are you ready now?"

There was no need to answer him.

A deep sigh already stated *yes.*

I picked up the cup, and after some timid sips of the warm liquid, I became a *non-contorted* lotus, drifting on aromatic balmy water. Jack La Lanne wasn't around. There may be woes in this world, but none of them had relevance to me.

How blissful to skim across this tranquil pond, with the freedom of an ethereal swan.

Events of 5/28/72

ENTRY 25:

MR. O'FLANAGAN *"He is already here."*

Focusing on anything, let alone figuring out this character, was difficult when you're seconds away from snoring. I relaxed as the delectable crackers melted in my mouth, along with the revelation that—with gobs of butter and caramel sugar floating on top—Ovaltine *is* a comforting beverage.

I wondered why he said it's a healthy *new* discovery from *Switzerland.* This nutritional punishment has been in my Tillagevale kitchen ever since I can remember. As for adding the butter and sugar, this touch exposed me to a delicious first.

The logistics of refreshments aside, the combination of everything—including the royal throne—started helping my headache ease-up. I felt so much better, but just couldn't quit slumping down in that luxurious chair. From this lazy position I said, "Do you *assist* Mr. O'Flanagan, here at this office?"

"Yes, to my misfortune I do. I cannot escape that exasperating man, no matter how hard I try. Day and night, he forces me to be at his disposal every moment. This includes weekends and holidays. He always comments how I am the sole person on Earth he can trust to keep his money and his secrets."

At this screwy point, facing the strong possibility of Mr. O'Flanagan turning out to be even zanier than his assistant, I sounded less than enthusiastic while piping up, "Will he be back today? Bertie said that Mr. O'Flanagan is the only person I should talk to when I'm here."

The unanticipated eruption of his hardy laugh shook both of our thrones. *"No,* Ginger, he *cannot* be back today. The truth is he cannot be back at all. *He* is already here. *I* am Mr. O'Flanagan."

Without permission from me, my mouth opened wide from shock. Could this strange man be the actual *Irish* realtor I've been wasting my afternoon waiting for? An Ovaltine waterfall seeped down my chin, with a definite resemblance to my father's famous stuffing-slobber episode.

Within seconds of looking like a toddler, who's in dire need of a bib, the perceived *Mr. O'Flanagan* handed me a brand new white-linen napkin embossed with the letter ***S.*** A tag in bold letters read, **Handmade in Ireland for Wanamaker's Manhattan.** The quality of this napkin intimidated me. Should I use the exclusive thing? I never saw a *Wanamaker's* department store anywhere here in New York City. I'm definitely going to find the place later.

I did make a cautious effort to use this napkin without ruining it. In so doing, I overlooked some of the sticky substance coagulating on my chin. "Wipe, wipe," he said, with sincere encouragement. Soon after, he nodded in approval of my restored dignity. With his chore of cleaning me up completed, he puffed out a forceful breath of resignation before telling me:

Yes, concerning my Irish name, naturally you are astonished. The truth is, everybody has the same reaction. I am quite used to this situation and I tell all who inquire about my name the reason why it came to be. And, since *you* have now given me the usual shocked response, I will now tell you as well.

Long ago, a tall and adventurous Irishman stumbled upon my peaceful village in India. The women of this village are famous for their exceptional beauty, intensified with luxurious raven hair and ruby lips. Their sparkling dark eyes illuminate like brilliant stars, besotted in the moonlit heavens. These alluring characteristics are inherent matriarchal charms, and my ancestor from the *Land of the Lepricons* succumbed when he saw one of these beauties whose characteristics even outshone all of the others.

As he continued I thought not even Star Trek could top this, and I was right:

Adding to your expected confusion, the spelling of my given name is **S . . . I . . . N . . . G . . . H.** The pronunciation is the same as in utterance of the English word *sing.* My name is **Singh O'Flanagan.** I cannot begin to tell you the gibes I hear due to it. 'What *do* you sing?' they taunt. 'Can it possibly be, *When Punjabi Eyes are Smiling?'*

Ginger, I ask you not to pity me, for circumstances could have been far worse. What would my fate be, if I had been born into a family with the surname of *Singh?* Singh happens to be a very popular first *and* last name in India. Many a Singh Singh lives in my indigenous village. Imagine what I would hear in America, if *this* were my name.

In replying, cajoling him felt natural. "I sure *can.* You'd hear, "Where's your ball and chain?" I also thought to myself did I just meet an individual who is even *more* name-challenged than I am. At this illuminating point, his second hardy chuckle—in prolonged response to my "prison" joke—continued rocking the room, and this is when I started liking the eccentric man in the garish turban.

While the pleasant lilt of his voice wasn't helping my noticeable lack of concentration, the headache was gone. Not even a slight throb remained. I'm sure the hot Ovaltine and those delicious crackers helped a lot.

He continued smiling at me before pulling a stack of filled folders from a cluttered shelf, behind one of the now rolled-up tambour doors. He dumped this jumbled pile of papers on top of his desk and spread them out in a random pattern. For the first time since I met him, he adopted the demeanor of a proper realtor about to conduct some serious negotiations.

Events of 5/28/72

ENTRY 26:

CALLIOPE

"Or is this the emergency treatment for hiccups?"

Even though a sleepy haze surrounded me, I still heard Mr. O'Flanagan's genial cadence communicating with me in the background. He hummed like a rhythmic sonata, setting me to music, until I heard the unbelievable words, "How would you enjoy living in an exclusive residence near the park?"

With genuine excitement I asked, "Are *you* talking about Washington Square Park?"

"No," he said. "That park will only be a bad influence."

My vexation came to the surface fast. "Yeah, that's right. Greenwich Village is *much* too good to be true."

He, however, continued shuffling those papers around, giving no hint of any offense. "I am speaking of the epitome of all parks, the most famous one—Central Park, on Fifth Avenue, located across from the zoo. The place is so close to their magical carousel that often you may hear the joy of its calliope."

This spell of hyperventilation was so severe that I needed a paper bag to put over my head. Or is this the emergency treatment for hiccups? On the verge of passing out *or* hiccupping nonstop, I still managed to relay my frustration.

"Mr. O'Flanagan—I don't know *what* Bertie told you, but trying to save every spare penny forces me to room with my cousin Shelley. I do have a job as a temporary typist for Kelly Services. I'm great at what I do and I earn good money, but can we come back to reality here. I'm telling you straight up, there's no way on any *Kelly Girl's* salary that I can ever afford a place on *Fifth Avenue* near *Central Park*. No way."

His raised eyebrows conveyed such a look of genuine surprise that his turban slipped down his forehead. "Dear young lady, you misunderstand me. All of my current apartments are *rent-free.* I am surprised Bertie did not mention this point, before you came to my establishment."

In a split-second flash of febrile fury, my face burned like I'd been in the hot sun for hours. I had this mental picture of accomplishing my desire to rip out the gnarly Bertie—cowlick, I once learned to drive on. I almost did manage the furious task, back in the third grade. I'll succeed now. Mr. Drench, with his overworked bullhorn, will no longer come around to break us up. I think.

While he adjusted the lopsided turban, and I simmered down, I told him I had no information whatsoever from Bertie about any rent-free places. I also asked him how he managed giving places to people without any rent involved.

"It is quite simple," he told me. "I find tenants who will act as apartment *sitters,* so to speak. In your case the owners are . . ." and his voice trailed off. He jumped up from the royal chair and adjusted his turban once again before saying, "Come along. Come along *now.* We are going to the place that I have in mind for you. I will explain details along the way."

Events of 5/28/72

ENTRY 27:

SMITHSONIAN MODE "It is the bee's knees."

While we left "Ripley's" real estate office, Mr. O'Flanagan spoke in the hushed voice of a man, creeping out of a sleeping baby's room. Even though he left it open a crack, before completely shutting the door, I could no longer see the powerful bright light from inside the office. He looked contented, proud of a job well done, when he said, "I know you will agree with me when I say how my workplace is an exquisite representation in time."

Thank goodness that the lock acknowledged him first, by snapping shut with a secure click. What could a person like me say, other than I thought the whole layout was more than a little eccentric, and this sure wasn't an answer he'd appreciate hearing.

When I felt the vibrant spring air patting my face, I couldn't believe the time was going on 4 o'clock. As we walked away from the building, my eyes riveted on the sidewalk's curb—where a decrepit small black car parked. Four strange rickety wheels, all hanging by a thread under bent metal, stared at me from a few feet away. The horrendous thought that the wreck I looked at existed as my mode of transportation, wasn't soaking in. Not right away, I mean. In hindsight, though, I shouldn't be so hard on myself. What else could I expect from my own non-porous bonehead?

The outlandish style of this ancient car's arched front fenders, as well as those two huge eyeball-headlights, gave this blight on the quaint Village landscape the look of someone who's been shook-up to the point of hospitalization. A petrified spare wheel hung at a crooked angle, while mounting on the side of this car. This vehicle didn't have a roof or windows and reminded me of a pathetic junkyard reject—with two front seats.

A lone-piece of floating framed glass, divided in half, tried to play the part of a windshield, while the round chrome mirrors—protruding on each side of this makeshift windshield—stuck out like Mickey Mouse ears, in need of a good plastic surgeon.

Examining the jalopy up close, I remembered seeing a car like this one, right after my famous tenth-birthday surprise party. With parents chaperoning, and the town chartering a bus, Tillagevale Grammar School sponsored a summer vacation trip to the Smithsonian Institution, in Washington DC. We had fun that spread out over several days, while we made many interesting stops on the way there and back.

I'll never forget the museum's lifelike manikin of Charlie Chaplin—sitting behind the steering wheel—of the almost exact vehicle in front of me. At the momentous summertime, some of my *friends* doubled-over with laughter and joked about the perfect *hotrod* for me. They goaded me to climb in for a spin around the museum. I had no interest in taking up their offer. That menacing security guard, watching my every move, wasn't in the mood for a drag race.

While looking at this version of that car in the here and now, I experienced the same sort of jitters but without any cop around to haul me off. I also did a great job of convincing myself that the car had nothing to do with me. Without a doubt, some movie production company must be filming here on Carmine Street today. That is, until Mr. O'Flanagan stopped short—right in front of the wreck.

"Here is my pride and joy that superior **Model-T Ford** *Roadster Pickup*. When I bought this opulent vehicle, I paid a staggering **$475** dollars. I never regretted my extravagant purchase. The little gem is worth every dollar I spent. As soon as I am able, I will purchase some of those amazing *Royal Cord* balloon tires, the cushiony new kind, made by United States Rubber Company. My little **Runabout** deserves the best."

He patted the roof of this *car* before reaching into the bulky briefcase he carried. With a flourish, very much like my grandfather once used when producing that mysterious beret, he pulled out a tin container with a spout. "See me holding this *Texas Motor Oil,* designed for the crankcase. It is the bee's knees. I could never drive without this new innovation that makes those inconsistent startups easier."

He shook the thick "motor oil"—made from the knees of an unlucky bee—and poured the black sludge straight into the so-called engine. While the slushy stuff went *glug—glug—glug,* memories of the old Edsel looked tremendous. I treaded on the thin ice of fear, shaking with the chilly realization that he expected *me* to travel in this piece of trash. My

Smithsonian buddies sure turned out to be intuitive and an awful lot rode on this situation.

If that qualifies as a pun—please live with it. I can't worry about this stuff now. I must get back to the inspired way I figured out an answer to Mr. O'Flanagan's proud statement concerning his contraption, without infuriating him with my true feelings about this moveable collision.

Score one for me. My mind races a lot faster than *his* old heap. "An interesting car, I must say. It's the first opportunity I've ever had to ride in anything like it. There will *never* be grounds for such an incredible drive again in the future."

Whew, I couldn't do better than this.

Perfect!

Mental congrats were in order. Never in all of my life have I pulled off being so gracious, while feeling the complete opposite. I've stumbled upon "generic validity" a sure-fire way of igniting the stink bomb of honesty, without the other party even smelling the stench. I can now translate actual fibs into polite words, enabling me to speak the unabashed *truth* without a single ramification. I think this is what that political correctness junk is all about.

I knew that my new discovery worked, when Mr. O'Flanagan smiled with his pride intact, plus some, while opening the door for me. Getting in this relic, without an army to drag me, tested how low I'd go to get that free deal.

While I flushed with embarrassment inside the thing, he remained outside for several minutes, hand cranking the engine. He turned the dumb apparatus around and around, exhausting me from just looking at him. The car made an obnoxious din, sputtering and choking, gasping for breath. I thought that whatever this Texas Motor Oil sludge *is,* Tillagevale was the manufacturer.

He stopped cranking and hopped into the driver's seat. My eyes smarted from the steam pouring out of the smoky radiator in front. Now I comprehend *why* he put on those big aviator-type goggles *before* he did the crank-up.

As the car gained enough power to mosey and bump along, like a poor turtle, missing one of its legs, I rubbed my irritated—already very red eyes. Where's Shelley's *Visine* eye drops, when I really need the stuff. I sputtered myself when I said under my breath, "Please don't let people see me now."

Not wanting anyone to notice, made my slinking down in the uncomfortable seat very easy. As is typical New York, nobody paid any attention to the noise or the car, while we cruised uptown at the Daytona Raceway speed of no more than ten-miles per hour. But it still sent my beret flying. If I rode in this automotive-relic along Main Street in Tillagevale, a sizeable crowd would gather to watch us. A full-blown, living-color picture of yours truly, with a major focus spotlighting her mussed-up hair, was bound to appear on the front-page of tomorrow morning's sold out Gazette.

I guess the most fascinating aspect of life in Manhattan is the idea how, because so many outrageous events transpire here on a regular basis, the population is discerning about their reactions. They keep their cool. The unofficial slogan, among these New Yorkers, has got to be **deal with it.** Trust me here, concerning the tenacity of New Yorkers, even more than Mr. O'Flanagan trusts his useless Tillagevale-concoction—clogging up the arteries of his ancient engine.

Are you still not convinced?

If so, all you need do is take my story about Fanny Faller from Coney Island as a prime example and she will persuade you how tough New Yorkers can be. After *her* rescue from the ditch, the first thing she did was to boss everybody around.

Living here is definitely *not* for wimps.

Events of 5/28/72

ENTRY 28:

LAP OF LUXURY **"Women were mad about him."**

I stayed quiet for a few minutes, taking in the atmosphere, before I said, "So—Mr. O'Flanagan, what's the story with the digs? You said you'd explain on the way. I assume we're heading straight for them now in your *Roadster.*" While he answered me, he paid careful attention to the heavy traffic:

There are *no* archeological digs where *we* are going! However—the superb dwelling I have in mind, especially for you, is a duplex condominium inside of an established structure uptown on Fifth Avenue. In real estate terms, the word 'established' acts as the primary euphemism for buildings that have been in existence for decades. This exclusive two-story residence is under the auspices of wealthy people living in England, as part of their holdings in the United States. It is located on the **14th** floor. There are twelve spacious rooms within its two levels, separated by a winding stairway.

Each bedroom is in the upstairs portion of the space and all include their own private bath, and magnificent views of the city. Quarters reserved for a servant, locate off the laundry area on the first floor near the kitchen. There is also a large wrap-around, walking-out terrace, with a spectacular view of Central Park. The same view is visible from several tall windows, throughout the magnificent residence.

While Mr. O'Flanagan's astounding words floated around in the air, I noticed a loud thudding noise. My heart acted like the Mexican jumping bean my mother complains about. This deal got better by the minute.

Imagine *me* living in the lap of luxury on Fifth Avenue, across from classy Central Park. There will also be no more nasty arguments with Shelley *or* Vivienne about hogging the john. I'll keep makeup in every one of these bathrooms, in case of an emergency.

I forgot real fast about my beauty-ritual daydreams, when hoarse sounds emanated from his throat. He cleared his voice for what was coming my way. More than eager to hear everything he had to say about the rich people owning the place, my ears bent forward. With a final deep rasp, accompanied by an even deeper sigh, he told me everything about its history:

The spectacular apartment belonged to a daring chap by the name of *Alistair Perry.* Mr. Perry was quite a dapper young man. Women were mad about him. Men envied him. Their attitude not only testified to his being wealthy and extraordinarily handsome, they also knew of his fame and fortune as a deep-sea treasure hunter. And, in turn, he knew not only the visible world, but he also understood complex stratification beneath its oceans.

As a very privileged teenager, he attended boarding school on the French Rivera where he befriended a younger lad, Jacques-Yves. In the future, Jacques' destiny also led him to fame in the world of oceanography.

Alistair and Jacques both dedicated themselves to the sea. They swam together for hours in Mediterranean waters, warm as a comforting bath, while learning not to fear the briny deep. Indeed, these boys were adventurous lads, and a crowd-pleasing spectacle, as they practiced their innovative diving showmanship.

Not too long after his graduation, at the age of eighteen, Alistair found his way to America. He received a degree in Aquatic Science from Yale University.

In **1924,** after he turned twenty-one, the **United States Navy** sought his expert assistance in developing daring experimental diving methods using helium oxygen. He became the very first diver to do so with valid scientific success. You can hear the pride in my voice, as I speak of him.

Alistair, the oldest in a large family of six children, went back to England for a visit with his parents, and five charming sisters, for a stay of two months. At the still young age of only twenty-five, after accomplishing so many extraordinary feats, he had been away from home for many years. He had definite commitments in America, so when his vacation was about to end he prepared for his return.

The passenger ship he booked met with ill fate and sank during a heavy gale. Although he was the strongest of swimmers, the veracity of the wind overpowered and he—along with over a hundred poor souls—died in the wreck.

When he finished relaying the tragic story deep grief crept over me, almost as if I knew people who boarded the tragic vessel. "What was the name of the ship, Mr. O'Flanagan?"

"The ship bore the name of **Vestris.** We, *er* rather *they,* almost made it back. Sometimes, when I think of this tragedy, the horrific details overwhelm me. However, on **November 12th, 1928**—just **200** miles off Hampton Roads, Virginia—the valiant mistress went down. I tell you now of the most disastrous day-of-days."

By some sluggish means, when he slumped over the steering wheel from exhaustion, after an explanation that apparently drained the life out of him, the car dawdled up to the curb in front of an impressive building. The tall and wide structure consisted of huge square blocks of gray cement. It reminded me of a medieval castle—without any mote or knights in shining armor—jostling around. Had we arrived at the final destination?

With what felt like no more than a second later, I stood underneath a black canopy that had four bright-brass poles supporting it. I had no memory of stepping out of the car. I think the cream of the crop, tree-lined block distracted me. The formal welcome by a tall doorman, with broad shoulders, was also nothing to sneeze at. His black uniform, loaded with starch, acted as a firm base for his flaring red cloak. Seeing that official looking gold-braided hat of his made me feel like a regular **VIP.**

"Pleased to meet you," the attendant said, while staring at me. "I assume you are the young lady planning to do the caretaking job for the Perry estate." Although this building employee looked diplomatic, he acted rude by ignoring Mr. O'Flanagan. He never even looked at him. I wondered what kind of charm school for doormen *he* graduated from. I made a mental note never to tip him, if I do live there in the future.

In less than a minute, I heard a clinking sound. This arrogant attendant was in the process of handing me a bulky silver-key, dangling off a metal chain tagged **Perry #14-C.** To my astonishment, I told him with a new kind of authority, "Time to check the place out."

I already acted like a girl, in firm charge of this Perry-pad.

Events of 5/28/72

ENTRY 29:

PEEPING POTTERY **"I'd even settle for Nibble Nuggets."**

The building I entered appeared more than what you'd call "established," with that old Victorian birdcage-type elevator crawling all the way up to the 14th floor. When we got off the waggling cage, I saw Mr. O'Flanagan's hands motioning to me—"Down the hall, right here."

I felt apprehensive twisting the bulky key in the lock. As soon as my hand quit shaking, I rubbed my eyes from astonishment, which made the irritation even worse. When the stubborn door opened, the most breathtaking space greeted me. I felt more than awkward, stepping on the lavish maroon rug—presenting like a work of art in the middle of the room. This carpet has the animated weave of an impressive red and gold dragon. Its thickness had my boots disappearing into the plush pile.

One whole wall of this palatial room is made of glass. There's no specific window treatment. Only a white-lace valance, entwining a lengthy dark wooden pole, spans the top of the window's matching wooden-frame. I hesitated to take a closer look at the curtain's beautiful simplicity. Inching toward it, I bent down and stroked the portion of lace, which touched the floor, being careful that the fingernail I broke—while trying to open this apartment's entrance door—didn't snag the delicate material.

The fabric, hand-loomed in England—at least according to the small label I spotted near the hem—appealed to me. I realized how this gossamer window treatment is uncomplicated on purpose, so as not to obscure daily pastel hues of a softening late afternoon sky, hovering over impressive treetops in Central Park. My legs trembled as the whimsical sound of a calliope rode the breeze through an open window, located *somewhere* in the huge place.

I wandered into the kitchen while Mr. O'Flanagan stayed in the other room, as he wrote with preoccupation on a piece of paper. This time he used a pencil. He'd never risk splattering ink on *that* carpet.

The kitchen is a scrumptious raspberry-sherbet color, with ceramic-tile counter tops in the shade of a sweet tangerine. Since a state of extreme starvation took over *again*—I salivated with the thought of food. Any food. I'd even settle for Nibble Nuggets. White bead-board cabinets, which stretch all the way to its vaulted ceiling, didn't appear to contain anything edible. They just brimmed over with vivid crockery of all colors. This curious array of empty dishes peeked out at me through square panels of clear pane glass. With equal curiosity, I peeked back.

A soaring orange and brown ceramic cookie jar, in the shape of a rustic windmill, sits on top of a notched butcher-block island in the center of the room. Visualizing the presence of cookies tempted me. After lifting the canister's heavy lid, I expected to find at least one stale biscuit or something. But no luck. Not even a single crumb sat at the bottom. "Got to keep this jar filled to the top," I said, talking to Mr. O'Flanagan, as well as myself. By now, he stood next to me.

A white squatty appliance, on tiny feet-like legs, stands next to the island. There's a noisy round motor on top. It could be an old-style icebox, except for the motor. I opened the heavy hinged door to check. The primitive refrigerator appears electric, but there's no freezer compartment. A prominent logo on the inside of the door reads **General Electric Monitor 1.** I thought, gosh, Shelly's dumpy kitchen has a more modern refrigerator than this thing. Her freezer is small, and filled with frozen fish for the cats, but at least it exists. I can always manage to squeeze-in my ice cream.

Back in Tillagevale, though, Mom has a new and huge *GE* refrigerator in the nauseating new avocado-green color—the current rage. And, in ultramodern addition, there's a sizeable freezer on top with its own separate door. She also has an electric stove and dishwasher to match, with everything being part of her recent kitchen makeover.

I wanted her to buy the also popular harvest-gold appliances. My father remained adamant, though, saying he couldn't let their scatter-brained daughter, that's me, influence this major renovation. So, since the brighter color wasn't on sale, an abundant crop of dull avocados grew in our kitchen.

Mom went vegetarian with her new interior decorating trip. She bought the same green color for the new linoleum and window curtains. Also, don't let me forget mentioning the ceiling light with green bulbs, the *agricultural* wallpaper designed with huge ripe avocados—splattering all over—and the matching colored tablecloth and placemats. She got corresponding Formica countertops from somewhere too. She also painted the legs on the kitchen table and chairs using the same disgusting green.

The best part though, is the showy portrayal of piles of avocadoes on the kitchen chair cushions. Whenever people sit down on them, they mash them into *guacamole.* In view of her disastrous gastronomic design, Daddy complains whenever he's in the kitchen about the distinct feeling of floating in a sizeable pot of pea soup—without the ham hock, unless, of course, *I* happen to be there. I ask you though, *who* is to blame for his perpetual cannibalization? Not *me* this particular time, *that's* for sure.

Letting busy cannibals have a rest, I'll get back now to *this* apartment's strange kitchen. Aside from the whirly fridge, there's a large old-style gas stove, made from a vibrant yellow color—tall and wide—with six big burners. I tested one of them by turning the sizeable knob, and the unit fired-up with a roar.

A brand name, etched in a metal strip on top of this stove, reads **Glenwood Deluxe.** I had fun, opening those three breadbox-like side ovens. I couldn't see a scrap of evidence that a cook ever baked, or roasted, anything in these mini-compartments. Still—assorted used cast-iron pans sat in the convenient storage cabinet at the bottom of the stove.

Everything about the stove, just like the rest of this kitchen, is sparkling clean. The Smithsonian should duplicate the entire room for an exhibition. They could place mannequins of Stan Laurel and Oliver Hardy, posing inside. Some of their old movies portray kitchens, very similar to this one.

Now, I'll return to the non-cinematic kitchen.

Here—a virtual jungle of lush green plants assembles on this room's window-ledge. I looked close, and the simple flat piece of wide timber, supporting this *garden,* didn't display any Zorro skull and crossbones. I only saw the same yellow paint color as the stove, and it aligns along the ridge of the elongated white enamel kitchen sink underneath it.

Mom would love all that shiny floral material wrapping around this sink, like a poufy vanity-skirt. I lifted the fabric and took a quick peek, noticing how it disguised the sink's bright brass-pipes. Not a single can of RAID hung around. I didn't spot any creepy crawlies under there, chubby or otherwise. What's *not* more, I couldn't find any dishwasher near the sink or anywhere else. I should suggest getting one. I'll broach the convenient subject later.

Shinny copper skillets and pots—with signs of loving wear and tear—hung from an oblong steel rack, suspended by four lengthy black chains. Although appearing heavy, the big thing had large iron bolts securing it to the kitchen's high ceiling. Somebody centered it over that well-used butcher-block island.

Standing on my tiptoes, I reached up and touched the cool exteriors of the suspended cookware and they spoke to me about pining for their chef. Meeting and greeting them caused me to salivate even more thinking about the thick egg omelet—with a heap of Double Gloucester melting in the middle—that I'd whip up in one of *these* very old Galloping Gourmet gizmos.

Okay, this will be my new place for practicing culinary art.

But what about the rest of this museum?

Events of 5/28/72

ENTRY 30:

ALISTAIR

"Profundity means depth."

A sizeable domed room, with dark mahogany paneling, is adjacent to the kitchen and appears to be a den. The flagstone fireplace, complete with logs ready to burn, reflects a cozy atmosphere. There are some old pictures mounting on the wall of this *den.* Something pulled me toward them with the force of an invisible rope. Most prominent, were several black and white snapshots of a tallish, well-built man with dimples and curly hair. I judged him to be in his twenties. No skinny and homely weakling in swimming trunks here, this much I know.

Another photo, enlarged in an elaborate silver frame, sits on top of an ebony **Baby Grand** in the center of the room. This specific photo, on the shiny piano, depicts the handsome guy barefooted. He's wearing a long tank-top shirt and short pants, as he stands between two people. In this rendition, he looked as rigid and serious as the austere fellow standing to the left of him did.

This military person is clad in what appears to be a regimental type of uniform. An oversized plumed helmet hides part of this mature soldier's stern face. Both of this militiaman's gloved hands grasp a sword, more menacing than ceremonial, and this graphic *weapon* dangles off a thick leather-like waistband around the hips of this man's stately fame.

An elegant, tall, and thin woman stands on the younger man's right. She wears a fluffy mid-calf sundress, skirting her high-heeled boots. Dark hair piles high up, under a very wide-brimmed straw hat. She holds short lace gloves in one hand, and a folded ruffled umbrella in the other. She gazes at him with a look of tenderness. In a strange sort of way, this beautiful woman resembles what could be a mature version of Vivienne.

Additional photographs capture the same younger man, frolicking on a pier with five spirited girls. Two of these young ladies are in their late teens and wearing Flapper dresses. The others are younger and prance in dainty pinafores.

A few more of the photos show him standing alone on the shore, with his remarkable profile looking with wistfulness toward the sea's vast horizon. I asked Mr. O'Flanagan, "Are these pictures of Alistair Perry?"

After I mentioned the name of Alistair Perry, his voice grew softer and more sentimental in tone, as he told me, "Yes, *yes,* the very same. He appears in photographs here, taken at the famous resort of *Blackpool*—while on vacation with his parents and exquisite sisters. These are indeed charming depictions, showing him on a family holiday, enjoying the North Coast of England. Two days later, he sailed on the doomed Vestris for his return to New York.

When a photographer from the seaside hotel took these pictures, the weather for late October delighted him with unusual warmth and sunshine—more like summer than autumn. Do you sense how Alistair's family had such pride in him? Although they did not take pleasure in his imminent return to America, they knew his fate aligned with the ocean's profundity."

I must have looked puzzled, because Mr. O'Flanagan educated, "*Profundity* means depth."

Now—if Bertie trailed here along with me, he'd answer him with something like, "Profundity is a deep word," followed by his phony pun apologies. But I only nodded my head before he continued to explain:

In some of these pictures, did you notice the look on Alistair's face when he stared at the horizon? I am sure he speculated about the vast amount of Celtic riches he might find, underneath the mythical Irish Sea. I am sure that if he had more days there, he would have arranged for an expedition in these waters.

When I speak of the dear ill-fated Vestris, I must tell you that he desperately tried to save the women and children who panicked on this capsizing ship. He paid no mind at all, to his celebrated young life. He dived into the cold, murky water several times to snatch many of these helpless wee-ones out of the ocean in time. Thanks to him, the one lifeboat left afloat was filled to its brim with shivering boys and girls, clinging to their grateful mothers—such a courageous chap—our young, Alistair.

After he finished relaying this terrible scene, the quiet of a graveyard descended on us. He bowed his head in a prayer, while six lingering memorial chimes resonated from somewhere in a distant room. Can it really be 6 o'clock, I thought. I checked my watch and the hidden clock was right on the button.

He stood there without saying another word to me. He just remained in the center of the room, with his eyes searching, almost as if he couldn't believe he was in the grand place too. With the last of those six loud chimes still echoing, I broke the solemnity of his current prayer-like stance by asking him the dumbest question in recorded history, "Got any *cats* here?" He ceased meditating fast when he said, "What is wrong with feline friends? You are not fond of them?"

Gosh, he thinks I'm against animals or something. I had to clear this up so I said, "My cousin Shelley rescued five, and I'm a little inundated in the cat area now, that's all. I don't hate them or anything."

"All right," he answered, "but you must not worry. Alistair had no cats. He traveled the world too much. And even if he did adopt any, after the event of his tragic drowning so many years ago, they, too, could no longer be with us."

I felt the warm blush of embarrassment spreading across my face before I blurted out, "If he died so long ago, why keep his place?"

It didn't take him more than a second to explain:

Ginger—let me tell you now that Alistair left his extraordinary mark on all who knew him. When the Vestris met its final resting place, on the furious ocean's sandy bed, Alistair's father, Viscount Reginald Perry of Her Majesty's exclusive **Imperial Guard,** could not accept that his precious only-son could never return. He made the heart-wrenching decision to keep the memory of Alistair alive—undisturbed for eternity.

This apartment will remain without variation, exactly in the same way his precious son left it before setting out for his last journey. A reliable caretaker like you will, at all times, watch over these outstanding quarters. Viscount Perry stipulated how, upon his death, the family must allocate perpetual funds toward its upkeep. Future heirs, who attempt to rescind this irrevocable requirement, will lose their inheritance.

"*That* will ensure loyalty," I affirmed.

I never anticipated his answer after I asked him, "Where do I come in?"

Events of 5/28/72

ENTRY 31:

SOUND MATTERS OF SCULLERY

"Now—let me see."

As soon as I asked Mr. O'Flanagan what function I'd have at the curious museum, he stiffened up even more. And, while he pulled a long list from his shirt pocket, he looked and sounded like my father—except much worse. With that recognizable expression on *his* face this time, lips pursed . . . eyes narrowed . . . eyebrows raised . . . nose twitching . . . jaw jutting out, he did everything possible to let me know how I'm sure in for a lecture.

MR. O'FLANAGAN'S DISCOURSE

Ginger—your job will be keeping this place neat and tidy. Each day you are to adjust your schedule, so that at the end of every week you have accomplished the following:

You are to water and fertilize all the plants in the kitchen. This watering also includes the trees and potted-palms out on the terrace. Do not neglect them. You did not go out there yet, but when you do, you will see how many of them await your expert attention. Should any of the abundant greenery here, whether inside or out, ever need replacement due to nature, please tell the doorman. He will replenish them as close as possible to the original ones. If the cause is your neglect, *you* are to finance new ones.

The weather is good now, but as warmth gives way to frigid—you are required to cover the outdoor garden with heavy burlap to prevent any frost damage. The doorman keeps this stored in the basement. He will help you bring the cumbersome rolls up on the elevator, and before the inevitable freeze comes, you are to reach up high and tie that bulky-burlap tight. If you do not, it will sail off to parts unknown—just like Christopher Columbus once did.

Keeping the entire kitchen sparkling clean is *mandatory.* Alistair prized his French copper cookery. In the kitchen's utility pantry, you will find a special caustic polish to maintain them as bright and new.

You are also to wipe down all the pictures and every curio you see. You will soon learn that Alistair had a wide-ranging assemblage of these sentimental dust-collectors, gathered from around the world. They are all still here, and looking as good as new. Your job will be to maintain them in this pristine condition. The special walnut oil, and soft polishing cloths for this extensive job, sits in the utility pantry as well.

You are also to polish *all* of the carved furniture. And, as you can see, plenty of intricate detail exists for you to contend with. You will need to dig into the furniture's deep crevices by using the strange new stick-probes, with cotton on their tops. I believe they refer to them as *Q-Tips.* Thousands of these widgets are also in the same pantry. I caution you, they deplete fast.

You will also be washing every window inside and cleaning every mirror—leaving no glass in the place untouched—including the kitchen cabinets. The vinegar and cheesecloth for this job locate in the same pantry. I read an advertisement recently, for something known as **3-in-One Household Oil.** They proclaim it as being the 'new way' to wash windows. Please utilize all the vinegar first, before you purchase that latest chemical composition.

Get yourself a strong pair of rubber gloves in the proper size, in order to clean all the bathrooms and to scrub down the kitchen—including every tile floor in this duplex. Speaking of the *tile floors,* there are also several other types of flooring throughout this mansion, which consist of assorted woodblock and modern Congoleum *Gold Seal* linoleum. To clean *all* of these floors in a proper manner, you must get down on your hands and knees with the heavy-duty horsehair brush. I recommend that you use the kneepads provided.

Rheumatism, at your young age, would be a terrible shame.

You will dip this brush up and down inside that industrial-sized bucket provided for you, after you fill it with powerful *20 Mule Team Borax Powder,* diluted with water—as hot as your hands can tolerate. Mops are *not* sanitary. You need what I call, *elbow grease.* Put your nose to the grindstone, now.

I had been very patient listening to all this junk, but when he talked about a stone grinding my nose, I almost turned around and walked out. Then, I thought—well, that's one way to get rid of the freckles. I smiled at this concept, and I think he felt I was being sarcastic, because he didn't look too pleased when he went on to say:

You will *also* need some real 'medical grease' on your aching elbows, upon completion of these obligatory chores. And—after what I just heard you thinking—some of it for your nose too. You can find powerful *Watkins Red Liniment* on the top shelf of the pantry. This soothing ointment has been a favorite since **1868.** You cannot dismiss exactly sixty years of merciful pain relief. When I played Rugby, back in those good-old-boy university days, I could not have scored as well as I did without this soothing medication.

We do think of everything!

Then—there is the crucial matter of all the carpets. Before he left for England, Alistair acquired the *Hoover Positive Agitation-Model 700* vacuum, and they have the audacity to advertise how their new invention eliminates carpet impurities claiming, 'Suction lifts the rug from the floor and floats it on a cushion of air, while the Agitator gently flutters out all the dirt.'

Vacuuming each priceless carpet every week with this machine is mandatory—no ifs, ands *or* buts. Even if those heavy Persian wool rugs appear as though they are *not* in need of the noisy contrivance, you *must* use the thing.

I, being of the old school, do not hold much stock in such namby-pamby carpet treatment with that sporadic electricity. Give *me* crisp sanitary air, carpets hanging on a strong outdoor rope every Saturday, and a hardy billy club to swing. In England, they refer to them as *bully clubs.* These substantial wood bats allow one to thrash carpets for hours, in order to do the laborious job with efficiency. A trusted vacuum cleaner from nature, if you ask me.

You *cannot* suspend these thick carpets out of the windows—or off the terrace railings—in order to beat the bedbugs out of the heavy things, no matter how much you are tempted to try it. We are too high up, and safety *is* a concern. As I always state, what shall one do.

Washing and ironing towels and linens, in Alistair's modern laundry room, will be easy. He had just installed an up-to-date *Maytag* washing machine. What a wonder that automatic wringer is, although you still must take the soaking-wet items out of the washer's tub, and place each one of them through it separately by hand. *All* you will need is a repetitious pump of the pedal with your foot, in order to operate the marvel. This certainly trumps turning that unyielding wringer by hand.

I must tell you though, even with this new method, doing the sheets and towels is quite a chore. Then again, like every other miserable thing in life, there often is a bright side. In truth, I hear some women claim how use of this nifty electric-pedal fosters delightfully trim ankles.

Following his comment about *trim ankles,* he emitted some funny *ah hum, ah hum* sounds, just before wiping perspiration from his forehead with the palm of his right hand. Next, he said, "My heavens, why am I perspiring like this? I am supposed to be beyond such titillating topics. To be safe, I will continue with more sound matters of scullery. Now—let me see, what *is* it that I am supposed to say now? Oh, yes, by George, I've got it! I will tell you that Alistair's iron is modern too, and it controls heat with one of those new *thermostats.* No more of those nasty ironing-day burns to material *or* fingers."

Right after his description of the dumb iron, making it out to be the latest modern wonder of the appliance world or something, an eerie silence permeated the room. He stood there like a statue again, still holding on to the inventory.

Is he done?

Nope.

I had only a brief respite, while he stopped his machine gun commands, to whip out a clean purple-silk hanky and wipe thick droplets of sweat off his brow.

He also made a loud honk, while blowing his nose.

Events of 5/28/72

ENTRY 32:

CINDERELLA "No snooping allowed."

During the precious two-minute interval, while Mr. O'Flanagan flipped with the thought of some poor maid's ankles wearing down to the bone, words to the "Cinderella Song" started buzzing around in my brain. I went off the premises, enveloping in a melodious cloud of:

Cinderella ♫♫♫ Cinderella ♫♫♫ Cinder . . .

"Ginger!"

"Oh yeah, Dad, *what* did I do now?
Um . . . oops!
I'm sorry, Mr. O'Flanagan."

He glanced at me very much the way my mother does when I give her what she calls *backtalk,* before continuing the gibber-jabber:

I was *about* to say—that you must see the doorman in order to file a prompt report of any problems. He will manage the issues as soon as possible. On occasion, he does come in to inspect the premises. He will tell you beforehand. He is also an excellent handyman *if* the need arises.

I mentioned before about the servant's quarters next to the designated laundry area. Well, it is windowless and quite narrow with a single cot, a small chest, a basic lavatory, and a utilitarian shower.

In your situation now, however, caretakers for the Perry family may choose any bedroom upstairs that they wish to use, with the exception of the one belonging to Alistair. This chamber remains locked and sealed, never to be touched. A metal plaque on the secured door warns **Do Not Enter.** Alistair's bedroom has not been touched in forty-four years, down to the rumpled sheets he left on the bed. I know you will respect this.

Hurrah, I said to myself, when I thought there might a chance it'd be quitting time, because even *he* slumped from exhaustion. Have you ever seen somebody who stopped talking to you in mid-sentence and stared into space, like being in a trance or something? At that moment, it could be a snapshot of *him.* I bet he has low blood sugar too. I sure know *that* stupefied look. But who's at fault? *He's* the realtor in charge. He should keep some good snacks on hand, shouldn't he?

While I had this chance, during another one of his stupor-stages, I gave him my puppy-dog look and said in my best coquettish voice, "Me? *Snoop.* Never happen."

Although I couldn't understand much of what he harped about for the past hour, and I had bigger and better stuff to dwell on, I still put on my dependable act. "Is this *enough?"* I asked him, in my practiced over a lifetime sincerity-tone. "Is this *all* I must do? I'm sure there are a few *other* things you *might* have in mind."

Hey—I kept a real straight face when I said the insincere words, and this cover-up still counts as willingness to comply.

No way, you say.

I guess you *do* learn something new every day.

Events of 5/28/72

ENTRY 33:

WESTERN UNION **"What could be simpler?"**

When my hopes grew high that the endless rub-a-dub-dub litany ran out of suds, my question caused him to blink his eyes, as if he were coming out of his unconscious state. Mimicking Cinderella's wicked stepmother, but now she wore a turban and showed off her nasty goatee, he answered right away. Just imagine the double earache I developed, while listening to him for a *second* time:

You need not question your obligation. I have informed you about the few *simple* things necessary that solidify your verbal contract to take this position. The estate pays the maintenance, as well as any regular bills, so you need not worry. I am also giving you very special permission to install a small—now let me think here for a second. *Hmm*—what *is* the term again, for that silly image-machine?

Oh, right. You may bring a *television.*

You may also play Alistair's new **Orthophonic Victrola.** He never really had a chance to enjoy those revolutionary *Victor Acoustical Records* he collected. They are indeed new wonders of sound to thrill you.

Do not mar these expensive recordings, designed exclusively for this Victrola. Speeding up the sound, by accidentally cranking the mechanism too much, will desecrate the illustrious tenor, Enrico Caruso. Even though he has left those of us here on Earth, we do not want his immortal voice gyrating into one of those new jazz singers.

The telephone here, on the desk, is at your disposal. Do not abuse the privilege. I know they are now developing the potential for a human voice to travel overseas, via the marvelous communication invention of Mr. Alexander Graham Bell. You might be impressed to hear that I met the distinguished Mr. Bell a few years ago, having the distinctive honor of shaking his hand. Quite a chap!

Now getting back to other wonders of today, I hear this miraculous European vacation, via telephone, incurs outrageous charges by the minute. Your type of chitchat will cost as much as flying over the North Atlantic, on the luxurious new *Graf Zeppelin.*

Do you know how this comfortable airship transports its fortunate passengers to Europe, in little over a week? This is why the price for Zeppelin trips is not feasible for most. So please *do* keep your calls in the **USA.** If for some reason you cannot, please contact *Western Union* for an economical telegram. Speaking of this vital service, I have a reliable tip, from exclusive sources, how in five years hence they will sing their greetings to people. Bad tidings will also be available in cheeky musical format. My stars, what *is* this world coming to!

At this point, he appeared to shock himself into another prolonged silence and returned to the statue routine. I wasn't frightened. I'm so used to Shelley. Otherwise, I'd think he went into a coma standing up. I took this quiet chance to think about how he could have met the inventor of the telephone. I recall from history class that Bell died in **1922,** and my father sent my mother one of those idiotic singing-telegrams when she had her "diamond earrings" birthday, five months ago.

Mr. O'Flanagan is lousy in math. The way I figure, the *liniment* he talked about has been around for **164** years, not the **"68"** he mentioned. Counting sums on fingers with the other hand—bad arithmetic or not—he *is* right about Western Union singing "bad tidings." I know this, because when that squirt of a telegraph messenger showed up at the door, with a big bunch of helium balloons for my mother, she was *not* impressed—and this is an understatement.

I think her ungrateful, and all-around lousy reaction to these festive white balloons, may have been due to the big, bright-red printing on them, announcing: **Today is a Milestone for Mary**. And for such a little guy, he amazed us all as he went on to sing, **Happy 46th Birthday to You** in a voice so loud, Mr. Drench's bullhorn mimicked a gentle whisper. This auditorium-style entertainment caused all of the neighbors on Azimuth Circle to open their windows and shout, "Congratulations, *you* don't look it!"

The next morning, I noticed *someone* had been sleeping on the living room couch. I guess not even Howard Johnson and Tiffany & Company could get him out of the doghouse. But that subsequent cruise to Paradise Island, in the Bahamas, sure did.

Referring to travel—what's with Mr. O'Flanagan's dumb idea about flying to Europe on a slow zeppelin? Why do *that* when you've got Pan American Airline's fast new *Boeing 707.* And how about all of the improvements going on now at New York's **JFK** airport? PAN AM is expanding runways and terminals to accommodate this new line of jumbo jets.

And people say I fabricate. *They* should hear *junk* like this. How dumb does he think I am? Zeppelins just advertise hotdogs and beer at baseball games. One will occasionally fly over Tillagevale's new professional sports ground, built on top of the overflowing garbage dump known to locals as "Perfume Inlet." If you're ever lucky enough to catch one of these clunky tanks advertising **United Cornpone Bank,** it'll take your mind off the lingering unpleasant smell at a typical *losing* home team event.

This recent stadium is a major overkill. Athletes with superior ability can use this place, and there aren't too many around. This is how well equipped it turned out. As a bungling result, the effort was the usual waste of taxpayers' money to the carefree tune of almost half-a-million. The governor got away with it, by sneaking the cost inside of some *pork barrel* under the guise of "special education for those with physical and mental challenges." He sure got that part right!

I *also* realized how contacting Vivienne later on, after she trots off to the Congo, wasn't going to be easy. I must face facts. Where *my* sister plans on heading, is as distant from the good old *U.S. of A* as any teacher of square dancing dares to twirl. Looks like the blazing question of whether or not Pygmies like the Virginia reel, will forever remain a mystery.

When he snaps back from wherever he *goes,* I'll reassure him that international telephone usage won't be a problem. And my reassurance appears to be imminent, because he just started continuing his lecture as if he never even paused.

"You are allowed to cook simple meals here. As instructed, be careful to clean up. No wild parties now, although you can invite respectful family members and friends."

All of a sudden, a frantic vanilla-bean alarm went off. "Say—since you're speaking of the kitchen—*again*—where do I put my ice cream? There's no freezer. And, I might add, there's no dishwasher. Even my cousin's dump, *er* I mean *place,* has a small portable dishwasher." Of course, I refrained from telling him that she bought hers *after* I moved in.

He scrunched up his brow more than ever, and speaking in that now familiar puzzled tone, he said:

What do you mean—there is no *freezer?* A wooden bucket, facilitating ice cream, is in the pantry. All the rock salt and sugar you need sits on the shelf, right along with it. Buy yourself the eggs, the cream, and anything else you want to put in the mix, and just churn away—not that I am an expert in this area. I never bother with the tedious chore myself. There should be plenty of the fattening frozen concoction in three hours or so, depending on that elbow grease.

Now, concerning this *dishwasher* drivel, you only need look at your own hands. Put on your sturdy rubber gloves and find the dishrag, along with the bar of handy *Palmolive* soap, like everybody else does—and scour away.

In conclusion, is everything I have explained, including your ice cream preoccupation, clear?

Clear, I thought. Is he kidding me? I had never heard such gibberish before in my entire life—not even from Vivienne and Bertie. The perfect opportunity had arrived for me to shine as bright as those coppery pots *before* they get all tarnished.

I scratched my head before I said, "*What* could be simpler? *I'll* be professional. *You* can rely on *me.*"

Events of 5/28/72

ENTRY 34:

IN THE CLINCH

"*He* can stay in the servant's dungeon."

With those three concise and ingenious promissory sentences, I had clinched the deal. When I came up with these useful declarations of sincerity, discretion prevented me from mentioning some stuff. Stuff like the way my mother called my room back in Tillagevale, "Ginger's version of the county dump." Or—how Shelley tells everybody she meets that since my arrival she could get spare money from renting her place out as an "obstacle course."

How relevant are these dumb family observations anyway? What does it matter, if I didn't comprehend much of his "scullery" gobbledygook? Who cares, the place is *free*.

Free. Free. Free.

Instead of frittering away the exhilarating moment to focus on tedious household garbage, I flew as high as a summer kite—buoyed by the windfall in front of me. I'll save most of my salary and, coupled with my scholarship, I might be able to study at New York University. After all, it *is* the famous journalistic hub for young career hopefuls like me, and I already know about what goes on in Washington Square Park.

My euphoria deflated, when Mr. O'Flanagan sauntered over to the fireplace mantle. He was on his way to retrieve the cumbersome door key I placed there, when we first entered the overwhelming place. Dangling it in front of my nose, he said, "Here, *you* keep this key and, before I forget, please tell your dear parents you will be safe here. The doorman was once a New York City policeman, and lives in the building's basement unit. He is almost always on the premises."

I thought about why he said my parents were "dear." Before I questioned his insane opinion, he went on to say, "Feel free to do that compulsive *snooping* on your own now. I must not be late for an appointment with some lofty people."

Gosh, I thought, he's dumber than I realized. He's willing to trust me alone in this historic slave-pit when he's aware of my true nosy-self. I couldn't think of anything else to say to him except, "Bye, and thanks so much."

"There is no need to thank me," he replied. "Instead, I suggest you thank your very good friend, Bertie Norman. He is the one who vouched for you, praising you to the skies, except for telling me how you are quite pugnacious."

"Yeah, you're right. I *will* try to thank him," I sort of said with sincerity, since I needed to check what the word *pugnacious* meant first. I had a strong feeling the adjective wasn't a qualifying trait for Miss America.

His effort to remind me about my obligation to my very *good friend* caused another eureka moment, hitting me like one of those Gantry lightening bolts. I could make some dumb Bertie-lemonade—out of Bertie himself. Where would I ever find anybody better than Bertie, to take the bait about living in this ostensible rent-free place here in the best part of New York? What they don't get in cash, they get from the sweat of your brow, along with the rest of your body attached.

He can stay in the servant's dungeon. He's already here in New York, and he'll be contacting me soon. Even you understand by now that I don't need any "trust me" on this one. He knows I'm rooming with Shelley, and her name is in the phone book. With *him* living somewhere in Manhattan now—I don't need any Western Union kid to sing me a depressing telegram. His counterpart with the initials of **BAN** will gladly do the job for him—on a daily basis.

You know what, it just occurred to me that Bertie's initials spell the word "ban" and gives great advanced warning for innocent people about to encounter him. I'll go and get a big pitcher from one of those crockery cabinets, and start squeezing those sour lemons. *He* will turn into sugar for the mix by becoming my very necessary cleanup-pigeon—my *indentured* pigeon, that is.

The poor creature can fly outside onto the terrace to spread its sore wings. It would be worth his while to break a lease if necessary, in order not to pay any *rent.* I'd be subjecting myself to his puns, but so what. With college and work, I won't be around all that much. I'll be fast asleep, locked upstairs in one of those great bedrooms with a private bath and magnificent views—far away from his scullery prison cell near the laundry room.

He won't care. After all, when a guy like him worships that nut **Diogenes,** who once loved living inside of a water barrel on the street, he'll think he's at the *Ritz Carlton.* Cinderella problem solved.

Events of 5/28/72

ENTRY 35:

GHOST OF YESTERYEAR "She swooned."

As I followed Mr. O'Flanagan into the building's hallway, I gripped the key so tight I pinched my fingers black and blue. I carried it to be safe, even though I left the apartment door ajar. I didn't want to hassle with opening the stubborn thing again without supervision.

Standing there in the dusky, narrow space, a muted light placed his remarkable, albeit far-out countenance, within a shadowy bubble. While looking up at him, I knew I'd never see him again. I didn't have a clue why.

The hallway looked as gloomy as I felt. I stared at his back, as headed toward the waiting elevator. His purple turban bounced around, giving the distinct impression of floating down the long hallway. In a trance, I watched its jewels fade like once glowing candles, ready to extinguish on their worn-out wicks. In a final flash, reminiscent of a shooting star, he disappeared. Nothing of him remained except his footprints on the hallway's thick carpet, and a strange glow of light radiating from the elevator shaft.

The place sure is creepy, and going back into the museum alone gave me the chills. I checked out the "modern" laundry room. Too bad everything is as he described, with the exception of a large utility sink's outdated scrub board standing by, a wooden ironing board standing up, and several clotheslines standing in wait.

That servant's quarters next-door, excuse me—I should now say Bertie's room, appears as though an interior decorator from Folsom Prison designed it. One look will have the great Johnny Cash composing a new jailbird's-lament to sing. I'd buy the record, would you?

I knew you'd agree. Johnny Cash is *so* great. I saw him perform in Tillagevale once, just because he got lost. His tour bus went far off the beaten track, when it ran out of gas three years ago, coming to a grinding halt in front of the remote old-folk's home I told you about; the facility near the railroad tracks. Nobody in town ever goes out there, unless they know somebody in the place. On this day though, when word spread about Johnny, a crowd gathered in front.

At first, Sister Gracie refused to believe Ferguson, one of the "senile" residents, when he rushed in to tell her how Johnny and his new wife, June Carter Cash, stood in the backyard gazebo while they sang *Ring of Fire,* accompanied by their entire band.

She checked.

She swooned.

She sipped a *medicinal* hot toddy.

She also danced with Ferguson and found out within a minute that he didn't suffer from dementia at all. Quite the opposite, I have heard. Later, she went around telling people how she understood, for the first time in her life, the meaning of the expression, "There may be snow on the roof, but flames still blaze in the furnace."

I don't get it, do you?

You do! I guess you'd explain, if you were here.

Hearing it might make me blush, you say.

Now I really, *really* want to know.

Hobbling back to octogenarians, the recent widow, that dear Blossom Biddle, who had not danced in twenty years, threw her crutches to the ground—before snatching Ferguson, right out of Sister Gracie's arms. The cute *new* couple *cut a rug* until around midnight, when Johnny and his gang, armed with a full tank of gas, maps, and complete written directions, continued their regular tour. He comes back to the home at Christmastime every year now, to entertain the residents and brings a ton of presents for them. He also makes sure Sister Gracie has a good supply of bourbon for those medicinal purposes.

Speaking about entertainment, I located that "Victrola" Mr. O'Flanagan mentioned. I hadn't noticed it before, next to the fireplace—near the piano. The manufacturer's name reads **Victor Talking Machine Company.** How far-out can you get? Answer—a lot more, and you'll see why later.

This tall and box-like device is made of furniture-grade wood with a mesh-paneled front. The top lifts to display an intricate turntable, if you want to call it that. There's also a fat book of usage instructions, suitable for a mechanical engineer. I'm not worrying, however, about my total lack of technical ability. I'd never play the thing—*instructions* or not.

And—what's with those big and heavy so-called "records" stored inside, the ones imprinted with a sizeable dog that barks straight into a gigantic horn. After inspecting all of these *recordings,* I found out Alistair sure loved the *Caruso* guy. Several of the record covers stated that the contents contained the *acoustical* voice of this Enrico Caruso.

The one that stood out the most depicted a colorful picture of a portly man with a big black moustache. He wore some kind of a clown costume. Underneath this picture, in bold writing, were the words: **INTRODUCING THE WORLD'S GREATEST PAGLIACCI.** I wondered what's so "great" about his being a *Pagliacci,* whatever *that* is. Also, I'm sure not familiar with any Al Jolson or Eddie Cantor. And what's with, "Lively Stable Blues for a Fox Trot?"

So, I'm happier than ever that I brought my great portable stereo to New York. This thick cement castle has reinforced soundproof walls, comparing to the cheap construction of Shelley's place. I'll play mine here, as loud as I like, without fear of rogue brooms. In these historic digs, with that dumb record player as part of the scene, I'd even be thankful for Doris Day if I couldn't play my own. I'll admit she has a gorgeous voice.

Because time grew shorter than Napoleon, I didn't go upstairs and pick a bedroom. I'll make my selection of the biggest and best *permissible* one later. Even though I'm capable of bypassing many obstacles, I'm leaving the prohibited chamber in literal peace. I won't even *attempt* a breach, no matter how curious I am. For obvious historic significance, Dance Macabre is *not* one of my favorite classical pieces.

I went out onto the terrace, using the French doors from the den. Tarzan and durable Fanny Faller could swing on all the shrubbery growing in this huge outdoor space.

Looking down over the railing, I observed a lot of skipping children pouring out on to Fifth Avenue from Central Park. They left the zoo before dark, after a long day's adventure of feeding and petting the animals. I pictured their excitement, and happy nighttime dreams, from reveling on that swashbuckling carousel.

I envied those blissful kids. Maybe being an adult isn't so hot. They looked carefree—running at a pace with helium balloons—while "grownups" couldn't keep up and slumped from exhaustion.

I remember being a kid, content with just a helium balloon. Unless, as usual, Vivienne got the bigger one—the sturdier balloon—that never broke away from its string or floated off to oblivion like mine always did. Or popped and stunned *her* into tears.

Since I no longer heard any drifting vibrations from the calliope, the zoo and the carousel had closed for their deserved rest. Tomorrow is Memorial Day. The park will be crowded with more visitors. I'll go there often, when I live across the street. Yes—looking around at that beautiful Manhattan skyline, convinced me to move in. I'd be foolish not to, wouldn't I.

The sun prepared to set. The glorious blue sky of the day had now turned scarlet red, with a metallic bronze-hue chiseling deep valleys, into waning white clouds. I know this is weird, but while looking up at this astonishing panoramic vista, I knew my grandfather stood out there with me. I heard his voice, as the late-day breeze rustled branches on some of those decorative potted trees. Within this swishing sound, he quoted the adage he relied on whenever planning a fishing trip. **Red sky at night, sailor's delight—red sky in the morning, sailor's warning.**

My notorious imagination was kicking in on high speed. I told myself to remember, how Grandpa once said that the wind plays tricks. I chocked back tears. Hearing something that reminded me of his comforting voice made abandoning the terrace difficult. He had a real presence, out there in the twilight. I could've stayed for hours, but soon night would fall. I *had* to go back inside the eccentric place for a few more minutes, to review what Mr. O'Flanagan told me.

As I closed the French doors, with all of those square panes of glass, I thought what kind of idiot uses oil to wash them. Even a domestic disappointment like me, knows a household disaster when she sees one. Didn't he ever hear about *Windex?* I'll buy some generic brand for Bertie. I might spring for cheap paper towels too. I don't want to risk collapsed wings on my pooped pigeon.

Also—what's with washing dishes with a Palmolive soap *bar?* "Madge the manicurist"—in all the TV commercials of the past few years—hasn't fed *him* the propaganda how doing the slave-chore of washing dishes with Palmolive *liquid* soap makes nails and hands as captivating as the most expensive beauty parlor in Hollywood does.

With those eight reverberating chimes, from the enigmatic clock I've yet to encounter, I handed the place back to the **Ghost of Yesteryear.**

Before grabbing my shoulder bag, now stuffed with pages and pages of notes and quotes, I turned off all the lamps. The least I could do was ensure the ghost returned to comfort in its accustomed darkness.

Locking the door was much easier than *opening* it.

Events of 5/28/72

ENTRY 36:

INCOMMUNICADO "Even for *you.*"

Rushing back up to The Bronx was easy. I had big Bertie-news for Vivienne. He's alive and kicking. And, for once, he actually behaved like a genuine pal by helping me get the best place on the globe. Of course, I had that major stipulation. He must agree to be my pigeon, and fly around the place.

My parents couldn't come up with any more arguments. I'd be safe and secure with *that* **24-hour** Gestapo-doorman. I bet the guy never takes a day off. Also, my father tells me how "reliable" Bertie is. This twisted opinion will be another weapon in my New York arsenal, and it's probable I'll put *myself* through college. How could he not be impressed with *this* kind of practical planning?

Yes, the museum-pad will be a soirée with my future fame and fortune.

When I opened Shelley's Bronx door, I dashed to the phone. Before I even dialed to make that call to Tillagevale, it rang on cue. "*Vivienne,* what a coincidence. I just got back here and was about to call *you.*"

She sounded tired when she said, "Yeah, Ginger, I bet. I've been trying to call you too—all day. Do you realize it's almost nine? Why the heck don't you and Shelley get one of those new answer machine thingies? I think they're cool."

"Vivienne—do you realize how much they cost? Shelley and I went to Macy's to check them out. The cheapest one is **$300.** All the models weigh ten-pounds, and using this contraption means changing two very bulky reel-to-reel tapes. I can't even change a dinky typewriter ribbon. Shelley wants nothing at all to do with buying or maintaining one."

"I guess not then, Ginger," she said with disappointment. "They're sure expensive, aren't they. I think this is the reason why Daddy won't get one, here at home."

I wanted to tell her she's right, for once in her life, but didn't. Instead, I said, "Speaking of home, Vivienne—I understand why you're calling. You want to tell me about the correction in The Gazette about Bertie. You don't have to. He told me himself, when I saw him on the bus this afternoon."

An abnormal silence permeated the other end of the phone, until I heard Vivienne drop the receiver with a loud clunk, and shriek like the maniac I'd soon be. *"Ma,* Ginger is *totally* spacing out. Daddy said she'd eventually inhale bad influences, but she's *already* smoking something. *She* says she spoke to *Bertie* on the bus *today!"*

You know what, when Vivienne behaves like this I understand why I squelch any infrequent emotions I may have about missing her. I heard exasperation in my mother's voice when she picked the phone up off the floor. "Ginger, *what* is going on? You have your sister in hysterics."

"Mom, I only said how I saw Bertie today and . . ."

As a rule, my mother allows me to finish a sentence, and even though she doesn't really want to listen, she'll throw her hands up in the air and do so anyhow. This time, though, she cut me right off with, "What do you mean that's *all* you said. I know New York has a reputation for being callous but this is too much, Ginger. Even for *you."*

Although Vivienne wears that **Out to Lunch** sign on a regular basis, I just got an obvious message how my lights are on—but I'm so far away from home I'm twirling batons in the jungle with pygmies. "Mom, is there something I should know that I *don't?"*

"Daughter of mine, you're lucky your father isn't home to hear this lunacy. Are you aware he has an open-ended airline ticket to New York City? He's able to use it at a moment's notice. Well, *this* is the moment. If he hadn't gone outside now, to walk Bertie's mother and father across the cul-de-sac, he'd be heading straight for the airport. Bertie's parents spent the entire day with us, poor dears."

As soon as I heard her call Bertie's parents, "poor dears" I knew something was *not,* in the words of Shakespeare's Hamlet-character *Marcellus,* "rotten in the state of Denmark." Whatever the "something" *was*—it had found a new home in Tillagevale.

Before long, I heard her telling me in an exasperated manner, reminiscent of my father—right before *he* loses it—"Now *what* on God's green Earth is your *latest* nonsense all about?" Search me, I thought. Since I had no answer to a question that I couldn't understand, I circumvented the riddle and said, "By the way Mom, what's the real deal with Bertie?"

Events of 5/28/72

PART 37:

MINCEMEAT

"She wants to know what he wrote."

Under normal everyday disastrous circumstances, and there are many, Mom almost never raises her voice—this goes for when I cleaned her renowned Tiffany earrings. Through *no* fault of mine, one of them slipped down the drain. Cesspool Brothers, Inc. got that half of her gift back after five hours. Dad wasn't even grateful. He said he could've bought her a replacement one—for less than that "crook of a plumber" charged him. On *this* draining occasion, however, my mother sure shattered my eardrums:

What is this phrase, the *real deal?* Is it some kind of new *hip* jargon for expressing concern? Poor darling Bertie, he was such a sweet and caring young man. I'm aware he wasn't your favorite friend. However, he did like you. His mother told us early this afternoon that a couple of hours before he died on Friday, Bertie summoned all his spirit to write *you* a lengthy letter, when he could hardly hold his pen.

Even with all of his young strength ebbing away, Bertie begged his mother to make sure you receive his letter this Monday. Although the post office closes for Memorial Day, he was adamant that she mail it for **special holiday delivery.** Vivienne wanted to warn you that Bertie's voice from the grave is coming your way *tomorrow.* Wait. I hear your father. He's *back.*

My mother mumbled something before I heard, in full Autry baritone-glory, "Ginger, this is your father speaking." Yeah, right—like I didn't *know* this. Why does he always tell me who he is? I'm certainly not going to forget, although often I'd like to.

"Um . . . hey, Daddy, how are yuh?"

"Don't you *dare* give me that 'um hey Daddy' business. Your mother is still trying to calm down your sister and if Viv doesn't stop hyperventilating soon, we will need a hotline call to Dr. Mendel."

I thought to myself that her acute overreaction must be because she has usurped my role of Drama Queen. "Is she *that* bad Daddy? I'm sorry. We just had a simple misunderstanding. All I *meant* to say was how I saw a guy on the bus today who looked *and* acted a lot like Bertie, that's all."

"Well, Ginger, you'd better be *real* careful from now on. Please don't make mincemeat out of your words in the future."

"I won't Dad, I promise, but are *you* telling *me* that Bertie Norman is really *dead?"*

I heard the frightening sound of my father gritting his teeth, as the vexation in his voice aimed for a crescendo even *I* never heard before. "Now you see, *Ginger,* this is exactly what I'm talking about. Of course, he's dead! A correction in today's paper simply explained how an elderly man with a similar name died on the same day. When such a young person leaves us there is considerable shock, and this kind of shock extends to the obituary personnel who made that confusing name transposition. Some people on the staff knew Bertie from childhood."

Well, concerning the word *shock,* this may or may not be true regarding **OBIT** sentimentality, but just ask the five startled cats what they experienced as I gave them a collective shove off the couch. Although I felt woozy, sitting on their prized territory, I found a squeaky voice to say, "I do apologize, Dad. *Honest.* Please tell Vivienne for me, and I'll send Bertie's parents a sympathy card."

"Wait a minute, Ginger. Your mother needs to talk with you again. Don't hang up."

There wasn't enough strength left in my body to hang up, even if I wanted to. Without the aid of any vampire—all the blood had drained from my body. The phone's receiver was a strange black iceberg, calcifying in my hand. Within a second, I heard my mother say, "Please give Vivienne a *rational* call tomorrow *after* you get Bertie's letter. She wants to know what he wrote." I shook when I told her, "Okay Mom, I will. I promise, and I'm really sorry for any misunderstanding."

"Yes, dear. We do know that. We're just out of practice here, since you've moved. We must adjust to you—all over again. I'm getting your father a migraine pill now. And, while I'm at it, I'll set one aside for Vivienne and myself.

Goodnight."

Events of 5/28/72

ENTRY 38:

TAHITI

"*She* needs a visit to the Mayo Clinic."

When I pried the icy receiver out of my stone-like hand, the phone emitted those pulsating off-the-hook warning buzzes. The irritating sound snapped me awake, long enough to hang up. The totality of what I just heard from my family sunk in. Everything was a way too much, even for me, and this says a lot.

The whole insane situation had to be true. My parents are right up there with the most annoying people I know, but they're not liars. They imbibe in moderation and they don't do drugs, with the exception of those prescribed on occasion by Dr. Mendel. They also don't cheat people—other than my father's penchant for those taller-than-regulation golf tees. They never act wild either.

That is—with the exception of the incidence when I heard them whispering about the Internal Revenue Service humiliating them. It happened while they took care of Uncle Eddy's brand new heated-pool, when he vacationed with Aunt Sharon and Shelley. He couldn't wait to go sightseeing up in the Grand Canyon, to test the traction of his flamboyant new canary-yellow *Porsche.*

I don't know if I mentioned this before, but although my dad studied accounting too, Eddy is the only *Certified* Public Accountant in Tillagevale. Each tax season, at practically the very last minute, a crowd of jumpy clients will lineup outside of his office at the mall. He's famous throughout the surrounding area for his expert knowledge of tax-loopholes pertaining to agriculture. He saves farmers a bundle. When the stroke of midnight signals the closing date of filing, he's ready to upgrade his lifestyle each year.

Returning now to the evil influence of income tax, Vivienne caught Mom and Dad skinny-dipping underneath this pool's—preset at 80-degrees—waterfall, with the enticing Tahitian-theme. How stupid were they to think she'd take a nap. Vivienne was young. She got over the revulsion. I think.

Now—I'll get back to the other gruesome reality. With Bertie *dead,* what kind of trip happened on that bus? What's with the Mr. O'Flanagan person that I spent this afternoon with? What about his offer for a dream pad? Trying to answer these questions would cause an ordinary girl to dial **911** and order the straitjacket in advance. But since I'm that exceptional pseudo-brave, natural-born snoop, I've decided to plunge right into my *own* hot water and explore what's going on.

I'm famous for finding the underlying cause of a mess, especially when I'm the one who makes the mess in the first place, so it's easy for me to find the culprit. You'll need to tune in later though, regarding my sought after sleuthing-expertise. This, too, needs to be a journal by itself.

Due to the Memorial Day holiday tomorrow, Kelly Services is closed. Day off or not, I'll go straight downtown to Carmine Street for a major chitchat with Mr. O'Flanagan or a reasonable turbaned-facsimile.

By now—I need one of those migraine pills myself. I'll just have to settle for a couple of Shelley's *Midol* tablets. She has a ton of them hidden. Of course, I know where they are. She's stupid enough to put them in a box of *Kotex.* I often question how somebody like her suffers from **PMS**—365 days-a-year. *She* needs a visit to the Mayo Clinic.

Sweet dreams Journal, 'cause you're the only one sleepin' tonight.

Chapter 8

THE DAILY ENTRIES

MONDAY NIGHT, MAY 29TH

Exhaustion took over. I'm not even going to check my watch. I need to think that it's early evening, instead of after midnight, in order to keep going. You'll understand why, as you follow along with what happened today. You're still in the year **1972,** of course.

Events of 5/29/72

ENTRY 1:

SNOW AND SAUDI ARABIA "I promise."

Can you imagine that I'm still intact on the morning after the craziest Sunday in the world. After everything that happened to me yesterday, I heard the announcer on the radio say how today is Monday, May 29th.—**Memorial Day.** He had a very solemn voice while lecturing his audience.

In addition to assorted historical trivia, he expressed concern that the day's significance was usually lost to people chomping on juicy burgers at family barbecues. He doesn't need to worry about *my* forgetting. I have a strong premonition that the one thing in my life people will chomp on today is *me.*

As predicted, sleeping last night was almost impossible. When I did manage to drift off, on my miserable sofa bed, I kept waking up from a nightmare at twenty-minute intervals. The same one popped up over and over, about Bertie being with me in Mr. O'Flanagan's ideal Roadster, but it now had the extraordinary power to fly.

We soared like a rocket over Tillagevale on a crusade to find Samurai Fuji, and Reverend Caesar O. Frisby was behind the wheel. The once slow and clunky—three-legged-turtle Model T—now raced like that jet-propelled Kolinsky Circus pony-cart ride. While the *Reverend* broke every conceivable speed limit, along heaven's highway, Charlie Chaplin sat on the holy speed-demon's lap.

I'll return now to yesterday evening *before* I fell asleep with that nightmare. I kept thinking how glad I am that my cousin isn't around for the coming crackup. She must be cold, snoring on that mountaintop. I don't think they have any kind of central heating in an austere-ashram. There's always a rugged fire though, where logs burn out around three in the morning. Then, you scrounge around in bed, or in her case on the scratchy mat, while looking for blankets that you don't have.

By now, while Shelley is experiencing this chilly summit-situation, her gratitude for dodging The Bronx is dwindling, just like that fire, while mine is on the rise. I was cozy *in* The Bronx, under my thick down-comforter, with the potential of her empty room beckoning me.

After the emotional exhaustion of what happened, I wanted the chance to sleep there. She has this new kind of wooden platform bed—with a firm foam mattress that she covers with soft Egyptian-cotton sheets. The customized thing has huge drawers underneath, where she hides oodles of stuff. Inside this cool upgraded-area of hers, I'd be comfortable with a quiet chance to assess my phenomenal situation.

I could *also* close the door and barricade myself to keep Daisy from jumping on my chest. Shelley, on the other selfish hand, has her exclusive bedroom protected with a foreboding crowbar-type of security device, riveted into the floor. She calls it a *Fox-Lock.* Everybody knows I'm able to outwit any regular fox, but I've never cracked this one. I sure broke my back trying last night. As a body-wide sore result, I realized that not even Harry Houdini could've managed the task.

I almost had a heart attack when I found out my cousin rigged the fox with a shrieking siren. Atomic decibels wouldn't stop blasting for an hour and woke up the entire borough. I think the neighbors' chipped brooms bit the neglected dust last night, once and for all, like the old Edsel did. Nah, forget it. The brooms, along with the neighbors, have eternal life—just like Barnabas.

Regarding annoying Daisy, I've learned from experience that if I barricade her in the bathroom, along with her food, water and a litter box, she still cries and cries. Hearing her wailing all night long usually makes things worse, and this was the last thing I needed. Also, what happens when I *go* in the middle of the night? The answer is this mini-cat will bolt out of the toilet like the *Road Runner,* and I have to chase her all over the place.

I'm never light-footed, so what I call the denizen-chorus will surely start their pounding routine, and plaster will fall from the ceiling. Since relaxing was hard enough, following the weirdness that went down, I couldn't add any more stress to the paranormal cauldron. I had no choice but to resign myself to that darned bedtime visitor. To my surprise, having Daisy drool on my chest worked out okay. In the complicated and lonely darkness of last evening, I had this compelling need for her to be with me. As I tried to nestle myself between the lumps and bumps of the saggy sofa bed, I found myself stroking her fur.

The only previous tactile contact I had with this cat, was grabbing her by the scruff of the neck when she tried using me for a pillow. Getting rid of her by depositing her on the floor was useless. I gave up the exhausting practice after only a few nights when, just like a true feline-boomerang, without fail she came right back every time.

Yet, while I kept petting her during last night, I learned that such a scrawny thing *could* be soft and cuddly. I used to think her penetrating dark eyes were spooky. Yesterday, while she verified *Mesmer's* theory of "animal magnetism", I found her once *spooky* eyes to be *perceptive.* She must be growing up.

Daisy's breath was sweet too, considering all of the homemade fish-chow she eats. Shelley, the pet food company, adds mashed up string beans, and who knows what else, to those simmering fish-heads. The brew smells worse than those Chitlins, but the little nuisance thrives on the stinky stuff.

Speaking of the fish in the brew, Shelley uses those gross flounder-heads she gets free from the supermarket to make this *baby food* for Daisy. The guy behind the counter "likes" her, but she says he's older than her father is so forget any potential romance. I think that because she enjoys the complimentary fish, she tolerates the flirtatious complimentary conversation. She leads the older salesclerk on. I've been with her and seen the way she smiles at him and flutters her eyelashes like Lillian Gish does, in one of those old silent movies. She denies any special *feelings,* but this is seafood for another day.

Her favorite movie is the Rogers and Hammerstein musical *Carousel.* She has the soundtrack and plays it loud enough to drown me out when I practice my hobby of yodeling and Swiss bell ringing. I won lots of State Fair competitions growing up. I'll tell you about my extraordinary talent in that future journal.

Yes, I will. I promise.

Now—yodeling back to Shelley, at full pitch or not, she sings one song in particular from this Carousel album. The title of it is *Mr. Snow,* and centers on Enoch Snow, the *mature* and robust fishing entrepreneur in the plot. I'll admit Shelley has a great voice. She stood in front of the chorus as lead soprano in the church choir back in Tillagevale, so her frequent apartment *concerts* are tolerable.

Every time I hear her *crescendoizing* with the song's reprise-lyrics—"When I Marry Mr. Snow"—I wonder could this really *be* one of those pseudo-soprano indicators—of a Freudian fugue-state's subliminal manifestation—of her obvious sublimated passion. Doctor Elmer J. Fudd might agree, but having to spit out this diagnosis would put *him* in the psychiatric party-ward.

I see why the supermarket "Mr. Snow" shows interest in her. She *is* attractive, when she tries to be. Often, when I catch a glimpse of Shelley in a certain light, she reminds me of an old oil painting of Grandpa Des. He looked strange posing in a navy-blue pea coat, while he stood in front of a tall building, located right here in lower Manhattan. A street sign in the painting pointed toward historic *Wall Street,* while thick flurries of realistic snow swirled all around. White flecks had landed on his hair and covered this pea coat that he wore.

In this early portrait, he appears to be around the age Shelley is now. His parents once commissioned an up-and-coming artist, by the name of Guy Wiggins, to capture this handsome mid-twenties son for them.

I loved looking at this picture of him, until one day it disappeared. My grandparents needed some additional money to build a new garage on their property, so they sold this artwork to a dishonest dealer. He said it would be part of a new museum. He also guaranteed them lifetime tickets for the family. They found out later that the beautiful painting was worth thousands-of-dollars, instead of the five-hundred he paid them. The crook shipped my young grandfather off to Saudi Arabia. I cried when I saw the big, spare spot on the wall and my grandfather said, "They liked it for the reason that they never experience snow there."

Work of art as verification or not, Shelley inherited similar features of our grandfather. I also remember his hair being sort of an auburn color like hers is now, before his turned that silver gray. She doesn't have the thick and long sideburns he had in the painting though. Ugh. The very thought.

Shelley's hair is also similar to Vivienne's color, but not as dark, long or thick. Or shiny. I tell her this damage comes from daily use of that hot hairdryer. But does she listen?

You already know the answer. By now, you're a Shelley expert too.

Getting back to her resemblance to our grandfather, her eyes are the exact brown that his were. Aunt Sharon also has similar eyes. Still, there's no denying Shelley has chubby Piggly Wiggly cheeks. I guess you *could* say they're a rosy kind of cute with no freckles that I ever noticed.

Now that I'm thinking about resemblances, she is, in many ways, a Doris Day look-a-like—with darker hair and eyes. I guess this is the reason why she adores this star, and the primary cause of her going around all day singing the *Que Sera-Sera* song, when she gets tired of *Mr. Snow,* both the real and the fictitious.

In any operatic case, getting back to allowing the pesky kitten to sleep with me, I found out, to my amazement, how the merciful rhythm of Daisy's melodic purring transported me into a deep—although brief—dreamless sleep.

Events of 5/29/72

ENTRY 2:

SPECIAL DELIVERY **"What next?"**

I'm writing this part very early, right before I leave to check out the status of Carmine Street. I've never been such a nervous wreck. Mail usually comes in the early afternoon. However, because today is a holiday, I'm not sure when a special-delivery letter will arrive or who will bring it.

To cover my bases, I'm pasting a note on the apartment door telling the post office that *if* I'm not home, and my signature *is* required, I give them permission to leave it in my mailbox.

What next?

Receiving communication from a deceased Bertie will be the most traumatizing event of my life. Right now, though, I'm thinking more about what I'll tell my sister. After yesterday, I know for sure I shouldn't say a thing to anyone in Tillagevale about the whole insane story.

I *could* open my big yap, and let everything spill out in a moment of desperation, but I'll sure look like the nut I'm supposed to be, trapped inside that butterfly net they use when snagging the crazies. A front-page picture of me, grappling with men in white coats, would sure sellout The Gazette. The presses will grind all night long, and the owner of the newspaper won't even complain about overtime sending him to the poorhouse.

Editorially trust me here.

No matter *what* I'm able to tell Vivienne, her subsequent reaction ensures how I'll relinquish my title of Drama Queen to her on a permanent basis.

I'll never get my glory back.

Events of 5/29/72

ENTRY 3:

MAD HATTERS' COFFEE PARTY "Abracadabra!"

I mentioned before how the radio played this morning, announcing trivia about Memorial Day, but I switched the thing on myself. No alarm needed to drag me out of bed *this* holiday Monday. I slept two straight hours without the Reverend Frisby nightmare waking me up, and then my eyes popped open very early on their own. I knew something even more paranormal waited for me. This sailor's Ship of Life morning sky glowed with such a bright red that a traditional Christmas poinsettia paled by comparison.

Going to Carmine Street isn't a problem for me now; I know exactly where to look. Breakfast never entered my mind. Getting out fast was all I thought about. I left my makeup and lipstick untouched on the bathroom shelf. Risking public viewing with an *au naturel* face was a definite sign of my frazzled state. I grabbed something from the closet, threw clothes on, and left uncoordinated—in many more ways than style.

When I got to the now familiar block, Carmine Street looked more or less the same. So far, so good. When I started walking toward the real estate office, I couldn't see the building. I only heard robust laughter.

Abracadabra!

The number **46-A** building was *gone,* evaporating overnight. A hard dirt alley remained in its place. Thick strips of wood, placed around this ally's strategic borders, formed a long narrow partition in the center of the dirt. Six elderly men stood near this partition. They all dressed alike, in long-sleeved white cotton undershirts, and baggy black trousers, shored up by wide black elastic suspenders. Large black-felt fedoras danced on top of their heads, trying to keep time with the men, who all laughed and gesticulated with gusto.

These seniors spoke to each other in an animated foreign language, causing them to flap their arms around in circles and slap their knees with force. They acted very energetic for their age, and choreographed those deep drags on their fat cigars—without missing a single synchronized-puff of smoke.

A much younger guy wrote on a blackboard, on the opposite end of the long alley. He wore jeans and a plain black tee shirt. Other men, belonging with the senior group, placed small iron balls on a tray. Metal folding chairs were also being set up, along the outside of the partition. My knees were shaking and buckling when one of the men noticed me and yelled out with a gruff accent, "You, *girlie,* you okay. You face too white."

A correct observation I thought. The way I felt, I knew my complexion could pass for an Alaskan snowdrift—not unlike the one my mother's long-lost uncle was under. I wobbled as I replied, "May I sit down for a minute?"

The short man who noticed me was bald, without his high fedora that now sat on the long wooden picnic table in front of him. While leaning over this table, he exhibited a bulging potbelly under his tight undershirt. He also pressed the handle of a large silver urn, dispensing steaming hot liquid into disposable cups.

While he measured what smelled like strong coffee he yelled again, projecting his booming voice across the alley—toward the tall youthful guy, I mentioned before. Since he spoke to him in what I assumed to be Italian, I couldn't understand a word he said. Even understanding him speaking English was tough.

The guy across the ally still occupied himself by writing on the blackboard. I guessed his age to be no more than twenty-five. By this nationalistic point, he had slipped a vest over the tee shirt showing a big picture of a red, white, and green flag, and underneath the flag were the words "Italy Rocks" so I got the language correct. He also wore a wide bandana around his forehead, which matched the same colors of the flag.

The man who befriended me snapped his fingers in the direction of this younger guy, before I heard him say, in sort of English this time, "Paolo, be nicea. Go getta this Signorina a chair." Then, in a clear and concise reply, without any accent, I heard, "Yeah sure, Nunzio, I'll do *anything* for a pretty girl."

After Paolo strolled over and winked at me, while he set up the folding chair—and a small tray table—the pudgy short fellow with the name of

Nunzio watched us. As soon as flag-bearing Paolo went back to where he stood before, Nunzio strolled toward me with caution, while carrying a tall Styrofoam cup in his shaky hand. "Girlie, you wanna cappuccino?"

I sat down on the chair and took the cup from his hands—so grateful to get off my wobbly legs. Then, I thought that perhaps I tottered—without any visa or passport—straight into a rabbit hole somewhere in Italy, to join a Mad Hatters' *Coffee* Party.

I could do nothing but stare at my whimsical surroundings, and hope I wouldn't pass out. He watched me for a minute, while I took cautious hot sips from the cup. I smiled at him, indicating the taste was great. Soon, he skittered toward the periphery of the alley and stood behind another long table. This one consisted of shiny aluminum that he covered with a clear plastic cloth.

"Hey girlie," he yelled, better than a microphone could, "I the *Nunzio Fusaro.* I take care the food. You wanna *cannoli?"* Within a second or two, this man bent over me while he held a mouthwatering confection. Whatever this was, it hid under a generous dusting of powdered sugar and waited on a small paper plate printed with yellow daises.

Was this a good sign or bad?

You're not really sure.

Neither was I.

He also brought over a paper napkin. Everything tempted me to say *yes.* However, the way things were going, I lived in mortal fear that everything, including me, would vanish in a puff of pastry.

"No. No thanks," I said. "I'm very worried about my weight. I'm hanging on to my figure."

"You! *You* no needa worry you weight, girlie. *Mangiare.* That mean, eat-um-up."

I looked at him as he stood there with that encouraging demeanor. I also reflected on the paper plate offering. I thought why not just go for it, because incredible odds told me not to bet against entering a dematerialization-mode. When I transmuted to some other nutty netherworld, it couldn't be weirder than this one. I'd go out happy, licking luscious cannoli cream off my lips.

I took a timid bite, and the only thing manifesting when I chewed away—was how my stomach ceased producing embarrassing growls. As I ate this cannoli, I looked down, watching that powdered sugar decorate the ground. This is when I noticed the bright yellow grid markers on the dirt, demarking sort of a bowling alley. I must have been staring when he said, "You likea the botchy, girlie?"

"I'm sorry," I questioned, "but what's the *botchy?*"

He raised his hands high in the air, in a gesture of complete hopelessness, before he said, "I no believea you no knowa the botchy. You spella it **B . . . O . . . C . . . C . . . E,** and bocce ball is numero uno in *Calabria*—where *I* from. I gonna tell you now, all *Italia* love the botchy, even them *Milano* people—with noses up the air so high, they drowna withouta the umbrella."

"I've never seen this before," I replied with irony, reminding myself how I've been saying this about an awful lot of stuff over the past two days.

Too bad the tasty diversion of coffee and a pastry ended so soon. I handed him the used cup and plate, along with the crumbled napkin, while asking him, "Why are you men here, doing this kind of *bowling?*"

He willingly explained, "We lova. We enjoya. We playa early morning. We playa afternoon too. We playa, playa, playa! We wanna playa in the dark, but we gotta no lights."

After this enthusiastic proclamation, he pointed and shook his arm toward the corner of Carmine Street. "This alley belonga Knights of Italia. We guys from biga church—over there. Seea? Acrossa the street, downa the block, neara Bleecker Strata. Our Lady of Pompeii. Seea?"

I looked toward the direction he aimed at, and of course recognized the dynamic building, but the banner was gone. Funny how the marble construction of the church itself looked much older—more of a dingy color than the newer bright white I saw yesterday, while hanging out of the office window and staring at it.

Before long, a feeble voice escaped my lips. "Oh—I do see the *church,* but isn't there supposed to be a building right *here*—where this *alley* is now?"

He looked shocked by my inquiry. Before answering my question, he crawled on his hand and knees, patting around on the ground, looking for something. He stood up after glancing toward the table with the coffee urn, dashed over to it and gave me a frantic glance while he straightened out sugar packets and plastic stirrers.

In preparation to leave, he also picked up his fedora that he had misplaced on this table, instead of the ground. Waving both of his arms in excitement he told me, "Oncea *I* heara abouta what you talk. I go getta my friend. *He* knowa."

Events of 5/29/72

ENTRY 4:

FORTUNATO "Buon Giorno, Signorina."

Fifteen-minutes lapsed before Nunzio Fusaro came back with his robust friend, also a senior citizen, but not bald. His bushy hair was a mixture of gray and brown like his eyebrows, and he had a very early five-o'clock-shadow.

This congenial person wore a long and wide black specialized oilskin apron. The bottoms of his kaki pants tucked halfway inside high rubber galoshes that were a similar color to the apron. Becoming aware of the sloppy presentation, he bent down to adjust his unruly cuffs. And, while he shoved them inside of these galoshes, I noticed that his dark blue corduroy jacket had an embroidered picture on its big front pocket, portraying a huge yellow swordfish. A disheveled and well-used white hanky, spilled out of this pocket. He's got a professional wife, I thought.

Soon Nunzio tapped on my shoulder as he said, *"Frankie*—she the one who wanna knowa olda place." At first, I thought maybe "Frankie" couldn't speak any English, because he took my right hand and kissed it saying, "Buon Giorno, Signorina." This continental touch had me flushing with shyness, until he said in perfect unaccented English, "Good Morning, Miss. My name is Francesco Fortunato. I am the owner of Fortunato's Famous Fish—around the block on Bleecker Street."

While I thought, here we go again with fish stuff, he crossed his legs and positioned himself on the folding chair that Paulo had rushed over and placed across from mine. With deliberation, this man cradled his face in the palm of his left hand—and bending over towards me—placed his jutting elbow onto his right knee before saying, "I'm very curious as to why such a young girl like you, has an interest in a building demolished over forty years ago?"

My brain wrestled with his fair question. Now how should I answer him?

"I guess you *could* say I enjoy researching any kind of history. Right now, I'm studying the olden times of Carmine Street."

In replying to my technical, as well as *truthful* answer, his enthusiasm was genuine.

"That's no surprise to me. Carmine Street has been an appealing, as well as historical place, for as long as I remember. I came here as a baby from Italy and never left. I can't imagine being anywhere else. I own a store around the block now, and live in the top-floor apartment of the building with my family. When I was young like you, I worked in the very building you're asking about. I clerked for a real estate agency."

I felt my felt eyes lighting up as bright as Reverent Frisby's abused pinball marbles. I'm actually getting somewhere. I looked at him and said with obvious excitement, "You mean *O'Flanagan's?"*

Gosh. When I mentioned the probable name of the place where he used to work, he looked like a ghost sat on his lap. With a face almost as pale as mine he said, "Mama Mia, how did you find out such old information?"

My having to answer him, without causing further suspicion, sure turned out to be a real test of my undercover prowess.

"Oh sure, Mr. Fortunato, it's because I, *well,* I . . . *yes,* of course, I saw an advertisement for it in an old newspaper stored on microfilm at the library."

Certain lies are necessary—the kind Lois Lane used on the investigative street of things. I'm just as crafty as she is I thought, until I saw the already inquisitive man scowling after my *crafty* answer.

"He advertised? I never knew *that.* People used to stream in all day. The office was Grand Central Station. 'Word-of-mouth, Fortunato, just one person informing another,' he used to tell me."

My throat grew drier than ever—along with my brain. Oh brother, I just made a big liar out of Mr. O'Flanagan. Now what will I say?

"I only saw *one* teeny-tiny, itty-bitty ad Mr. Fortunato. Maybe since that one announcement word of mouth took over and he never needed to advertise again."

I thought at that moment, putting my tendency toward modesty aside of course, that I should get a Pulitzer Prize for investigative journalism right now. I wiggled out of the advertising fiasco with more aplomb than any Lois Lane, Jimmy Olsen or even Clark Kent could ever do.

Mr. Fortunato looked relieved and when he spoke to me again. He smiled, ready to give me a detailed explanation:

That's more like the O'Flanagan I knew. When he died, I cried for days. He was like a father to me. I still miss him, after all these years. People knew that when you shook the hand of Singh O'Flanagan, blessings followed you for the rest of your life.

His real estate agency grew very famous, because, to help his business, he practiced **I-Ching,** a very old Asian skill originating from China. He told me often that some people call it, 'a philosophy of change.'

Mr. O'Flanagan was an expert at implementing this *philosophy.* When people came to him, looking for an apartment, a house—or even an office—he'd sit at his desk while he tossed certain coins in the air. He watched these coins, as they landed on the special green linen cloth he kept spread out on top of his desk. Using the random pattern of the way these coins landed on the cloth, he built hexagrams from secret codebooks.

Mr. O'Flanagan deciphered the meaning of each individual hexagram from his copy of *The Ancient Book of I-Ching* tailoring the information to individual situations, while helping people make important decisions. There is a misconception about this practice being *fortune telling.* It really acts as an intuitive guide. Mr. O'Flanagan wore his engraved I-Ching ring with pride. Not many practitioners have the honor of being a master of this art—the equivalent of being a black belt.

Finding prime Real Estate was his brilliance, and when he left this life the business went along with him. The church had an eye on the office building for years. As soon as they read that **FOR SALE** sign, their generous offer was accepted. Afterwards, they demolished the property for this bocce court.

He just gave me a lot of valuable information. I had to soften him up before asking the *crucial* question, without any more suspicion on his part. "It's a beautiful church. I understand why you're so proud. I'd love knowing more details, including the year it came to Carmine Street. You can help me with my research."

He nodded and smiled. I crossed my fingers behind my back, in anticipation of an informative reply.

Events of 5/29/72

ENTRY 5:

CORNERSTONE **"Are you a witch?"**

I had no idea what reaction he'd have, when I asked him about details concerning the church. Why should an outsider like me care? I only hoped that my question caused him to think that my teeth dig deeper into history than George Washington's wooden ones ever did.

He uncrossed his legs and brushed dirt around with his feet. Then, he said:

They set the cornerstone of Our Lady of Pompeii Catholic Church, here on Carmine Street, in **1926.** The challenge for architects and builders had begun. All of the people from Italy, living here at the time, supervised the construction—stone by stone. If workers were less than perfect, regarding its Italian Renaissance style, we let them know. Two years later, in **1928,** we dedicated this beautiful church to the people of our Italian community.

Further expanding my answer to your question, in **1923** Our Lady of Pompeii existed on Bleecker Street—not far from where my fish market is now. Everybody called this old one a "stick church" due to its wood frame and it looked nothing like the present one. My parents took me there as a child. The place was indeed humble by today's standards, but important to the community.

The pastor of this original parish, Father Antonio Demo, heard how road construction in the area would cause flattening of this older church. So he sought the expert help of Singh O'Flanagan to find another location where his dream of erecting a palatial new Our Lady of Pompeii—along with a private school—would come true.

Everybody respected and loved Father Demo, and they still do. More important to us all, he was an admirable man. A man made of pure gold. He never hurt or harmed a living thing, not like some other religious hypocrites I have known.

He died in **1936.**

I very seldom speak of these things and strange how I am compelled to tell you now. As a boy of ten, I became a victim of abuse by a young priest who had been ordained three months before. He came regularly from an upstate parish to teach local Catholic children their catechism in preparation for Confirmation. We gathered at various homes in the neighborhood every week.

One of them was mine.

I let him in on the day he showed up early. My mother went shopping to buy his favorite foods as an act of kindness. Whenever her chance to be the hostess came, she prepared for his lunch. He watched her leave and knew I'd be alone. He told me if I ever told anyone what he did to me, he'd make sure my mother suffered in hell for eternity.

This bitter experience showed me that assuming any act of *ordination* automatically guarantees *holiness* is a fallacy.

At this point in his conversation, I suspected the circumstances he meant, but didn't press him on details. Trusting me enough to mention his terrible incident was astounding. I could only say, "Yes, whatever happened was horrible for you. And I agree about the exceptional goodness of Father Demo. I know from personal experience, he was a great man."

This time, when he looked shocked about what I told him, his face didn't turn pale. However, he sure raised his eyebrows. "*You* understand about *him?* How is that?"

"If people designated a plaza in his name, he must have been everything you say. Earlier today, I stood in the park named for him. He helped me find Carmine Street. Sounds unreasonable—but I *know* he did. I also know you're right concerning the perceived 'holiness' of a person, basing it solely on their being a member of *any* kind of clergy. As you say, sanctioned rituals don't guarantee them automatic praise. Believe me—I'm aware of this fact."

Mr. Fortunato nodded in agreement and commented, "You are very bright for such a young age. Father Demo immediately had the choir priest defrocked—and my mother took care of the rest."

He took a deep breath before continuing with the proud history of the church:

While they laid the cornerstone I mentioned before, builders included a copy of this deed, rolling it into a small gold cartouche and placing it deep within the foundation. An Egyptian pharaoh would have received the same respect. Singh O'Flanagan had counter-signed the document. A small photo of Father Demo and Singh O'Flanagan shaking hands was also included.

I don't know why, but you bring out secrets I never expressed before. After the cornerstone ceremony, Singh told me in confidence that he and Father Demo also placed an I-Ching coin in this small cartouche along with the copy of the deed. They wanted the new church to carry along a special guide on its towering journey. If the church hierarchy knew this they would condemn them both as blasphemes, worshiping a craven image. No harm in telling *you,* though, since everything was so long ago.

How sad that Singh had to die and could not enjoy the magnificent structure for more than a brief period. He was kind saying that climbing its steps, and entering its grandeur, reminded him of the *Taj Mahal* in India.

When I heard the word "died" again—concerning those whom I thought for sure *lived*—no shocks ran up my spine. Spirits *are* playing ring-around-the-rosy with me, and they gave me confidence to ask him another crucial question. Being certain that he'd answer me, by telling me what I already knew, I'd have bet my deluxe cosmetic carrier on his reply.

"How did he die, Mr. Fortunato?"

"Oh—it was in such a dreadful way. He was on a ship when it capsized, almost forty-four years ago."

Like a fool, before I caught myself, I said, "You're talking about the **Vestris,** right?" I thought for sure he'd pass out this time. Instead his brow furrowed, and his eyes narrowed, as he moved his face even closer to mine and asked, "Are you a witch?"

"Not really," I replied, "although my sister frequently says I am. And, as I mentioned to you before, I do love researching any kind of history—nautical stuff included. That's all there is to my interest. I guess I'll go now."

Before I took a single step, all the bowlers at the bocce court started gathering around me. Those who spoke English really well said, "Tell us the whole story, Frankie. She wants to know too. We hear how that *wacko,* O'Flanagan, pranced around in a long skirt while a funny green turban performed an acrobatic act on his head."

"Yes—will you please tell us everything," I chimed in.

"Okay, I will," he agreed, "but you guys better get me an espresso. And while you're over by the coffee urn, add some of that *Anisette* Nunzio stashes in the empty milk carton."

Events of 5/29/72

ENTRY 6:

ORCHESTRATIONS

"Turn the page and see."

With everybody staring at Francesco Fortunato, like watching an outdoor movie screen, he accepted a tiny white ceramic cup, filled to the rim with what appeared to be black sludge, which reminded me of that Texas Motor Oil stuff. This time, however, a thin sliver of lemon rind floated on top.

This hot brew emitted a strong smell of licorice into the air. Starting to blow away steam from the cup—in preparation to take a sip—he had a faraway look in his eyes. *Eyes* that are the darkest brown I've ever seen, even darker than my father's are. With his brusque voice growing softer, he said:

O'Flanagan told me something like this. I will do my best to paraphrase his words, as I remember them. He never did call me Frankie. He referred to me as *Fortunato,* reminding me that my name means good fortune and it does.

Fortunato, he said, you are very young and do not know too much about this world. Someday, later on, you will become aware of the magnificent orchestra that plays for *your* ears only.

Sometimes this orchestra's violin will be mellow. Or it will be fast and furious. A violin makes you happy or makes you sad. At times, listening to it can also be boring. This is when your orchestra needs a tuba.

Drums and symbols are never boring. They crash with emotion, shaking your living concert hall until a smooth flute takes charge and puts you to sleep.

Your grand piano has the power to range from a soothing lullaby to a rousing march. This piano can accompany a cast of many, in your living opera, or just two young lovers, cuddling in a café.

The pipe organ in your orchestra is a versatile all-purpose instrument. It plays where you worship, and proclaims your potential when you graduate. When you go to a sporting event, it revs you up. And most certainly, this magnificent organ will play if you get married. And, when you depart this living recital, announce your arrival to the celestial.

Now—the harp—here we have a magical instrument. A legend tells that if you fall asleep hearing it play, an angel's wings will flutter in your heart.

Fortunato, I am very often sad, he said. My personal *O'Flanagan Orchestra* skips a beat. It can never play musical notes with total harmony, as long as I do not understand the essence of who I am.

Do you know, Fortunato, that a faithful Hindu never slaughters a cow. The endless milk and the yogurt, the cheese and the butter, and the heavenly cream, which the cow unselfishly gives, are a special form of nourishment from the Divine. I am ashamed to tell you that I crave corned beef.

I should be tapping my feet to Punjabi bangra. Yet I dream only of an Irish jig.

I should be comfortable in these pantaloons, but I really wish to wear kilts.

This turban is opulent, but I would soon trade it for a simple tartan cap.

A marigold is indeed exquisite, but I prefer the wild rose.

It is strange, Fortunato, how I know I will never rest in peace until I find my Irish roots. Only then will my life be that perfect symphony.

One day in late July of 1928, he came into the office. He waved a steamship ticket in the air, mimicking the excitement of a child showing off a birthday gift. I can never forget his exact words:

'I will sail for England in two weeks, and then, from a port in London, I am off to Ireland to realize a lifelong dream of seeking my Irish roots. In early November, I will return home to Carmine Street. I will board a ship taking me to New York City from somewhere in England. I do not know the exact vessel, port or sailing date yet.'

He revealed what a very generous man he was, telling me that I deserve a long, paid vacation.

'Fortunato, you've worked very hard and I care for you like the son kismet never gave me. Here is your full-salary for the period I am away. Enjoy this paid vacation. When I come back, your job will be waiting. Do not worry. I will write to you.'

He kept his promise. I always carry his letter with me in my wallet. Never parting with it has a miraculous effect. It brings me luck. Although almost as old as me now, we are both still in good shape. Should I read it to you?

Not a single person spoke. They just nodded there heads, indicating their desire for him to read the letter. All eyes and ears focused on him, as he took a minute to take another sip of his *espresso* refill, spiked with a generous spritz of the licorice smelling Anisette stuff.

He made a slurping sound saying, "*Delizioso.* Good. I needed that," before he pulled a yellowed letter out of his wallet. When he did, a small piece of something that looked like dried brown grass fell out and he retrieved it from his lap.

Seeing such a macho Mr. Fortunato with tears in his eyes made everybody uncomfortable. His voice was as soft and tender as a young father's would be, reading a bedtime story to his children.

Before I relay his words to you, if you wonder how I jotted down and remembered with accuracy everything he said to us, I applied the shorthand I complain about. I used the same method for recalling other exact dialogue in the journal too. I'll now make a formal apology to Sir Isaac Pitman and Mr. John Robert Gregg. The glyphs work after all.

Turn the page and see.

THE LETTER FROM COUNTY OF KINGS

Monday Morning
October 15th, 1928

Greetings to My Dear Fortunato:

I guess you thought I forgot my pledge to write. I did not mean to be negligent. While in Ireland, the task of finding my ancestors filled my days and nights. I also waited until I had some positive news for you.

I am now in Blackpool, England, where the magnificent Irish Sea embraces the shore. For the past week, I enjoyed myself at this beautiful resort before my ship, the Vestris, departs. I met some interesting people here who will accompany me on the return. One is a fascinating young man by the name of Alistair Perry. He is a deep-sea diver. I will tell you all about him later, when I get back.

Now let me explain about Ireland. It is the most spectacular place I have ever seen. A blanket of rolling green hills touches the sky and fairy dust floats in the air, making everything I see enchanted. Understanding why they call it, *The Emerald Isle* comes easy now.

When I first arrived, I did not know where to start. Yet my ancestral Irish-luck guided the way, when I met a man who knew the history of Gaelic surnames. He told me how the name *Flanagan* derives from a place that in times of yore bore the title of 'County of Kings.' He also said if the letter **'O'** is placed in front of an Irish name, we have a definite indication of past royalty.

Of course, his telling me I am a descendent from royalty was nothing short of spectacular. I took this chap to a nearby pub where there were many fascinating choices for us to drink. We decided on sweet and pungent apple cider, infused with cloves. We also partook of some delectable scones that floated in a bowl of thick clotted cream. I arranged my travel plans with him, to visit that place where kings once lived.

When I arrived there, I hired a respectable tour guide with the name of Danny O'Dowd. Danny is not only a descendent of royalty, as I am, he is also a skillful driver of his horse and cart. I had moments, I will say, longing for the comfort of my luxurious Model T Roadster. However, I grew used to the hard seat of Danny's cart, putting me in mind of the saddle on an elephant I rode as a child in India.

I found this hamlet to be a place of true enchantment, with medieval castles still nestling in their original misty-knolls. Danny took me to the County of Kings Courthouse, where hundreds of dusty and archaic linen-bound records are stored. I faced many wearisome days of tracing all of the O'Flanagan's but again, blessings abounded. The affable County Clerk, in charge of these documents, told me about persistent rumors of a tall, strapping man with thick chestnut brown hair. This man's name was Shamus O'Flanagan.

Shamus, well over six-feet tall, was renowned for his jovial personality. He could also twirl a shillelagh higher in the air than anybody else in the county ever dared. Thus, he led the marching band whenever they played.

And, since he also had an uncanny knowledge of medicinal plants, and curative flowers that grew in the woods, he never hesitated to help the unfortunate poor with his powers of healing. He saved many by nurturing them back to life with the simple garden herbs he cultivated. He boiled tree bark for bitter medicinal syrup that could drop a high fever. Many a person lived to savor morning's glorious light, thanks to *Doctor* Shamus.

In **1775,** Shamus sailed for India to study something he called "Ayurvedic Medicine." His family and friends could not understand why he left them for such a distant land. He came back home to Ireland several years later. This time his arms wrapped around the delicate shoulders of a foreign bride.

As rumors have it, when Shamus first saw her, he fell in love the moment she smiled at him. Her eyes glowed as deep and mystical as the River Ganges. Everywhere she went, throughout her new homeland, she wore her exquisite silk sarongs. They encircled her trim figure like a flirtatious breeze. To enhance her beauty further, she painted a small red circle—right in the center of her high forehead.

She placed a tiny ruby inside a small hole in her right nostril. Every so often, she alternated it with a little diamond or a tiny black pearl. She spoke to Shamus in a strange language and he replied in same. An exotic bouquet of sandalwood swirled in the air around her, wherever she passed.

All who saw her admired her lustrous black hair, braided and piled high, revealing a neck so graceful that swans envied it. She often adorned this regal hairstyle with golden marigolds. Shamus boasted about her to everyone. He said with obvious pride to all he encountered, "This is my bonnie bride—Mrs. Devindar O'Flanagan—the loveliest colleen in Ireland." All the women were jealous of her, and she knew it.

Devindar was lonesome. Precious letters from her family in India took months to arrive in Ireland. They came by ship, followed by horses, wagons, and weary feet. She kept her sadness a secret. Shamus never knew of her tears. Her love for him was stronger than any she had ever known. Soon this love within her replaced her empty isolation with a child.

On the morning when Devindar felt the pain of labor upon her, the husband she cherished suffered a strange fate. There is a legend of a sympathetic, courageous man, who heard the frightened cries of his brother's lost sheepdog. He knew the goodness of this dog, so without fear he followed its pitiable howls—straight into the shadowy and treacherous bog. The sole evidence the community found, was a leather pouch engraved with the initial ***S,*** floating on top of the marshy quicksand. Inside they found strange dried leaves and twigs.

When his brother's dog came home unharmed, later in the day, many believed the distressed howling really came from an evil pooka. It aimed to lure Shamus into *Far Liath,* the malevolent mantle of fog that kills without mercy. Far Liath can never stand the overwhelming light of a compassionate heart.

With midwives attending her, not a single person told Devindar of the horrible circumstances until the baby was born. The infant, an adorable boy, was healthy and to everyone's amazement, he looked as Irish as any Celtic lad—right down to his auburn hair, and those intriguing hazel eyes.

Devindar took the infant back to India as soon as she could arrange passage. Still, even now, the town immortalizes her beauty. This is evident from the accounting of the official County Clerk's conversation, I imparted to you. It is a coincidence how my own mother's name was also, *Devindar.*

Soon, several relatives in the area heard of my quest. They, like me, are all proud decedents of the same O'Flanagan family as Shamus. These kind people held a gala in my honor—a magnificent affair, under a colorful pavilion. This green and white tent sat on top of a captivating hilltop that locals call *Krilly-Dougal*—the embodiment of my heavenly ancestral nest—so high up in those fluffy shamrock-shaped clouds. The noble sound of bagpipes at this fete, echoed throughout the valley. The poignant memory of their cadence will touch my soul until I die, and maybe even after that.

Before I forget, I did get to dance a jig. It came easy to me, because I must confess young Fortunato that I sipped a smidgen of local foaming ale.

Thanks to my cousins, I now have yards of my own tartan wool cloth, bearing the official O'Flanagan Crest. I plan to sew a kilt and a cap when I return. I am also bringing back a special gift for you. But for now, I will enclose the real four-leaf clover that Danny's horse, Blarney, almost ate. Instead, I gave dear Blarney a big, tasty apple. I also handed him some cubes of sugar, telling him you sent them.

Remember to carry this very special lucky clover on your person and, as your name implies, *fortune* will be your constant companion.

See you soon and take good care of yourself—my son.

From Sing O'Flanagan

Events of 5/29/72

ENTRY 7:

PSYCHIC LEANINGS "What's *your* name?"

Developing self-control, concerning this blurting tendency of mine, was over. As soon as Mr. Fortunato finished reading the powerful letter, loyalty swelled within me. I stood right up and clarified, "I want everybody here to realize Mr. O'Flanagan did not wear a psychedelic *green* turban. A *purple* turban is more like it—with *real* sparkling emeralds. And he wasn't any *wacko.*"

Mr. Fortunato also stood now. He crooked a finger, motioning me to follow him as he marched over to the unoccupied side of the bocce court.

I guessed that he caught on to me:

Now—listen, young lady, I *know* you're a witch. But it's okay. You're a good witch like my mother, Dominica. God bless her, she is ninety now. In all her life, she has refused to put the powerful Sicilian evil eye on people—with one exception. She placed it on the catechism priest, I told you about. *He* got a double whammy from her. This was the first and only time she ever used her power in this way. Usually, it's her practice to *remove* curses from people. My mother is a good woman who protected her son, and other innocent children in the future.

We heard how, within two days of her incantation, he got so spooked he ran off to join the French Foreign Legion. On those barren and dry sand dunes of Algeria, his come-up-pance finally came to greet him. The reason why only the generous supply of rationed water in *his* canteen evaporated, will forever remain a mystery.

The rule of the Legion is . . . if you lose your water, you lose your life. The desert gives no man a second chance. Returning to Singh O'Flanagan, I am sure that you have seen him. You have had recent interactions with him, haven't you?

I looked into those now familiar dark eyes of his and didn't say anything. We both knew, he *knew.* He lowered his voice and almost cried saying, "I'll tell you something now that I never told anybody else before. *I* see him occasionally myself. He gives me expert advice. He is the reason why I bought the fish market on Bleecker twenty years ago—the best thing I ever did, so I know if *you* are able to communicate with him, it means you're a special psychic."

In that instant, Mr. Fortunato put a whole new perspective on every single bizarre episode I've encountered, not only now, but also throughout my entire life. The revelation that I'm psychic—not psychiatric—and I'm *special,* rationalized my entire life in a split-second. "Thanks for saying that, Mr. Fortunato."

"Call me, *Frankie*—like my friends do. What's *your* name?"

"It's Ginger. Ginger Autry." *"Hmm,"* he mulled. "Well—Ginger *is* the perfect name for *you.* You're a pepper-upper."

"I don't think it's a great name, Mr. Fortunato. *Er,* Frankie. It's the complete opposite. And when my parents tell me the same thing—they're referring to heartburn. Do you believe they debated whether to call me *Prudence?* It's a long story. I think they're sorry my mom didn't opt for their first choice, I really, really do."

The relief was tremendous as I went on to say, "I'll be going now. I have more psychic stuff on my agenda today."

His pleasant expression faded, giving way to disappointment. He dug into his pocket, causing the professional hankie, dangling out of it, to glide to the ground. He handed me a business card and said, "I like talking to you. Come and visit me at the fish market when you can. Let me know how Mr. O'Flanagan is doing."

I gave him a hug and told him, "I promise you I will."

Leaving Carmine Street made me emotional too. For some reason, while walking down the now familiar block, I had the extraordinary feeling an important part of me stayed behind.

Could it be my heart? I hope not. I sure need all of me right where it belongs, to support me when I get back to The Bronx and find that letter from the dead.

Events of 5/29/72

ENTRY 8:

POSTAL CONCERNS "Should I open it?"

My fears about not returning from the Carmine Street investigation, in time to get the letter, were unnecessary. When I arrived back to Shelley's apartment, Paul, our usual mailman, stood outside with his hand on the doorbell.

"I've got a letter here addressed to you, Miss Autry. It's marked for **special holiday delivery.** There's **25¢** postage due on it, and it's lumpy. If you weren't home now, I planned to pay the shortage for you and leave it in your mailbox downstairs. It must be important, if I'm delivering it *today.*"

"I see how lumpy it is," I answered. "Wait a second; I'll give you the money."

While I delved into my purse for the quarter, I was so shook up I forgot to thank the guy. My hands trembled as I clutched the envelope and headed for the kitchen.

Should I open it?

Although the bulges *are* creepy, I'm pretty sure Bertrand A. Norman's handwriting appears on the envelope. Too bad that before I got home yesterday, I tossed the gooey-gum portion that I originally ripped off the classified part of the newspaper—the part where he scribbled his note about the real estate office. I could make a comparison now if I still had it, but there's little doubt about his loopy scrawl.

Sitting down at the falling-apart kitchen table gave me comfort, knowing something *else* in the room was collapsing. As I opened the envelope, a piece of crayon fell out and left brownish marks while it rolled across the chipped white Formica top of this table. When I retrieved it, recognition whacked me. I held a scrap of the actual raw umber crayon, instigating all those fights with him in kindergarten.

Scrounging around further in the envelope, caused the two odd coins Bertie previously displayed in his penny loafers to hit the table with a loud thud—along with a narrow, shiny brass key. A **$20** bill wrapped itself around the letter itself, with the help of a thick rubber band.

Staring at the coins and the key, for at least ten minutes, put me into an almost trance-like state. I couldn't summon enough courage right away to remove the rubber band, unfold the money, and reveal the letter—written on several sheets of yellow copy paper.

Here it is, word for word, just as he wrote it to me—with underlines, and all.

I titled it, *Monoceros.*

MONOCEROS

My Dearest Ginger:

I'm not putting a date on this or anything. By now, you're very aware of the circumstances regarding this letter. You sure know when I wrote it. It will be a lengthy correspondence. I have plenty of explaining to do.

Let me begin by saying how sorry I am for all the upsetting circumstances. I never meant to frighten or deceive you. Over the past few days, prior to writing this, I've been in rehearsal with Singh O'Flanagan. We went over stuff, concerning how to handle my presence on the bus. I never told you a lie while I was alive, so why start doing it when I'm dead.

We had to figure out a way to skirt around the truth, and explain my brief transfiguration to previous human-form. He has been giving me tips about handling this delicate situation. It fits right in, because while I'm speaking with him, my parents think I'm babbling from delirium. But you know better.

While you're reading this, you must be curious as to where I am now. Me too.

I don't understand very much about this alternate plane of existence yet, except to say it is not frightening and it is real. I have only been popping back-and-forth to this strange new astral plane for brief periods, so I'm still not too familiar with it. As of this writing, I'm a visitor—not a registered voter. I do have the impression it's a place deep within a hallowed constellation of dim stars, going by the name of Monoceros.

Souls of all religions are here, even those without prior denominations or beliefs. They don't classify them under racial lines, as human bureaucrats do to people on Earth. Any *spirits* I have seen are photographic-like negatives of their prior mortal-forms. And these luminous cellophane images are capable of developing back into physical beings, as special emissaries to Earth—if ever necessary.

Precious family pets may also be here in this form. I remember reading an extraordinary true story concerning a parrot that came back a year after it died, to warn its beloved former owners about a lethal carbon monoxide leak. The raucous squawking in the middle of the night saved everybody. Later, they found several of its familiar gray feathers near an old space heater causing the trouble.

There is also a huge vault up here in Monoceros full of something known as Akashic Records. They are bound volumes containing the evolutionary progress of each soul. Animals and those family pets might be in it too. I'm not certain. Wouldn't it be amusing if little Carmen Miranda's buffet table episode happened to be part of it.

Thinking about your grandmother and her little hungry Chihuahua being together now, leads me to remember all those theories about death that upset you when your grandparents died. The ignorant supposition about death being the natural result of light bulbs burning out, without any hope for replacement, is bogus.

Further, concerning this constellation, it's in the shape of a mythological unicorn. The unfamiliar place is almost invisible and impossible to find with the naked eye, although you might be able to check it out with the small telescope I gave you once. I bet it's still under a pile of junk in the storage shed, behind 13 Azimuth Circle. It's not a problem, because you have plenty of time to find the ocular-gadget. Monoceros is only visible during the month of February—at 9 o'clock in the evening, not one minute before or after.

I know what you're thinking. Even now, when I'm no longer around, I've still got the knack of making things difficult for you.

It will be amazing as I ride on the bus with you this coming Sunday. I'll once again be that unenviable "dorky" corporeal-being you have known all of your life, but sad to say, never loved. It's appropriate how it will happen on Memorial Day weekend. I cannot believe I'll get to sit next to you and touch your hand once more.

Singh O'Flanagan has mentioned how Alistair Perry will transfuse me with any oxygen I'll need to write this dissertation. I'm thankful both of these great spirits are going to guide me when I make my permanent transition to the other world—sometime later this afternoon. It surprised me to learn how they're both big shots where I'm heading. I haven't met the Number One Boss yet, the Creator of the Universe and overseer of all Divine operations.

Singh is director of the I-Ching Division. He helps people make beneficial life-altering decisions. He is that familiar little voice, popping into people's heads, suggesting alternatives in a crisis. Do you believe he has picked me to be his chief assistant. I'll be contributing by serving the lives of people on Earth for the better. Of course, I know I need a lot of training. I'm sure a privileged guy, though, since Singh has given me a super eternal job—along with endless time to perfect it.

Come on. How could I resist.

Besides, lucky for me, but maybe not so lucky for you, you're my very first assignment. Here in this Monoceros place, as far as I know now, rookies like I'll soon be, receive some kind of a job description from various divisions. These jobs involve either helping the souls themselves or somebody still on Earth. I'm asking you to believe me when I say nobody here is burning in hell or anything—like Reverend Frisby spins around and screams about.

Do you remember his laughable "wild man of rock and roll" routine, when he'd gyrate like Jerry Lee Lewis concerning those "great-balls-of-fire?" Stuff like this doesn't happen. On the contrary, where I'm going, they are only concerned about raising awareness about certain issues in a non-punitive manner.

I've changed my mind about many things since visiting here. Although I still think it is a good idea for people to congregate in a building to pray as a group, I know now it really isn't necessary. All they need do is sit down outside on a bright and sunny day or look out of their window at night when the sky is clear and stars are visible. This is the free and open church of the Universe.

I have been learning too that when a soul occupies a human body, it resides within the scope of the conscience. I think that when it looks like a "conscience" does not exist in a human, it's because they do not have a soul in residence. This sure explains a lot about those who abuse animals, children, the weak, and the elderly. I also could never understand what drives murderous despots, until now.

I guess these empty-soul guys start at base one, here in Monoceros. I think it may also mean some of us, if needed, get more than one round at life to test for progress in this consciousness area. I'm not sure yet; I'm only guessing based on what I sense so far. And this huge Akashic library stores a lot of records. Lost souls will learn how somebody cared for them. They once received nourishment and were kept clean and warm, to some extent, by other human beings, no matter how imperfect the circumstances.

Getting back to those whom I know for sure are in charge here, Alistair Perry is the official head of the Maritime Division where he supervises the relentless service of his crew to protect his distinguished Navy. He also has responsibility for every intrepid United States Marine and the important Coast Guard. The endless traffic of the busy Merchant Marines, keeps him busy too. People on their recreational boats and cruise ships are never far from his watchful eyes. The dangerous area of commercial fishing depends on him, as well. He is in complete charge of all the ships at sea, no matter what country. Can you fathom what a busy job he has?

I have not lost my touch yet. Gosh, you're right. I am a pun geyser.

Every swimmer and diver is also under his watch. As I've mentioned, he's keeping me above water now since I'm sinking fast.

It is my claim to fame, so why stop now.

Ginger, I'll take a further dive here off my tenuous earthly-perch, and descend to the desperate need to tell you how much you mean to me. I never could find the guts to do it before. The first day I realized my cute powerhouse, Ginger Autry, could be with me in Miss Heller's kindergarten class, something hit me on the head and shouted out how you were the one. And, because I'm the sole half of us who received this blatant communication, fighting with you was the one way I had of getting you to notice me. Over all these years, I kept the little leftover scrap of our "battle royal" crayon, because your baby fingers touched it.

Speaking of school, I'm sorry I drove you nuts by sitting near you no matter what grade. How did I manage it? I have no idea, other than it being a childhood crush aided—for reasons becoming clearer to me every valuable second—by some of those lofty people. Ginger, I never sought out those seats. When they assigned them to me, I sauntered around school like the happiest kid in the world.

Still regarding school, do you remember the great class trip to Washington DC, when we went to the Smithsonian? I started feeling weird and tired after we got back to Tillagevale. One morning, a few days later, I woke up and saw ugly bruises on my arms and legs. Dr. Mendel was kind and sympathetic when he sent me to several specialists. I knew he suspected something was very wrong, but put on a brave face for me and my parents.

When we got to meet with these recommended doctors, all of these arrogant, so-called professionals, said I had a bad illness. A cancer of the blood they call "leukemia." There was little chance of a long-term survival. These <u>well-educated experts,</u> were the epitome of cut and dry. Like Detective Sergeant Joe Friday would say, on my favorite TV show <u>Dragnet,</u> "Just the facts, nothing but the facts." And let me tell you, they laid out these <u>facts</u> to my parents like machine-gun fire, quoting statistics from textbooks concerning medical doomsday. "Dr. and Mrs. Norman, the overpowering negative odds are, blah, blah, and more blah."

In the future, I hope there are better ways of controlling this terrible disease or even stopping it from spreading. There is a strong possibility it will be curable <u>someday,</u> if we have enough dedicated research scientists. For now, in 1972, all they do is treat kids like me with those awful steroid drugs. And these steroids have terrible side effects like puffing up your face to resemble a marshmallow, kind of the way you looked when you had to dress up like Alvin. On you, everything was cute and endearing. On me, well, it only added more spice to my prominent pumpkin pie caricature.

Give me a break I'm dying.

While all the leukemia junk happened, I pledged my parents to secrecy. I didn't want any pity at school or from the few friends I had. I already got plenty of morose concern on the home front. Over the past few weeks, I told them several times to respect my wishes concerning "final arrangement" stuff. There is to be <u>no</u> memorial service. I made them swear they will cremate what is left of my body and let me go in private.

Remember how I talk about life being a daily gift, so open your <u>present</u> each day and enjoy it. I'm now discarding the box my gift comes in. Why should my mom and dad pay money for a bunch of phonies to eat expensive catered food, while they tell my parents phony stories about what a great guy I was? Any true friends will do this kindness on their own. There's no need to bribe people with hoity-toity hors d'oeuvres. Besides, I think flowers should celebrate a person while they are alive, not when "waking up and smelling the lilies" is no longer an option. I asked them to donate the money they would have spent on such a superficial service, but not to Reverend Frisby.

At this point in my dissertation, I'd like to clarify some of the erroneous ideas you and everybody else had about me:

To start with, I could not risk wearing contact lenses due to dangerous eye irritation. I kept wearing those same stupid glasses, because I thought that if I made the outdated things into an <u>Arnold Stang</u> type of trademark, people might think of them as a comedic part of me. The illness also factored in with any dental work. My father said if he fitted me with metal braces my gums would swell and bleed. I'd be in even more serious trouble, and he could never forgive himself. It became a way of life for me to hide how I despised my atrocious "jack-o-lantern" buckteeth. The hardest thing of all was convincing <u>you</u> I didn't mind them. I kept hoping our mutual "dental challenge" might bring us closer.

Adding to everything else, my dad had the bum reputation of being that "uppity'" Orthodontist. To stay in the losing game I kept smiling, overriding insensitive people and their comments. Everybody thought I was a poster boy for the cognitively short-changed. I know how they made fun of me and criticized <u>phony</u> Dr. Norman. As a fantastic father, and an ethical professional, he agonized over everything, and there wasn't a thing he could do for me, other than respecting my wishes to keep the leukemia a secret and to love me.

I wore those crazy psychedelic long-sleeved shirts on hot days, and while swimming, due to the blood transfusions. I never wanted anybody to see my bruised, scared-up arms. I had a great excuse <u>up my sleeve,</u> when I told everybody I didn't want to get sunburned. I guess wearing all the bright colors, your favorite wild Bazooka-gum-pink above all, was trying to turn darkness into a bright experience.

Speaking of having to hide my pincushion arms, one night, due to the collapsing of my targeted artery, a transfusion went bonkers. Vital blood spurted out all over the hospital walls. The nurses always cared for me with kindness, but during this crisis, they gave me more moral support than usual. Still, these excellent technicians needed several attempts to get the torture-tube back in my arm at a better and safer arterial-location.

I heard my parents sobbing somewhere in the distance. Over all of the commotion, I understood their suffering was far worse than mine could ever be. The medical pundits predicted I'd die before reaching fourteen. At that moment, I made a vow to graduate Tillagevale High—even if it killed me.

This pun was my all-time greatest.

Now you understand why I invited you to be my escort for the Senior Prom, two years in advance of our graduation date. Clinging to an impossible dream like this kept me going. I wasn't at all surprised how you laughed like an attractive hyena, if there ever could be one, when I summoned the courage to ask you to go with me.

I'll never forget when you said you'd rather stay home alone with a TV dinner, and eat it frozen, instead of being at the future prom with me. I had a hunch your reaction would be something less than enthusiastic, but I gave it my best try. So, when Vivienne ran over to my house on Prom Night to explain your predicament, I could not believe my luck. We scrambled up in the attic to improvise some kind of a quirky black-tie getup. I didn't care about bumping my head on a beam. I was already dizzy from the anticipation.

Now keeping up with my truthful score, I did wish, when I heard you planned on going to the prom with the football-stud, that somehow, while he did his glorified thing on the field, a powerful thunderclap would scramble his conveniently mushy brains. The episode wouldn't be serious—only a brief incapacitation stemming from his burial under a team-wide pileup, owing to a sudden inability to decipher signals.

My stint at casting spells wasn't necessary. He had a very cooperative appendix. I didn't need any of my special mischief. Besides, I hear from exclusive sources that "Mr. Jock" is going to win the Heisman Trophy in a couple of years. While cooperative stars twinkled over the Majestic Hoedown Hotel, everything managed to turn out great. I know now that both of us were fated to get a trophy.

I got mine first on Prom Night, when you danced with me.

I apologize for trying to steal a kiss while we rode in the limo, but you looked awesome in your gown. You were a beautiful Brigitte Bardot doll, coming to life. I watched her on TV in The Girl From Ipanema movie about a month before the prom, and couldn't help thinking how much she reminded me of you. The way you looked on Prom Night, in your formal regalia, made me the luckiest guy in the world.

I don't know what kind of perfume-gunk you dumped all over yourself that night, but the intoxicating stuff made me even more nuts about you than I already am, so you can't blame a guy for trying to steal a kiss.

Remember, I wasn't dead—then.

You looked more beautiful than ever, when you struggled to do the fandango with me. You acted curious about my secret Latino status, so I'll tell you now. I learned those provocative steps by watching reruns of Arthur Murray's Dance Party. It's on right after Jack La Lanne's Sunday night exercise show. It wouldn't hurt such an adorable dancing-disaster like you to refrain from switching the channel to *Love Connection* on one of those pie-eating occasions, and stay tuned for a waltz with Arthur and his wife, Kathryn.

See how I need sensitivity training.

At least one thrill came my way, from my standpoint anyhow, when you tripped on those ridiculous spiked-heels and I caught you in my arms. I tried so hard to tell you but the words just wouldn't come out right. I sounded like I had a mouth full of crackers, didn't I. It's funny too, how the band played and vocalized the theme song from the Ipanema movie at that exact moment.

Above all, this part:

Oh, but I watch her so sadly . . .
How can I tell her I love her?
Yes, I would give my heart gladly . . .
But each day when she walks to the sea,
She looks straight ahead not at me . . .
I smile, but she doesn't see . . .
She just doesn't see . . .
No, she doesn't see.

Antonio Carlos Jobim wrote this song. I guess he had a Ginger in his life too.

Even if I did manage to wax poetic about my Ipanema emotions on Prom Night, I'm sure, as usual, you'd laugh. But you have such a bubbly laugh; a sip of Champagne that makes me giddy. I agree with you, how my dumb attempts at being "romantic" were pretty funny. Afterward, I'd also laugh about my lack of finesse. It's my last chance, so I'll get up the guts right now to tell you something I never could before. You're drop-dead gorgeous.

Yo, that was a major one. Yuh got to admit it.

You could have won the Bullsnake Lodge Junior Miss Tillagevale contest, if you had enough confidence to enter. I'll check out your mirror soon, to make sure some wicked witch isn't in possession of it; you sure don't see what other people are seeing when they look at you. You're beyond compare.

Do you remember when I'd sometimes be away with my parents on those protracted mystery trips? I was visiting St. Jude at his research hospital in Memphis, Tennessee. The one established by TV's compassionate Danny Thomas. They work hard at this place to cure all children in need, with or without insurance or the money to pay for it. If I had made it and lived, I would have been studying physical therapy. How great to do hands-on work with kids like those at St. Jude or somewhere like it, and help build them back up for a bright future.

I want my parents to donate the money they'll save on the dumb funeral to this extraordinary hospital. It's too late for me, but I have hopes it's not too late for all the others. Over the coming years, advances will emerge—not just for kids, but for adults too.

A day never went by at this hospital when I wouldn't think of you, even more than usual. Some real cute girls were there, around your age, who lost one or even both of their legs, due to medical amputation. I thought, wow—what they wouldn't give for Ginger's sturdy and healthy physique.

Open those remarkable blue eyes of yours. What you dislike about yourself, what you see as inferior, what you think is flawed, is in truth exceptional. Didn't it ever occur to you that those hateful comments coming from your friends are only because they're jealous. Don't get angry if they aren't acting toward you in the way you'd expect. Let them know you'll be more than happy to share your IQ and your beauty tips, whenever they want.

Getting back to beautiful chicks, please tell Vivienne she will forever be a kid sister, and I appreciate the prayers she is saying for me now. I hear all of them, but her voice is so sad. Please support her in efforts to celebrate my life. Don't always rag on her the way you do. Vivienne is a definite angel on Earth. So are you; you just don't know it yet.

The weird key in the envelope is from Alistair. He said you've got permission to go inside his secured room, and there is something important waiting for you in the top drawer of his bureau. You'll figure it out.

How much more of a snooping opportunity can you get?

Speaking of Alistair, I must say how dying has been a revelation to me. As a result, I coined a new term, "Die and learn."

Ouch—you do bring your sense of humor along with you whenever you go, and in my situation, this proved fatal.

Don't frown so much. You'll get nasty wrinkles on top of your cute freckles.

Returning to Alistair, I'm sure you remember how I never told anybody, including you, what my middle name is—what the **A** stood for, and all. Well, things were bad enough being called Bertrand. I accepted the name, because my father, in addition to his father and grandfather, carried it on before me. I never could be a Bertrand Norman, IV due to their further embellishment with the "Alistair" on top of the Bertrand. Like you, with your name-curse, my middle name grew to be a tad more than I was able to handle. My grandmother suggested it and my parents liked it. Now, since I've actually met an Alistair, I'm sorry I was ashamed of his name. He is the greatest.

I know what your middle name is. Vivienne told me when she was five. It's lucky how I never blabbed. If I had, your sister wouldn't be around now, saying those prayers for me.

Above and beyond names, I'll try getting back to the original premise of this letter. Do you ever think of Mr. Zahavi, our seventh-grade English teacher? Remember when he told us how, as we develop reading and writing skills, we become capable of entering an international time machine. Hearing his words then, I thought him kind of loopy. I understand his logic now.

I'd like you to understand—the same way I do—how writing preserves individual human brainpower over millenniums. The language in which one writes doesn't matter. Literacy, in general, ensures our ability to make a difference in the lives of people who read what we have written, after we've gone. Great works of literature still obtain the power to educate future generations or to make people laugh or cry.

I'm attempting to do something like this right now, by speaking to you and spanning my lack of mortal time with words. Don't get me wrong. I'm not comparing myself to the great D. H. Lawrence or anything as presumptuous as that. Mr. Zahavi was right, Ginger. Look at the specifics. I'm up here; you're down there, and it's my writing and your ability to decode it, enabling me to explain my everlasting future to you.

It blows my mind how important it is to write. I'm proud of you for wanting to be a writer. You'll be brilliant at it. Don't worry about the Pulitzer. It has your name on it.

I also think my view concerning the importance of writing applies to all traditional works of art including classical music, as well as ballet. Your scholarship encompassing the fine arts is what I'm talking about. Your Grandpa Des knew this. So when you were little, he introduced part of this creative world of the past to you via classical music. For instance, the way he tuned in Beethoven and the like on the little Creamsicle radio.

I liked hearing it too, whenever I'd get a prized invitation—along with my parents and grandparents—to one of those great Sunday pot-roast dinners. He also took the both of us to see Pirates of Penzance at the old community-theatre. The fire engine-red barn, once housing it, is long gone now. Do you remember what fun we had that afternoon? Why am I even asking? You could never forget how I was also there, sitting in the chair between you and Grandpa Des. I handed over my Raisinets when you gobbled up all of your own.

Thinking back as I lie here, unable to move out of this bed, my life, as I once lived it, was the best I could ever get. I'm not bitter at all. Since getting sick, I came to understand how when you're born into earthly existence, you start walking through this life on a rocky road. It's a road where, at all stages of the journey, you will stumble toward self-discovery. And you must travel this pathway alone.

In his existentialist way, Sartre knew the score. Everybody is alone within his or her designated realm. As they encounter their tailored terrain, they have an excellent opportunity to do superior things that make a difference. The trouble is, when people take these privileged steps, they fail to comprehend the significance about striding on unique opportunities pertinent only to them. Do you get what I mean? Others do stand alongside us as our guides, but each person is responsible for their own unique trailblazing.

All the same, it is sad how many of us choose a malevolent itinerary while we are on Earth. Some humans actually rejoice, as they walk along the way, being glad for the pain and suffering of others including animals. They even commit murder to get what they think they want. The worst among them are those who kill, exclaiming to all how their cause justifies innocent bloodshed. There is much work for them to do, on the Monoceros astral plane.

Ginger, you are still on Earth. You still have a chance to place your existence into an entire new perspective. Think back to when we grew up, and what went on behind the scenes on a regular basis. Who shows the most courage in life, those of us opting for gratification via an immoral quick fix—like cheating on a test or shoplifting for the fun of it—as small examples? Or is it those of us opting for the painstaking preservation of integrity?

Getting back to the trailblazing aspect, I don't understand yet about people who decide to cut their hike short and checkout on their own volition, although I do sympathize with them. I have the feeling, however, that suicide is a Monoceros no-no.

I do realize all the same, when people choose to end it before their full-allotment, they did not see the guiding light of hope that glowed for me. Even so, some of us—like me—do travel a short journey through no fault of their own. I often wondered why a baby or a young child died. I saw so many of them at St. Jude. It made me angry, watching families suffer.

But now I know that it's not the length of life's trip; it's the impact. Many parents go on to cherish their existing, or any further children, in much more of an enlightened way when their child dies. They may wind up adopting an abandoned baby, or underprivileged or abused kid, due to the pain of this tragic personal loss. It does not make it fair, but does make it better for me to understand the reason why I had to checkout so young. My departure will improve life for others, in some way.

If there is one thing my brief years taught me, it's that we all need a lot of courage to take charge of our lives. We need special moxie to stand apart from the crowd and do the exemplary thing. At times, it hurts so bad. However, the rewards are great. It's much easier for us to compromise ourselves or be spiteful and deceitful like all the others, because we want to join inferiority. What a sad waste of precious life.

After this long sermon, I'm sure you have no doubt I'll ace Homily 101. It's just that everything is so clear to me now.

Ginger baby, I'd love to go on talking to you forever. Very soon, I could, couldn't I. But in this very brief here-and-now, I need to save some of this benevolent strength from Alistair so I can stay with my parents a little while longer.

This brings me to the poem your dad quoted at your grandmother's wake—the one giving you so much comfort. And when your grandfather died, you received additional consolation by substituting the poem's real focus of a she, with a he instead. When Thomas Hood wrote this poem, his young sister was dying. Your dad read the first and last stanza of Hood's poignant observation of his sister's final hours.

There are two other stanzas in the middle of The Deathbed. If you substitute the word, "she" with a "he" instead—as done in the case of your grandfather—while you read these additional stanzas, the poem is a reflection of my parents' agony now.

So silently we seem'd to speak,
So slowly moved about,
As we had lent him half our powers
To eke his living out.

Our very hopes belied our fears,
Our fears our hopes belied—
We thought him dying when he slept,
And sleeping when he died.

What could be truer now, Ginger?

I want to kiss Mom and Dad before I get my Monoceros Green Card. Someday I hope to earn citizenship. My parents are going through a lot more pain than me. Although they tried hard for additional kids, I'm the only one they got. Tough break, huh.

Speaking of adoption helping, it may also be in <u>their</u> future. As you always say, you <u>never</u> know. I'm sure you understand how this death of their only child is the worst for them. Could you visit them, whenever you get a chance? They know I've been in love with you, ever since you pulled my ears and called me Dumbo. They <u>are</u> parents, but this doesn't render them <u>totally</u> unconscious.

Don't worry or be scared. After I get the necessary preparation, I'll do whatever possible to take care of you from up here. You may make it difficult for me. As both of us are aware, you're a bit hotheaded.

In "passing" here, I'd like to ask if you remember the chain that I gave you at your goodbye party. Being that usual pest, I confronted you about it on the bus, but never got an answer. I bet you stashed it someplace. I hope you brought it to New York, and it's not back in the shed with the telescope. When you do find it, put my enclosed <u>I-Ching</u> coin on it. This way Mr. O'Flanagan and I will always travel with you, next to your heart—<u>if</u> you want.

I'm also enclosing the matching coin for Vivienne. Please use the twenty-bucks I sent with this letter to buy her a fabulous chain, although it may have to be a gold-plated one. This is all the money I have now. I won't ask my parents for any. They know I can't take it with me. Tell her it's my gift. She likes weird stuff. She won't question it.

Before I end this letter, I should mention how I'm writing it in the special disappearing ink Mr. O'Flanagan gave me. Within a short while after reading it, everything will fade away just like me. It's not possible to Xerox it, so worrying yourself about anybody else seeing what I wrote isn't an issue.

I know you Ginger, better than you think, and the sad and sentimental nature of its contents makes this letter impossible for you to rip up. Not like the tons of airplane notes, I'd fold and dart your way during those twelve years of classroom flights. Or thirteen, if you count those handmade paper planes with the platypus pictures I drew on them, and flung at you during Miss Heller's reign. For some reason, she thought <u>you</u> started it and threw them at <u>me</u> first. I wonder where she ever got such an idea!

You're a smart cookie, Ginger. And, concerning this current astral-communication, everything will be a snap for you. I remember how much of a Trekkie you are, so will you pretend to be Scotty occasionally and beam me up a prayer? I guess what I'm saying is that since I'm the one walking toward a kind of sea now I'm hoping you will look up at me. I imagine John Keats felt very much like me when he wrote the sonnet When I have Fears. This part of it really gets to me now. He wasn't much older than I was, when he died.

And when I feel, fair creature of an hour!
I shall never look upon thee more,
Never relish in the faery power
Of unreflecting love!—then on the shore
Of the wide world I stand alone, and think
Till Love and Fame to nothingness do sink.

Being scientific, as I rocket back to Star Trek, please remember where you are right now. Never forget you live on a huge sphere of rock and water **4.5** billion years old. It suspends out there like a fragile blue and white ball—a dazzling Christmas ornament, hanging on a vast galaxy-tree.

You are also at the mercy of the sun's warmth and the moon's gravity. There are fiery asteroids, floating around out there. And their presence threatens where you live. They are truly a case of you never know. Keep these cosmological directives in sight at all times, and you will gain a new perspective concerning everything else in your life.

Before I leave you, I must tell you this. I went to Manhattan with my parents about two years ago. We followed a crowd of other tourists to a historic place called, Trinity Church. They have a graveyard there, dating back more than two-hundred years. It sits in perpetual peace and quiet, surrounded by grass and flowers, in the center of the financial district's hustle and bustle. I read this on one of the worn headstones. The name of the girl buried there was, **Ann Bond**—only twenty-four when she died in the year of **1796.** I wrote it down then, just as inscribed, and for some reason I kept it in my souvenir drawer:

"Heaven is my native aire. I bid my Friends a short adieu. Impatient to be there."

All my love to you for eternity and a day,

Bertrand Alistair Norman

{Before his letter was no longer visible, I traced his signature so it would appear here in the journal. He deserves his stamp on these profound words. *I* could never have written them.}

Events of 5/29/72

ENTRY 9:

UNDER THE TREE **"It's too late."**

I held the letter and stared at it for ten minutes before copying it word-for-word. I had to work faster than ever. My fingers flew across the typewriter. The ink started fading sooner than I expected, and my tears falling on it didn't help.

Bertie's gone for good, like I always wished him to be, but I never wanted it *this* way. He was so brave, joking around with me until the very end. I told you before how I resented being Alvin at the Bullsnake Halloween Party when I was small. I didn't mention he came dressed as Gene Autry. Maybe because he acted similar to him, dodging those bullets and arrows, which life, as well as those perpetual rustlers, continued to fling his way. And, throughout everything, he kept on singing.

Maybe this is the true purpose of a cowboy, who sings while adversity surrounds him. I never had this wholesome outlook before. Viewing Gene Autry in a positive manner in the future will help convince me I'm a singing *cowgirl.* I admit he has a harmonious way about him, in both the capacity of his voice and handcuffing the bad guys. I'm sure I'll be buying some of his record albums.

I realize now, those puns and stupid practical jokes were doubtless the only form of communication Bertie could have with everybody. With me, there's no other way I'd have given him the time of day. "Negative attention is better than no attention," as infamous Miss Heller from kindergarten used to say.

Thinking here of Bertie and kindergarten, he's the one who gave me those chattering Godzilla teeth. He left it up to me, what to do with them. He never required Mrs. Bulwark's smelling salts. *His* hysteria resulted from laughing so hard that he needed a fresh pair of underpants. The school nurse kept a supply of those in her infirmary cabinet too.

Also—concerning summer school typing class—Bertie kept changing my typewriter ribbons for me. He did it so fast—one-two-three, done. Miss Fairweather didn't notice him doing it. Or if she did, she never let on.

I'm getting it *now.*

What good does it do us?

It's too late.

When Vivienne talked about the Samurai Fuji incident, she didn't mention how, soon after it, Bertie spearheaded the successful fundraising drive to help relocate the restaurant. The Texas Department of Highways planned an interstate to veer right through the crossroads where the eatery located.

I'm also realizing he was there for me whenever I had a problem—even when I made it more than plain, I didn't want him to be. He got me out of a lot of potential scrapes. A major one came at Brad Patterson's graduation party. I wanted to try the potent beer the kids dispensed out of a barrel—and then drive *myself* home. I had never tasted an alcoholic beverage in my life, due in large part to Dr Pepper I guess. Curiosity had me wondering why everybody there kept talking about "suds" being "it."

I had also gotten my permanent driver's license the week before, and the first time Dad trusted alone with the Mustang. Bertie blasted me when he saw me tapping the, by this point, half-full keg. He snatched the large glass of foamy beer out of my hand, and poured it on a poor little shrub. It wilted before my eyes.

He also proved on target in other ways during the night. The beer-guzzling crowd, who managed to empty the keg, vomited on the grass. They had difficulty standing up from mixing all that beer with the hashish, and the assortment of other alcoholic beverages stashed around the yard. With Bertie shadowing me like a second skin—tighter than my old Huns' swim-team suit—I wouldn't dare venture into the marijuana department.

One of the girls on my cheerleading squad was there, smoking the pot. She drank a lot more than beer and was alone in the gardener's shed with a popular basketball player. She left Tillagevale several weeks later to help her sick *aunt* in Wisconsin. When she came back, she lived to cry. Everybody knew what happened.

Concerning my *own* garden department, if the shrubbery didn't get the beer first, and I did smoke one of those *weeds*—who knows. Maybe it would have been me, taking an extended trip to *help* a relative. Or I could have contracted a sexually transmitted disease. I heard that a girl had to leave gym class last year, because she had one with the name of "crabs" where a specific kind of *lice* was living in her hair. And I'm not talking about on her head. Yuck. Others can make you really sick, and more and more of them manifest every day, at least according to the newspapers.

Nobody ever mentions it within the family, but I know Aunt Sharon was pregnant with Shelley while she was still in high school. I guess around the age of sixteen. She and Uncle Eddy married immediately. My aunt was one of the lucky ones in a relationship that didn't crack under the stress. Both my aunt and uncle were good and responsible parents. They represented exceptions to the rule. It doesn't usually turn out this way, and they had to work really hard to keep it together. My aunt had to finish high school at home, away from her friends. But she did it.

After Shelley came along, and Uncle Eddy had graduated, he worked at the Piggly Wiggly during the day and went to college at night to become a CPA. Later, when Shelley grew old enough, Aunt Sharon had her turn. She is now an accomplished Family Court Attorney and works as an advocate for children. Did I tell you how proud of her we all are? Daddy calls her, "My sister, the Esquire."

Bertie often lectured me concerning my stupidity about jumping into dangerous territory, *that's* for sure, but he never expected—or ever got—a "thank you." He told me more than once how most guys live, sleep, and breathe to exploit a girl's vulnerability just to "hop in her pants."

With regard to this straight-talking "facts of life" topic, I remember with strange clarity, when we were by ourselves watching a 4-H track meet in Town Square Park early in the month of August. On this occasion, we sat under the big magnolia tree. I was a recent fifteen. Bertie would turn sixteen the coming October.

I'm recollecting the soft summer wind, blowing with the force of an oscillating fan. Sitting here as I type now, I can feel it bouncing my curls around. I also recall wearing those white short-shorts. The welcome breeze cooled off my sunburned legs and my face had a tan, allowing my freckles to merge into the uniform look of a Coppertone ad. I kicked off my sandals and admired my professional pedicure, pleased about trying bright-red nail polish on my toes. I wondered if anybody except me noticed how wild the color looked. I also thought the race was real slow to kickoff.

That uncharacteristic afternoon under the fragrant tree, we returned from swimming as a group at the lake earlier in the day. Bertie's thick hair framed his face with damp strands. Without gobs of greasy Brylcreem, the usual carrot-red was more brownish, with bright reflections of amber, and longer than I imagined with waves I never saw before.

When he removed his glasses, to wipe perspiration off the bridge of his nose, for the first time that I can recollect I gazed into his eyes without that tinted frogeye-barrier blocking them. These eyes were an unexpected shade of beautiful green—as green as the dew on the same grass at dawn and looking at him with this new kind of intensity made me uncomfortable.

When he closed his mouth, which even he would admit was a rare occurrence, his lips were a sensuous kind of full, almost magnetic—soft and enveloping. Why didn't I ever realize this enthralling detail before? I thought the sun got to me, when a warm flush spread across my body. I squelched this seductive sensation fast, and never allowed myself to think about it ever again—until *now.*

It shook me up, at that moment in the past, because I found everything about Bertie very desirable, even his voice. When did it get so husky and manly? I hear it now, floating in the warm air exactly the way it did that day:

See those jocks over there on the track. I hear them bragging in front of me on purpose, thinking they're doing that pathetic Bertie-nerd a favor. How else could *I* ever experience their selfish exploits?

Don't *you* fall for their testosterone loaded "I love you" crap. It really means they *love* what they *want* from you. They brag to each other how the duped girls keep crying and calling them up after the idiots use them to make a conquest. They ridicule them by mimicking a squeaky, high-pitched voice saying . . .

'You said you love me. You said you love me.'

I try to stick up for these girls when I quote the jocks, 'to the victor belong the spoils.' Of course, these guys are clueless. They look at me and go, 'duh'. On this subject, I recommend an old movie titled *The Apartment.* I want you to catch it on TV. It should be required viewing for every teenage girl, and young women too. It says it all.

As soon as he gave me heads-up on jocks, he tousled my curls. Under normal conditions, I'd have said my usual "bug off" except I didn't. I couldn't. His gentle touch felt softer and warmer than the rippling summer breeze, as he told me, "Please keep that special part of you, Ginger—until love is mutual, and love is real. Put an esteemed price on yourself. Why not save it for a future with somebody like . . ."

He never did finish that sentence. The crackle of the pistol, signaling the race, startled us both.

"Let the players begin," he mumbled.

Events of 5/29/72

ENTRY 10:

TIES THAT BIND

"He smiled at her in a virtuous way."

Reflecting back on how my parents comforted Bertie's parents on the day after he died, was natural. Doctor Bert Norman, and his wife Tessa, are lifelong friends. Now that I think about it, our grandmothers also grew up together in Tillagevale.

I remember Grandma Ava telling me those funny stories about her best friend, little Jean Dejoy. She'd say that while they played together, the future Mrs. Jean *Norman* loved to joke around just like Bertie, her someday grandson, trying to make the best of things for everybody.

How could Bertie love *me?* I behaved horrible toward him. It hit me, and it hit hard. I treated him like scum. I never took time to understand him. While he was sick and suffering, he still made an effort to protect my welfare—even though I acted like a total wasteoid.

Oh, my God! Was *I* the "guiding light of hope" that he talked about in his letter? If so, I never switched it on for him. While we rode on that mysterious bus, he took my hand for a second and caressed it like that summer breeze I mentioned. I pulled it away fast, as if he contaminated me. I shouldn't have. He meant it only as an innocent final gesture on his part.

Or perhaps his touch reminded me of the strange attraction to him, I experienced under the tree—feelings I'd been suppressing for so long. Maybe I didn't want to admit how I longed for his familiar presence; the sound of his voice; the annoying quintessential boy-next-door, who, in spite of everything, continues to be a part of me.

Over these past years, I should have realized what went on. I should have given him support and made his life better; maybe I might have extended it. I'll never know for sure. Instead, I made it worse. I should have helped him. I should have helped his parents. I'm sure he would have confided in me, if I had given him the opportunity. He needed me, and I never remember being cheerful with him without an agenda.

Who is the ditzy Autry now? It is *not* Vivienne. *I'm* the one who's been behaving dumber than anybody has. She saw deep into Bertie right from the start. She knew all along he was special and tried being kind to him, even later on when her friends told her she was a "nerd lover."

I remember once when we were much younger. I saw Bertie crying in the schoolyard. I ignored it, along with everybody else. Kindergartner Vivienne was the only one who went over to him. She handed him her favorite *Snickers* candy bar. He smiled at her in a virtuous way. It is this look on his face, captured from a moment so long ago, which has now burned itself into my memory—an expression articulating, "What a good friend you are."

My sister, what will I tell her about the letter?

No lies, but no truth either.

The chain Bertie gave me—where did I put it? I know I brought it with me, only with the thought that I might be able to sell it in New York, if I needed money. I'll search for it now.

I found it underneath the original receipt for the cashew nuts, inside my "Epicurean" black-velvet box. I lifted it out of the little lavender gift box and pressed his neglected present against my heart. The metal felt cold. After really looking at it, I saw a quality piece of jewelry. While I slipped the coin on the chain, and placed it around my neck, it felt warmer—like a teardrop defrosting. I made a vow to wear my beautiful necklace—forever.

A sense of peace came over me, dialing home to Tillagevale. Vivienne must have been sitting by the phone. She picked it up on the first ring. Without elaborating, I told her that Bertie wrote to thank me for going to the prom with him, and to tell her he loved her as a kid sister, saying she is his *angel.* This time, when Vivienne cried, I cried with her. I also told her I'm wearing the "lucky coin" Bertie had included with the letter, and he had sent her one too. She expressed her happiness when I mentioned I'd bring hers in person, since I'll be coming home for my eighteenth-birthday. His gift was too precious to risk mailing.

"Goody-goody-gum-drops, Ginger!" she said, with childlike glee. There was such innocence in that exclamation. I had not heard her use this phrase since she was little. Vivienne started to laugh—and so did I.

How great to be laughing with my sister, and not in her face or worse yet behind her back

When I bring her Bertie's gift, I want to put it around her neck myself. Bertie's right about Vivienne. *She* is an angel for sure. About *my* status as an angel, well, as usual, he was much too kind.

I glanced at my watch, and couldn't believe the hands rested on 2 o'clock. I must scrounge up courage to get back to Alistair's museum and look in his room.

Why did he give the key to *me?*

Why?

What would the sealed room reveal?

Events of 5/29/72

ENTRY 11:

LITTLE BIRD

"Then, I took this job here."

The building stood there, just as I remembered it, on Fifth Avenue across from the Park. I was relieved owing to all the stuff happening to me in recent days, because as I've been finding out for sure lately, you *never* know. The doorman rushed over to greet me.

"Good afternoon, Miss Autry. Nice day. Gettin' ready to move in?"

Oh, if you only knew the truth, I thought.

"I'm not here for the moving part," I said. "I came back to check some things out. I wondered when I first came here yesterday, was I alone?"

The strange look on his face wasn't a surprise. I anticipated it. "Yes, of course you were alone. Did you expect somebody to meet you here? I told property management how I'd take care of your arrival *for* them."

With concern in his voice, he continued with, "Didn't you see the list of detailed instructions taped on the apartment's front door for you?"

"Oh yes, the list," I replied—with as much sincerity as I could gather—before continuing to say, "I just thought this morning that perhaps *somebody* from a real estate agency came here yesterday, to help me sign a lease or something. Believe me, I got those instructions."

"It makes sense," he stated. "Don't concern yourself. There's no reason for any kind of *lease.* The family trusts my judgment."

I must have been staring at his cloak when he said, "Don't mind all this dust on my uniform. I was down in the basement with the exterminator a few minutes ago. There's a definite problem with mice. Don't worry; they won't make it up to the 14th floor. We arranged for traps to catch them, and later I'll set them free somewhere in the park. I don't like to kill nothin', if I don't have to. I'm not that tough guy people think, but don't tell um."

"I hope they work," I said. "Mice are smarter than any exterminator."

My shoulders slumped like deflated tires—giving away how I thought—this is the *least* of my worries. *"Ah,* I'm sorry. We've spoken so many times, but I still don't know your name."

His stern look softened for a moment when he said, "My name is Sergeant Mitch Purdy, retired from *New York's Finest.* That's the city's police department. A proud man in blue I was, for over thirty years, until I cashed it in five years ago.

Before too long, after I got the old gold watch, my wife divorced me. I guess she couldn't take me hangin' around the house all day long and cross-examining *her.* I wound up givin' her the place. She kept telling me how she managed our home, and raised four kids, without prior supervision from law enforcement. Then, I took this job here. I made a new life for myself, in my cozy unit downstairs. Downstairs with the mice, I should now say."

I got a delayed clear message that this all-around building attendant is a good person, concerned about my welfare. Although long overdue, a classic better late than never, I said, "Thank you, Sergeant Purdy. Thank you for *all* of your help."

"No trouble, Miss Autry. Let me know whenever you need me."

"I will," I said; knowing I wouldn't.

He stood there looking at me, offering me protection, all of the while I tiptoed down the hall toward the elevator. I know this, because I spun around several times to check. I hesitated pushing its button indicating 14th Floor. As the thing creaked and jerked its way up—my grandmother's faint voice competed in the background but I still *heard* it. She sang part of the refrain to an old song she loved.

She's only a bird in a gilded cage
A beautiful sight to see
You may think she's happy and free from care
She's not though she seems to be . . .
Arthur J. Lamb

Standing there by myself in the Gatsby elevator, things were as clear as could be:

Grandma's 'little bird in a gilded cage' was me.

Events of 5/29/72

ENTRY 12:

THE SANCTUARY "Why me?"

I never really understood the word *weird,* until I entered the apartment alone without Mr. O'Flanagan as a buffer for the ghost. But in spite of being shaky, I took responsibility by checking on plants in the kitchen. Some of them drooped. I adjusted the curtain a tiny bit, to lessen the sun and gave them a generous watering.

I went into the den again, to study those Perry-family pictures. While briefly glancing at them again yesterday, everything about them bugged me. Something about Alistair's face is very familiar from my past, but I couldn't recall what. Even now, with plenty of time to inspect them up close, no bells rang. It only made me more positive about their peculiar nuance.

The scary time to go upstairs to this cryptic room caught up to me. I could no longer postpone the fear of entering this burial chamber. Reaching into my jacket pocket, I groped for the shiny key Bertie sent me. Nobody's been in this room for over forty years. Why should it be *me* breaking the spell? The one thing I *was* certain of, is how some special "lofty people" counted on my courage. I failed Bertie in the past. I won't repeat my callousness in the future.

The door to the room unlocked with the ease of someone on the other side, turning the knob for me. My eyes had to adjust fast. This room is very dark in contrast to the sunny kitchen. Heavy black velvet drapes, covering the two floor-length windows in this room, block any daylight, giving it the look of a proper mortuary. I flipped an electrical switch, as fast as possible.

The reassuring flood of light revealed a surprise. The large room's bright and beautiful color of golden wheat, contrasted in a delightful way with the chocolate brown carpet. Stylish drawstring pajama bottoms, with big black and white stripes, crumpled on the floor—along with a dark gray suede slipper. I bent over them, very tempted to delve into everything. I didn't. These personal items might disintegrate like Oscar Wilde's *Picture of Dorian Gray.*

I noticed that the matching slipper sat on the Colonial four-poster bed, beside the pajama top. Rumpled white sheets, trimmed with brown lace, rested on the bed too, just as Mr. O'Flanagan mentioned before. Alistair had been in an obvious hurry when he left that final morning, so very long ago.

A familiar aroma drifted throughout this eerie space. And, like those haunting Perry photos, I couldn't identify it. I kept trying to put a name to it by savoring the air and inhaling deeply, but no luck. The scent hovered there, and I surely knew it well yet not at all.

Adding to the informal atmosphere, an empty steamer trunk is wide-open on the floor in the center of this room. I saw the expensive cedar lining. The outside of this trunk displays a collection of global travel stickers. I squatted close to them. They represented seaports and countries from all over the world—exotic places I had never even heard of before, and I wished then how I could go and see them all myself. I guessed Alistair decided not to take it at the last minute. Or maybe there wasn't a single space left for another sticker.

Someone—I assume Alistair—had left the bathroom door wide open. I found the huge white metal bathtub, raised high on claw feet, to be shiny clean—like the rest of the spacious white-tiled room. One exception to the sterility was the crusty mug, sitting on the sink's ledge. A large mohair shaving brush still stands upright inside of it. I inched closer to it and looked. Not wanting to be disrespectful, I left it alone.

Next to it—resting on the counter—is a short natural-bristle hairbrush with a mahogany handle. This brush still exhibits long strands of brownish curly hair. Had somebody used it yesterday? An icy sensation crept along the nape of my neck. I told myself to get a good grip or I might not go through with everything.

Bertie said I should look in the top drawer of Alistair's bureau. It stands on the wall, between the two long windows. My heart pounded out of my chest once again, as the dynamic black lacquer chest drew me toward it. I put my hand around the mother-of-pearl handle. It felt icy cold and I started to tremble, as the large deep drawer opened. Scared of what I'd find inside, I peeked fast with my eyes halfway-closed.

Since I squinted out of fear, I thought it looked empty at first—until I took note of some green and blue plaid material tucked into the deep drawer's corner. Sitting on top of the material, was a small gift box and next to it of all things, a bottle of Evening in Paris perfume.

I soon spotted a large brown paper envelope—lying flat in the middle of the drawer.

In an eerie way, it reminded me of that envelope my parents received, warning them about future tornadoes. However, this one read . . . in large authoritative letters:

<u>OPEN ONLY WITH PERMISSION</u>

Events of 5/29/72

ENTRY 13:

THE REVELATION ______________ **"You come straight to the point."**

Taking the envelope out of the drawer, I held it up to the light—shaking and unsure if I really do have his permission. He's *asking* me to do it. Still, what's in this envelope that possibly relates to *me?* I'll find out in a minute, if I don't faint first.

I opened it fast. Only a simple short cord, looping through a wide hole, preserved it. I pulled out an official looking document stamped with a bureaucratic wax seal:

®Certificate of Marriage
September 3rd, 1928

Miss Ava Arden Warren, aged 22 of Tillagevale, Texas

To

Sir Alistair Perry, aged 25 of New York, New York

Officiated by: Captain Destrehan Autry

Witnessed by: Mrs. Jean Norman

Time for me to crumble, with the closest accessible place being on the bed. Ava Arden Warren was my grandmother. I kept staring at the document. First Bertie's letter, now this. Shelley picked a good week to visit the Pocono Mountains. I'm sure those lofty people had a great deal to do with it.

There are also two small black and white photos kept inside this envelope. I took them out, taking special care not to bend them. How incredible for me to be looking at a picture of my very young grandmother, with her adorable short hair and square cut bangs. These thick wisps of hair are pressing against her forehead, and they're flattening with style under a wide, beaded headband. She wears short lace gloves and looks beautiful while holding a narrow bouquet of what appear to be roses, with very long stems.

I stared at her dress with more intent than anything else in the picture. I recognized it. When I was eight, I took tap lessons at the Bullsnake Lodge. We learned a dance called the *Charleston.* I wore the best *Flapper* costume at the recital, because my grandmother cut down the white dress, appearing in this photo. She made sure it fit me like a miniature version of the real one, with that snug-around-the-hips style, and a puffy, balloon-like sleeveless top. That short pleated skirt *did* flap around while I danced.

She referred to it as an "exclusive dress" lent to her long ago by a dear friend, who later told her to keep it "owing to a broken heart." I never questioned those circumstances. Now I realize how *exclusive* this dress really was, and who suffered the broken heart.

In the other picture, she looked the same. Except in *this* one, she sat down in a high-backed cane chair. A very macho Grandpa Des stood next to her. He wore some kind of an official uniform, along with the very beret I remember him pulling out of the recliner's pocket, and showing to toddler-me.

Even then, he stood tall and stately in the photo. His face didn't show a hint of a line. He had a thick head of hair, along with a handlebar mustache, as well as those youthful sideburns I had seen in earlier pictures of him. But in this rendition, they appeared much thicker and bushier under that familiar beret. I had *never* seen him look like he did in this picture. Even the one where snow fell all over him, on New York City's Wall Street, couldn't compare.

Before I could even catch my breath and recover from the shock of seeing this photo of my grandfather, a flood of spongy white light filled the room. At first, this apparition appeared similar in shape to that legendary Kolinsky Circus cotton candy, until it took the outline of a human form. I clutched Bertie's coin, expecting him to stand at the foot of the bed any second.

But Bertie hadn't come.

Alistair did.

He was a carbon copy of his youthful pictures in the den downstairs, but now he wore a long white satin robe. The embroidered words *Port and Starboard* floated all over it in vibrant gold thread. I couldn't tell his height while he floated about three-feet off the floor. I know you'll find this hard to believe, but I was speechless—*me,* the verbose Ginger Autry, speechless. There *is* a first for everything.

Being so close to his face, I thought—is *he* for real? Soon he answered my silent question with the sensation I had of his breath being frail, while he tried to catch it. I stared into his round azure-blue eyes—exact duplicates of mine. And yes, in "person" he is *beyond* handsome. He spoke in a soft voice, "Hello, Ginger. I hope you are not frightened of me."

When I managed the words, I heard wonderment in my voice, *"No.* No. I'm not afraid at all. Mr. O'Flanagan and Bertie told me how special you are. I feel like I know you, *Mr. Perry,* and now you're going to tell me a fantastic story about my family, aren't you." I had no idea what he'd say. Surprisingly, when he spoke, his first words were of me.

"*You* are a girl after my own heart. You come straight to the point. In my form of 'reality', I supervised at the hospital the night you arrived. You screamed so loud, the doctor could have used earplugs. I also drifted around when Vivienne arrived. And back on the day when your father made his stubborn way into the world, I was there for my wife and child. While I held Ava's hand, and placed my head on her chest, she told the nurse to close the window, because of the strange breeze near her bed. Later, over the years, I had to decide who screamed the loudest in the family infant-group. I now congratulate you, for winning the title hands-down."

As he continued, I heard the exhilaration in his voice. "It may be a simple story I will tell you, Ginger, but it is a *romantic* simple story."

Seeing his broad smile, caused another stir of recognition concerning those mystery pictures that plagued me, yet not quite. There is *something* so familiar about him—somehow, somewhere.

As he sat down next to me on the bed, I noticed the cavernous dimples, and the extraordinarily deep cleft in his chin sucked me in like quicksand. He held both of my hands, while he revealed the story of a lifetime. Here it is, just as he told it to me, sounding like the British actor *David Nivin*—light, crisp, distinguished, and extremely well-educated.

MEIN SCHATZELCHEN

On Saturday evening September 1st, back in the year 1928, I honored a kind invitation from Tillagevale University's renown Department of Oceanography. I came along with my good friend, Destrehan Autry.

I am sure you know Destrehan grew up in Louisiana. I often remember him telling me how, as a young boy, he would roll—right along with the Mississippi River. He would also have a laugh about my British accent. And I, in turn, spoofed his southern drawl. He held that his one little tugboat the *Armada* had more power than 'a whole dang fleet.'

We both spoke to the audience about our maritime adventures, and afterward we mingled with the students and the faculty. Your grandmother, Ava, was in charge of the Alumni Hospitality Committee. When she served me punch, I noticed my hands trembling. Her hands trembled too. I never did wash those purple stains of spattered grape juice, off my best white shirt. I know that this sentimental shirt still hangs here now, in the same sweet condition, somewhere in a closet.

Ava's good friend, Jean, also attended the lecture—along with her new husband. She had married Bertie's grandfather only one month before.

Ava and I spent the evening at the university, exclusively socializing with each other. We both failed to notice anybody else in the crowded room. Before we parted that night, I told her that I must sail for England on Monday, September 10th for a two-month visit with my family.

The next day after we first met each other happened to be a Sunday, so Ava and I picnicked at the local lakeside. It is endearing how I still taste those delicious egg salad sandwiches she made. Being alone together was enchanting. We talked for hours. It did not take long for us to understand how *Fate* had entwined our souls.

My previous plans had myself and Destrehan initiating our return to New York by train, on the coming Monday morning, September 3rd—but we did not. Instead, he stayed on doing research at the university's maritime library, while Ava arranged a vacation day from her work to be with me. As you know, she was the best pediatric nurse at Tillagevale Memorial Hospital.

On this day off, we could not wait to meet again. This time though, we sat beneath the delightful magnolia tree in Town Square Park. It is still there, the same as before, only much taller. I knew, that magical day under the tree, destiny chose Ava to be my wife. We asked Captain Autry if he would give us the honor of marrying us, and perform the ceremony later in the day.

Ava informed Jean of our plans, requesting her to keep our pending marriage confidential and act as our gracious witness. Out of kindness, she loaned Ava *her* recent wedding attire. While Ava and I bought our traditional matching gold wedding bands—where nobody she knew could ever recognize her—Jean went to a local florist to purchase a bouquet of beautiful long-stemmed red roses for me to present to Ava before the ceremony.

Although the marriage officiated by Destrehan was legal worldwide, we also intended a small church service and formal reception to occur later on. We hoped her relatives and friends, as well as my family abroad would attend—*after* I made my return to America.

First, I would explain about Ava to my parents while I visited in England. Later, Ava would introduce me to her ultraconservative family in Tillagevale. We often laughed about their future reaction to the wild, globetrotting 'pirate' with the 'snobbish' tone of voice—the *Continental* bloke, who mysteriously popped into her life.

We all traveled together to the town of *Dublin*—an hour's train ride from Tillagevale. With Destrehan presiding, and Jean borrowing Ava's 'something blue' handkerchief, to wipe away tears, Ava and I exchanged the vows we wrote. As we held hands, a tender twilight blanketed the sky with warmth—in motherly preparation of nightfall.

During this brief ceremony, the four of us stood inside of a private library, filled with the dim light of lilac-scented candles, inside of a German inn named *Mein Schatzelchen,* meaning *My Little Treasure.* This inn is now part of times gone by, but your favorite Dr Pepper factory still locates there in this town of Dublin, Texas.

With everything that Fate allowed, we were joyous newlyweds. Afterward, we had a magnificent celebratory dinner with Destrehan and Jean at this inn. I remember we ate marvelous sauerbraten for our main course and, with a heartfelt toast from Destrehan, we washed it down with fine European *Vevve Clicquot* champagne. The owner's wife at the inn baked as good as she cooked. She presented us with a small marzipan wedding cake. At nine that evening, our dear friends took the last train back to Tillagevale where Destrehan waited for me at his hotel.

Ava and I spent our first and only night together in a room on the top floor of this charming inn. We slept in a high featherbed that almost reached the ceiling. We laughed, because, in order to get into it, we needed the ladder attached to this enormous bed's long footboard.

The next morning, we took the earliest transportation available to Tillagevale. We held hands inside the back of a rickety truck—filled with crates of rambunctious chickens. When we said our sad goodbye, Ava went back to work. I made my departure for New York with Destrehan.

Soon after, as scheduled, I did sail for England. The pain of leaving without her was physical. A vicious force ripped the heart out of my chest. I stood on the ship's top deck as it left port. I could not stop sobbing. Ashamed others would notice me I leaned over the railing and looked down into agitated water. I watched my cascading tears become one with it, in the same way Ava and I were now one. The driving force of the ship's horn warned passengers of imminent departure with such shrillness the deck quaked. Never before had I felt the tangible power of this sort of reverberation, in all my years of traveling by sea.

I was, against my abandoned will, under sail with a voyage rougher than usual. I realize now how it portended the future. I never became seasick, no matter how violent the seas. On this trip, however, I rushed like clockwork to my cabin's loo every morning to deposit my breakfast.

Upon arriving at my ancestral manor in Lancashire, I told my parents of the marriage. My father reacted with anger. Ava was not acceptable. A 'mere nurse' from a rural town in crude 'Wild West America' could never replace the sophisticated British Countess, he would handpick for me in the future.

Matters worsened when I told my father the *Warren* family traced their roots back to passage on the Mayflower. He said in retaliation that it only affirmed her traitorous heritage. I found keeping control of my temper, while my father criticized her, and jumped to those erroneous conclusions, to be extremely difficult. But for the sake of my mother and sisters, who were thrilled I came home for a brief visit, I kept silent.

When my mother—the beautiful and gentle woman she was—saw my photographs of Ava, she understood why I fell in love. It is not a simple coincidence, in one of those puzzling pictures downstairs, how your sister Vivienne, and my mother *Natalie,* are so much alike. At the age Vivienne is now, they could have been identical twins.

Within two weeks after I sailed to visit England, Ava believed she was expecting. She could not share the happy news. Communicating with me was impossible and she had not yet confirmed her suspicions about the pregnancy. Without definite medical validation, she kept circumstances to herself. She felt confident that upon my return to claim her, at the time when a baby *could* be on the way, she would be only two-months along. Her supposed pregnancy went undisclosed. She told no one, including dear Jean Norman. She could not announce it until she was sure, and we formally started our married life together, here in New York.

Captain Autry came back to Tillagevale alone in mid-November. He held Ava in his arms when he told her I had succumbed on the Vestris. He and Jean were her sole consolation, as she came to grasp the enormity of the situation. Telling them both, about the definite pregnancy, was not the joyous occasion she planned.

Under these tragic circumstances, as my long-standing, loyal friend, he proposed marriage to Ava. Destrehan earnestly desired to protect her and the unborn child. She was grateful to accept. Remember—she had not told any of her family or friends about her hasty elopement and who, other than immediate family, would even believe her if she did say anything. In those years, this was a delicate situation.

Society was not as tolerant as it is today. It would not be easy for her to raise a child alone in a small, rural town, where perpetual whispers and rumors clouded her life. And starting over somewhere else on her own with an infant was not an option. I remained forever gone from her life. I could do nothing of an earthly-nature for her.

In order to raise necessary money, *Destry*, as people in Tillagevale knew him by this time, sold his beloved tugboat as soon as Ava agreed to accept his proposal. He made tremendous sacrifices to do for my new family what I surely would have done for them, if I could have. Many times, he said to me about himself, 'That old Mississippi River runs through my veins and gives me the strength I often need.'

His legendary 'chariot', was once a prominent part of the Captain's Quarters on the Armada.

In days, with the happy blessings of the entire Warren family, they married. Relatives and friends only thought about the culmination of a whirlwind courtship. After all, everybody of importance knew she had met the strapping, dynamic southerner two months before—at the university lecture that past September. The brief occasions she spent alone with me, were private. Nobody of relevance to her in town, other than Jean, knew of them. At the decisive time of Destrehan's sincere proposal, and the subsequent marriage, he started his profitable *Armada Travel Agency,* in Tillagevale.

When Ava gave birth to our precious 'premature' baby boy, on June 12th, 1929, she chose the name of *Alex,* which happens to be an earlier derivative of Alistair. At least, my versatile Gemini son was able to share the same initial as his father. Of course, the child's legal surname became—*Autry.*

Alex was a feeble baby. He had difficulty breathing. Things were touch-and-go for a month. I am certain all of the terrible emotional stress Ava endured during the pregnancy played a significant part in his four-pound birth weight. Due to this fragile weight, no one questioned his two-month 'premature' delivery. Ava's excellent pediatric training pulled him through, laying the delicate matter to rest forever in the family cradle.

Two years later, Ava and Destrehan had their own daughter, Sharon. They had become a true, loving couple. They are together now for eternity, as they should be.

Indeed—he took my place as a devoted husband to Ava, a true father to my son Alex, and a caring, loving grandfather to both you and Vivienne. He never showed any preference for his biological granddaughter, Shelley. All three of you were the same in his eyes, representing a unifying part of Ava. I know though, that deep in his heart of hearts, somehow *you* were able to get into his blood like a replacement for his venerated, Mississippi River.

I realize you have several inquiries about being here with me. Among them is the reason why I am revealing these family secrets. And, when you ask your questions, please do not call me *Mr. Perry.* I can never replace Grandpa Des in your heart, and I do not wish to, but if you call me, *Granddad,* while we are briefly here together, it will be a beautiful gift.

Events of 5/29/72

ENTRY 14:

GENEOLOGY **"Why did I act so horrible to him?"**

The power of his words stunned me. *Alistair Perry* is my biological grandfather. In all my life of imagining the stories I'd write someday, and the award winning journalistic investigations I'd be in charge of, I could never imagine what just happened to me now. Unlike Bertie's icy hands on the bus, his felt warm while touching mine. Maybe I allowed my *humanity* to transfuse him—being the crucial measure I never supplied for Bertie. I desired to hug him and put my head on his shoulder. He typified a real person to me—a person looking so much like me.

Alistair read my thoughts, because looking into my eyes he said, "When a spirit-being takes on human-form that entity *is* alive. There are only two significant differences between spirits and humans. The first is how spirit-beings train to use their extraterrestrial powers with caution. The second is how they all display boundless generosity of heart—unlike most of their counterparts on Earth."

"There are so many questions Mr. P . . . *er, Granddad.* I don't know where to start. Is Bertie okay?"

"Yes, Bertie is adjusting well. He told me you're the one girl on Earth who could go through these past few days without, in his words, *cracking up."*

"Don't be so sure of that, "I said. "All of my life I've suspected something on the Autry family tree, besides tea, gives me hives. Now I know why. I must take after your personality, as well as your physical features, right?"

Although he looked young, at least in spirit-life manifestation, his tone took on an air of lighthearted wisdom. "This observation is spot-on. You *do* look like me when I was your age. And terribly ostracizing for any Brit, I had an allergy to tea—just like yours. Before you made that decision to consult Miss Clairol, we shared the same type of hair. I will confess to you now that I also disliked my mundane, as you say, 'crowning glory.' In those days though, chaps hesitated to experiment with any type of hair dye. I did not need any more speculation concerning my flaky creditability."

We both laughed, and I felt secure enough to express my thoughts.

"Why did *Bertie* have to die? Why did I act so horrible to him?"

He was gentle, and not at all judgmental, when he answered me. "Bertie had been placed here for a short while, to make life better for others. You will come to comprehend this later on. You were not horrible to him. You were *indifferent.*"

When he told me this, I knew he tried to soften the blow . . . to be kind, the way a grandfather would. So not hesitating to speak up like a *true* granddaughter I said, "Yes, I *was* indifferent, and this translates to horrible. I was a bad friend, and a big disappointment to him."

At this special moment, he touched my cheek with such softness it reminded me of the brush of one of those angelic ostrich plumes on my mother's hat, I once told you about.

"You should not worry yourself. Bertie no longer attaches to these trepidations. He did ask me to help you understand how dancing with you wiped out every one of what he calls, 'your strong willed rejoinders.' Believe me when I say, he is at peace with everything."

Although he tried hard to make me feel better, his efforts weren't working. I had to get my swell of conflicting emotions in check, but hard to do, when talking to such a magnificent apparition. I needed to focus on something, other than Bertie.

"Why did you keep that Evening in Paris perfume in your drawer?"

Along with his gorgeous eyes, those dazzling dimples danced again as he answered, "Conflicts with my image of a masculine diver, doesn't it."

I felt comfortable enough to roll my eyes and say, "Sure does, Grandpa."

A look of adoration captured his eyes when he told me, "Ava loved that perfume. It represented the essence of her *aura.* Before I left Tillagevale, I went to Woolworth's and purchased three bottles. I gave her one, and took the other two for sprinkling on bed linens. I kept one of them in my drawer here in the city, and the other came along to England. In this way, she stayed with me no matter how far away I had to be. At night in England, alone in my bed, I felt her there. I could almost reach out and touch her."

"What about the small gift box and the plaid material?"

"Yes," he said, with an awkward nod, as he levitated off the floor. He attempted to walk over to the open drawer. Holding on to it for a minute, he stabilized himself enough to carry the material and the gift box back over to the bed, and place the retrieved items on my lap. Before he sat down next to me again, his hands shook. He regained his composure, right before continuing with our conversation:

Mr. O'Flanagan was very excited about this tartan material from his newfound cousins. He also had this little gift box, containing the special present he purchased in Ireland for Mr. Fortunato. He brought these two items to my room at the Blackpool hotel, the night before we sailed. He was excited to show them to me. In an absentminded rush the next morning, we both failed to notice that he left them behind in my room, after his visit the previous evening.

The Vestris sailed early in the morning. My father waved a conservative goodbye to me from the dock, his fingers moving very little. My mother was signaling me with both her arms outstretched, and for some reason she ran back up the ship's ramp to hug me one more time. She whispered in my ear how she loved me more than life itself, acting as if she would never see me again. I now know she was right. When they motored back to the hotel, the staff told them I had forgotten some things. So naturally, my parents forwarded Mr. O'Flanagan's gifts to me here in New York, thinking they were mine.

Completing the arrangements for this place to be my perpetual memorial, my father placed Mr. O'Flanagan's mistaken things in my dresser drawer—sealing them forever. They were destined to become a natural part of my commemoration. He thought *I* had left them in Blackpool.

After hearing his explanation, it made me realize the true significance of the fabric. I reached down and stroked the tartan. I felt close to Mr. O'Flanagan and his dream of having his own kilt, the long-held dream that never came to be.

"What's going to happen to this material? It meant so much to Singh how his family in Ireland gave it to him. And—what about this special present for Mr. Fortunato? May I bring Frankie his forgotten gift? It will be better late than never. I'm sure he'll want to wear it. He already knows I've seen and talked with Mr. O'Flanagan and everything."

"I cannot answer this question, as I am giving *you* a special mission. The nature of it speaks to figuring everything out on your own—including the status of Singh's very belated gift for dear Mr. Fortunato."

He looked at me with the kind of admiration I had never seen directed at me before, when he said, "I am confident you will succeed with your mission, and gratified how you care about Singh O'Flanagan. He tells you of my bravery on the Vestris, but never mentions how he swam in the rough waters, right along with me, and rescued many passengers himself."

It didn't surprise me at all that Singh exemplified an extraordinary hero too. However, it did amaze me that Alistair could have this sort of faith in me and *my* ability to carry out any kind of "special mission." I told him I'd live up to his expectations—no matter what.

And I meant it.

Events of 5/29/72

ENTRY 15:

ZEROSEN **"His name is, *Everett.*"**

The heavy mist in the air surrounding us placed *me* on a Tomorrow-Land cloud. But where was I floating? I soon had an idea when he told me, "I wish to thank you for allowing me the privilege of acting as your grandfather for this brief, but precious moment in mortal-time."

After letting me know that he felt grateful to *me,* and thought it a *privilege* to be *my* grandfather, tears came fast.

I kept choking back these warm tears while he continued with:

My delightful granddaughter, if you will further indulge me now, I am going to give you some simple grandfatherly advice:

You are certainly aware of the carousel in Central Park across the street. Its cheerful sound often fills these rooms. Well, you should be aware of another carousel and it spins endlessly. Many people will not get on this additional carousel. They worry about what others will think of them. Due to this fear, they never have an opportunity to catch the prized *brass ring.* They are anxious about falling off of this wonderful, colorful ride that we call, 'The World.' They will never experience the music of its living calliope.

Your special quality is the unique spirit of inquisitiveness you carry in your heart, and the ability to be who you are—no matter what. Do you remember when your teacher read the children in your kindergarten group the colorful picture book about a carefree mermaid? I stood behind you in your class that day when you jumped up and asked a very startled Harriet,

'How *does* a mermaid take care of her bathroom-business?' I knew when Miss Heller let out her latest shocked gasp that *you* are a definite chip off *this* old block.

Regarding your first name, it represents your adventurous spirit. I know you are thinking about changing it. I believe you prefer the name, *Victoria.* It is not a bad name. I am very familiar with a queen of this nomenclature. Even in the spirit world, we are to call her, '*She* who must be obeyed.'

The name of 'Victoria' is not for you and it *never* will be. And your original middle name, the one with the 'P' suits you. It is not, as you say, *the pits.* It is truly the core of you.

About your last name, you will get to change it in seven years. I cannot reveal all of the details, but *will* tell you that your future husband is now, as we speak, a skillful test pilot with the Navy. He graduated with highest honors from *Annapolis.*

After graduation, he entered Navy pilot training and earned his wings. The new captain took a **Grumman F-14 Tomcat** on a long test flight last year, maneuvering it off an aircraft carrier's runway. As happens, during the course of such a dangerous trial, major defects manifested owing to the initial long-distance flight. As a terrible consequence, the engine malfunctioned, along with all of the communication instruments, while far into the test.

Putting on his life jacket, he ejected over shark-infested waters near Rarotonga in the southern Cook Islands. When the menacing gray shadow under the clear water bumped against his legs, he said prayers that his life would end swiftly without pain.

To his astonishment, he found it not to be a shark but rather a large dolphin. This strong and friendly creature gently maneuvered him onto its back. He rode this dolphin through the violent current, until it placed him on the craggy volcanic terrain of a remote, uninhabited inlet. I know this dolphin well. Her name is *Cosmina.* She is part of my Pacific Ocean rescue crew.

At first, he thought he was fated to become a modern-day version of *Fletcher Christian,* on a new *Pitcairn Island.* There, existing alone on the jagged black rocks, surrounded by heaving waves—inhospitable to even the sturdiest of ships—this downed pilot discovered evidence of old *Zerosen* plane wreckage. Japan used this fighter aircraft during the Second World War.

The Zerosen's cockpit entombed skeletal remains of its pilot. A passport claimed the name *Shigeru Nakamura,* and its picture showed a young fellow, only twenty-three at the time of his death. The handwritten words, 'Belongs to Garry' were on the first page of a brochure titled, 'Speaking English with Yankee Captors.' This educated pilot had been familiar with the American penchant for nicknames. Who had once dubbed him *Garry,* and why?

The American pilot also found a book of matches advertising *Magome Bar and Café,* along with the small photograph of a pretty girl who wore a modern-like dress for the era. On the back of this photo, his Japanese counterpart had printed the name *Midori,* encircling it with a heart. He had delighted in his young life, until his duty ended it.

In preparation for burial, the responsible American showed respect for his fellow aviator by covering him with the *Flag of the Rising Sun,* discovered near the bones of the succumbed youthful warrior. He made a vow to return all the personal items of this soldier to the Japanese Consulate, if he ever got out of the situation alive. At least, *that* horrific war had ended.

In this cockpit, he also found pieces of a shortwave radio, scattered next to a large bamboo container filled with gingerroot—once preserved in sake. In the main, this crystallized ginger, along with speared roasted fish, seaweed, and rainwater—kept him alive. Only sweet ginger each day offered him something delicious. Something special to keep him going. Later on, he found out how 'gingerroot' is a true curative food, rich in nutrition and Vitamin C.

After the excruciating five weeks, he established contact with his aircraft carrier. The Zerosen's old shortwave radio, although full of static, finally worked after he utilized salvaged electronic instruments he found inside the cockpit. I guided him from above. He would not join me for sixty years.

When you are to meet him in the future, he will be almost thirty-three—and you twenty-five. It is a big age difference to you now. Later on, it will not be. Destrehan, also eight years Ava's senior, handled his responsibilities with maturity.

On the day that you first see him, he will be flying with the Navy's famous Demonstration Squadron **The Blue Angels,** for an appearance in Tillagevale. A winning ticket to share a boxed-lunch with one of the eligible pilots has them announcing *your* name to share *his* lunch, part of which will be, by the way, your favorite bologna hoagie. He will leap to the bandstand when he sees you and almost drop the delicious lunch.

It will not be too long before you are a beautiful bride. He will proclaim at the alter of the Annapolis Chapel, while he slips Ava's plain gold wedding band on your finger, 'Nutritive ginger once saved my life, and now *this* beautiful *Ginger* will *be* my life.' The joy of that day will remain with you for eternity.

He was quiet now, perhaps thinking of his own wedding day long ago. While caught up in this staggering moment, I didn't mean to be abrupt. It's just that I couldn't find any words to question him other than, "My future *husband!* What's his *name?*"

"Everett," he said. "His name is, *Everett.*"

"No, I'm sorry, but I mean his *last* name. I hope it's not Candy, Cake, Brownie, Pie, Fudge, Bread, Jam, Crisp, Milk or Bun. Are you aware these are real surnames of actual people listed in phone books?"

I also could not help, at this astounding instant, to reflect on this pilot's fantastic adventure. It put the old Gene Autry legend, about riding Champion across the English Channel, right into a plausible category.

After my maniacal flare-up, concerning confectionary nomenclatures, Alistair smiled one of his biggest and broadest smiles ever when he said, "Yes, I am telling you about your someday husband. *He* is a lucky man. When you see him in the future, it will not matter to you if his last name just happens to be that of *Danish,* and keeping up the family tradition, you will share this future boxed-lunch under the very magnolia tree where your grandmother and I fell in love."

Events of 5/29/72

ENTRY 16:

DOMANI

"Let me protect today."

Unbelievable as it continued to be, talking to Alistair about so many personal things, when he mentioned the Magnolia tree I had to find out more about its magic. I realize now what a special tree it is, not only since it's been standing there for a century, but also over this long span it absorbed the emotions of so many people.

"Can I ask you kind of another personal question about Bertie? Maybe you already know of my strange feelings for him, when *I* sat with him underneath the same tree—so important to you and Grandma. I realize it's too late, and a lost opportunity from the past, but do you think if he hadn't been so sick, and I hadn't acted so dumb about him, we might have been a *real* couple in the future."

Alistair looked contemplative as he nodded his head and said:

It is obvious how Bertie hoped and wished for a miracle making it possible for you to one day become *Ginger Norman.* I am going to interject some relevance here concerning your question about your supposed *lost* relationship with him.

Young people accuse their elders of preoccupation with 'living in the past.' Concerning this, in **1928** when I sailed on the Vestris, I brought along a new book to read titled, *Generally Speaking* by the English author *G. K. Chesterton*—very renowned then. I will now paraphrase what he mentions, in this compilation of essays.

He said if those of us who are alive talk of the past as *irrelevant* because it is 'dead,' this is a serious misconception. In truth, it is 'the past', which 'lives' as those who still exist know of its ever evolving details. They read of it in history books. And now—much more than in the world Chesterton and I shared—your generation will hear it, and see it in the present, via television. In the coming years, there will be even more astounding ways for the past to return before your eyes. You will sit in your living room and participate in history. You will experience it live as it *occurs,* before you see it again later on, as it once *existed.*

It is the 'future', which does not exist. Human beings can never predict it, other than to, in Chesterton's own words, 'calculate it in a mathematical fashion by averages and tendencies.' They can never ever envision *precise* details of tomorrow. They can only record with complete accuracy, those tangible ones of yesterday. Please carry this impression with you, when you think of your lost 'future relationship' with Bertie.

"Yes," I said, "you're right."

After that, followed by a moment of reflection, I went on to say, "Bertie mentioned something like this idea a few times. Stuff like the past being *history* and the *future* being a mystery. And he spoke of our still learning from those who die, and how they continue talking to us, and entertaining us, through their previous writings and their musical compositions.

Their influence also lives on with the legacy of their works of art. And now, that I'm thinking it over, what about their plays and movies? I love watching old Laurel and Hardy movies. I laugh and laugh."

After a moment of silence he said, "Very perspective of our Bertie, and you too." He then went on to elaborate concerning my question about a "lost" future *relationship* with Bertie:

"In further answer to your question, about any romance with him, it is through his friendship that you learned how 'love' comes in many forms. He, and the lessons he taught, will live in your heart.

In essence, the fleeting moment of tenderness and attraction you felt for Bertie, while sitting under the tree, is your validation how you already *were* in a romantic relationship, if not a conventional one. Nothing is lost. It exists in your memory. Does this make sense to you?"

"Yes." I said. "*Yes,* it does. Everything I've been fortunate enough to experience with Bertie in the past will continue to be a part of me. Yet *you* told me about my future. You told me about Everett. I guess you're capable of doing this because you are no longer a human being."

When I said this to him, it bothered me. I thought he might take my reference to his not being mortal in the wrong way. He didn't. He answered without hesitation:

You are correct. Since I *am* no longer mortal, I am privy to specific aspects of the future, concerning those whom I guide from above. Remember, though, I used to be—as you humans say—'flesh and blood.' This is why you should live the next seven years enjoying this enriching age of your young life—without obligatory thoughts of Everett. I want you to experience normal social dating now.

Once I leave you, you will remember pertinent details of this meeting, with the exception of the account concerning the matrimonial prediction. Like that disappearing ink, Everett will fade from your consciousness. It will be gradual, but it will be gone. When the portended time comes, you will experience an overwhelming urge to attend an aerial performance of The Blue Angels over the sky of Tillagevale. An impulse will compel you to buy that raffle ticket for a boxed-lunch, and even though you do not want anything to do with it, you will find yourself walking toward the bandstand and paying for raffle ticket number **529.**

As you gaze into each other's eyes, as if you have been doing it all of your lives, Everett will tell you the same story concerning his experience in the unfamiliar waters of Rarotonga. To you then, it will be the first you have ever heard of it. As a youngster, I too—like Everett—spent time in unfamiliar waters on the French Riviera where I attended school. Of course, I had to learn French. Speaking in Italian is also popular in this area of Europe. Within a few months, I became adroit enough to switch back and forth between the two languages without even thinking.

I had a certain affinity for one Italian word, *domani.* It means *tomorrow.* While the freezing waters constrained me, after the Vestris capsized, somehow I returned to the blissful warm waters of my sentimental Riviera, where I once loved to swim. My contentment there as a youngster, surpasses anything else I had ever experienced before. I wanted to stay forever, but knew it could not be. To console myself, I composed a little rhyme in Italian. I would often recite it. I will translate it for you now.

Domani
Domani
Keep away!
Let me protect today.
Domani
Domani
Don't come my way.
But if you do, please let me stay.

I spoke these last words, as raging water swirled around me. I could no longer breathe. The next day had a different agenda for me. My ideal life, and my ideal wife, is forever lost to domani. The invincible power of the youth that I held such stock in, equaled nothing other than a temporary investment—with no compounding interest for this uninsured account.

Remember to make the most of your *today,* as it is all you are certain of.

Fire it up!

Do your best.

Never take advantage of it.

Use it for the good of yourself, and for the good of others.

He looked tired—exhausted I guess—from the horror of reliving the last tragic moments of his life. With his voice breathless and weak, he said, "Since today is where we are *both* at now, I have just received telepathic word of another horrific storm. The coast of Malaysia is threatened. This coming situation calls for me to return to my post. We must ready ourselves to say *goodbye.*"

Events of 5/29/72

ENTRY 17:

GLOW OF THE NIGHTLIGHT **"No reading glasses."**

Hearing him say he'd soon leave me made my hands tremble, much more than when I opened the life-altering envelope. Part of me implored him not to go, as the light surrounding him dissipated. How useless my runaway emotions felt. Things had gone way above anything *I'm* able to control.

As he spoke, I could only let the endless supply of tears I kept choking back, pour like rain desperate to quench dry land.

"Ginger, as I vanish, your tears will make it difficult for me to cut the human-bonds again. I feel such pride for you and Vivienne. Indeed, I have two beautiful granddaughters. My thanks go to you, most of all, for allowing me to act like the mortal grandfather—I never had a chance to be. Holding this sentiment, I will now admit how our Alex *is* difficult. But always remember, so are you."

With these final grandfatherly words, I watched his captivating eyes turn into a *clear* crystal ball. Within this profound sphere, I recalled *why* Alistair's pictures in the den downstairs looked so familiar to me.

As a little kid, I feared the dark. I still do, I guess. Every night, even if it's difficult to imagine now, a young father came to my room to reassure me, and tell me I'd soon be having pleasant dreams.

I saw my daddy with no crinkles around his eyes.

None of those forehead-furrows.

No receding hairline.

No reading glasses.

No little paunch for Mom to pat with devotion—way back then.

I saw the tender daddy, who read his little girl her *bestist* Uncle Remus tale—prior to hugging her tight and saying goodnight. He'd plant an affectionate kiss on her cheek, before turning on her night light. I know he often worked late, but never failed coming back on time to tuck me in.

In my sleepy toddler haze of innocent days gone by—in the soft glow of a tiny pink 15-watt bulb—I looked at my dad's face. This tender childhood gaze focused with intensity on an exact replica of the youthful countenance of Alistair—with one exception, the dark brown color of my father's eyes.

When I looked around the room again, he had left me. Nothing of Alistair remained, except the poignant memory. For the first time in my life, I realized how important my own father is to me, and *he* is still here waiting for me.

Events of 5/29/72

ENTRY 18:

A FRAGRANT BLANKET "They grounded me to reality."

After Alistair left, I remained alone in the room for an unknown period, until the illusive clock chimed six-times. The bureau drawer, still in the open position, beckoned me. I put everything back in the envelope, just as I found it before, placing it with reverence next to the bottle of Evening in Paris that would forever keep it company. I also dropped in the room's key, and the door glided shut without my touching it.

With renewed purpose, I scooped up the material and the gift box from where it still rested on the bed. Before I flipped off the light, I set the door's automatic lock. Then, I slammed it shut—securing the entrance for at least the *next* forty years.

Lost in my thoughts, going back to Shelley's place, I tried to reconstruct who I am. I sure know who Ginger Autry is, I've been living with her long enough. But who is Ginger Perry? And being *Ginger Perry* places me in an exclusive club, where my membership will forever remain private.

For once, it felt good seeing the familiar cats even with their raucous meows for dinner. They grounded me to reality. I forgot to feed them earlier. All of them, except for Daisy, complained about their hunger pains. Do you believe I picked up that pesky little kitten, and carried her over to my bed? If Vivienne is an earthly angel, Daisy must be an angelic earthly-cat.

Decisions wait for the making. A good night's rest will help. I still felt Alistair's hug warming my soul, as I snuggled under the covers. The comforting scent of Evening in Paris followed me home. The bed wasn't lumpy any more. In a mere minute, I drifted off to a blissful and dreamless sleep, cocooned with Daisy in a fragrant blanket of love.

Chapter 9

THE DAILY ENTRIES
TUESDAY NIGHT, MAY 30TH

So many things needed figuring out today. I'll tell you again, I'm very glad you're here with me in **1972.** This *Divine Mission* gig is *not* going to be easy.

Events of 5/30/72

ENTRY 1:

DECISIONS **"I have other plans."**

What a weekend. I called Kelly Services the first thing on this Tuesday morning, asking them for the day off, citing pressing family matters. And this sure is no fabrication. I realize you can't help me decide stuff, but you can project good vibes my way. I'll count on receiving as many as you send my way.

My job supervisor mentioned things were slow after the holiday. Therefore, not coming in today for a job is okay, but I'd *better* show up tomorrow. This is good in a way. I function better with a deadline. Oh no, I'm starting to sound more and more like Bertie every minute. And you know what, it's fine with me. I'll head back to Alistair's place now, and tell the doorman I've decided not to take responsibility for the apartment. I have other plans.

Last night, while feeding the cats, I admitted to myself how hard Shelley tries to find homes for them. I remember her asking me to help with the task, if I could. I just let it fly by me. Well, her sincere request has now landed in my lap. I'll call her at the ashram first. She left me the phone number in case an emergency arises. Now, if this situation isn't a literal "rising emergency", what is? If she says okay, I'll use that big cat carrier in the closet to bring the "Sergeant" a special present.

Timid sprinkles fell, when I arrived on that beautiful Fifth Avenue block. I found Mitch Purdy stooping under the awning, busy flicking raindrops off his coat. "What kinda round ball of brown fur yuh got there, Miss Autry?"

"Sergeant Purdy, I'd like to introduce *Bruiser.* He's a tough former alley cat. I bet his presence will be a great deterrent concerning any more mice. He's one of my cousin's five strays. He deserves a good home. I know he'll love the freedom of the basement. If there is ever any police squad for cats, *he'd* be their chief investigator."

The doorman gave me an excellent response when he reached out for the cat carrier, before I even handed it to him. I stood with him under the awning, while a now heavy rain cascaded down its sloping sides, and felt assured about his official presence protecting Bruiser, along with me.

"How about this hardy guy! What a great idea Miss Autry. I shoulda thought of gettin' a cat myself. You're not just taking care of the estate; you're helpin' the entire building."

It took me a second or two to get the courage to give him the news. "Well, the truth is, I came to tell you I'm not moving in. I realize it's much too much for me to handle. But I *do* have that kind cousin I mentioned. I'm going to help find a good home for *all* of her cats. Her name is Shelley Marie Cherubim. I bet she'll jump at the chance to live here, *if* you ask her. She's already 26. She's single too, although I don't think she wants to be. She's honest to a fault. She's the utmost in reliability. And don't worry she's very pretty. She doesn't look a thing like the Piggly Wiggly Mascot."

"Like what?" he questioned, leading me to believe he had never been shopping at the Piggly Wiggly.

"Oh," I said, "just a silly offhand comment that I shouldn't have made, and nothing worth giving a second thought."

"Well, if there's one thing I'm certain of—it's how, with *any* family resemblance at all, your cousin is a stunner. I'm sorry you won't be keepin' me company here, but you young people gotta do what ya gotta do. I've been there once myself."

I told him, "Thank you for understanding. Thank you also for your compliments. But in reality, concerning family resemblance, I look more like my father. Shelley takes after our grandfather—a handsome former tugboat captain. Like you, he wore a special hat and uniform. Before I forget, I judged you in the wrong way at first and I'm sorry. I realize now, you're an okay guy. Here's Shelley's phone number and you can take Bruiser out of the carrier. I need it for other deliveries today."

While he held the cat, he made several *p'seu-p'seu* sounds at him, before continuing our conversation as if I never hinted how I needed to rush:

No problem at all with this gang buster; he'll have a good home here. The basement's huge. It's got several windows too. It's only halfway under the ground, so there's a lot of bright light and sun. Even on a cloudy day, I read my newspaper without turning on a lamp. If he ever gets sick, he doesn't have to worry. There's always my son the vet—Dr. Mitchell Joseph Purdy, Jr. Not too long ago, he used to be a cop like his old man. He worked on the canine squad. After loving the dogs so much, he went to veterinary school. He pushed hard, going evenings, weekends, and vacations—while working on the job too. He graduated last year, on his thirtieth-birthday.

The day after the cap and gown, he quit the force to start his Purdy Animal Hospital out in the town of Port Jefferson, on Long Island. Half of the time, I don't think he charges. He's been eatin' a lot of them peanut butter sandwiches—without the jelly. You tell your cousin, if she ever wants a good residence for her strays—contact my son. Here's his card.

When he put it in my jacket pocket, he gave me a sly wink. "He's *not* married and he's lookin' for a gal who loves animals as much as he does, so please make sure Shelley knows about him."

I told him how I did call Shelley earlier, to inform her about this potential new home for Bruiser and, as soon as I see her, I'll mention Long Island and the history of Dr. Mitch Purdy when I hand her that card.

"I really do have to leave," I said, waving an enthusiastic goodbye, while he now nuzzled Bruiser in his arms. Sheets of rain became a waterfall of stinging pellets, as I hurried to the Lexington Avenue subway station.

Events of 5/30/72

ENTRY 2:

CLADDAGH

"You've waited long enough."

When I phoned Shelly earlier, concerning Bruiser's relocation, I also told her that since the carrier can hold two cats I'd return back to The Bronx after I drop him off at his new prowling-grounds. I planned on making another round of deliveries, and if okay, I'd refill it with her strays, Felicity and Lola. Shelley agreed with my idea, but asked me never to place her "little Sophie"—the first stray she ever brought home. She was a definite keeper.

When I left swinging the again heavy carrier, I headed downtown. When I found Fortunato's Famous Fish on Bleecker Street, I was an angler myself—dressed in a traditional yellow rain slicker—but sure carried a very bizarre bate box.

Mr. Fortunato didn't act surprised when I showed up at the door of the fish market. He just smiled at me, as well as the cats in the carrier, and asked about their names. Somehow, he knew we were arriving. "They'll eat good here," he said. "I hope these girls like fresh salmon. You've given me a useful gift."

"There's *another* gift," I said, while I pulled out the small box from my shoulder bag. My raised voice startled us both, when I propelled the box toward him. "This is the actual gift Mr. O'Flanagan bought for you in Ireland—the very one he mentioned in the old letter you carry in your wallet. Pease don't ask me any details about how I got it. If I explain it to you, I won't believe it myself."

He didn't even look shocked about my whipping out the little box. Instead, he took my hand and led me to a spotless kitchen of bright stainless steel toward the back of the store, where we sat down at a round terracotta table. This time, he poured both of us one of those espresso concoctions—but in large mugs—dumping half of a full bottle of anisette into his. Mine came with just the lemon, and several packets of brown sugar.

"Open your gift," I encouraged him. "You've waited long enough."

His hands trembled as he removed the green tissue paper, and then the lid of the box. A typed gift card sat on top of the soft green velvet pouch inside this box. He hesitated a minute before reading it to me:

To My Trusted Fortunato:

The enclosed ring is 22-karat gold,
the same as you are. The Irish call it a
Claddagh, and this crown, with two
hands holding a heart, is the symbol of
eternal friendship.

It comes from captivating Killarney.

I look forward to assisting you, when you
open this gift, and then watch you wearing it.
It is a token, thanking you for your loyal
help, and for being a fine young man who
will always be a son to me.

Singh O'Flanagan

As Frankie slipped on his once lost ring, it fit him like it had just been pre-measured. Our mutual gloom ebbed away—along with the cleansing spring rain. A big, bright, and glorious sun chased away the showers, while radiating its healing warmth on a shimmering Bleecker Street.

I left the fish market, lugging a much lighter carrier—with only my raingear inside it.

Now the biggie comes.

It's back to The Bronx, to call my father.

Events of 5/30/72

ENTRY 3:

LOGARITHMS

"Do my aging ears deceive me?"

A quiet place, with three less hungry cats waiting, greeted me when I returned. A sulking Sophie, missing all her pals, didn't even let out one crotchety meow. I know how thrilled Shelley is about my arranging to place the others in great homes. She agrees how they will be much happier in their spacious new digs, than they ever were in these cramped rooms.

Due to some kind of weird motivation, I looked forward to speaking with my father. An accommodating Providence arranged for him to answer the phone on the first ring. He sounded happy, until I asked him to sit down for some very "big news."

I could hear him shouting to my mother. "*Mary*—Ginger is on the phone and she's got some of that *big news.* Get my emergency migraine pill, and bring a glass of water. I need it on hand, just in case."

"*Daddy*—you know how I constantly tell you that I'd prefer living my life as a pathetic ignoramus, rather than stoop to Tillagevale U. I've changed my mind."

A stunned silence permeated the other end of the phone. I could hear him take a deep breath before he said, "But their Journalism program *isn't* so hot. You're right. I checked into it."

"The thing is Dad, I won't be studying *Journalism.* I've decided to take *pre-med.* After all, Tillagevale U turned Grandma into a great nurse, so they'll lead the way toward making me a great medical-research scientist. I can do it, Dad. I always topped everybody in my classes for biology, chemistry, and logarithms. Remember?"

I guess I put him in a good mood. I heard him laugh before he said, "How *could* I forget. Don't *you* remember when it drove your sister nuts, the way you're able to understand *rocket science.* I won't ask why you're making such a drastic **90-degree** academic turn like this. Extensive experience as a parent has shown that no matter what the explanation is, I'll pay the price. I'm trying to wean off my headache medication. Dr. Mendel says in order to succeed I must remain calm at all costs. Will *you* now facilitate my breaking his orders?"

I have so much experience in the area of ignoring zingers that I just let this one slip by and said, "Speaking about Vivienne—how is she?"

"She's excited over the gift from Bertie," he replied.

"I know she is, and I want to tell you and Mom how I'm hanging out here for the next few weeks, until I wrap stuff up with Shelley and Kelly Services. After that, I'm coming home for good."

For the first time in my life, as I spoke with my father, I could recognize a mature and confident tone in my voice, one that expresses a belief how I'm growing up—in spite of myself.

My new sense of credibility helped me say, "I've already contacted the university concerning their pre-med requirements. They told me I could enter this coming fall semester. The Gazette also said I could have my old job back, whenever I want. At least, it will help pay for books. I assume it will be okay with you."

I guess he responded to my mature stance. His usual cranky voice now sounded gentle and reassuring—similar to Alistair's—without the English accent.

"Sure, Ginger. *Sure.* It's straightforward education-wise; it doesn't involve Pygmies and flaming batons, and even better—you're more than able to handle the curriculum. So go for it kid. Maybe they'll allow you to *minor* in fine arts, and not chuck your scholarship. You *are* a talented writer. As your father, I should have told you so—long ago."

Emotion overwhelmed me when I said, "Thanks for saying I'm a talented writer. And—as Mom often tells *you,* 'better late than never.' It means a lot, and it's worth more than millions of dollars in scholarships to me. Also, your idea about using fine arts as a minor is brilliant. I know for sure, no matter what I do with my life in the future, part of it will always involve writing. Wow Daddy, two great heads *are* better than one."

"Do my aging ears deceive me? Did I just hear you call me great and brilliant?"

In answering him, I found *myself* bewildered when I said, "Come to think of it, Dad, I guess I did." I also told him to, "Please tell Mom and Vivienne the news, okay."

"Don't worry, I will," he said in a quiet voice—a voice very much reminiscent of those old days when he'd reassure me before bedtime, about reading me those Uncle Remus tales.

"Vivienne's off shopping somewhere," he continued. "Those Memorial Day sales drag on all week."

"Oh Dad—speaking of shopping—please go to the Piggly Wiggly and buy a big box of treats for cats. Any kind will do, although she *is* partial to ones with vitamins. I'm bringing home a little kitten.

Her name is Daisy, and she's the cutest thing."

EPILOGUE

At the beginning of July, I once again took the trusty Greyhound. I caught that infamous New York City cold and coughed up for an expensive express bus back to Tillagevale. On this trip, Providence was pleased with me. You really *do* get what you pay for. She placed me next to an elderly woman named Dot. For most of the trip, she crocheted a shawl with shiny yellow thread. It smelled of the delightful cherry-almond Jergens hand lotion she used.

Before I left, Shelley presented me with a roomy new pet carrier for Daisy. She equipped it with a small litter pan and a large bag of expensive dried cat food for kittens. For most of the trip, though, a contented Daisy sat on my lap. Dot loved her and crocheted "the little one" a cute collar with some leftover thread.

I didn't take the completed journal and bury it, as once planned. I had a distinct feeling things weren't over yet and it might need another entry. Instead, I placed it in a secure locker at the Greyhound bus terminal—right before I boarded the bus for home. I'm now back working at the newspaper. They said I could stay on part-time, if I want, after the fall semester starts. Tillagevale U accepted me without any problems. I'm looking forward to starting my new academic life, one not including the aid of smelling salts.

Guess who'll be joining me in a couple of years. It's Vivienne. She got over her benevolent Pygmy-fixation, deciding on majoring in performing arts instead of Belgian Rain Forest lore. Now that I know the whole story, Vivienne couldn't help being attracted to globetrotting. She's also Alistair's granddaughter.

Mom surprised me by saying she had a job lined up too. The library asked if she could come back, now that the kids are grown, and set up a new mobile book van that will travel around the county on different days of the week. She was thrilled about not only the new fun job, but also knowing they forgave her for the notorious encyclopedia scandal. I overheard her tell Aunt Sharon that she feels younger, and has a new lease on life with something exciting to look forward to in the future.

The best thing happened at the quiet celebration of my 18th birthday. Owing to Bertie and all, just the family gathered for a barbecue in the backyard. Aunt Sharon and Uncle Eddy came. Shelley couldn't make it, but Dr. and Mrs. Norman did. My mother told me how much they wanted to be with us.

At one point, a strong urge propelled me over to the legendary hammock. My father once mentioned how Mom brought it with her from the old Boston house. She couldn't part with it, and leave it with the new owners, because her deceased parents received it as a wedding gift. And, as newlyweds, they often reclined in it together—lost in their world of dreams.

The closer I gravitated toward the aging heirloom, the more I realized how tough it is. In spite of being open to the elements, in different climates over the years, it weathers all of the seasons. It keeps on swinging. This familiar mainstay and me, well, we both swung our way through life unaffected by wear-and-tear. I hope this trusted hammock will still be around for me to rest in with *my* husband someday, and comfort us when *we* are old.

I remember now that I once saw a small snapshot of me lying in it as a newborn. The handwriting on the back of the photo belongs to my mother. She wrote how Dad took it on the very day they brought me home from the hospital. She also wrote that while growing up, she herself, rested in this hammock—feeling how being there enabled her parents to still cradle her. And, far into the future, on the day of this picture, showing *me* in it, they could cradle their first grandchild.

Inspecting the hammock further, I wasn't at all shocked when a faint outline of Bertie materialized—while *he* swayed in it. Like a haze lifting from my eyes, I saw his fantastic image grow brighter. The glasses were gone. His hair had grown into a long and flowing style, similar to Alistair's—with not a drop of Brylcreem in sight. His new and improved smile revealed teeth, no longer a yellow-enamel hodgepodge. They were white, straight, and *even.* He wore a long frock, also similar to Alistair's, except for the brown color—with beige I-Ching coins embroidered on it.

I just knew that he couldn't miss my special emancipation-day. If he had, it would be the first birthday of my life when he didn't come around. I also knew it would be the last time I'd ever see him, outside of my heart—to be precise. Within a second, Vivienne darted behind me—poking me in the ribs.

"Hey Sis, did you hear about Shelley?"

She got me in a ticklish spot, so I giggled when I said, "No. What about her?"

"Well, I just overheard Aunt Sharon tell Mommy how Shelley had this great offer as caretaker for a free apartment and she decided not to accept it, just so she can go every weekend to this *Port Jefferson* place. She's spending a lot of time with some *vet.* I think his name is *Mitch,* and wedding bells might be in the air."

Acting surprised about Shelley's potential change in status I said, "You don't say!" Vivienne grabbed my arm when she went on to speculate, "Ginger—maybe she will ask *you* to be her maid of honor, and *me* to be her bridesmaid. You think?"

"Yeah, I think," I assured her, with complete confidence.

Although I couldn't mention this to Vivienne, I knew for sure if it weren't for everything happening to me—to change *my* life—Shelley wouldn't even know about a place called Port Jefferson. My wearing a gorgeous maid of honor gown, of my own choosing, is a given. Remember, I also have connections for a gorgeous church in Manhattan to hold the wedding ceremony. The address is **25** Carmine Street.

Vivienne moved alongside of me, squeezing my hand. "Hey, look at the hammock. It's moving. Maybe it's Bertie's ghost. You think?"

I looked over at a beaming Bertie. Since everything concerning the hammock, including him, swayed with jet prolusion, I thought for sure he'd fall out onto the dirt. If spirits *can* fall, that is.

"Well, Viv," I said, "you're right. He sure did like our hammock. There *is* a ghostly sort of breeze but that's all it is. Just a breeze. I wouldn't get freaky about it."

I wanted so much to tell her the truth—to say, "Vivienne, look! Bertie is *here,"* but I couldn't. She, by her very kind and sympathetic nature, had already completed her mission without realizing it. I had only just embarked on mine.

So—I gave her a kiss on the cheek before she said, "I guess you're right about the heavy breeze being just that. Concerning the part about Bertie liking the hammock, you forgot he only *liked* it until the day he fell asleep in it at your tenth-birthday party—and you flipped him out of it. His knees bled from the scuffs. Remember his embarrassment from blubbering like a baby in front of all the giggling Girl Scouts. It's sure a good thing Mom had that peroxide and gauze handy."

I looked over at Bertie again. He stood with his arm around the old willow tree. He laughed and made a "thumbs-up" sign with his right hand. Within seconds, he unfolded his fingers. He put them to his lips and blew a gentle kiss toward his parents who sat at the picnic table.

Within a second, he did it again. This time though, he aimed his gesture of affection toward Vivienne. I admit I felt jealous, until—with a lingering flourish from his lips—now puckered into more of an intimate pose—he imparted that final kiss toward *me.* And, reminiscent of one of those old paper platypus planes, it drifted toward my face like radar programmed it.

After I felt the gentle guided-breeze tickle my lips, a subsequent overpowering gust of air, in the clear form of a chariot, surged around him. It came to carry him home. Although he was gone, I said in a whisper, "Thanks, Bertie. Thanks for the very best *present.*"

I noticed Vivienne had some goose bumps on her arms when she asked me, "Did you just say something, Ginger?"

"Nope," I replied. It must have just been rustling from the breeze."

She shivered a little before saying, "There sure *is* a breeze, isn't there."

I nodded my head in agreement and said, "You're making it worse now, by swinging my arm back and forth like you are."

Acting like little kids, we skipped hand in hand toward the family where we joined them at the table. A kaleidoscope of color encircled us. Everybody looked up at the sky. The beautiful rainbow was breathtaking. "Did you ever see anything like it before?" they said in unison. Although not really directing the question at me, I answered it.

"Well—yes I have, a long, *long* time ago."

My mother stood up with a jolt. "*What* is that blowing under the willow tree?" She darted over to check something drifting around across the lawn. The expression on her face combined complete shock and absolute joy.

Picking it up, she said, "It's my parents' wedding picture! It used to be in that old frame of mine, the one with Ginger's baptismal picture in it now. When I moved to this house as a newlywed, I carelessly misplaced it. I tore the place apart for years, trying to find it. I thought I'd *never* see it again and was heartbroken. My goodness, how did it end up here, today, under the tree?"

I knew Bertie gave it to her as a special gift but just told her, "It must have been that big gust of wind before. I saw it blow the shed door open. It's still open now, Mom. I bet it came from somewhere, deep inside the shed."

Daisy looked confused by the commotion, but she continued sitting on the welcoming lap of Bertie's mother. I felt especially sad for Mrs. Norman. She didn't know her son had been there to visit us all—one final time. Daisy made herself at home on that soft wool skirt for most of the afternoon. Now, the kitten crouched on the grass while she lapped up a spoonful of whipped cream off a paper plate.

"I hope my cat's not pestering you too much, Mrs. Norman."

Picking up Daisy and hugging her tight, she said, "No, Ginger. *She* is a little doll, and not bothering me at all. By the way, starting now, please call me, *Tessa.*"

Dr. Norman came over to where I stood. He carried a small shopping bag. Making an obvious effort to keep quiet, he said with a whisper, "Moments before Bertie died, he asked me to give you this. He said you could understand its meaning. When I went into his closet to find what he wanted you to have, the jacket looked brand new again. How strange. He must have spruced it up sometime before. I also want to say I haven't seen my Tessa so relaxed or laugh so much since, well, you understand."

I nodded before peeking into the shopping bag. I saw the famous Ty Cobb jacket. As he noted, the denim looked bright and new, along with everything else about it. I took his hand and said, "I understand *everything,* Doctor Norman." He looked at me with respect when he told me, "Ginger—I'll have no more of that *Dr. Norman* business. I agree with Tessa. You're an adult now. From this moment on, please call me, *Bert.*"

I looked over at Mrs. Norman. *"Um . . .* Tessa, I'm thinking that since I'm working at The Gazette fulltime now, and taking some college prep-courses at night, maybe you might like to have Daisy come live with *you.* I could visit her, and take care of her, if you ever go away and stuff."

Dr. Norman squeezed my shoulder. "Thank you, Ginger. Bertie had exceptional taste."

I felt humbled when I said, "Thank *you,* Bert."

When he rushed over to give his wife a hug, I rushed inside to get all of Daisy's gear, including those vitamin treats my father bought her. I knew at that moment, Daisy is an *avatar.* I only acted as her temporary caretaker. She belongs in the safe arms of Bertie's parents.

So now, loyal reader, I'm up in my room—typing the finish of this journal. When I retrieve the bulk of it from the Greyhound locker, I'll add this epilogue to its binder and it will be off to Central Park Zoo—as planned from the start. While Dad and I cleaned up after everybody left, I told him I'd be going back to New York for a couple of days, to tie-up some loose ends. He went inside of the house for a minute. When he came back, he handed me an envelope.

"Here are those open-ended airline tickets I had on reserve. I don't need them now. Use one of them to fly back to New York, to do what you need to do. Use the other when you're ready to return. You won't be taking that tired old Greyhound out for a walk, when you come back home again."

He also said he'd switch the registration of the Mustang over to me for as long as needed. Yesterday, my uncle sold him his almost new metallic-brown Volvo for a great price. Edward Cherubim, CPA, purchased the new black Cadillac of his dreams. Toward the end of an already great windfall, droves of last minute farmers came into his Mall office before April 15th. He rented a stack of additional chairs to accommodate them all.

As for me now, just like Singh, I have my own little Runabout. It will come in handy when I volunteer to work at Sunday school. If the Bible Villain's Hoosegow corkboard is still hanging, I'm going to replace it with *Portraits of Bible Stars* along with a backdrop of the constellation, **Monoceros.**

In closing, I'd like to tell you that someday in the future, if you hear about advances in the cure for leukemia, you could bet I played a part in it. It won't just be due to my anticipated medical degree. I'm also intent upon studying Ayurvedic Medicine and Homeopathy. I also want to explore nutrition, and healing with medicinal herbs. I'm sure Shamus will help me out. With such an overwhelming disease as blood cancer, I think doctors need every available weapon inside of their medical arsenal. I know you agree.

I'll still snoop around and do investigations whenever I can. Now, instead of writing for a magazine, I hope it'll be for some prestigious medical publications. I'm not giving up my chance of getting a Pulitzer Prize. Remember, Bertie said it's a given.

If you're wondering about Singh's beautiful wool material, I've donated it to Tillagevale's *Ancient Order of Hibernians.* They have promised to make a special kilt with it. They're going to name it "The Singh O'Flanagan Memorial Tartan." The tall shillelagh-twirling leader of this local Hibernian Marching Band—will be wearing it down Main Street, at every future St. Patrick's Day parade.

Please know how much I appreciate your loyalty. I never could have made it through the past three days without the special angels in my life and this includes you. We won't be sad. This is not the finish; it's just the beginning. If there's one thing I want you to take away from reading my journal, it is how stories never end—they just cruise away toward a new adventure. Time *does* sail, and every unique Ship of Life must chart its own course.

In conclusion, I say with conviction that dear Providence follows everybody around as stagehand behind our lives. And *Luck* is her faithful partner. They're both busy shifting the scenery. When Luck sometimes behaves in a bad way, if we really analyze it, we may have brought it upon ourselves. Even if we didn't, there's still a lesson we can learn from the situation. Before we say goodbye, I have one more important thing to tell you.

Never push back when an angel shoves.

And, when you check around for *your* angels, remember that one of them may turn out to be a very persistent kitten or a special person next-door. Take care of yourself. Don't be afraid to reach out and grab Alistair's brass ring. *You* can catch it. *I* did.

With love to you always,

Ginger Peachy Autry

P.S. You were thinking **Prudence**—weren't you.

ACKNOWLEDGMENTS

To my parents, you are forever in my heart . . .
To Eizo, for his unwavering patience and support . . .
To Mori and Renzo, who taught me not to give up on a dream . . .
To Amy, for her perpetual belief in my ability . . .
To Ariel and Taiko, in hopes you will be proud of me . . .
To Patricia and Michael, for always being there . . .
To Betty, for her enthusiasm . . .
To Erin, for her encouragement . . .
To Simon, for his fantastic sense of humor . . .
To Margie, my inspiration . . .
To Pam D, my role model . . .
To the Borough of Brooklyn, I owe ya . . .
&
All the loyal passengers on my own Ship of Life, as well as the guardian angels and spirits, sailing along with us . . .

Since the formal printing of the journal, there is an email address attached to it:

SailtoMonoceros@aol.com

Cinema, music, television, and many of the other historical references in this journal, including metaphysical, are accessible on www.YouTube.com

ABOUT THE AUTHOR

Marilyn Ninomiya holds a doctorate in holistic ministries, as well as a master's degree in natural health. She also holds a bachelor's degree and an associate's degree in the area of behavioral science, and has won awards for her research. After working in the natural health field for several years, she is concentrating on her new career as a writer. Her short stories have won outstanding recognition. This is Ninomiya's first novel.